FLORIDA MAN

MIKE BARON

**WOLFPACK
PUBLISHING**
— EST 2013 —

Published in the United States by Wolfpack Publishing, Las Vegas

Wolfpack Publishing
6032 Wheat Penny Avenue
Las Vegas, NV 89122

wolfpackpublishing.com

Paperback ISBN 978-1-64119-749-6
eBook ISBN 978-1-64119-748-9

FLORIDA MAN

1 | NOTHING IN THE FRIDGE

Gary Duba and his best friend Floyd Belmont sat on the deck of Gary's deluxe double-wide, raised four feet above Florida on cinder blocks in case of flooding. Two-hundred-foot tractor chains stretched over the house like massive belts, anchored in concrete plugs in front and back, in case of hurricanes. The night was hot and humid, with squadrons of mosquitos dive bombing the deck, oblivious to the citronella candles, tiki torches, yellow wrist bands, and ample applications of Deet on both men's fully tatted arms. Homemade mosquito traps hung like obscene fruit from Gary's hand-made awning, stitched together from Harbor Freight tarps.

It was just past eleven, Little Big Town playing on WBCW, Florida Country Radio through the tinny speakers of an old Sony boom box. The boys had been drinking shine, smoking reefer, and snorting a little crushed oxy since nine, when Floyd had arrived in his eight-year-old Chevy van with Belmont Pest Control emblazoned on the side, along with its logo, a dead palmetto bug in a mint green oval.

A sign in front said, THIS PROPERTY PROTECTED BY SMITH AND WESSON.

Another sign said, TRESPASSERS WILL BE VIOLATED.

Floyd hawked and spat a loogie over the rail. "That fuckin' bitch still owes me three thou for her boob job. Only reason she dated me, so I'd pay for her fuckin' boob job."

Floyd was five feet six, built like a fire hydrant, sideburns like a Civil War general, chest, shoulders and back covered with black fur like a bear. He wore bib overalls and no shirt.

"You gotta admit," Gary said. "She's got a nice rack."

Gary sipped shine, causing his Adam's apple to bob up and down like a bouncing ball. Tall, bony, with thick, knobby wrists, a brush mustache, and a full mullet concealed beneath a Confederate cap, Gary was the picture of Southern manhood. He wore a sleeveless Lynyrd Skynyrd T-shirt showing off his tatted arms which included a skull with a dagger through it, a skull with a snake through it, a heart with the legend "Mom", Johnny Cash, and barbed wire bracelets.

"My advice to you," Gary said, "is not to worry about that skank. She gone. Be grateful she's out of your life and didn't give you the clap or something."

Floyd lit a Camel. "I just wish I had that three thou. I could really use it."

"Look at it this way. It's worth three thou just to have her out of your life."

"Now she's dating some Cuban slickee boy from Coral Gables who says he can get her modeling work. My ass. Only modeling she does is on a pole with a G-string."

"That's what you get for dating a stripper."

Floyd sucked a Dixie dry. "She told me she loved me!"

Gary barked. "You told her you'd take her to Jamaica!"

Floyd belched luxuriously and reached inside his coveralls and scratched his balls. "Got anything to eat?"

"Dubious."

"If I order a pizza, will they deliver out here?"

"Depends on the driver. Good ol' boys will. Them Indians and Iranians and all won't come out here. Not even with the fuckin' GPS guiding them. Say it's not worth the trouble."

Floyd blew a ring. "What trouble?"

"Fuck if I know. Lemme go look in the freezer. I might have some frozen catfish."

Floyd bent forward, put a finger down his mouth and made a vomiting sound.

"Well I'll look. I might have some tater tots or something."

They sat there.

"Well?" Floyd said. "You goin'? I mean, I could do it, but you got shit in that fridge that looks like sea foam. Looks like something from Alien, y'know what I mean? I mean, you oughtta clear some of that shit outta there before it breaks free and kills you in your sleep."

"Yeah, okay."

They sat there.

"Well?" Floyd said. "Are you goin' or not? 'Cause I go in there, omma just start throwin' shit out the window. We'll let the raccoons eat it and see if it kills 'em."

Gary gripped both armrests of his home-made Adirondack and heaved himself to his feet, holding on to the bannister while his head swam, waiting for things to focus. He shuffled through the tinny aluminum screen door, letting it bang shut behind him, and paused in his living room as if seeing it for the first time. A yellow and brown plaid sofa, listing at one end faced his flat screen television, resting on a worn wood kitchen table. He'd snagged both the sofa and the table from Goodwill for eight-five bucks. One wall was decorated with a Dolphins pennant, the Gators, a framed poster of Dale Earnhardt Jr. A shelf made from cinder blocks and wood planks held his bowling trophies, DVDs and CDs and a stack of American Angler, Sport Fishing, Outdoor Life, Field & Stream, Big Black Ass, Monster Titty, and Monster Truck.

He hovered for a moment wondering why he was there. His gaze fell on the yellow refrigerator.

Right.

He went to the fridge, opened the main compartment and bathed in the cool air and light. Plastic containers of noodles, green chicken salad, and one lone yellow bacon strip. He shut the main and opened the freezer, trying to find meaning in the monolithic chunk filling most of the space like an iceberg. He jammed it with his hand, busting loose a package of Jimmy Dean's Pork Sausage and Muffin Breakfasts which had lain there since Clinton was president.

He went through his mostly bare cupboards finding only a can of chicken broth and a box of croutons. Well fuck. Gary was hungry too. He wondered if he offered a big tip, if the Caesar's in Turpentine, twenty miles away, would deliver.

He pulled out his wallet and filed through. He had seventeen dollars, barely enough to pay for a pizza and a tip. And then he was broke.

Gary worked as an off the books roofer for Big John Schermerhorn, but he hadn't worked in two weeks and soon he'd have to pay mortgage, four hundred and twelve dollars, and utilities. Gary did not plan to remain a roofer forever. No sir. He had a dream. His dream was anchored in reality.

His dream was anchored in four concrete plugs sunk into the earth, in the front and back. Gary had invented a system to prevent houses from being blown away in harsh weather. House suspenders. Massive cables running over the roof, keeping the house pinned down, like a seatbelt.

He was just waiting for a big blow so he could take his results to the authorities and get the ball rolling. Gary figured he needed a hundred thou to get started. All he needed was an opportunity.

Uncertain how to break the news to Floyd, for whom he sometimes worked ridding the earth of vermin, Gary realized he had to piss. Steadying himself against the wall, he went down the short corridor to his bathroom and switched on the light.

A snake stared at him from the toilet, head upright and tracking like a periscope.

Gary blinked. It might be a bull snake. It might be a rat snake. Or it might be a poisonous water moccasin. He couldn't tell in the dim light. In any case, he had no intention of wrangling the snake just so he could take a piss in his own house, so he turned off the light, shut the door, and went back outside.

"I got nothin'. Why don't you pay for the fuckin' pizza?"

Floyd pissed and moaned and dug out his fat Harley wallet, connected to his bib overall by a chain and clamp. "Awright. I got enough. You call 'em. I left my phone in the truck."

Gary dug in his pocket. "Fuck," he said. "I musta dropped it. Hang on."

"Where you goin'?" Floyd said.

"Take a piss off the back deck."

"Whyn'tcha piss in the toilet?"

"There's a snake in the toilet."

"You want me to get my magnum and shoot it?"

Gary turned the corner and stood at the end of his wrap-around deck, which he'd built with Floyd's help. The rail covered three sides. Here, on the fourth side, an end piece facing the swamp, he was free to piss as the good Lord intended.

Gary hung ten at the edge, unzipped his fly and sent a golden arc into the sand, seeing phosphorescence coalescing along his dock, stars intermittently reflected in the open water of Fortier's Landing, heard the chorus of frogs, the heron calls, and as he adjusted to zip, slipped. His feet shot out from under him and his head hit the edge of the deck like a melon on concrete.

2 | RABID

Gary woke. He was lying on damp earth that smelled like urine. A metallic green beetle marched by with a leaf. He watched a cockroach scurry up one of his cinder block risers. He'd sprayed the bricks with the most virulent of Floyd's toxins, but rain had washed it away and the roaches filed to and fro like Rome's legions. He saw a bottle cap for Dixie beer, and beyond that, a fat rectangle covered with mud.

His phone.

Slowly, Gary sat up, head throbbing like an unmuffled Harley panhead. He put a hand to his scalp, and it came away smeared with dried blood, where he'd hit the deck. A low moan escaped his lips. He was thirsty enough to drink swamp water. Shoving the phone in his pocket, he crawled out from under the deck. The sun was up, slanting in over the mangrove and striking the face of his home. Shakily, Gary got to his feet and used the handrail to drag him the four steps up to his deck where Floyd slumped on his nylon chair snoring with metronomic precision.

Kkkkkkkkkk...GRONK

Kkkkkkkkkk...GRONK

Kkkkkkkkkk...GRONK

Gary went in through the screen door straight to the kitchen, filled an empty Big Gulp from the 7/11 with tepid brown water from the tap and glugged it down, Adam's apple oscillating. He refilled it and drained it again. Then he had to piss.

Remembering the snake, he went back out on the deck. It was too early for the snake. This time he was more careful and successfully relieved himself with no further damage. Leaning on the rail he returned to his pale green chair and sat with a scrape and a bump. He pulled out his phone and saw that he had two calls. The latest, at nine-thirty last night, was from Krystal 's mother Trixie.

"Gary, dear, I'm so sorry to bother you, but Krystal 's in the Glades County Jail. She's been there all day. She's been trying to reach you. She needs five hundred dollars bail. Apparently, they've charged her with indecent exposure. Something about a Waffle Hut. Please call me, Gary. I'm so worried."

The second, older call was from Krystal and must have been her one call from jail.

"Gary, baby..." She burped. "I'm in Glades County on a bullshit charge! I never hurt that fucker! He put his hands on me, and I was naked, baby...anyway, please come down here and get me out. Please! It stinks down here, and I have to pee in front of all these other women, and some gross guard who comes back here just to stare..."

"That's enough," said a male voice, and the call ended.

Gary groaned and shut the phone. "Fuck."

Floyd snorked.

"FUCK!" Gary said.

Floyd twitched. Gary reached out with one long leg and shoved the chaise lounge on its side, spilling Floyd on the deck, his mason jar dumping shine on the pine, attracting thirsty palmetto bugs.

"What the fuck?"

"Wake up. It's ten the fuck o'clock."

"So what? What's going on?"

"Krystal's in jail. I gotta bail her out."

Floyd sat up, legs splayed, leaned forward, reached inside his coveralls and scratched his nuts. "I have got a king hell motherfucker of a headache. Any shine left?"

"If there is, it's in the kitchen. Don't go in the bathroom."

"Why not?"

"Snake in the toilet."

"Fuck. I've gotta take a dump. You got a bucket?"

"Man up! Just squat and shit!"

"Easy for you to say, but I'm wearing these coveralls."

Gary raised his left hand and gave Floyd the finger. "There might be a bucket under the sink."

Floyd pulled himself to his feet and shuffled inside, letting the screen door slam shut behind him. The report bounced around Gary's skull like a BB. He squeezed his temples with the heels of his hands. Hoisting himself up off the armrests, Gary stumbled through the living room into the kitchen. He could hear Floyd grunting in the back, toward the swamp. Gary filled the Big Gulp with more tepid brown water, drained it, did it again.

Problem. The ibuprofen was in the bathroom.

Gary went into his bedroom, already too hot with the shades drawn, opened the drawer in his press board night-stand, burrowed through Anal Antics and Guns & Ammo until his hand closed on his

Taurus .357. He checked the cylinder. Fully loaded.

Problem. If he shot the porcelain toilet, it would flood the trailer.

Well fuck. These things were never simple. Jamming the pistol in his belt, he returned to the kitchen, took a broom from the closet, and used it to open the bathroom door. He peered in. If the snake were there, it was lurking below the rim, waiting like a Chinese sub. Gary used the broom handle to bring down the lid, ran in and put the wastebasket on top. He opened the mirrored medicine cabinet, grabbed the ibuprofen and closed it.

Who was that squinty fucker staring at him? His hair looked like Jan Michael Vincent's. He splashed tepid water in his face and used a comb to smooth back his mullet. Gary put a hand on the crown of his head. He could feel himself going bald like his old man. He was only thirty-six.

Wait a minute. Hadn't he been wearing his Stars 'n Bars? It must have fallen off when he fell. Returning to the kitchen he slammed down four Ibuprofen and went out on the deck. He heard the distant sound of traffic from the Dixie Highway, the honk of birds out in the swamp. Floyd shuffled around from the back and came up on the deck.

"Did you rinse out that bucket?" Gary said.

"Of course. You think I'm some kind of animal?"

"You got five hundred I can borrow?"

Floyd looked at him as if he were a palmetto bug.

"Fuck. Omina have to sell one of my cards."

"Aw mannnnn," Floyd said.

"You gonna come with me?"

Floyd scratched his left armpit. He reminded Gary of a bear. "Fuck what else I got to do?"

Gary went back to his bedroom, slid open the accordion closet door, and retrieved one of several three-ring binders holding sports cards. He sat on his bed and flipped through the pages, stopping when he came to his 1987 Topps Barry Bonds Pittsburgh Pirates #320. He pulled out his phone and went online. Fuck yeah. A cool two thou. He didn't have time to put it up on eBay. He'd just have to get what he could from Billy Bob. He removed the card from its plastic sleeve and inserted it in an individual plastic sleeve.

Floyd was smoking a doobie when Gary came out. Gary held out his hand. Floyd passed him the doobie and Gary inhaled. Purple paisleys filled his skull.

"You ready?"

"Let's do it."

A rabid raccoon hissed at them from the front yard. It

stood on its hind legs, jaws dripping saliva, in a direct line with Gary's twelve-year-old F-150.

The boys froze.

"Fuck," Floyd said. "That's a rabid raccoon."

Gary drew the pistol. "Well hang on. Just hang on."

Resting his arms on the wood rail, Gary gripped the gun in both hands and sighted over the top.

The raccoon hissed.

Gary squeezed the trigger, a puff of dirt appeared next to the raccoon. The left front tire of his truck whistled and flattened.

Floyd leaned on the rail. "Don't you got a shotgun? What happened to that sweet little Judge you had?"

"I sold it."

Floyd held out his hand. "Well give me that thing."

Gary handed him the pistol. Floyd went down two steps and sat on the top level, arms on knees, taking aim. The raccoon charged, spraying spittle.

"Shoot it! Shoot it!" Gary said.

Floyd squeezed off three shots, the last one drilling the 'coon through its thorax, sending it tumbling.

"Well shit," Gary said. "We'd better take your van."

"You got a shovel? We'd better bury that fucker."

Gary went around to the Suncast resin outdoor storage shed he'd bought at Lowe's, and took out a garden spade and a pair of leather gloves. Putting on the gloves, he used the shovel to carry the raccoon a hundred feet from the house, onto a slight hummock among the mangrove. By the time he'd dug a hole big enough, his clothes were damp from the wet. He thought about taking a shower, but time was of the essence, and that snake was probably waiting to throw back the toilet seat like a stripper coming out of a cake, leap into the shower, and sink its fangs into Gary's calf.

It was half past eleven when they hit the road. Floyd stuck a Camel in his mouth and lit it, as he jockeyed the van up the rutted string of puddles that was Gary's driveway.

"Let's get some breakfast on the way."

3 | ROAD RAGE

Traffic was heavy with trucks, tourists, and trailers on Eighty as they headed toward Turpentine under an overcast sky. They rode with the windows open to minimize the heavy chemical odor.

"Looks like rain," Floyd said.

"Yup," Gary concurred, switching on the radio to Norm Busby's Morning Talk.

"We're back. This is Norm Busby for Great Day in the Morning, and we're talking to Earl Abellard of LaBelle, who claims to have seen a UFO last night hovering over Hoover's Pond. Earl, you were saying?"

"That's right, Norm. Your basic flying saucer, and it made a weird humming noise. I took some pictures with my phone, but the light wasn't very good, but I still got some good video of it slippin' in and out of the clouds. I'll send it to ya soon's I get off this call."

"Now this isn't the first time you've encountered these

strange flying saucers, is it Earl?"

"No, it's not, Norm. I been seein' 'em all my life, and I been reportin' 'em too. But they don't want the news to get out, so they just ignore what I got to say, and they ignore my proof. It's a well-known fact that the Air Force has been tracking these UFO's since the fifties, and we all know about Area Fifty-One, and the fact that they got alien bodies hidden in a secret lab in the mountains of Southern Colorado. My theory is, we're already being invaded but if the news got out there would be a panic. Your Zionist Occupational Government would lose all control if people start thinkin' for themselves so there's no lengths to which they won't go to keep it buried. I fear for my life, Norm. I truly do. I don't go nowhere unarmed, and a couple times, I've had to do some pretty-fancy driving to escape from government agents who are intent on silencing my voice.

"Oh beep! I'm being followed. I'll have to call you back, Norm."

"Earl, stay safe out there. Emma Cruz from Fannondale is on the line. Emma, welcome to the Norm Busby Show."

"Norm, I was abducted by aliens six years ago. They are not good people."

"Tell us about it, Emma."

"I was driving by myself on Fitch Road out by Congers Lake, about nine pm. Couldn't see the stars it was so overcast, when outta nowhere, I hear this weird humming noise, and then I see lights, flashing lights, bright white lights, coming down from above, and a flying saucer landed smack dab in the middle of the road. Good thing I was going slow or I would have hit it. So, I stopped my car. All of a sudden, my headlights went out. I locked the doors. I feared for my life. I got two kids and my first thought was I wasn't never gonna see those two kids again. I dialed 911, but all I got was this weird screeching noise, like when they do the county-wide test thing.

"I bout pissed my pants, excuse my French. Then I see them, just like the pictures, little men with big heads and big eyes, coming toward the car. I prayed to Jesus they would leave me alone, but on that deserted road, there was no Jesus. They ripped the door off and dragged me out."

"Did they sexually molest you?"

Floyd looked in his rear view. "Look at this asshole."

Gary used the side mirror to look behind at a fast-approaching black Lincoln. They were doing a scrupulous seventy-five in the left-hand lane, passing a convoy of tractor trailers, English Movers, Petco, Walmart. Floyd couldn't risk any more points, or they'd lift his license. The Lincoln flashed its high-beams and honked. There was no place to pull in without accelerating and passing two more semis so Floyd held it steady. The Lincoln flashed its lights and honked. They continued thus for a minute until at last Floyd pulled ahead of a Mayflower van, turned on his blinkers, and pulled in about ten feet in front of the semi's bumper.

The Lincoln pulled adjacent, its blackened front passenger window sliding down. Floyd and Gary looked over at an angry woman in a buzz cut and green cat's eye glasses screaming something and flipping them the beard. Floyd flipped her the bird back. The woman faced front, rummaged around on the seat next to her and held up a revolver, which she pointed at Floyd. Floyd sprang the center console, grabbed his Beretta nine, pulled back the hammer, and stuck it out the window. Down the road a hundred yards, a semi filled the lane coming straight at the Lincoln. The Lincoln sprang forward, its right rear window slid down, and the driver squeezed off two shots, one of which splanged off the van's roof.

Floyd transferred the pistol to his left hand, stepped on the gas and fired back. The Lincoln sprinted at over one hundred miles an hour and pulled into the right lane in front of them, as the semi laid on the airhorn. The driver held her pistol in her left hand upside down out the window, firing back.

"Gary! Where the fuck's your gun?"

"Well I'm sorry, Floyd. I left it back at the house."

"Crazy bitch! Get her license number."

The Lincoln suddenly stood on the brakes and came to a near halt in front of them, just ahead of the Highway Nineteen turn-off. Floyd worked the wheel and the van veered right, nearly going up on two wheels, as it took the exit off the highway into a light industrial area filled with auto repair shops, plumbers, and waste management companies.

Floyd pulled over to the side of the road and shut the engine off, sweating heavily.

"Jesus fuck!" he exclaimed.

"Crazy bitch!" Gary said. "Gettin' so it's not safe to go anywhere these days!"

"Did you get the license number?"

"Fuck no! What, you gonna track her down? You can't track down every stupid fucker who takes a potshot at you on the highway."

Floyd lit another heater. "It's enough to make your liver turn white. Where we goin'?"

"Billy Bob's Pawn Shop. You jes' follow this frontage road 'bout five miles, hang a louie on Trax Avenue. You been to Billy Bob's, ain't you?"

"Not in a coon's age."

It was already in the mid-eighties with heavy humidity. Both boys were soaked through. Gary stuck out a hand.

"Gimme one of them heaters."

Floyd handed him the pack, started the engine, and pulled out into traffic. They passed two auto parts stores, a Wendy's, an Arby's, a Taco Bell, a Popeye's Chicken, two check-cashing places, five liquor stores, and Florida Pawn.

"You ever go into that Florida Pawn?" Floyd said.

"Nah. I'm a Billy Bob's guy. I do a lot of business with Billy Bob."

Floyd pulled partially into the oncoming lane to avoid two cyclists riding side by side wearing blue and yellow spandex, teardrop helmets, butts in the air, calves flexing.

"Fucking cyclists. Think they own the road."

Gary leaned out the window. "SINGLE FILE, SHIT-HEADS!"

As they pulled back to the right, both cyclists flashed the middle digit.

They passed the Dangle Lounge on their right, a two-story windowless stucco that looked like a charcoal briquet in harsh morning light.

Floyd hawked a loogie out the window. "That's where I met that bitch Priscilla."

"Put her out of your mind, bwah!"

"Man, I ain't been with a woman since. My right arm looks like a ham, I been jackin' off so much."

"Hey, man, that ain't right. There's no need to swear off women just because she robbed you."

"Man, she dropped a roofie in my drink. I woke up in my undershorts in a ditch."

Gary pointed. "There's Trax. Hang a louie."

They turned north on a strip of leprous blacktop, passing a billboard for LAW OFFICES OF HABIB RODRIGUEZ with a huge picture of Rodriguez, a bearded good ol' boy wearing aviator glasses, a ten-gallon hat and chomping on a cigar.

Have you been in an accident? Do you think you have not been fairly compensated? Contact the Long Arm at Rodriguez Law Offices to find out how much your injuries are really worth. You don't pay us unless they pay you.

A neon sign with a palm tree that flashed sequential rings

up from the bottom, orange and brown for the trunk, green for the fronds, hovered over the road. Across the street was LIVE GATORS, BABY GATORS FOR THE KIDS, STUFFED GATORS, parking lot filled with license plates from up north and rentals.

Billy Bob's was a long, low, one-story shingle-sided building with two big front windows showcasing everything from stuffed gators to gold coins. The parking lot held a half dozen vehicles, mostly pick-ups. Four skateboards leaned against the wall next to the main entrance, a glass door with two signs: OPEN, and PROPRIETOR IS ARMED. Signs in the window offered best prices for used firearms and lay-away plans.

Four teens stood off the far end of the building, knee deep in weeds, in a circle, laughing and pointing. Floyd parked the van in front, and they got out.

"Just a second," Gary said. "I want to see what those boys are doing."

He sauntered down the cracked concrete, across the shredded blacktop to the weeds fronting a drainage ditch. Four teenagers surrounded an adolescent alligator, keeping it corralled with branches.

"Hey fuckwads!" Gary said. "Wha'd that gator ever do to you?"

A thin, gangly youth with nose, lip, eyebrow and ear piercings turned with a sneer. Gary, no stranger to street fights got in his face.

"What's it to you?" the piercer said. "We ain't hurtin' it

none."

"We can sell that gator to that gator joint across the street," said a stocky skinhead with Japanese lettering running up his neck.

"Well pick it up then!" Gary said.

"Hey, Gary!" Floyd called from the front door. "Are we gonna do this or what?"

Gary turned and walked.

"That's right, pussy," the piercer said under his breath. Gary whirled. The boys studied their shoes.

They entered Billy Bob's, air conditioning chilling their skin. The big front room was chock-a-block with used bicycles, band equipment, motorcycle helmets, skateboards, and power tools. An island of glass cases displayed jewelry, watches, binoculars, and cameras. Two employees worked the counter, a man with face like a pepperoni pizza and a thick woman with long brown hair and a butterfly inked on her bare shoulder.

While Floyd examined the instruments, Gary approached the woman.

"Hey Darlene. Billy Bob around?"

It took her a minute to recognize Gary as a repeat customer. "Sure enough, Sugar," she said, picking up the phone. "I'll get him."

4 | BILLY BOB'S

A door in the back opened and out came Billy Bob, a lovable bear whose dense black beard concealed no chin, wearing a fisherman's vest from which pockets protruded pens, knives, and pliers. He wore a pair of 40/32 Levis held up by a silver belt buckle the size of a saucer depicting a gold-plated bronc buster waving a hat. Billy Bob went behind the counter and fronted Gary.

"Mister Duba. What can I do you for?"

Gary fished in his pockets and handed Billy Bob the Barry Bonds rookie card. Billy Bob looked at it, turned it over, held it up to the light, looked at it upside down. "Yeah, that's a real nice Bonds you got there. You want to sell it?"

"I ain't here to play euchre."

"Hang on. Let me consult my books." Billy Bob exited the island, went in the back door emerging a minute later with a thick, well-worn copy of the Beckett Baseball Card Price Guide, set it on the counter, consulted the index, and turned to page 542. His fat finger traced down the page until it came to the card in question.

"I can give you three hundred," he said.

"Are you shittin' me? Gimme that." Gary wrested the book from Billy Bob's grasp and turned it around. "Says here it's worth one thousand nine hundred and ninety dollars! Look at it! That there's mint condition! I bought that in a sporting goods store back in the nineties. It went straight into a plastic sleeve! That there's an uncirculated Barry Bonds rookie card!"

"'Cept it is circulated, or how else would you have it?"

"Listen, Billy Bob, my girl Krystal's in the pokey. I need five hundred to get her out. I'll give it to you for five."

Billy Bob made a face, pulled his beard. "Sorry, Gary. No can do. It's just not worth it to me. It sure ain't gonna sell here, and puttin' that shit up on eBay takes too much time and is too much work. Why don't you go on eBay? You'll get a better deal there. Now if you had any more of those He-Man figures we could do business. You got any more?"

Gary shook his head in disgust. "Man, I been comin' here for years."

"That's right. We been doin' business for years. You got nothin' to complain about."

Gary put his hands on his hips and swiveled to survey the crowd. The old man in a long-billed fisherman's cap examining a casting reel. The young mother clutching a snot-nosed toddler by the hand, looking at some Hummels. A Mexican Goth with a purple Mohawk getting the feel of an old Stratocaster.

Gary held up the card. "Hey, all you good people! Any baseball fans in here? Any of y'all collect cards? I got here a mint condition Barry Bonds rookie card! Book says it's worth two grand, but I'll let it go for half that, or your best offer!"

"Shut the fuck up," Billy Bob snapped. "The fuck you think this is? Your own personal auction house? This is where I do business, not you."

Gary walked among the shoppers holding the card to his forehead like a sacred relic. "I got it rightchere, anyone want to take a closer look. You buy this, you can turn right around and sell it for twice what you paid! Easy money."

Billy Bob turned purple. "How'd you like me to come out from behind this counter and throw your punk ass out the door?"

Floyd looked up from the electronic drum kit where he'd been silently playing, mouthed the words, "oh fuck," and stood.

"That's it!" Billy Bob thundered, coming out from behind the glass island. The exit was opposite the storefront, so he had to come all the way around, his progress impeded by several golf bags. Gary was still hawking the card when Billy Bob seized him by the scruff of his neck and the back of his belt, propelled him forward, used Gary's face to push open the heavy glass door, and tossed Gary to the pavement like yesterday's trash.

"Fuck you, Duba! Don't come back here. I don't need

your business." Billy Bob went back inside, the door sighing shut behind him.

Gary tucked the card carefully into his pocket and got to his feet, the injustice burning in him like a coal fire, like acid from too much spicy Mexican. He'd been a good customer! The boys stopped tormenting the gator to look at him. One of them made a snide comment and they laughed.

Gary steamed their way with blood in his eye. They took one look at his gangling form, bulging biceps and thick wrists and skedaddled, some of them leaping the drainage ditch, landing in the water, soaking their high-zoot sneakers. Gary arrived at a circle of trampled grass. The adolescent alligator regarded him with a beady eye. Gary seized the gator by the neck and just behind its back legs. It thrashed madly for an instant, and then stopped resisting, sensing futility.

Floyd sat in his truck as Gary returned gripping the gator.

"Put that down! Come on! Don't do something stupid!"

As a customer exited, Gary entered. The customer did a double take, double-timed it to his truck without looking back. Billy Bob was nowhere in sight.

Gary stood in the front of the shop holding the gator above his head like a WWF belt. "You don't want my business, Billy Bob? You don't want anybody's business!"

He whirled, thrust the gator at an obese woman holding an Elvis plate. The gator clacked air. The woman screamed. The plate shattered. Gary moved counter-clockwise around the store, thrusting the snapping gator at all who came near.

The clientele stampeded, screaming. A bony blonde meth freak paused to capture the precious moments on her iPhone.

Billy Bob erupted from his back office like a badger, pointed at Darlene. "Darlene, call the cops."

Billy Bob had played tackle for Everglades High, and for the Gators. The shop was filled with Gator paraphernalia. As the one-time tackle circled the glass counter like an angry tractor, Gary gripped the gator's tail with both hands and whirled it around his head like a lariat. Billy Bob paused.

"Take one step and omma toss this gator in your ugly face!" Gary said.

"You stupid redneck! How'd you like me to go back in my office and get my forty-five?"

"Do it, you gutless piece of shit! You're the reason the Gators lost to the Wildcats."

Billy Bob extended a trembling finger. "I was sick that day! I told the coach and he made me play anyway!"

Sirens intruded. Floyd popped back in.

"Drop that fuckin' gator 'less you want to end up in jail with Krystal!"

5 | HABIB

The Law Offices of Habib Rodriguez occupied the pillared centerpiece of a strip mall on Highway Twenty-Seven, sandwiched between All American Karate and Virgil's liquors. Floyd parked his van in the lot between a Lexus and a modified Chevy truck whose bumper perched three feet above the pavement. Floyd went into Virgil's while Gary sought counsel.

"Habib, man, I ain't got no money, but if you loan me the five I need to bail out Krystal, I'll do whatever you ask."

Habib leaned back in his executive chair. Pistons plunged, compressing air. Springs adjusted. It sounded like a trampoline in progress.

"What do I look like, a bail bondsman? Go to Herkimer's."

"Man, I'm in a jam. Come on, man! She's been in there for a day and a half! I've got to get her out. I done paid you every cent I owed you, didn't I?"

"Last time you gave me stationary bicycles, if I remember correctly."

"Well you took it. Howzat workin' out? You using it?"

"Gary, I don't have time to take a shit, much less pedal a stationary bike. What I want with that bike when I have a new Fat Boy in my garage."

Gary was sweating. His eye twitched. "Please, Habib. There must be something I can do for you that's worth five hundred!"

Habib lowered his head and peered from beneath the Stetson. "Can you take a picture?"

"Can I take a picture?! You know I can!"

"Show me."

Gary slapped his pocket and scrolled through pictures. Krystal and he shit-faced at the Dew Drop Inn. Gary shit-faced in the yard in a photo taken by Krystal. Gary's bunion. He knew it was in there somewhere.

"Listen, I told you about my idea, how to protect your property during hurricanes and shit. If you'd come out to my place, you'd see what I mean. It's a stroke of genius, man. If I can get backing, I'll clean up! Wait...wait...here it is."

Gary turned the phone around and held it up. Habib took the phone and squinted. He turned it sideways. "This looks like some shit hole trailer with chains over the top."

"House suspenders, man! Only instead of holding your pants up, they hold your house down! I need somebody to help me put together a crowd-funding campaign, and to do a documentary on what I've already accomplished. I'll use my house as an example."

"Your house looks like something that's due to be de-molished. Even if this crazy ass idea was worth something, you'll never sell it with what you got here, which looks like an old rusted trailer chained to the earth. You'd have to show a nice house in a nice neighborhood, and ideally, show the fuckin' thing in action with hundred mile an hour winds and other houses whipping by."

Gary sat back. "I hadn't thought of that. But I know how to take a picture."

Habib delicately slid Gary's phone back across the desk, reached into the middle drawer of his gun metal gray gov-ernment surplus desk and withdrew a manila envelope. He shook out several color photos printed on his office computer. The first showed a demure couple in their thirties, she with a brunette bob, sultry eyes, and a Jayne Mansfield sweater, he in a sharkskin suit, hairline mustache, and snarky grin. There were photos of the couple separately.

"Missus Kelso has asked me to represent her in her divorce proceedings with Mister Kelso. Missus Kelso has worked like a dog to build her mail-order cosmetics business up into a six figure business, and now Mister Kelso, former-ly employed as a chef at The Olive Garden, a racetrack tout and inveterate gambler, has employed a barracuda named Harlan Sandusky, who intends to go after Missus Kelso's assets, claiming that she has been trying to gaslight him throughout the two years of their marriage.

"Yet every night, Mister Kelso cavorts with whores at the

Starlite Motel. I need some crisp pics of Mister Kelso with his dates, ideally, in flagrant delecto."

"I can do that, Habib, no problem. Can you advance me the five?"

Habib sat back and stoked his stogie, eyes on the yellowing acoustic tile ceiling. "Do I look like a sucker to you, Gary? I'm a criminal attorney. Get your shit together. If you stay sharp, you can get those pics to me tomorrow morning. I'll pay you then."

"All right. I guess Krystal can stand one more night. She does pack a mean wallop. You want me to use my phone, or do you have something else you want me to use?"

"These photos have to be visible and recognizable to a jury, if it comes to that." Habib opened the bottom right drawer on his desk and pulled out a device the size of a cigarette pack. He slid it across the desk. "That's the latest Fonebone. That isn't even on the market yet. I'm loaning it to you because it takes crisp photos, even at night, and you can send them to me immediately. Take it. Turn it on. It's intuitive. Flip up that little viewfinder."

Gary turned the object over in his hands, held it to his eye and peered through, framing the lawyer against the backdrop of a black velvet painting of a ferocious wolf perched atop a rocky butte, like Batman brooding over the city. To the right, framed testimonials and photographs covered Habib's Ego Wall. Habib with three governors, Habib with Miami running back Roebuck Simms, Habib with Brian Flores, Habib with Debbie Wasserman-Schulz, Habib with

Dale Earnhardt Junior. Various movie stars.

On the wall behind Habib, flanking the noble wolf, were his degrees from the University of Florida and Duke, where he'd earned his Masters in Law.

"That camera is a prototype. I shouldn't even have it. Don't let it out of your sight."

Gary looked at the logo, a telephone receiver wearing a dunce cap. "What is Fonebone?"

"You've never heard of Fonebone? It's a multimillion dollar tech, started by Orin Houtkooper in his garage. It does everything the Smart phone does, only simpler."

Gary stood, sliding the device into his pocket. "I'm on it. I'll get you something tonight."

Gary found Floyd scratching off lottery tickets in the liquor store. "Dude, can we stop at the jail on the way home?"

"Naw, dude. I got a gig in an hour. You got a spare tire at home?"

"Yeah. Awright. Thanks, Floyd. Thanks for being a good friend. You can leave. I'll hitch home."

6 | THE STARLITE MOTEL

Gary walked down the street to Big 'O' Tires, helped himself to coffee and stood at the counter behind which an open door led to the garage bays. A plump man in Big 'O' coveralls and a soul patch came out.

"Whaddaya need?"

Gary recited his tire specs, which he knew by heart. "Omma need a wheel and a tire. What's that cost?"

"You bring in the wheel, we can switch it over."

"That ain't happenin'."

The man poked at his computer.

"I can give you a deal. One hundred twenty on a Hankook, comes with a six-month warranty, and that includes mounting. Where's the vehicle?"

"Back at my place. I ain't got no spare at the moment."

"Hang on." The man disappeared into the garage and returned a moment later, heaving the heavy black tire up on the counter. Gary inhaled the heady scent of fresh rubber.

He wouldn't mind working there.

"How you wanna pay for this?"

"You a baseball fan?" Gary asked.

"Hells yeah. Big Marlins fan. I'm stoked about Wetzer."

Gary reached into his pocket and pulled out the Barry Bonds card. Fifteen minutes later, he stood out front with the tire at his side and his thumb in the air.

A Seminole Indian named Ed picked Gary up on Twenty-Seven in an old white Ram Truck, dropping him at the intersection of Partridge Way. Kicking the tire before him like a hoop, Gary walked three miles to Weldon Way, a dirt trail that ran five miles past Wokenoki Trailer Park and Ralston Salvage, pausing to admire the elegant roof line of a '67 fastback Barracuda, eventually reaching his place. The end of the road. Beyond his trailer lay swamp. His Ford F-150 listed in the yard, the once beige finish bleeding rust. Gary had installed lifters to raise the chassis six inches over stock. The truck looked like an old Conestoga wagon abandoned on the trail to California.

Leaning the tire against the truck, Gary went to his tool shed and grabbed his wrenches and a heavy-duty Harbor Freight jack. Didn't trust those toothpicks they called jacks. No sir. He grabbed a six pack of ice-cold Dixie from the refrigerator and pissed off the deck. No sense messing with that snake.

He climbed into the truck, set the parking brake, got out, and loosened the lug nuts holding the wheel. He slid the jack behind the front wheel well and pumped until the flat tire sagged an inch above the clay. Removing the lug nuts, he slid off the tire and rolled the whole wheel away. He mounted the new wheel and replaced the lug nuts.

He lowered the vehicle, removed the jack, and tightened the lug nuts. Good to go. He thought about heaving the old wheel into the swamp, but it would just sit there, and he'd have to look at it every time he went to the end of his pier to smoke a doobie. Gary retrieved the wanton wheel, rolled it into the mangroves and heaved it on his burn pile, a ten foot clearing in the center of which lay a pyramid of charcoal, the remains of cans, a lamp, odd pieces of lumber, shoes, and a GE coffee maker that had pissed him off.

He went up on his deck, settled back in the Adirondack, sucked the Dixie and called Trixie.

"Hey there, little lady," Gary said. "Just want you to know I'm workin' on that bail money and with any lucky I'll have her outta there in the morning."

"Oh, thank God!" Trixie said. "I'm so worried! I went down there this morning. The poor thing looked exhausted. I told her to pray to Jesus and with God's help we'll get through this."

"Krystal's a tough broad. She knows how to throw a punch."

"Her father was a boxer, you know, before he vanished in the middle of the night, goddamn him to hell."

"Yup. You told me."

"Where did you get the money?"

"Well I don't have it yet, but I'll get it. I got a job."

"What job?"

"I'm a bonaroo private eye!" Gary told her about his job for Habib Rodriguez.

"Well you be careful out there, Gary. I'll pray for you."

"Yes, ma'am. I'll letcha know when I'm goin' down to the jail."

Gary used the broom handle to open the bathroom door and raise the toilet seat. He duct-taped a broken rear-view to the end of the broom handle and used it like a periscope to look in the bowl. The snake was gone.

Gary showered in tepid water the color of tea, toweled off and went into his bedroom, pulling on black jeans and a black T. Wouldn't do to be seen. No sir. He'd watched Cheaters. Best get in and out without causing a ruckus. Gary used his cellphone to locate the Starlite Motel, a hot sheets crib on Manatee Boulevard. Habib said the mark didn't appear until after nine.

Damn, he needed some money. He should have asked Habib for a thou. No, two. Gary hadn't worked for five days, ever since the job at Cobalt Estates ended. That had been a good gig, repairing Spanish tiles and shingles in a gated community after a hurricane. From his perch atop the estates, Gary had a clear view of the swimming pool, in which a septuagenarian clad in a sinister black wetsuit, skull cap and goggles swam laps for an hour every morning, and the nine hole golf course beyond, where geriatrics cruised in light yellow golf carts in white shorts and knit tops. A hearty few walked the course with their Mexican caddies.

Gary fell asleep in the Adirondack, woke when a yellow jacket perched on his nose. Gary and the yellow jacket were eye to eye. It tickled. Slowly as a melting glacier, Gary reached up with his right hand and grabbed the bill of his Stars 'n' Bars cap. In one fell swoop, he brought the hat down in an arc, swatting the yellow jacket into the air.

"FUCK ya! Fuckin' yellow jackets. Nobody likes you."

It was dusk. It was time. Gary went through his dresser and all the cabinets, but he was out of meth. Filling a water bottle, Gary put the Fonebone in his right front pocket and booked, negotiating the rutted, potholed, sinkholed road with his lights on. Twenty-five minutes later, he parked on Manatee Boulevard up the street from the Starlite, which he could see through his windshield. It was still in the mid-eighties with high humidity.

A lanky black kid leaned against the street sign down the block. A light blue Volvo pulled over, there was a brief exchange, and the Volvo purred away.

Well damn. If he needed it, there it was. Gary looked at his watch. It was nine forty-five. The mark should show any minute. He wondered if he had time to run down there, score some speed, and get back in position. Well sure. Gary was fast. He'd run track at Manatee High in Belle Glade, where he'd grown up.

He was just about to open the door when a Mercedes sedan passed him on the left and pulled into the Starlite parking lot. Fuck. That was Kelso. The buzz would have to wait. When Kelso went into the office, Gary eased out of his truck on the passenger side and lingered in the shadow of Doc Johnson's Adult Sex Toys. A pair of teenage boys in hoodies shuffled by. Gary rubbed his hands together as they passed, and they kept on moving.

Quiet as a ninja in his Wal-Mart sneakers, Gary advanced until he had a clear view of the parking lot and motel, an L-shaped two-story late fifties mod job with external stairs. The neon sign advertised FREE CABLE AND INTERNET ACCESS. A small sign declared VIBRATING BEDS/ WIDE SELECTION OF ADULT ENTERTAINMENT.

Gary watched as Kelso returned from the office, got in the Mercedes and drove in Gary's direction. Gary pulled into a doorway. The Mercedes parked in front of a room far from the office. Kelso got out, went around, and held the door for a big, raw-boned woman whose platinum wig clashed with her dark skin. She looked like she played center for the Atlanta Dream. The woman lit a heater while Kelso unlocked the door. They went inside. A light went on. There was one big front window, with the shades pulled down, leaving a two-inch gap at the sill.

Well all-rooty. Gary thought maybe he ought to look into private investigator work. Sure as shit beat roofing. He waited until the lights dimmed and crept forward, hugging the stucco wall of the strip mall behind him until he was level with the end of the building. He pulled out the Fone-bone, opened the viewfinder and looked. With its infra-red application, everything was clear as day. He nonchalantly strolled up the sidewalk to Kelso's room, knelt, and peeked through the gap.

The monstrous woman straddled Kelso wearing nothing but pink panties which showed her bony ass and appeared to be playing patty-cake with the client, who lay with his head on two pillows. He had them in profile. He began clicking. A car turned in behind him, its headlights flashing against the front of the hotel, throwing his shadow into the room, onto the back wall.

"WHAT THE FUCK!" the hooker said.

7 | PATRICE

Gary shoved the Fonebone in his pocket as the front door opened. The woman was six feet four, with startling aquamarine eye shadow and palm frond lashes, wearing only the pink panties. She had negligible breasts and a package. She pointed a bony finger at him.

"Hold it right dere, fuckface."

Gary booked. The creature ran him down in three strides and shoved him to the cracked asphalt. He chipped a tooth, turned over on his back but the woman was already on him raining down punches.

Gary used his elbows, frantically twisting to throw off her weight, got a leg free, heel-kicked the monster in the sternum and struggled to his feet panting. His clothes were soaked through. The hooker sprang up. Maybe she did play basketball. They circled. The hooded teens leaned against a rental Ford, smoking and elbowing each other. A Lincoln Town Car stopped, the passenger window lowered, and a cell phone appeared.

Gary faked a hook and lunged in low, but the hooker brought up her knee, stunning Gary in the chest. He got his arms around her and took her down. Unnoticed, Kelso ran out of the motel room carrying his shoes, got in the Mercedes, and booked.

A dot Indian came out of the office. "I have informed the police," he called from a distance. "They're on their way."

The combatants rolled apart, panting. The hooker got to hands and knees. Gary ran for his truck   fumbled with the keys, leaped into the driver's seat. As he inserted his key in the ignition, he heard the doppler whoop of cops. The passenger door opened, and the hooker scrambled in, clutching a North Face backpack.

"What the fuck?"

The hooker slammed the door. "Drive, mon! Drive!"

Gary started the engine and pulled out as the flashing bars appeared in his rear view four blocks back.

"Fuck you doing, mon?" the hooker demanded. "You taking my picture?"

"Not you. Kelso! I'm a licensed private investigator representing an attorney representing Kelso's wife."

"You a licensed private investigator."

"That's right."

The hooker snorted. "And I'm the Queen of Ethiopia."

Gary scrupulously obeyed the speed limit as three police vehicles stopped at all angles in the parking lot of the Starlite.

"I'm just trying to make a living," Gary said.

"I'm just trying to make a living too."

Gary looked at his dash. "Fuck. I'm outta gas."

"Well you can just drop me wherever, noble mon. I'll find my way home."

"Got any money? Listen, if you loan me twenty bucks, I'll take you wherever you want to go."

The hooker regarded Gary like the state insect. "Are you for real, mon? First you break up my evening and now you want me to loan you money?"

"I wouldn't be doin' this if I didn't need the money."

The hooker barked contralto. "What about them pictures, mon? I don't need no vice beef."

"The law will never see these. Listen. Jordan Kelso's a real shit heel. His wife's a fuckin' saint, and she's beautiful. What's he doin' soliciting prostitutes?"

The hooker pointed to herself in defiance. "You don't think I'm beautiful?"

Gary glanced over. "I don't think you're even a woman."

The hooker grinned, flashing a grill like a Rolls Royce. "I is saving for my trans op. I got fourteen thousand to go."

"Is that a no on the twenty?"

The hooker dipped into her backpack, removed a wallet and took out a fifty. "This all I got, mon. When you gonna pay me back?"

"Soon's I turn in these photos. Tomorrow morning. Only reason I'm doing this is because my girl Krystal's in jail and I need bail money."

"Tell de troof, now. You ain't no licensed private investigator."

Gary grinned and offered his hand. "Gary Duba. I'm a roofer."

"Patrice Talley. Pleased to meet you." Patrice had a grip like a longshoreman.

Gary pulled up to the pump at a Kwik Trip. Patrice grabbed her pack and headed for the store. Gary followed her in, gave the cashier the fifty.

The tank topped out at forty-one dollars and sixteen cents.

Retrieving his change, Gary bought a five-dollar lottery ticket. Not enough for cigs. Getting in his truck, he rummaged through the glove compartment and door wells for a butt, a roach, anything. Looking through the greasy frosted windows, he saw a tall black man purchasing items. It wasn't until Patrice came out that Gary realized who it was. Without the wig and the makeup, Patrice was just a big guy.

Patrice pushed a plastic shopping bag onto the seat and removed a pack of Carltons, handed Gary a Slim Jim and a Red Bull. "Okay. Take me to the Lip Lok Lounge."

"Where is it?"

"It's in Belle Glade."

They headed east on the Interstate. Traffic was light for Wednesday evening, and they reached Belle Glade at eleven-thirty. The Lip Lok Lounge was a louche hole on West Canal across the street from Martini Tacos, sandwiched between EASY CASH and BURT'S TATTOOS. It had a stucco facade, a horizontal window hosting a neon Dixie Beer sign, and an ancient air conditioner perched above the front door like the Sword of Damocles, dripping water. Gary parked in the side lot next to an ancient Citation.

The cool interior smelled of beer, sweat, and makeup. Customers sat at the bar or in the booths wearing studded black leather. The Mexican bartender, who wore a black leather vest and gold chains against his furry chest, waved.

"Patrice! Sweetheart! Where did you find Storm Front Commander?"

Patrice threw an army around Gary's shoulders. "This my good friend Gary Duba. Gary is a licensed private investigator. We met on a case."

"What are we drinking?"

"I'll have a Cuba Libre," Gary said.

The bartender's hands moved. "Duba wants a Cuba. You?"

"I will have a shot of El Tesoro and a Dos Modeles."

Patrice used a gold AmEx card to pay for the drinks and took them to an empty booth. "I will add these drinks to what you owe me," he said, sliding in. Gary slid in opposite.

"No prob. Where you from?"

"Kingston, Jamaica. Come here three years ago, save my tips for my trans op. Some day I want to open my own club."

"What kind of club?"

"A classy nightclub with a select clientele."

"Fags?"

Patrice's lip curled in disgust. "No, mon. We don' refer

to ourselves as fags. A fag is what you smoke, mon. We are transsexuals."

Gary looked around, smelling tequila, beer, cigarette smoke and Ax Body Spray. A gilt-framed photo of Marilyn Monroe gazed at their booth. A row of panties was thumb-tacked to the fake wood paneling above and behind the bar, beneath black and white photos of Elvis in leathers, Tom Jones, Freddie Mercury, Liza, and Divine.

"Is everyone in here a transsexual?"

"No, mon. Lip Lok welcome all kind. Even you."

Gary pointed a finger across the table. "Hope you're keepin' track, 'cuz I need about two more drinks."

8 | PALMETTO BUGS

Gary tasted vinyl. His eyes opened. His tongue lay on the bench of the Lip Lok Lounge's booth. His head pounded like a military parade. Light filtered in through the blinds covering the horizontal window facing the street. A palmetto bug confronted him from six inches. He didn't have the energy to smash it. Lou Christie's "Lightning's Striking Again" played on the sound system.

Inch by inch, he returned to a sitting position, his bladder full. His head throbbed like Ginger Baker's bass drum. The Lounge was closed, yet he remained. The chairs had been set upside down on the tables and a man in a black leather vest swept the hardwood floor.

The bartender.

"Oh, you up, now? Man, you was snockered. I tried to pry you outta here when we closed, but there was no pryin'. No tryin', no pryin'. No lyin'."

"Where's Patrice?"

The bartender made a poof gesture with his fingers. "He disappears at the crack of dawn."

"Fuck. What time is it?"

Without looking up, the bartender pointed to a clock on the wall. Eleven.

Gary felt his way to the restroom, leaning on tables, tipping a chair to the floor with a clatter that sent shock waves through his fractured skull, and emptied his bladder. He splashed water on his face and looked in the mirror. He had a nice shiner, a chipped tooth and a fat lip. He washed his hands, went out, grabbed a glass from behind the bar, and drank three glasses of water. He eyed the liquor bottles. A hair of the dog was in order.

"Would you pour me a drink?"

"Pour yourself. Leave five bucks on the table."

"Oh mannnn, I don't have five bucks. I owe Patrice fifty."

"Well that's a first, gotta say. Never known Patrice to loan nobody nothin'. Are you and him..."

"Of course not! Do I look like a fag?"

The bartender looked over with weary eyes. "Son, in here, everybody looks like a fag. What's a fag look like, anyhow?"

"You know! Some mincing ponce in high heels."

"Like Patrice?"

"He's a trans! Not a fag."

The bartender grinned. "Now you learnin'!"

Gary wiped his mouth. "Yeah. Sorry. What's your name?"

"Clarence. And you're Gary Duba. From Libre Cuba. Tell you what. I'll pour you one on the house. But that's it. After that, you're on your own."

Gary shuffled to the bar, settled on a red vinyl stool and tossed down the glass of rum. He pulled out the Fonebone, checked his pictures. Yes! Kelso was clearly visible with Patrice atop. He pulled out Habib's card and sent the photos.

"I need twenty bucks."

Clarence swept. "Yeah. Good luck with that."

"I don't suppose I could borrow twenty."

"Hah!"

"How 'bout you give me the broom and let me clean up. And I'll pick up every scrap of shit in your parking lot."

Clarence looked up. He forked over the broom. "Lemme know when you're done."

"You got any rubber gloves?"

Clarence went behind the bar and handed Gary a pair of heavy-duty yellow gloves.

The interior was neatly swept but the adjacent parking lot looked like the aftermath of an Occupy Wall Street rally. Gary filled a jumbo garbage bag with cigarette butts, used condoms, nitrous canisters, advertising fliers, receipts, plastic bags, syringes, beer bottles, peppermint schnapps bottles, empty cans, two pair underpants, a sock, four used batteries, two AA and two AAA, a torn Man Date, a discarded tire, and a Nike sneaker.

Sweating heavily, Gary walked around to the rear and stuffed the bag in a steel dumpster that reeked and squeaked.

Two rats dove for cover as he shut the lid. A commercial alley ran behind the lounge and the backs of the buildings facing opposite on Hunt Street. A dusty date palm grew through a crack in the asphalt.

Reentering the lounge, Gary shivered at the sudden drop in temperature, acutely aware of his slovenly appearance and rancid aroma. Clarence was behind the bar washing glasses while Smokey sang "Soulful Shack". Gary did a little two-step as he vamped toward the bar, snapping his fingers.

"All done."

"Yeah? Lemme see." Gary followed Clarence behind the bar, through the warehouse and out the steel back door. Clarence stood with hands on hips surveying the pristine lot.

"Holy shit. Well I guess that's worth twenty bucks. Come on in."

As Clarence handed Gary four fins, Gary said, "I don't suppose you got a shower here. I smell like a Tijuana whorehouse."

"Come in back."

Gary followed Clarence back into the warehouse. Clarence pointed to a corner where a shower head extended from the wall over a concave floor with a steel drain in the center. "Place used to be a feed storage facility. There's towels in that cardboard box along with clothes, anything you want to borrow."

Gary stuck out his hand.

"Thanks, man. Thanks a lot."

Clarence waved over his shoulder.

There was no hot water. Gary took a cold shower, toweled himself off and plowed through the discard box, pulling out a pair of black socks, blue Fruit of the Looms, and a Green Day T-shirt. He put on his jeans. A man didn't part with his jeans.

Gary went out front to thank Clarence. "Y'know, if you want to get rid of those palmetto bugs, I know a guy."

"That's a pipe dream, essay."

Gary drove west on Twenty-Seven past the Beauty Buffet, Krav Maga, Lorenzo's Liquors, Dealin' Doug's Used Cars, KFC, Arby's, Taco Bell, Taco John, Taco Avocado, Taco Jocko and a Waffle House. Three blocks ahead he saw police vehicles scattered randomly in front of Habib's office like children's toys. Parking down the block, he approached on the sidewalk, passing homeless people curled in abandoned doorways. A phalanx of police surrounded the building. Seconds later, two burly cops came out with Habib between them, handcuffed, and deposited him in the back of a police cruiser.

Gary went up to the nearest cop, a kid in short-sleeved blue and aviator shades.

"That's my lawyer!" Gary exclaimed.

"Better find another one."

"What happened? What did he do?"

"You can read about it in the papers."

Stunned, Gary walked back to his truck and looked

across the street at the Waffle House.

FIVE DOLLAR BREAKFAST

He went inside. A signed photograph of Burt Reynolds hung behind the cash register. The place was half-full with the lunch crowd. Gary took a corner table and ordered a five-dollar breakfast which included a three egg omelet, hash browns, and coffee. What was he going to tell Trixie and Krystal? He stretched breakfast out an hour, compulsively consulting the Okeechobee News website. At two fifteen, the first story appeared.

LOCAL LAWYER ARRESTED ON
COCKFIGHTING CHARGES
ALSO CHARGED WITH DISTRIBUTING
CHILD PORNOGRAPHY

Gary ran a mental inventory. He had nothing at home as valuable as the Barry Bonds card, but perhaps the whole collection, which included dozens of uncirculated cards, would fetch seven hundred and fifty. But where? He burned his bridges at Billy Bob's, and he didn't have time to do the eBay thing, even if he understood it, which he didn't.

There was a weekly swap and flea market in the parking lot of the Piggly Wiggly, but that wasn't until Saturday. Krystal couldn't wait until then. He thought about selling his blood, but that barely scratched the surface and they'd probably turn him down anyway, due to a preponderance of meth, alcohol, and weed.

He looked down. A palmetto bug stood atop his omelet like a commencement speaker, waving its feelers to quiet the audience.

A woman screamed. It was a real wall piercer, loud enough for a hurricane warning. She ran toward the door. Several others got up, spilling coffee and silverware.

"PALMETTO BUGS!" a child wailed.

The stampede was on.

9 | BELMONT PEST CONTROL

Gary followed, without paying his bill. Out front, he found the manager, a squat Mexican woman in a beige dress with Rosalita embroidered on her breast in red, dialing nine one one.

"Yes, it's an emergency!" she screamed into the phone. "The Waffle House has been overrun with palmetto bugs!"

Beat.

"The Waffle House on Main!"

Beat.

"What do you mean it's not an emergency? A woman fell down running out of here!"

Rosalita went wide-eyed. She gestured at the heavens. She turned to Gary in astonishment. "They hung up on me."

Gary fished out his wallet and handed her a five. "That's for breakfast."

He found one of Floyd's cards. "Here. Call Belmont Pest Control. Insurance will pay for it."

She took the card. "Fuck if it will."

"Whatever. Belmont does a good job and they guarantee their results for thirty days. You got to call them again, they give you a discount rate. You can look up their business rating."

"I don't have time for that. I only been managing this place two months. This is just my focking luck. I should call national."

"Screw national! They'll just dither around while you lose customers. Go ahead. Call Belmont. He'll get the job done by the end of the day, guaranteed."

She peered at him. "What are you, his brother?"

"I work for him. Gary Duba."

She stared at the hand a minute then took it. "Rosalita Bermudez."

She dialed the number.

Floyd arrived at two-fifteen, his van emitting a vast gray cloud. Only the manager's Kia, Gary's F-150, and an abandoned Chevelle remained in the Waffle House parking lot, which like most lots in Gary's acquaintance, was filled with trash. Floyd parked near the back entrance where Gary and Rosalita stood. Floyd emerged in a pong of Canoe, wearing crisp gray pants and a puce Belmont Pest Control shirt with the logo and his name emblazoned on the chest in green. He'd trimmed his beard and washed.

"Floyd," Gary said. "This here's Rosalita, she's the manager."

Floyd shook hands. "You have a pest problem?"

Rosalita crossed her arms. "Palmetto bugs! They have always been here, but they knew their place! Now, all of a sudden, today they decide to mount a revolution. They are crawling on the tables and up customer's legs. No one can eat like that."

Floyd waved them off. "Nothin' to it. We're gonna need several hours."

"You might as well. I put up the closed sign and informed regional. They say they can't get their guy here for forty-eight hours and gave the green light. Now, this isn't going to poison my customers, is it?"

"Belmont Pest Control is licensed and certified by the Florida Department of Agriculture. We are bonded and fully insured. If pests return during a thirty-day period, Belmont will go through your property again at no charge."

"How long is this going to take? Tomorrow's Friday. We do most of our business on the weekend."

"How big is the property, ma'am?"

"It's about ten thousand square feet."

"We go through the property. We use caulk to stop further infestations, stop any leaks, look behind the refrigerator, under the sink, crevices in cabinets and shelves, closet door corners, restroom cabinets and closets. We use permethrin, a biological based component. It's very safe. And Boric acid. I suspect it will be dark by the time we finish. You can take off if you like, and I'll phone you when the job is done."

Rosalita threw her hands in the air. "Great. Focking great."

"If I didn't have Gary here, it would take twice as long."

Gary and Floyd put on rubber gloves, carried all the dirty dishes into the kitchen, rinsed them off, and put them in the jumbo dishwasher. They wiped off the tables and set the chairs on them upside down. Palmetto bugs ran for their lives. The Waffle House was old with peeling stucco and a photo of its grand opening, in 1970. There were several photos of Burt Reynolds, one with the original owner, signed. Ancient framed color photos showed proto surfers, hula girls swaying under palm trees, and Don Rickles. The place smelled pleasantly of bacon and coffee.

There were still orders waiting to be picked up. Gary helped himself to some bacon.

They caulked the seams, fixed a drip in the kitchen, sprayed permethrin at the base of every wall as well as a mixture of boric acid and baking soda. At the back of the kitchen, partially covered by a refrigerator, was a walk-in closet that looked as if it hadn't been cleaned in thirty years. Floyd and Gary rocked the refrigerator away from the wall far enough to open the door.

"I'll do this closet," Gary said. "You start on the rest rooms."

Inside, he flipped the switch, but the light was burned out. Using a flashlight, Gary surveyed the crowded space, with two sets of floor-to-ceiling metal shelves facing each other, a three-foot corridor extending five-feet to the back wall, covered in old cardboard boxes. Palmetto bugs streamed from the light. Gary got down on hands and knees and located their passages, using caulk to seal them.

There was a three-inch gap between the cement floor and the bottom shelf. Gary got down and shined his flashlight on the squirming mob. Palmetto City! The Mother Lode. The beetles gleamed root beer in his light as they scrambled for cover. Gary forked out three ancient mouse traps with desiccated remains, and several tape traps encrusted with brittle brown husks, stuffing all into a plastic garbage bag.

Lastly, all that remained was the wall of moldering goods against the back wall. He didn't even look. He hauled them out two by two, out the back and into the dumpster. One box fell open as it fell, releasing a clatter of tin cans so ancient, the labels were indecipherable. Pulling out the last box, Gary spied a brown paper bag wedged in the corner. He picked it up. There was something inside. He shook it. He feared it. Wharf rat mummies? A dead iguana? Carrying it out into the kitchen, he carefully opened it and looked inside.

It was as he'd imagined. The fur of some dead animal. But wait. It was too uniform and nicely combed to be an animal. Delicately, he pulled it out. It was a wig. A black wig for a man. Gary stared deep into the bag where a curled yellow sheet lay. He pulled it out and spread it open on the kitchen counter.

It was a receipt from Skylines and Hairlines in Miami Beach, dated June 12, 1986. The custom-made wig cost two hundred and forty-nine dollars. The receipt was signed Burt Reynolds.

It was nine p.m. as Gary stood in the parking lot by his truck and dialed Billy Bob. The temperature had fallen into the low eighties.

"Fuck you want?" Billy Bob answered.

"First, I want to apologize for chasing your customers away."

"Fuck you. You know, I got that shit on video. I'm still deciding whether to turn it over to the cops."

"We been doing business for years, Billy Bob. I want to make amends."

"How you gonna do dat?"

"I have something you're gonna like."

"My ass." Billy Bob's voice faded as he turned away and yelled, "I'm on the phone!"

His voice returned. "What is it?"

"Burt Reynolds' wig."

"Oh, my ass! Burt Reynolds' wig. Are you high or something? You doin' crystal again?"

"No. I swear it ain't a hoax. I found it in an old closet at a Waffle House Floyd and me was fumigatin'. It comes with a signed receipt. Burt Reynolds. Skylines and Hairlines in Miami Beach, dated June 12, 1986."

"Are you shittin' me?"

"It's real. It's been hidden away for decades. At least let me come in and show it to you."

"Call me tomorrow."

Billy Bob hung up.

It was nine-thirty when Gary finally pulled up at his place. He went up the steps, unlocked the door and turned on the lights. Palmetto bugs scurried for cover. He rummaged around beneath the sink, found a box of baking soda, and laid it down along the baseboards.

In the bathroom, the snake was gone. Gary took a long, tepid shower in brown water, toweled himself off and tossed his dirty clothes into the overflowing wicker basket. He had to get to the laundromat soon or he would be out of clean clothes. He collapsed on his bed, turning the wall air conditioning unit up to the max.

Up at seven, Gary pulled on clean jeans, automatically transferring all the receipts from his old jeans into the new jean's back pocket, and turned on the morning news on WINK in Fort Meyers. All their newscasters began each broadcast by winking at the audience. A vivacious redhead appeared. "This is Aphrodite Cruz for WINK in Fort Meyers. The Florida Highway Patrol has arrested an

Okeechobee man for defecating on traffic from a light pole. Fort Meyers Police have taken a woman into custody for tackling another woman who cut in front of her in line at the Motor Vehicle Department." Venezuela was in flames. The Coast Guard had intercepted seventeen boats of fugitives. Aphrodite winked. "We'll be right back after these important messages."

Habib appeared during the commercials, standing in front of a hip-hop Lady Justice, the word "justice" rendered in vivid blue graffiti. Habib wore blue jeans, a white dress shirt with turquoise bolo and leather vest, wearing his Stetson and sunglasses.

"Have you been injured in an automobile accident? Is your insurance company not giving you what you deserve? Call me, The Long Arm, Habib Rodriguez. All initial consultations are free. You will not be charged anything unless we win a substantial award."

A young black woman, her hair in cornrows, said "I was sitting at a red light when a driver T-boned my car. The insurance company didn't want to give me what I deserved, so I contacted Habib Rodriguez, and he got me two hundred and fifty thousand dollars."

Next up was a beautiful blonde in a swimsuit posing against a Caribbean sunset. She splayed her long fingers over her lovely face. The camera moved in for a close-up of the lush lips, the charming dimple. "I wasn't always this beautiful. In fact, I looked like a gnome. I look now as God intended, thanks to Doctor Vanderly Mukerjee, plastic surgeon to the stars."

A slight Indian in a brown suit and glasses appeared before a wall of certificates. "Greetings. I am Doctor Vanderlay Mukerjee. I have been blessed with an unusual facility for enhancing your natural gifts. If you are displeased in any way with your appearance, or your performance in the bedroom, contact me, Doctor Vanderlay Mukerjee. Keep our beaches beautiful. Thank you."

When the news returned, golfers fled alligators in electric carts.

Gary turned to his phone, bringing up Lake Okeechobee News.

ATTORNEY HABIB RODRIGUEZ BUSTED FOR COCKFIGHTING.

Local criminal defense attorney Habib Rodriguez, known for his aggressive advertising, was taken into custody yesterday on charges of animal cruelty and operating an illegal cockfighting operation. He is also being investigated for possible involvement in a child pornography ring.

"Well fuck," Gary said.

Habib would be out by noon, but Krystal had waited long enough.

At nine, Gary put on his stars 'n' bars and booked. Gary turned to WCAW music out of Fort Meyers playing some Hank Williams. At nine-thirty, a food truck was parked in LIVE GATORS offering LIZARD ON A STICK. Tourists were lined up waiting to get into the popular reptile attraction, which sold stuffed alligators in several sizes, from sewing kits to suitcases. Adults hung on to sniffling children, some adults wearing infants on their backs and fronts like papooses. The parking lot was jammed with license plates from all over the Eastern United States.

Billy Bob's parking lot held several vehicles including Billy Bob's GMC Yukon with the license plate, GIMME. Gary parked a row removed from the building and got out, heat and humidity wrapping itself around him like plastic. He grabbed the bag with the wig and turned toward the building when a black Lincoln pulled up adjacent, one space away. A stout woman in a buzz cut and green cat's eye glasses got out. She wore a sensible suit. She carried a leather barrister's bag.

"Hey," Gary said.

The woman walked toward Billy Bob's.

"HEY," Gary said. The woman stopped and looked back at him.

"What's your problem?" she said in a gravelly voice.

"Aren't you the bitch who took a pot shot at us the other day 'cause we didn't get out of your way fast enough? Remember the van with a green logo?"

The woman peered, mouth pursing, shoulders hunching. "Youuuuuu..." she growled, reaching into her leather barrister's bag and pulling out a six-shooter.

Gary backed away until he bumped into his van. "Put that gun away, you crazy bitch!"

The woman held the pistol in both hands in a shooter's stance. "You're a public menace! You're supposed to get over when somebody flashes their lights. It's you who are the menace! Get down on the ground and put your hands behind your head!"

Injustice a sword through his heart, Gary grabbed the wig and hurled it at the woman, striking her in the face. She gasped. Gary was on her in a second, wrestling for the pistol. She was surprisingly strong. They danced around the parking lot, oblivious to tourists across the street who decided this was better than LIVE REPTILES and approached clutching their cell phones.

He wrenched the gun away and tossed it end over end like a shuriken at the scrub at the end of the lot. The woman kicked him savagely in the leg.

"I'M A JUDGE, YOU MORON!" she yelled as Gary grabbed the wig, got back in his truck and peeled out, spraying the judge with gravel.

11 | BELLE GLADE PAWN

Gary had stopped in Belle Glade Pawn on Charteris Street five years ago and scored DVDs of Smokey and the Bandit, Convoy, and Git R Done starring Larry the Cable Guy. A buck apiece. It was just past eleven as he pulled into the parking lot of a strip mall housing Minute Maid Cleaning, Haley's Comics, Joyce's Fabrics, and the pawn shop. The parking lot was almost full. Two board punks in shorts and tank tops did tricks in front of an empty storefront. Out front, a line of used lawnmowers vied for space with knobby-tired mountain bikes and backyard grills, all chained to steel bolts sunk into concrete.

Belle Glade Pawn had once been a bar and stretched back like a shotgun shack with a long glass counter on the left. Half the right wall was covered in peg board displaying guitars, basses, and hockey sticks. The rest was devoted to shelves of electronic appliances including numerous flat screen televisions. The center aisle was jammed with bicycles and exercise equipment.

Inside, an anxious Mexican holding a gold watch spoke Spanish with a young Mexican clerk in a Gators shirt. Two boys checked out the long boards while an old white woman, her hair in a bun, carefully picked through a bin of Beanie Babies. A middle-aged Asian man stood behind the cash register staring at his phone. He had close-cropped hair and wore a short-sleeved Hawaiian shirt featuring the Beach Boys, with photos of the band interspersed with Deuce coupes, 409s, and surfin' babes.

Gary went up to him. "You the manager?"

The man looked up. "Whaddaya got?"

Gary carefully placed the toupee on the counter. The manager wrinkled his nose. Gary pulled out the receipt and carefully flattened it out on the glass. The manager looked at it, looked again, picked it up. He looked at the wig. He poked it. He bent forward and sniffed it.

"Hmmmm."

"DNA analysis should prove conclusively that's Burt's."

"Where do we get a sample?"

"Are you shittin' me? Just go on eBay. Look for Burt Reynolds' hair. Dozens of women were scrapin' it up off the sheets during the day, believe you me. They knew he was somethin' special, and that someday, a lock of Burt's hair would be worth a pretty penny."

The manager extended his right hand.

"Alex Chow."

"Gary Duba."

"Why don't you have a look around? This is going to take a few minutes."

Gary went to the DVD section, moving past multiple copies of American Dreamz, The Matrix, and Batman Begins, pulling for possible purchase a John Wayne collection and two Rob Zombies. He went over to the CD racks. Gary didn't do downloads and had no use for streaming. He could barely operate his hand-held device. He sneered at electric vehicles and automatic transmissions. What was the world coming to? A bunch of soy boys afraid to ride their bicycles without helmets, for Chrissake. He feared for the modern generation.

And yet, what was he doing about it? He had no kids. At least none of his exes had ever come back to him with a squalling brat, but it occurred to him from time to time that he ought to spawn at least for the sake of the family name. Sure, his older brother Philip had two kids, one an assistant manager at a Jiffy Lube, the other married with two children.

Gary seldom saw his old man, who lived in Pensacola, where Gary grew up. Frank was a lifelong navy man who liked to stick close to the base. He'd been absent through most of Gary's growing up, and his mother Joan had not been much help. Someone nudged him. He looked down. A Mexican boy of about six looked up.

"Can you recommend any good country music?"

"Kid, you come to the right place."

Gary riffled through the CDs, pulling The Best of Toby Keith and Merle Haggard.

The boy took them. "Can you loan me two dollars?"

Gary laughed. "Sure. Come on, kid."

They returned to the long glass counter where Alex was still absorbed in his search, holding up a finger to ask for patience. Gary looked at the pistols neatly laid out on black velvet beneath the glass. They had two Judges, only two hundred dollars apiece. Gary missed his Judge. There was no better tool for yard critters. Well that would have to wait until he won the lottery. He looked lustfully at a Donald Trump Commemorative .45 automatic from Auto-Ordnance. Six hundred bucks. Behind the counter on the wall were a number of Mossbergs, Remingtons, and Winchesters. Gary looked around. Camera globes hung from the ceiling at the front and the back, and the tell-tale tape of an alarm system framed each glass panel. The place was probably wired into the local PD as well. He couldn't help it. It was the way he thought.

In seventh grade, Mrs. Milman, his home room teacher, told him he had the mind of a career criminal and if he didn't get his priorities straight, he'd end up in prison. He dropped out of high school in his senior year to go to work as a roofer. No training required. A plump Latina with purple hair approached.

"Migelito! Let's go."

The kid turned. "Aw, Maaa...this man is buying me some CDs."

She turned big brown eyes on Gary. "Pay no mind to him. Come on. Let's go."

"It's no problem, ma'am. Frankly, it thrills an old redneck

like myself to find someone young who likes country music."

"Country music, oh yes, he's just crazy about it. I don't know why."

Gary headed for the other cashier near the front. "Come on. Let's get this out of the way."

He paid two dollars and eighteen cents for the CDs. The woman thanked him profusely while Migelito beamed. When Gary turned back, Alex had his hand in the air.

"You are correct," Alex said. "Tufts of Burt's hair are available, but they're not cheap. That, plus the DNA testing, is going to cost me four hundred dollars."

"Yeah but come on. Burt Reynolds' wig with a certificate of authenticity and DNA testing? That's gotta bring in a couple thou at least."

"The last such toupee went for ten thousand dollars in 2017."

"Well there you go."

"I will give you one thousand dollars right now. Cash."

"Deal."

Alex took the toupee and receipt into a back office and returned a minute later with a green vinyl money bag, out of which he counted ten crisp hundred-dollar bills. He placed a form receipt on the counter, listing hairpiece as the item and acknowledging receipt of one thousand dollars. Gary signed. They shook hands.

He called Trixie from his truck.

"I got the money. Meet me down at the jail at three o'clock."

12 | FRAZZLED

The jail was in Moore Haven. It was hotter than a sumbitch. Gary parked in a lot a block away and walked past
the Lizard On A Stick truck as he headed for the building.
The smell of sizzling lizard made his stomach rumble. He'd
never eaten lizard, but it smelled like chicken. As he was
about to cross the street to the jail, Trixie called. She was
running late because she had to stop at an ATM machine on
the way. Gary returned to the lot and stood in line between
two construction workers in hard hats having a late lunch.

A Latino kid with a shock of black hair stood in the window, wearing a bandanna on his head like a gang banger,
and a white chef's jacket. Gary scanned the board menu.

"I'll have the lizard on a stick with a side of sweet potata
fries and a Coke."

The kid handed him the items one by one. "That'll be
nine-fifty."

Gary peeled off a hundred-dollar bill.

"I can't break that."

"Well shit. That's all I got."

They stared at one another.

"You go get change."

Gary hefted his lizard on a stick. "You want this?"

"No, you eat it. I trust you."

"What kind of lizard is it?"

"Iguana."

"Where you get it?"

"I trap it. I got friends who trap it. It's very popular in Dominican Republic."

"That where you're from?"

"Yes."

Gary retreated to the shade of an east-facing mortgage lender while he ate his lunch. The lizard on a stick tasted a little like chicken with a salty, fishy undertone. It wasn't bad. And the iguana were free, right? No one raised them. You trapped them. That kid was cleaning up. Of course, Gary didn't know what he'd invested in the truck, or how long he worked. All Gary thought about was money. How to get it, what he'd do if he had it. An iguana restaurant wasn't so far-fetched. They always made a big fuss over every new restaurant because a.) advertising, b.) they were bored, and c.) the constant turnover of restaurants in the area.

Not your chains. Waffle House, Cracker Barrel, McDonald's et al were for the aeons. Once they set-down they never left. It was all the other restaurants, the one offs, the dreams of cooks, the pretentious French places that came and went with startling frequency.

He chewed and swallowed his lizard, ate the sweet potato fries, washed it down with the Coke, wiped his hands on the paper towels and deposited the litter in a city trash can.

"Gary!" Trixie called from down the street.

Trixie looked like a bag lady in her voluminous gray dress, wearing a wide-brimmed straw hat and carrying a feedbag-sized purse. She was five foot two and built like a beehive.

"Oh, I'm so relieved! I can't wait to see my little girl."

"Aintchoo been down here?"

"No, I couldn't get away. I was cleaning all day and when I get home at night, I'm just so exhausted it's all I can do to feed the cats and fall asleep. I'm supposed to be cleaning right now, but I explained the situation to Folana and she gave me the rest of the day off. Where did you get the money?"

"I sold Burt Reynolds' wig."

"No, really."

"I'll tell ya about it later. Come on. Let's get your little girl out of the hoosegow."

The jail smelled of pinesol and piss. Gary had been arrested twice, once for disorderly conduct and another for DUI. He'd had to take a course on anger management and do twenty hours of community service to get his license reinstated.

Glade County Correctional Facility was a white, one-story stucco on Moore Haven off Highway Seventy-Eight.

Smokey-hatted sheriff's deputies were coming out when Gary and Trixie arrived. The last deputy held the door open for them.

The inside was a refrigerator. Ten feet in from the door stood a rectangular portal identical to those at airport security. Either side had been walled off with portable units. A sheriff's deputy sat on a wood stool, reading a Vince Flynn novel. He set it down and handed Gary a plastic bin.

"Cell phones, knives, sharp metal objects, etc. No drugs, no cigs, no prescription pills. You'll get it all back."

Gary dropped his keys, cell phone and his Kershaw in the bin. Trixie placed her purse in another. The deputy waved them through the metal detector. It was less intrusive than a TSA pat-down. They went to the linoleum desk behind which sat a broad-shouldered black woman in a sky-blue shirt, hair pulled back in a bun, entering reports into a data bank. She turned toward them.

"Help you?"

"We're here to bail out Krystal Clanagan. She's been in here since Saturday."

The woman rose, went to another computer on the desk and entered data.

"May I have your name, please."

"Gary Duba."

"I'm Krystal's mother, Trixie. But my last name is Thompson."

The woman printed off a couple forms, showed Gary where to sign. Under relationship, he wrote "boyfriend". He gave the clerk seven hundred and fifty dollars and she gave him a receipt.

"Wait here."

Two cops entered with a meth freak between them, a live wire, hairless as newborn rat, massive cables flexing under his neck, frothing at the mouth, twisting like a galvanized frog leg.

"I WANT A LAWYER YOU PIG FUCKERS...I KNOW MY GODDAMN RIGHTS..."

The deputy on the stool slid off and opened one of the portable barriers. The cops hustled the meth freak through to the other side where a door buzzed. The freak emitted an acrid, acid smell. They went through, the door shut. They could hear the meth freak cursing. His cursing cut off mid fuck and there was silence.

Minutes later, a tall woman guard with freckles and red hair came out with Krystal, who looked frazzled but beautiful, with almond eyes beneath a burgeoning unibrow, her long brown hair tied back in a ponytail. She rolled her eyes.

"About fucking time."

The clerk showed Krystal where to sign for her property, and her agreement to appear in court on a charge of disturbing the peace and indecent behavior. Finally, the clerk raised the counter and Krystal emerged. Gary and Trixie surrounded her in a group hug. She smelled of cigarette smoke, body odor, and cheap perfume.

"God do I need a shower," she said, as they went through a turnstile to get to the door. Reclaiming their belongings, they passed a Turpentine police officer sipping coffee from a paper cup. He held the door for them as they exited into the heat, humidity, and sun. They all put on sunglasses.

As they walked toward the street, a black Lincoln with tinted windows pulled up in front of two more Turpentine police officers, one of whom hustled around the front and opened the driver's door. A stout woman in a buzz cut and green cat's eye glasses got out. She wore a sensible suit. She carried a leather barrister's bag.

Gary froze. The woman froze. She hunched and pointed, her mouth twisting.

"ARREST THAT SON OF A BITCH! HE ASSAULTED ME!"

13 | THE VIEW FROM INSIDE

One cop was a young Latino. The other was older with a gray mustache. They seized Gary painfully by the arms and cuffed him. Trixie and Krystal stared, dumbstruck.

"What the fuck?!" Krystal said.

The little judge steamed up incensed. "This is one of the individuals who fired on my vehicle on Tuesday and assaulted me this morning. Take him inside and book him. Show him what we think of scofflaws in Glade County."

"Yes, Judge Murphy!" the young cop said, hustling Gary back toward the jail.

"Call Floyd!" he yelled. "Call Habib Rodriguez!"

"What the fuck?" Krystal demanded of the judge's back as she followed. The older cop got in her face.

"You'd better move along unless you want to join your boyfriend."

"What did he do?" Trixie wailed.

"You heard the judge."

Inside, Gary was searched, finger-printed and photo-graphed. The clerk at the computer printed out his record and handed it to the arresting officer, whose name tag said Morales. On the way to the cell, Morales kicked him in the back of the knee, drove him to the floor, and slapped the side of his head with the flat of his palm. Morales heaved Gary to his feet, backed him up against the wall and drove his fist into Gary's gut. It was the hardest blow Gary had ever felt. Only his spine prevented Morales fist from punching through to the wall. Gary bent over, gasping. He vomited on Morales' shoe.

Morales kicked him in the face. "You motherfucker. What does it take to piss off a judge? To take a shot at a judge? You miserable cocksucker. We don't like your kind in Glade County."

"Fuck you," Gary mumbled, earning him a knee to the gut. He looked up. He hoped the dark glass hemisphere re-corded everything for his suit. Nah. They'd just erase that part.

The cop marched him through a buzzed door into a big holding room with six rows of benches bolted to the floor and a dozen prisoners. A single horizontal window high up on the rear wall. The cop removed the cuffs and propelled Gary into the room with a shove, sending him sprawling. He stumbled into a stocky Latino with a Zapata mustache, who shoved him away. Gary landed on his ass.

"Welcome to Glade County," someone said.

Gary stood. There was a stainless-steel sink in one

corner of the big room, a stainless steel toilet in the other, covered with feces and urine. If you wanted to shit, you had to hover. A flat screen TV on one wall was covered with steel mesh. The room stank of body odor, feces, urine, and Pinesol. Three black kids huddled against the back wall.

Gary took a seat next to a middle-aged Asian man with short hair, wearing a rumpled long-sleeved white shirt with the sleeves rolled up to reveal tatted arms. Jeopardy played faintly on the TV.

Without looking at him, the man said, "They bang you up?"

"I've had worse."

"What did you do?"

"I assaulted a judge."

"For reals?"

"With a wig."

The man laughed. "Bobby. Bobby Watanabe."

"Gary Duba. What you in for?"

"Porn."

"Just porn?"

Bobby half turned. He wore blue suit pants and a black, leather loafers. "I'm a filmmaker. I specialize in erotic manga. It's an art. It should be recognized as an art. It's not a bunch of sweaty meth freaks holding an orgy, there's a story, there are characters, there are character arcs. It's erotic. Japanese pornography is nothing like the American stuff. It's wrong to even call it pornography. My stories are made with exquisite taste. I also publish erotic manga."

"What's wrong with American porn? At least we feature real people."

"I use real actors and actresses. Some are very young. Some just look young. No one is coerced, no one is forced to perform against their will. I don't offer them drugs. I pay good wages."

"Man, have you ever seen classic American porn? Debby Does Dallas? Blueberry Stud Muffin? That's tasteful!"

"I'm not talking about the classics. I'm talking about shit like All Ass Access and Cock A Doodle Don't."

"You braggin' on how tasteful porn is, you ever consider maybe that's the reason you lost World War Two?"

"How so?"

"Well like you say, everything in Japan is so tasteful and understated, whereas we Americans are just crude and disgusting, maybe that's what it takes to win the fuckin' war."

Bobby's eyes narrowed. "Are you saying the Japanese soldier is not the equal of Americans?"

"Nope. I'm sayin' we got the bomb, and we're not afraid to use it. And another thing, you people are too goddamn polite and it's costing American lives."

"What are you talking about?"

"I'm talking about the so-called horns you put on your motorcycles. Say you're cruisin' the Interstate, goin' down to Miami for a Dolphins game. Some motherfucker's trying to edge you out of your lane. You ridin' a rice burner, you lay on the horn, what do you get? Nothin'. That's what you get. Like a kitty meowing. 'Cause you're too goddamn polite to lay in a real horn, that people can hear. You ever ride a Harley?"

"You're saying the Japanese motorcycle horns are weak?"

Gary formed a pistol with his hand. "Bingo."

Bobby put his chin in his hands. "I never thought of that."

"You ride?"

"No."

"I had to sell my Harley to stop the bank from foreclosing on my fuckin' house. I'm the inventor of House Suspenders. I'm looking for investors."

"What are house suspenders?"

"They're big chains you lay over your roof that are anchored in concrete. That way, if a hurricane comes along, you won't lose your house. They're like regular suspenders, only instead of holding your pants up, they hold your house down."

"An intriguing idea. But what if the house is so shabbily built that the wind destroys it and it flies away in pieces?"

"I've thought of that. I'm thinking of adding a huge tarp with openings for chimneys and shit. Cover the whole thing. A house straight jacket. Know anybody who might be interested in that?"

"Maybe. Let's exchange contact info."

"I ain't got nothin' to write with."

"I'm very easy to find. Bobby Watanabe on Facebook."

"Ain't on Facebook."

"How do you expect to raise interest in your project if you're not on Facebook?"

Gary shrugged. "I hadn't thought about that."

The outer door buzzed open. A deputy conducted a tall black man in a Hailie Selassie T-shirt, hair done in tight cornrows, to the cell and opened the door.

Gary got to his feet. "Patrice! The fuck you doing in here?"

They exchanged the soul grip. "Same old story, mon. Straight arrow bidnessman hire me to give him blow job. Then he not pay me, so I have to teach him some manners."

14 | FLOYD COMES THROUGH

They sat on the last bench. A Mexican weather girl on the TV drew most of the room's attention, men hooting, stroking invisible Johnsons and whistling.

"I can pay you back when we get out," Gary said.

"Where you get de money, mon?"

Gary told him about Burt Reynolds' wig.

"Oh yes, mon. I only know him from The Best Little Whorehouse In Texas. He was a great actor."

"Well you should see Boogie Nights. It's right up your alley." Gary tapped Bobby, who was sitting on the bench in front of him. "You should too."

Bobby swiveled. "Should what?"

"See Boogie Nights."

"It's very good, but it's not porn." He turned around.

"It is good you have the money, mon," Patrice said. "For I am broke."

"Don't you worry. I'm good for it. You got any skills? I

mean aside from whorin'."

"I can play de saxophone."

"Ain't no money there."

Patrice thought. "In Jamaica I grow de ganja. That I can do. But I am in enough trouble as is."

"Well now see, that's where you're wrong. This state's gonna legalize marijuana any day now, and when that happens, you'll be in demand. Shit. I know some good ol' boys would be happy to have you tend their crops. But right now, it's illegal, you understand?"

"Oh, I understand all right. In Jamaica, it is still illegal, but they will not arrest you for small amounts. They understand that the tourist trade depends on drugs."

"In Jamaica, we play the plants reggae. Make them grow faster."

"Is that indoors or outdoors?"

"Both. I sing to dem. Dere is bad police near Kingston, Felipe Fulgencio, trying to close us down. I write a song for him. Attencio Fulgencio, your plan is reprehensio, don't keep us suspensio, or make us strike our tentsio. I'll plant you face first in de ground, you will not like dat ugly sound, your face and private parts I'll pound, and then I'll build a fencio."

"That's beautiful, Patrice. But even if you have all the talent in the world, trying to make a living at music is just a crap shoot. I know some good ol' boys pick like Jerry Reed, they can't make it work. Shit. If I could get all the musicians I've worked with roofing, I could put together a pretty good band. Ain't nobody plays the blues like a good ol' boy."

Bobby Watanbe swiveled. "That's absurd. Blacks invented the blues. Are you saying these so-called good ol' boys play better blues than BB King? Albert King? Freddie King?"

Gary quickly back-tracked. "Now hold on. I ain't sayin' that. Lemme say, no fuckin' punks or Brits can play the blues as well as some good ol' boys, but some good ol' boys can't play the blues as well as your genuine black blues man."

"Who dis?"

Gary introduced them. "Bobby's in tasteful Japanese porn."

Patrice's eyes rose. "I have done some acting."

"I only use children."

"No problem. Maybe I could provide the music."

"I had to suspend production until after my court date."

"When is your court date?"

"They have not yet informed me. Now if you gentlemen will excuse me, it's time for my daily meditation."

Bobby turned around and slumped forward. The clock on the wall opposite the holding cell said it was six. Gary looked around. Two inmates sprawled against the sideboards, heads cradled in their arms. The three black kids played scissors, papers, stone while rapping loudly.

"My stone got a bone for your paper, my name is Don Draper and I'm a baby raper."

"My scissor got a quiver for your liver, 'cuz I'm a lover, not a giver."

"Don't fock with the rock or I'll give you a shock."

Gary was exhausted. He'd hardly got any sleep the previous night and he sure as shit wasn't going to get any in here. He hoped Krystal had called Floyd or Habib. He prayed she hadn't gone straight to her meth connection. The bitch had been on and off the shit as long as he'd known her. He thought if she moved in with him, he'd be able to keep an eye on her and keep her off the shit, but it hadn't worked out that way. More often than not, she'd cajole him into doing a line, and then they got to fucking, which could take hours. It left them both exhausted and wanting more.

The only reason Gary had been off the shit for the past week was because Krystal wasn't around.

The next thing he knew, Gary was on the floor cradling his head in his arms and Patrice was shaking him.

Gary jerked, disoriented. "What?"

"Get up, mon. It's morning. You are bailed out."

Tepid sunlight streamed in through the gun slot. Gary got to his feet. He needed to pee, shower, shit, shave and eat. He went to the front of the cell where a deputy waited.

"Let's go, Duba."

"Who bailed me out?"

"Fuck if I know."

The deputy conducted Gary through two doors to the front room where Krystal waited with Floyd, in his work duds.

"Floyd! God love ya! I'll make it up to you!"

"Fuckin' A," Floyd said.

Gary signed forms and retrieved his belongings. It was eight-thirty.

"You are due to appear in court on this date to answer one charge of aggravated battery, do you understand?"

"Yes ma'am."

"Sign here."

Gary signed. The clerk gave him copies of everything. A deputy raised the counter and Gary walked out, into Krystal's arms.

"Where's my truck?" Gary said.

"It's impounded. It's in your paperwork."

They went out through the turnstile.

"How much?" Gary asked.

"Seven hundred and fifty," Floyd said.

"Goddamn!"

Gary looked at her eyes and nostrils. She appeared straight.

Krystal had parked on the street a block away. When they reached her Pontiac, Floyd kept going toward his van. They got in the Pontiac. Krystal started the engine, lowered the windows and lit a Carlton, passing the pack to Gary who slid one in his mouth. The air conditioner didn't work. She promised to get it fixed, but neither of them had the money.

"Did you call Habib?"

"I left a message. Then I called Floyd and he said he'd bail you out."

"Floyd's a fuckin' rock."

"What about this judge bitch? What happened?"

Gary brought her up to speed beginning with the road rage. "But they won't mention that. She pulled on us first! I wish I had video."

"Hey, pull into that Arby's. I'm hungry enough to eat a baby's butt through a park bench. And I gotta pee like crazy."

"You got any money?"

Gary checked his wallet. He still had two hundred dollars. "Let's go!"

Krystal ordered while Gary visited the men's room, washing his hands and face and running through ten feet of paper towel. When he came out, Krystal sat in a booth with two jumbo roast beef and cheese sandwiches and big cups of Coke.

Gary tore through the sandwich like a feral hog in a vegetable garden.

"You need a shower," Krystal said.

"That ain't all I need. Let's go."

15 | MATCHING TATS

Krsytal knelt on the bed wearing nothing but a Richard Petty T-shirt, showing off her pert breasts, her long bottle blonde hair hanging straight down to her ass. Tats like wooly caterpillars climbed her thighs. Gary suspected they belonged to former boyfriends and had been repurposed. He could almost read the name Mervin or something.

Gary came straight from the shower and dove on her with a snarl. She squeaked. Gary slid right in and fucked her for a few minutes, then pulled out, flipped her over and fucked her doggie style, Krystal hanging on to the wood headboard, the trailer shaking like a maraca.

"You're a monster!" she shrieked. "You're a beast!"

"I am the beast of the apocalypse!" Gary roared.

They lay panting.

"Got any money?" he said.

"Fuck no. But I will next week. I'll be workin' with Ma for the Merry Maids."

"Soon's we get some money we should get matching tats."

"Oh, that would be so sweet. I also think maybe we should each wear tiny vials of each other's blood around our necks."

"That's class, Krystal. Pure class."

"We can engrave them with our blood types so that in case of an accident, they don't have to mess around."

"That's a good idea for everybody. That there might be a money-making proposition. You should write that down. You and me, we're a fuckin' brain trust. I got a million money-making ideas."

"Like what?"

"Like motorcycle helmets that automatically massage your head while you ride. All-natural hearing aids. No drugs, no electronics."

"How you gonna do that?"

Gary sat up, cupped his ears in both hands and bent them forward. "You ever try this? You ever hear how much more you can hear when you do this?"

Krystal cupped her ears. "Wow. You're right!"

"I can build these cheap out of plastic. You fit 'em over your head on a band and they stick out from your ears providing all around sound enhancement."

"Yeah, except they make you look like an idiot."

"Well you already got all these cyclists wearing blue and yellow spandex."

"Your point being?"

"Well they ain't afraid to look like idiots. And neither will people who need a little hearing adjustment but don't want to shell out the big bucks for electronics. They'll come in a variety of fashion colors. Tiger striped. Paisley. Camo for the hunters. Black for evening wear."

Krystal got up, T-shirt swinging, and headed for the kitchen. "You want a beer?"

"Sure."

Gary pulled on his pants it wasn't even noon and he'd already been laid. Now he had the rest of the day to worry about money. The mortgage was due in three days and he had an unpaid electric bill to the City of Turpentine, and he owed six hundred and fifty-nine dollars and nineteen cents on his Visa card. He only had the one card, unlike Krystal, who had a half dozen. Gary just hoped she didn't get caught.

Gary heard the TV go on.

"Come out here, Gare. Judge Swinehart's on."

Gary went into the living room, closed the front door and cranked up the rooftop AC unit. He sat on the sofa next to Krystal and twisted the cap off a cold bottle of Dixie.

Judge Swinehart was a no-nonsense black former Marine appointed to the court by Bill Clinton before he quit to become one of the most successful television adjudicators in history. Judge Swinehart had twenty-two million viewers. Judge Swinehart earned two hundred million dollars a year. Judge Swinehart didn't give a shit.

The defendant was an uptight ingenue dressed to meet the Queen, long black hair clasped at the nape of neck, wearing black-framed glasses. She'd changed the locks on a former roommate and posted pictures of the roommate engaging in sex with a person, although in truth, since both were dressed like giant squirrels, it was difficult to identify either.

"I knew we weren't going to get along when she tried to kick my cat," the defendant said primly.

"That's a lie," said the plaintiff, a sad homely girl in a huge sweater.

Judge Swinehart was a massive man with a chin the size of Rhode Island. "You had no right to lock the plaintiff out of her own apartment. She had paid you the rent. In fact, from what I heard here today from the witnesses leads me to believe you shouldn't be out on your own. You are a menace to yourself and others. Judgement for plaintiff for five thousand dollars."

Bam!

The defendant stomped toward the exit, firing her Carpathian shot. "This isn't finished. It's just beginning."

"We will get the litigants' reactions in a moment, but first, here's a word from our sponsor."

A lissome young Latina appeared. "I was minding my own business driving, when a car ran a red light and struck me. The insurance company only wanted to pay me one thousand dollars for my injuries and damage, so I went to Habib Rodriguez, and he got me seven hundred thousand dollars."

Cut to Habib, standing proudly, arms crossed, in front of the graffiti Justice.

"I can't guarantee you that your case is worth seven hundred thousand dollars, but if you don't call, you'll never know. If you don't win, you owe us nothing. Call the Long Arm, Habib Rodriguez today."

Gary called Habib Rodriguez. Brenda answered.

"One moment, Mister Duba. I'll see if he's available."

Habib came on the line. "The pictures are fine. Come on down and I'll cut you a check."

"How'd it go with the cops?" Gary said.

"They got nothing. Cockfighting ring my ass. That's my brother's deal. Everybody knows it. Total bullshit charge. And the kiddie porn? That's all evidence I've been collecting for a case. They don't got squat."

"That's good to know! See you soon."

Krystal flipped through channels, pausing to watch a Japanese hot-dog eating contest at which the contestants sat at a groaning board filled with hundreds of hot dogs. When the referee blew his whistle, six people began maniacally stuffing their maws with hot dogs.

Krystal flipped to a soccer game.

Krystal flipped to two women fawning over a gadget that looked like a combination ice cream churn/bullet loader. The woman on the left had long platinum hair, a generous décolletage in which nestled an enormous emerald, and wore a sleeveless gold lamé dress. She was somewhere between thirty and sixty. The other woman, a buxom brunette, wore a form-hugging sweater and a black pleated skirt that rode up her thigh as she crossed her legs. Her elegant fingers rested on the device between them.

"I'm telling you girls you cannot live without the Perkiset. It brews coffee, processes food, and opens cans. It does the job of a half dozen other appliances. You can even toast bread in it."

"Muriel is so right," the blonde said. "Once you have one, you'll wonder how you ever got along without one. And it's only available here, on Purchamerch."

Krystal changed the channel. A gorgeous redhead in a yellow sundress stood before the Florida Lottery Logo, including Megamillions, Gold Rush, Cash4Life, Jackpot, and Powerball flashed her chiclets. "As of today, no one has claimed Tuesday's Scratch Off Prize, which is now up to seven million five hundred thousand dollars. The number is four, one, two, one, zero, four, nine, four, five. That number is up on our website."

As if in a dream, Gary reached for his Scratch Off ticket.

Friday morning, Gary appeared at the Florida Lottery District Office in West Palm Beach where he turned the signed ticket over. A lottery official told him it would take twenty-four hours to process the ticket, and then they would electronically deposit the funds in his bank account.

"Make sure you save the paperwork, because Uncle Sam will want his cut. And congratulations. I hope you enjoy your winnings."

Outside the office, Gary leaped in the air and clicked his heels together three times. "WOOO!"

He took Krystal's hand and they skipped like Dorothy in the Wizard of Oz back toward Gary's truck.

"Looks like our luck is finally changing," Gary said, heading west toward Turpentine.

Krystal slid over and squeezed his arm. "Can we move out of the trailer?"

"That's the plan. I got my eye on some nice properties in

Hendry. And I still got to collect from Habib for the photos!"

"Gimme some money!"

"No. You'll just spend it on meth."

"I won't, I promise!"

"Krystal, you know you got a problem. And when you got a problem, I got a problem. Ain't neither of us need that problem so the answer is no. I'll give you twenty so you can get something to eat."

"What the fuck? All of a sudden you're a millionaire, and you won't give me a couple hunnert bucks?"

"I ain't got the money! Not yet! My credit's shit! I owe six thousand dollars on my Visa bill!"

"Show 'em the fucking papers! They'll change their tune."

"You prove to me you can keep your nose clean for a week. Howzat? Then I'll give you some money."

"You're so mean!"

"You prove you can stay clean for a week and I'll buy you a new car!"

"Really?"

"I ain't no bullshitter. You know that, Krystal."

She slid back and threw her arms around him, causing him to swerve into the oncoming lane. He jerked back just in time to avoid a head-on collision with another pick-up. The dude honked at him and stuck the finger out his window.

"Jesus, Krystal! You nearly got us killed!"

"Baby, you take me right home. I'm going to fuck you silly."

At two p.m. Gary pulled into the Law Offices of Habib Rodriguez. He carried a manila envelope with his prize documents. The waiting room held a half dozen prospective clients including a middle-aged Mexican couple cradling a pit bull, a hairless dude in Hodaddies and a Hawaiian shirt, who grinned with a blank stare, a morbidly obese woman in a red wig, a man in blue work shirt and Renk seed cap and his daughter, a sullen gum-chewing teenager with exposed midriff.

Gary went up to Brenda the receptionist, a stunning Latina brunette.

"Brenda."

She looked up with a million-dollar smile. "Mister Duba, Mister Rodriguez will be with you in a minute."

Gary sat in one of the cheap steel folding chairs and shuffled through a meager selection of magazines: Lake Okeechobee News, Glade County Realty, Sunset, and Modern Poultry.

Flipping through Glade County Realtor, he circled likely prospects.

A window looked out on the highway, blinds down but open to permit light. None of the chairs matched. The father and daughter sat on a bright brown and yellow plaid sofa. You could play checkers on the black and white linoleum floor. The wall behind Brenda held a Leroy Neiman print of trotters at Hialeah Park. Gary recognized the frame from Hobby Lobby.

Habib's office door opened. A frazzled redhead came

out, then Habib.

"Come in, Gary."

The Mexican with the pit bull looked like he was going to say something, but Habib shot him a look. Habib had wrestled in college and tried out for the Falcons. He wore a sleek, navy blue suit that draped his body like a well-dressed walrus.

Gary followed Habib into his office and shut the door. Habib brought up the images on his desktop. He put on horn-rimmed glasses. He took off the glasses. He faced front, hands neatly folded.

"Good enough. I'll have Brenda draw you up a check for five hundred dollars."

"Could you make it a thou?"

"Why?"

"I had to fight a fucking six-foot four transvestite! Look at my lip!"

"That pleases me no end. All right. I'll make it a thou."

"Whaddaya think, hoss? Think I could be a private eye?"

Habib smiled. "Gary, you never cease to amaze me! Universities now offer that as a four-year program. You have to obtain a state license which involves a written test and scrupulous background check. Licensed private investigators are agents of the court, no less than lawyers."

"Is that a no?"

Habib smiled.

"Listen. I've decided to pop the question. You can marry us, right?"

"What brought this on?"

Gary handed Habib his award certificate.

"Holy fuck," the lawyer said.

"Yeah."

"Well, sure, I can perform the ceremony. When's it gonna be?"

"Let's make it next Friday. I'll throw a party. I'll hire a band."

"Where?"

"I'll rent out Thorson's."

Thorson's was a popular C&W joint with a mechanical alligator.

Brenda knocked and opened the door. "Mister Rodriguez, your two-thirty is here."

"Thank you, Brenda."

Gary and Habib shook hands.

As he stood in line at the bank Gary checked his messages.

Sherri Lee Clip wrote, "Hi."

Kitty Flawless wrote, "I see your profile and think we make great friends please answer me back."

There was an urgent message from the widow of General Akbar Al Bakbar of Tunisia asking for his bank account so that she could send him ten million dollars.

At the window Gary faced off with a dimpled dot Indian clerk named Iva.

"How can I help you?"

Gary showed her the Lottery statement. "I'd like to open

a line of credit."

Iva oohed and ohed. "Wait right here, Mister Duba."

Minutes later, the Cuban manager appeared, a dapper man in a gray banker's suit with a narrow burgundy tie, his gray/black hair slicked back like a thirties movie star.

"Mister Duba, I'm Jaime Stevenson. Please come into my office."

Stevenson's office contained a framed photo of his pretty wife and two teenage children. The window overlooked a parking lot. Stevenson sat behind his desk and looked at the statement.

"First of all, congratulations! I see you've been banking with us for five years."

"Yassir."

"Have you thought what you're going to do with your winnings? You may wish to place some of them in an interest-bearing account or certificate of deposit."

"Wahl, we'll see about that. Right now, I'd just like some credit."

With ten hundred-dollar bills in his wallet, Gary skipped out of the bank with some temporary checks on which he could draw up to five hundred thousand dollars. He'd taken out a new credit card with a million-dollar limit. It would arrive shortly.

When he got to his truck, he phoned Krystal.

"Babe, let's pick you out a ring."

17 | TIT FOR TAT

They chose a French-set Halo from Jared for fourteen thousand and thirty-seven dollars. Krystal walked out of the jewelry store in the Turpentine Mall holding her hand aloft for all to see.

"I'm famished," she declared as they approached the food court, a large circle surrounded by Chick-Fil-A, Arby's, Hardee's, Taco John, Panda Express and Sicilio's Pizza beneath a stained-glass dome depicting Ponce de Leon first stepping onto Florida soil. Krystal grabbed a circular table while Gary scored two chicken sandwiches.

Skate punks rolled through the tiled court drowning out the muzak.

"You need to compile a list of wedding guests," Gary said. "I'm thinkin' of hiring a band. Who should I get?"

"Elderberry!"

Gary shot a finger. "Bingo."

A skateboard shot out from beneath four hundred and

fifty-dollar sneakers and went airborne, striking a skater in the thigh. The offending board punk wore a pea coat and had fashioned his hair into a purple ten-inch coxcomb arcing over his pierced and tatted face. The strikee was a black boy built like a praying mantis, all legs and gangly arms, wearing a gray hoodie, and gray sweatpants with a red stripe.

"YO MOFO," called the strikee.

"What up, dog?" replied the striker.

Without preamble they came together like two battling robots, swinging their boards like Knights Templar. A board sailed loose like the silver surfer, bounding over Sicilio's Pizza counter and striking a Latino cook in the chest. Young and old gathered to film. It was better than Jerry Springer. It was better than The Bachelor. With a shrill whistle, mall security arrived, a mesomorph with a hairline mustache and a police academy flunkee in a buzzcut.

Gary and Krystal stopped at Thorsons on Twenty-Seven on the way home. Thorson's was a free-standing faux Alamo with viga poles, that in a previous life been a Mexican restaurant. The marquee by the door advertised Serene Green, Country Fiddlers, and Hank Williams III.

The present owner was an old biker named Pete. Gary reserved the venue for Sunday, August 14, and left a hundred-dollar deposit.

"Let's get shit-faced and get matching tats!" Krystal gushed.

Fortunately, Thorson's was two doors down from Wirtz

Tattoo, run by a hairy biker named Nate Wirtz. His motto: What's the wirtz that can happen? Pete served them three boiler makers apiece. They were professionally shit-faced. Pete made Gary give him the truck keys before turning them loose on Nate. It was five pm as they stumbled down the crumbled concrete to Wirtz. Two chops lounged in front of the former Standard Oil Station, its glassy front office converted into a tattoo parlor, its garage now housing a half dozen chops in various states of undress.

A '57 Panhead with an elongated front fork and teardrop tank on which Wirtz had painted a spectacular Lady Death sat in the front window framed by four signs. BEWARE OF DOG. TATS FOR TITS. SPEAK MURICAN, DAMN YE. MOLON LABE.

Inside, Wirtz bent over a young Latina with gleaming black hair, wearing Daisy Dukes and a man's shirt tied over her taut midriff. He didn't look up as Gary and Krystal entered.

"Have a seat! Have a beer. I'll be right witcha."

Wirtz was finishing up a spot-on Betty Boop. Marijuana scent entered from the garage, from which the boom box blasted Jason & the Scorchers. Wirtz admired his work, cleaned it with an alcohol swab.

"You're good to go."

The girl got up, admired herself in a floor-length mirror, and squealed.

Wirtz rotated on his swivel-topped mechanic's stool. "Whaddaya need?"

"We want matching tats. He wants Pepe LePew holding a flag that says 'Krystal.' That's me. I want Fifi La Fume waving a flag that says Gary."

"Who's Fifi La Fume."

"Pepe Le Pew's girlfriend. I thought everybody knew that."

Wirtz rolled to his computer and brought up Fifi La Fume. She was pink, with white stripes and quite attractive, for a skunk. He printed it off. He brought over a big book of tats and they discussed size, location, colors. Gary's arms were pretty much taken but he had a place on his chest.

Gary sat in the chair. Wirtz produced a bottle of Buffalo Trace and three Harley shot glasses.

"Libation?"

"Can you ink while you're drinking?" Gary said. "You gotta nail Sam. You can't go wobbly and give me something looks like it was drawn by a kid."

Wirtz stared at him with deep-set blue eyes.

"Okay, okay, go ahead."

They downed the shots and Wirtz went to work while George Jones sang "Bartender's Blues".

When he was done, Wirtz wiped it off with an alcohol swab and held up a mirror.

"Nailed it," Gary said. It was Krystal's turn.

Wirtz eyed her thigh. "Who did these cover-ups?"

"Those aren't cover-ups! That's the original design."

Wirtz cloaked his mirth.

On the way home they paused just past the trailer park to

allow a gator to cross the road. At the turn-off, someone had dumped two bald tires, a trash bag filled with shit that was now blowing in the breeze, and an old water heater.

"Motherfucking cocksucker!" Gary said. "That's the third time this year!"

"Maybe you should put up a camera, find out who did this. Then we'll gather it up and dump it back in their yard."

Gary turned on to his own rutted driveway. "Don't worry about it. We're moving. Just as soon as I find the right place."

They went inside. Gary cranked up the AC.

"I'm starving," Krystal said. "What's there to eat around this place?"

"Go look."

Krystal went into the kitchen and opened the freezer. There were some desiccated breakfast burritos and two cans of frozen orange juice. The refrigerator contained green slime in a plastic container, a box of baking soda, and a bottle of beer.

"Ain't shit!" she sang.

"I'll order a pizza."

"They ain't comin' out here for no five-dollar tip!"

"They will for fifty."

Gary phoned the Blackjack in Turpentine and ordered an extra-large with pepperoni, ham, and mushrooms. Krystal found a bottle of Jack in the cupboard and they got shit-faced. The pizza arrived forty-five minutes later. The delivery man banged on the door for five minutes then left in disgust.

18 | A BEAUTIFUL CEREMONY

Krystal went crazy at the Party Store, decorating Thorsons with helium balloons, a banner that said CONGRATULATIONS KRYSTAL AND GARY, crepe paper, centerpieces with plastic dinosaurs, party hats and whistles. Bullard Bakery provided the three-tier wedding cake, decorated with green alligators on the sides and Jed and Ellie Mae action figures on top.

First to arrive were Elderberry, four dudes who lived on the same dead-end street in Palm Beach Gardens, all veterans of bands, all skilled musicians, all with regular jobs. They unpacked amps, drums, guitars, keyboard, and banjo and set up on Thorson's small stage at one end of the long room in front of a wedding banner.

Next came the caterer TexMex Lunch in an ancient van spewing volcanic clouds of gray smoke that quickly dissipated. TexMex was Maria Fuentes and her son Roberto, who set up buffet tables and began hauling in steel tureens.

Guests began arriving at noon, including Krystal's two bridesmaids, Jen and Barb. Jen was a tall redhead, hair done up in a regal wave, a blue dolphin leaping off her right breast, wearing an emerald green dress and high heel boots. Barb was a statuesque bottle blonde with a serious tan, bobbed hair, ruby lips and brown eyes. The girls made frequent trips to the ladies' room and brought their own flasks.

Trixie arrived with her boyfriend Stanton, a wizened homunculus with a potato nose and red skin, wearing an ancient cowboy suit with yoked breast, mother of pearl buttons, and a beige Stetson. Floyd arrived on his Fat Boy, in jeans, hand-tooled boots, saucer-sized belt buckle depicting a leaping marlin in silver, plaid shirt, and leather vest, hoping to score with either Jen or Barb.

Patrice arrived in a diesel Volkswagen with Bjorn Borklund, a Swedish flight steward for United. Patrice hefted a plastic tub filled with firecrackers, rockets, and Roman candles.

"Is tradition in the islands, mon. We toast the newlyweds with fireworks."

By one, the parking lot was jammed. Gary and Krystal had to park in the weeds beyond the pavement next to a drainage ditch. Gary wondered whether he should strap on the Taurus in the glove compartment, in case they had to battle alligators to get to their vehicle.

Gary wore a sky-blue leisure suit, his hair slicked back, amber aviator's glasses, and cowboy boots decorated with red roses and green cacti. Krystal wore a diaphanous, form-hugging dress that was little more than a cotton doily showing vast amounts of skin, tats shining through like signals from a distant galaxy. They waited outside on the deck.

Krystal joined her pals in the ladies' room.

Presents piled up on a table opposite the bandstand. Big white rectangles with gold ribbons, gay bespoke wine bags, envelopes.

Gary wouldn't mind a boost himself. He eyed the crowd, settling on El Cheapo, Diego Albuquerque, a transplanted Columbian and one-time low-level cartel stooge, who claimed to be a professional gambler. El Cheapo was notoriously tight with the nickel. You could find him most Saturdays and Sundays at Hialeah or Gulfstream Park, where he sold a little blow on the side.

"Diego!"

El Cheapo turned toward him beaming, arms outstretched. "Mi hermano!" They embraced El Cheapo wore an expensive gray track suit with crimson stripes and carried a pound of gold around his neck, rubbing his hair chest. He was five-feet six and built like a sumo, with a thick, dense pompadour of black hair and a caterpillar mustache, smelling of citrus and peppers.

Gary ran his finger under his nose. "Got a picker upper?"

"Come with me, my friend."

They repaired to El Cheapo's Cherokee and did a couple lines. When they got back, the guests had assembled in the main room where Habib stood beneath a wedding bower decorated with lilies, wearing an undertaker's suit.

"Let's get this show on the road," Habib boomed. "Here comes the groom. Where's the blushing bride?"

Krystal emerged giggling from the women's room with her cohorts and took her place, backed by Jen, Barb, and Trixie. Floyd and Patrice formed up next to Gary.

Habib consulted his notes. "Gary, you have something to say?"

Gary cleared his throat. "I never thought I would ever meet my soul mate! When it comes to girls, I was about as clueless as a pig in a whorehouse. I think I done trashed every relationship I was ever in, or she did, and I've been fired from every job I ever had, 'cept for Floyd here, but I sure lucked out when this here gal shoved her shopping cart into the side of my F-150 at Walmart. I think I still got the dent! That there dent's a reminder of the luckiest day of my life, the day I met my soul mate, Krystal."

The ladies reached for tissue. Habib turned to Krystal.

"My love, (SNORK!)...you are the ideal man. Ever since I saw you yelling at me in that parking lot, I knew you were the guy for me and you have not let me down. Every time I needed someone, you were there, like last week when you bailed me out of jail, and I want to explain, the only reason I took my clothes off was because that fucking Waffle House was infested with palmetto bugs, and one of them got in my shirt! They knew I was gonna put that shit on Facebook, and that's the only reason I was arrested. And I never licked the manager. I stuck my tongue out at him and he lunged at me."

"WHOO!" Jen said.

"You go, girl!" Barb said.

Habib recited the required words to which each participant responded, "I do."

Habib put their hands together. "By the power invested in me, 'neath a bower infested with fleas, I pronounce you man and wife. You may kiss the bride."

Gary bent Krystal back in a salacious lip lock, hands gliding over her firm buttocks.

Elderberry broke into "I Knew the Bride When She Used To Rock and Roll." Guests slid back the chairs and boogied. They did the Texas two-step, the frug, the monkey, the dirty boogie, the mashed potato, the backpack, the bloc boy, the macarena and the floss. Sixty people rotated from buffet, to the tables, to the restrooms, to the dance floor and back again.

A string of firecrackers erupted sending El Cheapo to the floor. Others laughed and pointed as two men aimed bottle rockets at one another with empty beer bottles, lighting them with their cigarettes. Bottle rockets careened off the walls and blew up helium balloons. The proprietor, an old biker named Wally Mathis, grabbed Gary by the throat.

"You get control of your guests or omma throw them out on their ass."

Gary shimmied through the mob to where the two men now faced each other with Roman candles protruding through their unzipped pants.

"Huey! Brad! What the fuck are you doing? Take it

outside!"

Huey, all sticks and knobs in blue jeans and Hawaiian shirt waved a cigar. "This motherfucker says I don't have the nerve! I'll show you nerve, you motherfuckin' cunt!"

Huey stoked his cigar to a warm glow and touched the fuse protruding from his pants.

19 | UP THE FALLS

The first fireball erupted from Huey's pants with an incoming whistle, soaring past Brad's head and landing behind the bar where the bartender stamped it out. The second landed in a trash can against the wall igniting used paper plates and cups. In an instant, the flaming garbage can spread to the crepe banners, which spread to the ceiling.

"AIEEEEEEEEE...UNG! UNG! UNG!" Huey cried, his pants aflame, as he ran for the exit.

Men shouted. Women screamed. They flowed out of Thorson's into the parking lots, stumbling, shrieking, carrying their drinks. The flames spread quickly, consuming the entire building as the wedding guests retreated and stared in horror.

Wally Mathis was so mad he was spitting. He shoved Gary, who fell on his ass. Gary got up and they traded hands. Gary connected with an overhand right that whipped Mathis' head, but Mathis came back with a monstrous right hook cracking a rib. Guests separated them.

Mathis was crimson. "I'm suing you for every dime you have!"

Habib got between them. "Did Gary sign a liability document?"

"You can sue Huey Gunderson! He's the motherfucker started the fire!"

Patrice and Bjorn drove away as the firetrucks arrived, followed by the police.

The wedding gifts had turned to ash. Turned out the only person Mathis could sue was Huey Gunderson, and he couldn't sue Huey because Huey had run to the drainage ditch in back of the bar to douse the fire, threw himself in the water, and was eaten by an alligator which dragged his body into the swamp. Only his hat remained.

The next morning Gary and Krystal flew from Palm Beach to Negril, boarded a bus where they were plied with drinks, and arrived at Sandals Royal Caribbean on the north shore. They showered, made love, and strolled the broad pristine beach on which beach boys with dazzling smiles offered them sailing lessons, parasailing, snorkeling, and water skiing. The beach was a thousand feet long, bordered on the east and west by a hurricane fence festooned with charms and ribbons beyond which clamored a mass of miscellaneous merchants hawking everything from Bob Marley paraphernalia to cocaine at sixty dollars a gram.

At Sandals, everything was included in one price. Drinks, food, parasailing, the works. Only the drugs cost extra.

They ate outside at Eleanor's, one of eight restaurants. They had the seafood ceviche, snapper, shrimp, calamari, bell peppers, cilantro and lime served on faux British colonial china. Gary ordered the Blue Mountain coffee-rubbed strip loin with creamy mashed potatoes, market vegetables and Cabernet reduction, while Krystal ordered the pan-seared snapper with Scotch bonnet lime broth, black mussels, carrots, leeks, and boiled potatoes.

They stayed up until three in the morning snorting coke and watching Mexican soap opera.

Wednesday afternoon Gary and Krystal lounged by one of the big pools where members of the Brockton, Massachusetts Fire Department, most resembling Chippendale dancers, also held sway. After consuming a quarter gram of cocaine and four Long Island ice teas, Gary elected to cannonball the pool, drenching several firefighters and their wives and girlfriends sitting nearby.

"I'm so sorry," Krystal explained. "He's drunk."

A firefighter said, "No worries. And if you're going to the falls, steer clear of the transvestite with the burro."

That evening they dined at the Jerk Shack, comforting dishes served steps away from the Caribbean Sea.

On Thursday, they signed up for the Konoko Falls Rainforest Trek, joining a dozen other vacationers in an old jitney that took them west toward Margaritaville, where they turned south toward Shaw Park Botanical Gardens. The parking lot, shaded by palm trees, was chock-a-block with rentals and buses from other resorts. A hurricane fence surrounded the property, beyond which the locals clustered selling everything from Toots and the Maytals shirts to fine Columbian blow. Eager guides, some wearing multicolored knit caps, descended. Each resort had a deal with a different set of guides. Gary's and Krystal's guide was a gangly youth with a gorgeous smile, wearing baggie shorts, sandals, and a Dred Zeppelin shirt.

"Greetings, my friends, and welcome to Konoko Falls. I am Jason, and I will be your guide today. Please watch your footing as the falls can be slippery, and do not stray far from our group. You will have much opportunity to take pictures, and I urge you all to visit the restrooms now, as defecating in the river is frowned upon."

"Can we smoke ganja?" asked a vacationer from Connecticut.

Jason grinned. "This is Jamaica, mon. You do what you like."

They marched up a set of broad, natural rock stairs down which the river flowed, passing other groups returning. Jason pointed out the colorful foliage and exotic birds with historical notes.

"On this spot in in 1954, Sir Ian Fleming, creator of James Bond, slipped and suffered a fractured wrist."

The river leveled out for a hundred feet surrounded by smooth stone steps rising into the forest. A natural level platform on the west housed several souvenir huts selling shirts, sandals, hats, juice, grilled lizards, and beer. Nearby stood a brown Buddha wearing a polka dot pink and white tutu and his burro, on which sat a laughing little girl as her parents took a picture. The burro was dyed black, green and red and wore a knit cap of the same color, with holes for the ears.

When she was done, the Buddha lifted her down and turned to the visitors.

"Who is next? Who would like to be photographed with me, Ernesto Xavier, and my famous magic burro Chiquita? Who among you? Who?"

With a girlish squeal Krystal bound forward waving her arm.

Gary stared. "What the fuck?"

She arrived at the burro whose back was a mere forty inches above the ground. Ernesto Xavier gripped her beneath her arms and placed her on the burro as if he were setting a table.

"And who is taking the picture?"

Gary reluctantly held up his phone.

"Wait, wait," the Buddha said, moving around behind so that he could be in the picture. His left hand casually draped over Krystal's shoulder and rested on her breast. Krystal brushed it off. The hand resumed position. Gary froze.

Krystal jumped off the burro. "Forget it, creep!"

As she and Gary started to walk away, Ernesto Xavier pursued them.

"Wait. Wait. That is ten dollars you owe me for the photo."

"I didn't take no fuckin' photo, you fuckin' perv!"

Ernesto Xavier got in Gary's face. "You cannot abuse me like this. You white people think you can just come down here and treat us like we were still your slaves, well Ernesto Xavier is not having it."

A crowd formed around them, tourists eagerly recording the historic event.

One of the vendors cried, "Pay the mon!"

Jason came toward them with a worried expression.

"Fuck off!" Gary said, turning to go.

Ernesto Xavier grabbed him by the arm. Wappo! Gary turned and slugged the Buddha in the kisser, sending him down on his broad ass.

The burro heehawed, put its head down, and galloped, butting Gary in the breadbasket and sending him onto his butt. Jason remonstrated with Ernesto Xavier.

"You cannot harass my tourists. You cannot charge him for a picture he didn't take. I have warned you about this before, Ernesto."

Ernesto got to his feet. "How is an honest man to make a living then?"

Two park police arrived wearing Navy blue shorts and light blue short-sleeved shirts with epaulets, and crisp black brimmed hats. They huddled with Ernesto Xavier, then with Jason, and finally with Gary and Krystal. Back and forth they went. Finally, one of the police, who looked like he was about nineteen, held out his hand.

"Okay, here is the deal. Ernesto is willing to forget about this incident for twenty dollars."

"Are you shittin' me?" Gary said. "I never even took a fuckin' picture!"

"Nevertheless, you will go home, and Ernesto will remain here trying to make a living. Otherwise, we will have to bring you both to police headquarters in Negril and question you for several hours. Also, you must pay us a twenty-dollar mediation fee."

"What?"

Krystal kicked Gary savagely in the shins. Jason whispered in his ear. "This is a good deal. You should take it."

Cursing softly under his breath, Gary reached for his wallet.

Back at the resort, Gary and Krystal continued to snort coke and drink until Gary decided to catch and grill his own iguana. How hard could it be? Everybody was doing it, and the iguanas were everywhere. They would be easy to catch in the morning, before it got too hot but where would he find them?

Fingering a monster doobie, Krystal inhaled on the bed, crossed her legs Indian style, placed her palms together and said, "I will pray to the goddess Gaia to guide you in your search for the iguana."

Gary gave her a thumb's up. "Sounds good."

She passed Gary the doobie. "This ganja is so much better than what we get in Miami."

"Yeah, I don't like to buy that Mexican shit. They lace it with paraquat and fuck knows what all. I sure would like to take an ounce of this shit back with us. Maybe you could hide it in your vagina."

Krystal held up the package of rolling papers they'd brought. "Look at this package of Zig-Zags. Jesus smoking a joint. If that ain't proof God intended us to get high, I don't know what is."

"This is sure as shit God's own reefer."

He didn't wake from his Valium induced sleep until noon Friday, but quickly brought himself up to speed with rum and blow. Looking out onto their private patio, he spotted the fat yellow lizard sunning itself on the stucco wall. A seasoned gator hunter, Gary left their unit by the front door and crept around the house keeping to the meticulously tended shrubbery until he lurked five feet from the animal, armed with a stout club.

As Toots and the Maytals drifted upward from the beach, Gary exploded from the bushes, ran forward and clubbed the lizard across the head, killing it in one blow. What a beaut! Had to weigh five pounds. Holding the dead lizard by the tail, Gary entered through the open patio door and tossed the beast in Krystal's lap, where she sat Indian style texting and scrolling.

"YEEK!"

"Skin it. We're havin' iguana for dinner."

Krystal picked it up by the tail, twirled it around her head and released it. With reflexes born of too much coke, Gary caught it in his left hand with the sound of a baseball hitting the catcher's glove.

"Fuck you, Charlie Brown! You caught it you skin it!"

"You're about plum worthless, you know that?"

"Oh yeah? You tell me that the next time you want some pussy."

"Well why don't you just go off with Mario the cabana boy? I seen you makin' eyes at him."

"Is that what you think of me? That I'd go to bed with a Jamaican?"

Gary rethought his position. "Look here. If I prepare it, will you eat it?"

"Is that all you're gonna serve? Just the iguana? No jerk sauce or salad?"

"Look here. I caught it, I'll skin it, and I'll cook it, but you got to bring something to the party. Why don't you take your sweet ass over to one of those restaurants and get us a big platter of greens to grow. Salad, rice and beans, jerk sauce, you know the drill."

"How you gonna grill it?"

"Omma go buy me a grill and some charcoal from those dudes on the beach."

When Gary explained what he wanted, the dudes on the beach were only too happy to oblige. They told him to meet them back at the wall in one hour and they would have everything. One hour later, they passed over a table-top Weber, a bag of charcoal, a flensing knife, and a gram of fine Columbian cocaine, all for the low, low price of two hundred dollars.

When Gary returned to his cabana, Krystal had procured the salads, side dishes, and two bottles of Ron Rico. Gary set to work on the patio, gutting and cutting up the iguana, leaving the head intact as he'd been taught by his father.

"You wanna leave the head on the fish so you know what you're eatin'."

Soon, the not so heavenly aroma, fish-like, in fact, of grilling iguana wafted among the cabanas. Krystal set the patio table with silverware borrowed from the resort and they sat down to eat. They had hardly taken their first bite of grilled iguana when there was a knock on the door.

Gary found Assistant Manager Leotis Harrison waiting politely, wearing crisp white trousers and a blue blazer with gold buttons, the Sandals logo emblazoned on his chest.

"Yes, Mister Duba, I am very sorry to bother to you, but we are receiving complaints that you are cooking. Perhaps you did not read all the rules, but it is forbidden for you to cook in the patio. That is why we have provided eight restaurants."

"I'm sorry about that, Mister Harrison. We won't do it again. I just wanted to sample some of the local game in my own way. I'm a hunter and fisher from way back. When I was growin' up, half what we ate came out the swamp."

"What is it you are cooking, if I may ask? The local markets can be unreliable when it comes to hygiene."

"Come on back! Try it for yourself!"

Gary held the door as Harrison walked through the airy living room out the open patio door to where Krystal stood to greet him.

"Hi! You want some rum and a line?"

Harrison froze at the edge of the patio and stared at the

room service platter which occupied the center of the table.

"Dear God," he said.

"Yup, that's one prime iguana! Tastes just like chicken."

Harrison took a step toward the table. "My God. That is a Jamaican iguana. They are on the endangered species list. Only three hundred are believed to exist."

"No shit. Well I guess they're down to two hundred and ninety-nine now."

"Mister Duba, this is very serious. We at Sandals are committed to the Jamaican ecosystem and preserving our biosphere. I must ask you to stop cooking right now. Do not take another bite. I am afraid there will be very serious repercussions. Wait here. The manager will be in touch with you shortly."

An hour later they were ordered to pack their bags and leave, the first couple ever evicted from Sandals.

Tired of the cookie-cutter contemporary homes ubiquitous to today's housing market? Magnificent Chateau Ami will steal your heart with its exquisite artisan details, European flair & craftsmanship. Inspired by the splendid chateaus of France, this lavish estate is a rare luxury retreat melding timeless architecture with finest 21st century comforts, conveniences & technologies. Sprawling entertaining spaces flow to the outdoor living room past the tennis courts & guest house, to the stunning pool & tranquil forest beyond. Extensive upgrades include breathtaking new landscape design, new interior/exterior paint, new electronics & 150kw whole house backup generator!

Set on 2.5 acres of premier lakefront, this sprawling oasis is the crème de la crème in prestigious Turpentine Ranch! Your search is over! If you've grown tired of the cookie-cutter, all white and stainless contemporary homes ubiquitous to today's housing market, come see this magnificent estate with exquisite artisan details and European flair and craftsmanship. Inspired by the splendid and romantic chateaus of France, this lavish estate is an extraordinary luxury retreat melding European sophistication with timeless architecture, while offering everything the 21st century has available in convenience, comfort and technology. The ornate automatic gates open to welcome you to the home of your dreams. Sprawling entertaining spaces flow to the outdoor living room, past the tennis courts and guest house to the stunning pool with a programmable color fiber optic lighting system, and the tranquil forest beyond. Upgrades include, but are not limited to, breathtaking new landscape design, new interior/exterior paint, new electronics, and a 150kw generator capable of powering the entire home!

Renowned architect Randolf Stofft & Cudmore builders have created a masterpiece of meticulous design and craftsmanship, featuring rare custom amenities including inlayed onyx, hand-planed hickory wood floors, intricate hand-painted ceilings (with a 30 ft dome in the grand entrance hall), custom crown moldings, arched windows & doors, a hand-carved fireplace by Barbara Tattersfield, onyx, granite and marble flooring & countertops, gorgeous crystal chandeliers, and an opulent iron stair railing leading to the upstairs. The entire home is customized with intricate 24k gold leaf design elements on the walls and ceilings. You will also appreciate the floor-to-ceiling custom wood built-ins, custom bar in the study/library, huge walk-in wine cellar (BYOB), and private elevator to transport you to the 2nd floor where you can sip that wine and enjoy a good book in the reading nook that peers out to the stars above.

With fresh paint inside and out, and the tennis courts resurfaced, no detail has gone untended. Additional upgrades include all new electronics, a new pool and pool equipment, and a 2nd backup generator ensuring backup power in the event of an outage. Entertain elaborately in the dramatic living room with coffered ceilings, regal formal dining room and large family room with vaulted wood ceilings. Hand-painted rare hickory wood floors in the family room and kitchen afford an inviting French country feel. The chef's dream kitchen is equipped with 3 Wolf ovens, 2 dishwashers, a built-in Miele espresso maker and butler's pantry. The luxe master suite is indulgent with a sitting room, huge custom walk-in closets, his/her bath with steam showers and hers pink onyx bath & Jacuzzi, as well as an enormous chandeliered walk-in closet, newly painted with new floor covering. A fully equipped home theatre, gym, state of the art lighting system and security and mu-

sic systems optimize comfort. The oversized pool &
outdoor Jacuzzi, covered summer kitchen with wood
ceiling, tennis court and putting green are perfect for
outdoor recreation. A customized climate-controlled
4-car garage will satisfy even the most discerning car
enthusiast. The whole estate has been meticulously
maintained by a full-time housekeeper and property
manager, making it move in ready. Guests and staff
enjoy privacy in the separate guest house with a full
kitchen and separate servant wing. Hurricane im-
pact glass windows ensure protection from even the
harshest weather.

Chateau Ami was the only house in Turpentine Acres, which was to have been an upscale gated neighborhood southwest of Turpentine. The brick pillars for the gate had been installed but not the gate itself. Chateau Ami was a spec house built by a fly-by-night developer named Soo Kim, who'd disappeared six months previously leaving the Central Bank of Florida holding the bag. Hence the cut-rate price of only five million dollars. Lakefront was a euphemism for swamp, the same swamp near which Gary's trailer sat, some five miles away.

The first thing Gary did was to tether his new house to the earth with six massive steel cables, two over the main house, and two over each wing, anchored in concrete plugs sunk deep into the swampy ground.

The Dubas held a housewarming party on the Sunday

following their eviction from paradise, inviting all their friends. Parked in the turn-around before the chateau's grand front entrance was Gary's new Bullitt Mustang, a trailer containing two new jet skis, and a new electric Harley Davidson which Gary bought on a whim while drunk. Parked on the lawn nearby was Gary's new Lamborghini Urus, a bright yellow SUV capable of traversing the Baja peninsula. Visitors parked all over the capacious driveway and the broad concrete apron fronting the garage.

It was really a football party, as the Dolphins were playing the hated Jaguars at the Hard Rock Stadium. By ten-thirty, a dozen men and four women gathered in the spacious living room to watch the pregame show on the giant flat screen TV. El Cheapo sat front and center wearing a cobalt blue jump suit with gold stripes and five pounds of gold around his neck, hair pomaded to great heights, nine hundred-dollar Gucci Men's Distressed sneakers on his feet, waving money.

"I got a thou says Roebuck'll run over a hundred."

"I'll take that action," Gary said, one arm on the mantle of the marble fireplace, over which rested a black velvet Steve Rude Elvis in a gilt frame. "Burnett'll shut him down like an unlicensed taco stand."

"No way Jose."

"Who is this Roebuck?" Patrice said, reclining on a lounge wearing a crisp white Guayabera and flowing beige cotton slacks.

"Roebuck Simms is only the greatest running back in

Miami history," El Cheapo said. "He is Heisman trophy winner and set an all-time record for rushing yards at the University of Alabama."

Jen and Barb giggled in the back row. Krystal had said there would be eligible bachelors. Jen and Barb surveyed the field. El Cheapo was okay if your taste ran to gangster shlock and you liked nose candy. Floyd was trailer trash and smelled like he'd been fermenting in Ax Body Spray. Habib was the catch of the day.

Jen leaned over. "Let's hit the pool, girl."

"Okay," Barb replied.

All eyes were on them as they walked through the room toward the patio entrance in the rec room. As soon as they were out, Jen said, "I found a two-foot black dildo in Krystal's closet."

Barb's laugh sounded like silver coins landing in your hand. "I gave her that, to make up for what she lost in the fire."

"I don't think she'll need it. I find Gary kinda sexy."

"He is, in a Dukes of Hazzard kind of way."

Outside, they put on their sunglasses and tossed towels down on the chaise lounges and sat at the edge of the pool, dangling their slim legs in the clear blue water. An alligator eyed them from the mangrove swamp fifty feet across the perfect lawn.

22 | GATOR IN THE POOL

Jen pulled out a pack of Carltons and offered one to Barb. Jen lit their cigarettes with a Bic and exhaled a luxuriant cloud of smoke. "Rhonda called me yesterday to see if I'd give her a ride to a wine tasting."

Barb barked. "She'll have consumed a bottle by the time you pick her up."

"I said I couldn't do it. I'm sick of Rhonda always calling me to give her rides, and she's always late, and she always drinks too much, and then she has to call Hugh to come get her."

"Poor Hugh."

"That man is a saint."

Jen gestured at the house, the lawn, everything. "Can you believe this shit? Well it couldn't happen to a nicer guy. Krystal really lucked out with Gary. I hope she doesn't blow it." She took out her phone and did a slow video pan.

Barb laughed again. "That's Krystal's modus operandi."

Jen gazed across the bright green glass and noticed a disturbance. "What's that?" she said, pointing.

Barb peered. "What the fuck...RUN! IT'S A GATOR!"

Shrieking, the girls jumped up and ran toward the house. The gator slithered at lightning speed toward the pool, a saurian torpedo in the grass. As the girls ran inside screaming, the gator plopped into the pool.

Barb and Jen ran into the media room.

"THERE'S A FUCKING GATOR IN THE POOL!" Jen said.

Gary leaped to his feet. "You're shittin' me!"

"IT'S ENORMOUS!" Barb said.

Gary strode toward the rec room, in which he'd installed a vertical glass gun cabinet that held a Mossberg twelve gauge, a Remington .22 rifle, and a Sears .30 - 06, which he grabbed along with a box of ammo, loading it on the dining room table. El Cheapo reached beneath his shirt and removed a Colt .44 revolver. Floyd ran to his Harley and retrieved his .45 1911. Jack Hansen, whom Gary knew from roofing, ran outside to his truck to get his bolt-action to get his Savage Axis II. They all ran out to the patio where the gator swam, tail undulating in the crystal-clear water. The boys took up position around the pool and blasted away. Gouts of blood erupted from the hapless gator's hide as it was struck numerous times.

"GOT THE SUMBITCH!"

"LOOK AT THAT FUCKER!"

"YA-HOOO!

"Yeeeeeeee-HA!"

The fusillade lasted several long seconds after which the boys held their guns staring into the darkening water as the gator bled out. Everyone was a little hard of hearing.

As Gary's hearing returned, he heard this.

"Fuck me! I've been shot!"

It came from the house.

Tucking his rifle under his arm Gary went through the open patio door, through the rec room, across the hall to the media room where Patrice leaned forward on the sofa clutching his calf which oozed blood on the hardwood floor and a white carpet.

"Oh fuck, man!" Gary said. "I'm sorry! Wasn't me! I had my back to the house."

Krystal grabbed her new Coach purse. "Come on. I'll take you to the hospital."

"No hospital, mon! I have no green card! Take me to Kildeer Veterinary."

Krystal grinned. "What?"

"I am very serious! Doctor Kildeer is a good man. He knows how to treat puncture wounds."

"All right. Can you walk? Let's go."

Krystal waited for Patrice to catch up. They got in Krystal's new Ford Edge and drove down the perfect blacktop that was to have been the highway to a neighborhood of gazillionaires, but now served only one house. Blood seeped onto the floorboard.

Krystal stretched over the back of the front seat and

snagged a towel which she handed to Patrice. "Don't bleed on the seat."

Patrice dutifully tucked the towel under his leg.

"How'd your operation go?"

"It is the first of three, and it went very smoothly. I cannot tell you how grateful I am to you and Gary for paying my medical expenses. Otherwise it would have remained a dream."

"Thank Gary. It was his idea."

Patrice directed her to the far side of Turpentine, a busy commercial strip containing a full complement of fast food joints and a strip mall in which Kildeer Veterinary was sandwiched between a coin op laundry and Verizon outpost.

Krystal pulled into the parking lot. Patrice winced as she went over the curb.

"How do you know this Doctor Kildeer?"

"He takes care of my chiweenie, Fernando, I love him so much."

They exited into the stifling heat and humidity and entered the veterinary with a hiss of its door piston, like stepping into a freezer. In the waiting room, an elderly man sat in a folding chair cradling a Jack Russell terrier. Two doors, one on either side of the counter opened into the back. Behind the counter sat a middle-aged woman in a baggy shirt, working at a computer, a pair of cat's eye glasses with blue frames hanging on her ample bosom.

She looked up. "Patrice. What can I do for you?"

"Eleanor, I must see Doctor Kildeer as soon as possible

on a personal matter."

Eleanor couldn't see his flesh wound from where she was sitting. "Please have a seat. I'll tell him you're here."

They sat. The old man stared at the hole in Patrice's leg. Patrice nodded at him.

"It's just a flesh wound."

The Jack Russell growled.

The décor consisted of the doctor's framed certificate from Colorado State University School of Veterinary Sciences, and a framed print of six dogs sitting around a poker table holding their hands, with a spaniel wearing glasses looking over a weimaraner's shoulder at the viewer, winking. The weimeraner held a straight flush in Diamonds.

A rear door opened and a young woman with pierced chin, tongue, and nose, wisteria vines crawling up her arm, exited with a spotted pig on a leash. She went to the counter.

"And how is Porque?" Eleanor asked.

"He's in the pink, Eleanor. What do I owe?"

Eleanor told her and the woman handed over her credit card.

A young man in a brush cut, wearing a white lab coat appeared in the door.

"Is that Herman?"

The old man stood and went through the door, which shut behind him.

The door on the other side of the room opened and a man in his late forties, fit, lean, with gray short cut hair wearing a doctor's coat came out. "Patrice. Come on back."

Krystal followed. Kildeer shut the door and gestured to the sofa. Patrice sat.

"What the fuck happened to you?" Kildeer said.

"It was an accident. They were shooting at the gator. This is my friend Krystal."

"How do you do, Krystal?" They shook hands.

Kildeer got down and examined the wound. "Well you're lucky. It only grazed you and passed right through. Missed any important stuff. Now you've got a nice groove in your leg. Maybe when it heals, you can use it to hold a pencil. I'll clean it and dress it, but the only antibiotics I have are for animals. Among those, the safest for humans is probably the amoxicillin. I'll give you a supply of those, but really, I urge you to see a real doctor and get some human medication."

"I can't do that, Doctor. They will deport me."

"I see." Kildeer went to work cleaning and dressing the wound.

"That's the best I can do. Wait here and I'll get you five days' worth. How's Fernando?"

"Fernando is doing well, thank you Doctor Kildeer."

Kildeer returned with the antibiotics. "Here you go. Eleanor has your bill. Is there anything else I can do for you?"

"Could I buy some horse tranquilizers?" Krystal said.

23 | FWOOSH

The once limpid waters of the swimming pool roiled with gator blood, red at the source, changing to a queasy brown as it drifted toward the pumps. Gary, Floyd, and Habib regarded the dead reptile floating in the pool.

"That's a ten-footer," Floyd said.

"Got to weigh five hundred pounds," Habib said. "You might be able to get some boots out of it. Too many holes for luggage."

"I may get it stuffed," Gary said. "But first, I've got to get it out of the pool."

"Well fuck," Floyd said. "Let's tie a chain around it and drag it out."

Gary pointed at him. "That there's a good idea. I'll get the Lambo."

The Urus cost two-hundred and thirty-two thousand dollars, had all wheel drive and a six hundred and fifty horsepower four-liter V-8, weighed four thousand eight hundred and fifty pounds, boasted three TFT screens, and leather seats. It had been designed to cross the Sahara and pull gators from pools. Gary went into his four-car garage and rummaged through his cabinets and closets, securing fifty feet of steel cable, a can of WD40, a roll of duct tape, and a vise grips. It was the same cable he used to anchor his house to the earth, so it ought to be strong enough for a gator. He drove the yellow Urus around the house and backed it up to the shallow end of the pool, fastening the cable to the trailer hitch with a steel clamp.

Gary got out of the car. "Now, Floyd, you get down in there and fasten the other end around its neck. Here's a cable clamp, duct tape and a vise grips."

Floyd stared at him. "Fuck that. That ain't my pool."

"I didn't hear you bitchin when I bought you a new van."

Floyd stared and puffed, then peeled off his wife beater. He wore baggy cargo trou and sandals. "Gimme the fuckin' shit."

Floyd waded into the murky waters, grabbed the gator by the tail, and swung it slowly around to face him, like a recalcitrant compass. He fastened the cable around its neck, using the clamp to snag it tight, held up the OK sign with thumb and forefinger.

Gary said, "Okay, Habib, can you help him ease the gator up over the steps?"

"Where you gonna drag it?" Floyd asked from the water.

Gary pointed toward the jungle from whence the reptile came. "I'll drag it back there and we'll bury it in the weeds."

"I thought you were gonna have it stuffed."

"Nah. Look at it. It's all scarred up and shit. Probably suffering from some parasites. I don't need no stinkin' gator stinkin' up the house."

With Habib and Floyd attending, Gary drove in first gear until the cable was taught. The Urus effortlessly dragged the monster lizard from the water as Gary made a wide turn toward the forest. He drove across the lawn, the reptile leaving a wide groove, until he was bumper to plant. The jungle sprang up ten feet, mostly palm trees, saw grass, mangrove, cypress and banana. Gary got out and looked.

"I don't think I can drive through this shit. Omma burn a path."

Habib and Floyd caught up. "Burn a path with what?"

Gary opened the Urus' tailgate and pulled out a fat white and black cylinder with a pistol grip. It looked like a toy ray gun, or one of the Army's new experimental particle beam weapons. THE BORING COMPANY was written on the side.

Gary stepped away, aimed the device at the plants, flicked a switch and pulled the trigger.

FWOOSH! A ten-foot gout of flame leaped out and began to devour the plants, which browned, shriveled and blackened within seconds.

"Holy shit!" Floyd exulted.

"Careful you don't set the forest on fire," Habib cautioned.

Gary blazed away, working the device side to side, clearing a path for the Urus. "Yeah, fat chance. It rained last night. All this shit is too wet to burn."

"Where the fuck did you get that?" Floyd asked.

"Off the internet. Six hundred bucks. Same dude who makes that electric car, the Edison."

Like a brave marine clearing the Okinawan caves of Japanese soldiers, Gary methodically worked his way into the jungle, flaming from side to side, wearing sunglasses. It was slow going. He had to stop and refuel the flamethrower from a can of compressed propane. Eventually he reached a bald spot where he was just able to drag the gator, with no more room for the Urus to proceed. He unchained the gator and turned the Urus around with a Y turn, running over the gator's head in the process.

Parking the Urus facing back toward the house, he said, "Let's dig that hole."

Habib and Floyd looked at each other.

"With what?" Floyd asked. "Our hands?"

"Wait here."

Gary drove to the garage, lifted the tailgate and loaded three spades and a pick-ax. He drove back across the rear lawn and carefully backed the 4X4 up his alley, stopped, opened the rear gate and handed out shovels.

After fifteen minutes of shoveling, they had only managed to penetrate six inches because water kept flooding back into the holes, and the ground was filled with tough, fibrous roots.

Floyd leaned on his shovel and dragged an arm across his forehead. "It's too swampy. We're gonna have to figure out something else."

Habib had stripped to his pants revealing a pale white barrel. "Gary, you know it's illegal for you to hunt or kill a gator without a license."

Gary pulled out the flamethrower. "Fine. I'll cook that sumbitch. When I'm done, it will fit in a shoebox."

"Is that a good idea?" Habib said.

"Why the fuck not? It's my land. It's my gator. This baby reaches temperatures of over six hundred degrees."

The boys stood around expectantly. This was better than nude female mud wrestling.

"Maybe you should douse it in charcoal fluid or something," Floyd said.

Gary got back in the Urus. "Good idea."

He returned with a gallon container of gasoline and doused the gator.

"Stand back, boys. This'll singe your eyebrows."

Habib and Floyd backed up on opposite sides of the gator, fifteen feet apart. Gary pulled the trigger.

FWOOSH went the gator.

FWOOSH went the clearing.

FWOOSH went the Urus.

FWOOSH went the forest.

"Run!" Gary yelled.

The boys gathered on the patio to watch the conflagration. The Urus exploded, hurling beautiful shards of fine Corinthian leather, maple dashboard inserts, and fender parts hither and yon. The blast knocked Floyd into the pool where he shrieked, hauled himself out, and ran for the main house to shower, lest dead gator cooties infect his bloodstream.

Gary could only shake his head in wonder at nature's mysterious ways. Well fuck. A black plume rose over the swamp.

"What the fuck!" Krystal called from the deck.

Fifteen minutes later, the sound of sirens filtered through the warm and humid air. A Turpentine ladder truck arrived with two police cars. The ladder truck drove across Gary's once-pristine lawn and backed up to the swimming pool where two firemen deployed a fat intake tube.

A fireman wearing a yellow helmet, canvas trousers and thick suspenders over a T-shirt, and a porn star mustache turned to Gary. "Why's the water all red and brown like that?"

"Ah, we're still trying to figure out the ph."

A police officer in a short-sleeved light brown shirt and TPD cap came up to Gary.

"What happened, Gary?"

Gary knew Officer Drake Garland from a previous arrest for disturbing the peace. He had only wanted to bring a little joy and happiness into the lives of those who dwelt in Turpentine. He had only wanted to share with them his deep love of Drowning Pool's "When the Bodies Hit The Floor". At midnight, on Main Street, with a bullhorn.

And for that he was unjustly fined two hundred and fifty dollars. But that was many moons ago and Gary was not the same person. Now he was a man of means.

"Officer Garland, I was clearing some scrub on my property with a flamethrower..."

"A flamethrower?" Garland was a solid five eight with a buzz cut. His utility belt creaked as he adjusted his position. The air was redolent of burning trash and the smell of burnt meat.

"Yes sir. It's perfectly legal. Elon Musk makes them."

"I see. I'm not certain your property extends beyond your lawn, which makes that patch of burning swamp the property of the county. I'm afraid I'm going to have to issue a summons."

"You do what you gotta."

"Maybe you oughtta stay away from matches for a while,

know what I'm sayin'?"

Gary hung his head in shame. "That deal at Thorson's, that wasn't my fault."

The firetruck had driven to the edge of the blaze, intake hose unraveling, where firefighters pumped pool water on the flaming weeds. It looked like a meteor had struck.

Garland wrote out a ticket. "Try to stay out of trouble, Gary. I'm happy for your luck."

The cops departed. The fireman with the porn stache came over with a clipboard, "Sir, we're going to have to bill you for our efforts. Please fill out these forms."

Gary took the clipboard, filled in his personal information and handed it back. "Can I pay you now? I got cash."

"No sir. First, we have to do a damage assessment study. We'll send you a notice. Did you know you got a cooked gator back there?"

Gary's eyebrows rose. "Are you shittin' me?"

"No. You got a big one back there. Looks to be ten feet long."

"You ever eat gator?"

The fireman smiled. "You have a good day, sir."

Gary went into the house where Floyd and Habib sat in the rec room, drinks in hand, having showered and changed clothes. Floyd kept a fresh set in his saddlebags. Habib kept a fresh set in his trunk.

Gary poured himself four fingers of Buffalo Trace, added some ice, collapsed in a leather armchair and glugged. "How's the game goin'?"

Floyd shrugged. "Fuck if I know."

All the other guests had left when the sirens sounded, including El Cheapo.

Habib brought up his personal device. "Fourth quarter just started. Dolphins lead by three. Roebuck runs for one hundred and nine yards."

"Shit!" Gary said.

Krystal came in wearing pedal pushers and a Not Lame T-shirt, red hair blazing, and sat on the arm of Gary's chair.

"How's Patrice?" Gary said.

"He's fine. The veterinarian patched him up and when I got back here, he left with his friend."

Gary bent over and rooted around under the chair, pulling out a smeared mirror.

"Fuck. We got any blow?"

"I was gonna ask El Cheapo," Krystal said. "Shit."

"Well fuck."

Floyd and Habib rose.

"Later," Floyd said.

Gary looked up. "Hey Habib. What's happening with the cockfighting charge?"

Habib snorted in disgust. "Somebody snitched me out. Some informant. It's not a problem. I was just a spectator. They got nothin'."

"Yeah okay. Hasta, you guys."

Seconds later, they heard Floyd rev up the Harley. Krystal dug in her purse and pulled out an amber vial. "Want a trank?"

"What kind of trank?"

"It's a horse trank. I got 'em from Doctor Kildeer. I just did a quarter and I'm feeling fine."

Gary held out his hand.

The next thing he knew it was the following morning and his face was glued to the floor as his cell phone played "Margaritaville".

As he stretched for it on the coffee table, elephants stampeded through his skull. With a groan he rolled over on his back. "Yeah?"

"Is this Gary Duba?" said a crisp male voice.

"Who wants to know?"

"Mister Duba, this is Victory Collection Agency. You owe twelve thousand dollars on your VISA bill. If we have to garnish your wages, we will."

"What wages?"

"Mister Duba, I'm curious. How did you blow through five million so fast?"

"Fuck you, that's how."

Gary ended the call. He phoned Habib and left a message with his secretary. In retrospect, perhaps he had been a bit profligate. He'd planned to invest in his house suspenders, but somehow, things got out of hand. A new van for Floyd. The Bullitt. Patrice's operation. Jet skis. A new car for Krystal. The flamethrower. He looked in his wallet. He had five hundred-dollar bills and some change. He knew he was overdrawn at the bank.

The phone rang again, number unknown. He canceled

the call.

Krystal handed him a beer. "Howzat horse trank workin'?"

"It's workin'! I just hope I can get it up."

Krystal drew her hand upward from his crotch. Little Gary leaped at her touch. "I never have to worry about that, baby. Let's go upstairs."

Gary felt woozy. He looked at the sofa. "Why?"

Gary woke to steady pounding on the door. He lay on the sofa, naked from the waist down, with a splitting headache that throbbed in unison with the pounding. It was dark out.

"KRYSTAL YOU BITCH! I KNOW YOU'RE IN THERE!" a male voice shouted from outside.

Gary fished around, found his jeans and pulled them on. He tried to summon some energy. Krystal stormed into the room wearing a terrycloth robe.

"It's my ex, Herman."

Gary blinked. "Herman? What Herman?"

"I dumped that loser years ago!"

Krystal strode through the elegant foyer and yanked open the arched oak door.

"What do you want, Herman?"

Herman was a wide body with lank blond hair, wearing coveralls and a John Deere cap. "You owe me seven hundred and fifty dollars."

"My ass. For what?"

"For bailing you out two years ago."

Gary staggered to his feet.

Krystal turned toward him. "Do you have seven hundred and fifty? It's worth it to get rid of this asshole."

Herman looked around the foyer. "You done well for yourself."

"How'd you find me?"

"You had quite the wedding. Read about it in the paper. Did she tell you we're still married? She never signed the divorce papers. You won't miss seven hundred and fifty bucks. Hell. Make it an even thou."

"Fuck you, Herman!"

Gary entered the foyer. He was taller and in better shape than Herman, but Herman outweighed him by sixty pounds. "Get the fuck outta here. I don't owe you shit."

"Oh yeah? How'd you like me to contest this wedding? Whaddaya gonna do then, smart guy?"

"How'd you like a fat lip?"

Krystal stormed out of the foyer. Gary heard her tromp upstairs.

"You're trespassing. Get the fuck outta here."

"Or what, tough guy? You gonna call the cops?"

Gary punched Herman in the face with a compact straight right. Herman staggered back, put a hand to his mouth, looked at the blood, put his head down and charged, ramming Gary in the chest and carrying them both through the foyer into the living room where they fell on a glass coffee table, which Gary hated, shattering it and going down in a tumble. They rolled. Shards of glass stuck to Gary's back. Herman got on top and tried to punch, his blows landing as ineffective swats.

Krystal reappeared wearing blue jeans and a Toby Keith T-shirt, gripping a two-foot black hard rubber dildo in both hands.

WHACK! She struck Herman across the back of the head, causing him to stagger sideways allowing Gary to escape.

WHACK! WHACK! She struck him forward and backward, wielding the dildo like a samurai sword.

WHACK! She struck him on the elbow causing Herman to howl in pain.

WHACK, WHACK, WHACK! She drove him back through the foyer and out the door.

Herman ran for his truck.

"ADIOS, DOUCHEBAG!" Krystal crowed as her ex peeled out in his ten-year old Camaro. Gary could tell by its exhaust it was a six.

"Loser!" he yelled, thrusting a finger to the sky.

They went inside.

"Why didn't you sign the divorce papers?"

Krystal shrugged. "I'll sign them now if I can find them."

They sat in the living room where Krystal produced a mirror and a vile of blow.

"Where'd you get that?"

"I found it when I got the dildo."

"Where'd you get the dildo?"

"Jen gave it to me. She thought it was funny."

"Lemme see."

She passed the two-foot hard rubber shaft to Gary, who hefted it, took a few practice swings. "You could do some serious damage with this!"

"Yeah. I'll put it in the front hall closet. It may come in handy."

Gary looked up. A feral pig stood in the open patio door looking around. He leaped up!

"Fuck! Where's my rifle?"

"Forget the rifle, Gary! Just scare it away!"

Gary ran toward the pig waving his arms. "Go on! Get!"

For a second, he feared it would charge. It stood two feet at the shoulder and displayed some impressive tusks. It turned tail and ran toward the high weeds, disappearing near the black spot made by the unsuccessful gator burial.

Gary went into the kitchen and drank two quarts of water. When he returned to the living room, Krystal was cutting up lines.

"Wha'd he bail you out for?"

Krystal bent over the mirror and snorked. "They said I attacked a manager at Popeyes, but that's a lie. She swung at me first."

"What were you fightin' about?"

Krystal leaned back, shutting her eyes in ecstasy. "Fries." She handed the cut soda straw to Gary, who sat next to her, slid the mirror over and did a line.

The coke rampaged through his head, chasing away the headache and the doldrums. He knew he'd pay for it later, but he could always take another horse trank to get to sleep.

"You got any more horse trank?"

"Yeah, but you gotta wait. We're outta cigs. Go up to WaWa and get a carton of Carlton's."

"Why don't you go?"

"I'll wreck the car. I don't drive drunk as well as you. You can take my car."

"Thanks. Thanks a lot."

"Come on, baby. You can do it."

Gary looked in his wallet. He had five hundred dollars. What the hell. He wanted cigs too. He put on a shirt.

"See you in a few."

The WaWa was ten miles up the road, at the intersection of Weldon Way and the highway. Gary could drive it in his sleep. Taking Krystal's keys off the marble table in the foyer, he went out into the cooling night, got in the Edge, and booked, the headlights cutting across two more feral pigs on the way out. He leaned on the horn and out the window.

"GET THE FUCK OUTTA HERE, YOU PIGS!"

Gary tuned into WWKA on the run. They were playing the New Country, which all sounded alike to him. Ten minutes later, he pulled into the parking lot of the brightly lit WaWa and went inside. The store belonged to a dot Indian named Singh, who was behind the counter.

"Good evening, Gary."

"Hey Singh. Gimme a carton of Carltons and a couple

Megaball tickets, willya?"

"I, for one, would be very much surprised if you won again."

Gary slid a hundred across the counter and collected his booty, stuffing the Megaball tickets in the breast pocket of his Western-style shirt. "I won before, didn't I?"

"Yes, you did. Good night, Gary."

"Hang loose, Singh."

Gary headed back. Now they were playing some fucking country/rap hybrid. Gary stabbed the CD player. Little Big Town, "I'm With the Band". At least it was music. He pulled a Louie on Weldon, onto Grange Road, which led to the turn-off to Elysian Fields. As he approached a dense overhang of oak, his headlights picked up an old station wagon parked on the other side of the road facing him, its hood up, something lashed to the roof, emergency lights feebly blinking. Gary pulled off the road onto the broad shoulder on the right side of the road, put on his Stars and Bars cap, and walked across the road, where a man bent over the engine bay, his back to the woods.

Gary went around the back of the station wagon.

"You all right?"

An elderly black man with white hair and a white mustache stood up and looked back at him, seeing his cap. The mans' eyes went wide. He held up a finger, opened his passenger door, reached inside and straightened up. Now he too was wearing the Stars and Bars.

"Just quit on me," the old man said in a gravelly voice. "Started stutterin', like it wasn't gettin' no gas, and then it stopped. I was barely able to pull over to the side."

"Lemme take a look at it," Gary said. "I'll be right back. May need a little WD40."

Gary crossed the dark road, popped the hatch, and removed a can of WD40, a roll of duct tape, and a vise grips from a cardboard box he'd put in back the day they brought it home. There was a similar box in all his vehicles.

"Turn off your lights," Gary said. "Save your battery." The old man complied.

The old man held a flashlight as Gary looked. It was a 1989 Buick Estate Wagon with the three-oh-seven-inch V8, a round air cover covering a four-barrel carb. Gary removed the air cleaner uncovering the carb. He leaned way over, getting eyeball to eyeball with the carb.

"Lemme have that light."

He peered.

"You got palmetto bugs in your carb."

"What the fuck?" the old man said.

"Omma have to take it off and blow it out."

"How did palmetto bugs get in my carburetor?"

"Where do you store it?"

"In an old detached garage. Fuck me runnin'. I ain't never heard of such a thing."

"Maybe somebody put 'em there."

"Who'd so such a thing?"

"Some psycho. All sortsa crazy people running around these days."

"Well look here," the old man said. "I'm Quincy."

Gary straightened up and shook hands. "Gary."

"I appreciate it. Most people wouldn't stop."

Gary returned to the carb. "I been in this spot before. That's why I always carry some WD40, some duct tape, and some vise grips. That shit'll fix 'bout near anything."

He got the carb loose, took it into the weeds, Quincy following with the light.

"You got a pipe cleaner?"

Quincy squinted. "How you know?"

"Just a shot in the dark."

Quincy fished around in his glove compartment and returned with a pack of pipe cleaners.

Gary ran them through the carbs, blew on them, sighted through them at the moon.

"Let's hope this works."

He reattached the carb and sprayed WD40 on the throttle cable. "Pump the gas a couple times. See if it'll start."

A sports car blew past, right down the center line.

Quincy pumped the gas and turned the key. The car whined for a few seconds then caught, exhaust releasing a dense gray cloud.

"Boy howdy!" Quincy said, turning on the lights and getting out. "Gary, how'd you like season tickets to the Dolphins?"

Gary scratched his chin. "Tell you the truth, I'd rather watch on television. You see more."

"You ain't wrong. Well at least let me pay you for your time."

Gary looked at the twenty-five-year-old vehicle. "Nah, keep your money. Pay it forward."

They shook hands again, Quincy got behind the wheel and headed north. Gary got back in the Edge and drove toward home. Five minutes later, his headlights picked up a slow-moving log crossing the road. Gary stopped.

"Fuckin' gators. They're harassing me." He leaned out the window. "GET THE FUCK OUTTA HERE! WE DON'T WANT YOUR KIND!"

The gator took its sweet time, disappearing in the saw grass on the opposite side of the road.

When he got home, Krystal was passed out in the living room, her legs sprawled, the smeared mirror on the table. Gary felt jittery from all the coke. He wanted to do another line, but the relief was temporary, and he'd end up even more jittery. He'd wasted countless nights lying awake, heart pumping. He found Krystal's amber vial of horse tranks. Half a trank. Couldn't hurt.

Gary sprawled in the living room waiting for the trank to hit, flipping through channels. Habib appeared in a three-piece blue sharkskin suit.

"Have you been injured in an auto accident, and the insurance company refused to pay what your injury was worth? At the Law Offices of Habib Rodriguez, we specialize in automobile accidents. I've been an attorney for fourteen years and the insurance companies don't scare me. To find out what your accident is worth, call me. The consultation is free, and unless we get you a substantial settlement, there is no cost to you."

What's Your Snoblem came on. It was a game show in which contestants had to act out their grievances before a celebrity panel. If the panel guessed the grievance, the contestant won awards. They weren't A list celebrities. They were D list celebrities. Dr. Grim, a late-night horror host. Miss Citronella, an aging beauty queen and essential oils spokesperson. Frank Funk, a life coach and inspirational speaker. The host was Major Sutton, a stocky, black comedian with a gleaming, bald head.

The contestant was a big, bony, middle-aged woman who sat in a folding chair driving an invisible car. She mimed talking on her phone. She got up, walked behind the car, and goose-stepped forward while throwing out her arm in the sieg heil. She sat in the seat again, rolled down an invisible window and tried to explain. She stood, goose-stepped, and wrote out an invisible ticket.

"Talking on your cell phone!" Dr. Grim exulted.

The contestant shook her head.

"I got it," Miss Citronella said. "I got it. Putting on makeup."

The contestant clapped her hands, smiled hugely, and pointed.

"We have a winner!" Major Sutton boomed. Takes one to know one, eh, Miss Citronella?"

Miss Citronella, a willowy bottle blonde in an evening gown, dimpled. "You know it, Major. Joan was putting on makeup in her car."

The contestant blushed. "I was late for a date."

"That's three in a row, Joan Marks. Your total winnings come to nine thousand eight hundred and thirty-five dollars!"

The audience applauded. The TV swam. Gary was zonked.

He woke on the floor, his head at a slight downward angle, due to the slanting nature of the media room. His tongue was glued to the carpet. A panzer division carried out a training exercise in his skull. Ringo bashed away. Gary always liked Ringo, but he didn't think he was a very good drummer.

Gary tried to open his eyes. Finally, he had to use his hands. From a foot away, an evil, fleshy alien stared back at him, its eyes black holes leading to hell. Gary froze, not out of fear, but the purest confusion. What was it? What was it doing here?

It was a feral-pig. It snorted, misting Gary with hog boogers. Behind it, two other feral pigs egged it on.

27 | THE CLEANERS

Gary rose up like Moby Dick. "GET THE FUCK OUTTA HERE!"

The feral pig squatted and discharged liquid feces all over the floor, its smell a radioactive cloud. Gary sprinted for the gun cabinet, grabbed the Mossberg, and ran back into the living room where a pig was eating the remains of last night's pizza. Gary snugged the butt into his shoulder and squeezed the trigger.

BOOM! Went the gun.

SQUEAL! Went the surviving pigs, running around in confusion. Gary chased them into the kitchen and fired, striking the bronze-colored refrigerator door. Pigs squealed in terror! They ran for the exits! Gary chased them out the open patio door where they skirted the now empty swimming pool and raced for the safety of the jungle.

Muttering, Gary returned to the house, shutting the sliding patio door behind him. Krystal stood in the living room, hands on the hips of her three hundred-dollar jeans, staring at the dead pig lying half on, half off a once white throw rug.

"What the fuck?"

"Did you leave the patio door open?"

"I don't know! What are we gonna do about this?"

"I can butcher it. Them's good eatin'."

"No, you fool! The blood! We can't have this shit in here! I'll have to throw out the whole rug! And look at that sofa! That's a nine hundred-dollar sofa!"

"I know a guy can get rid of blood stains."

"Who? Harvey Keitel?"

"El Cheapo."

"Well get him over here."

Gary reached for his phone. "Lemme as' you something. Have you opened up any new credit card accounts?"

Krystal stared daggers. "So what? We can afford it."

"No, we can't. I got collection agencies on my ass. We're a month behind on the mortgage."

Krystal held out her hand. "Then give me five hundred dollars."

"Not until you fork over all your credit cards."

"I got a hair appointment this afternoon!"

"You know, some of those salons would pay a lot of money for your hair. You want to help? Sell your hair."

"Fuck you!" Krystal stomped up the stairs.

Gary phoned El Cheapo and explained the situation.

"I'll be there in a couple hours," El Cheapo said.

Gary got a wheelbarrow from the garage, took it into the living room and hoisted the dead pig. It weighed about one hundred and twenty pounds. He wheeled the pig back into the garage, with a workbench running the length of the back wall except for a door in the middle. Stripping to his skivvies and putting on leather gloves, Gary slit the hog stem to stern on the floor next to a grated drain, pulled out the entrails, put them in the wheelbarrow, and walked it out the back door, past the patio and the empty pool, fifty feet to the blackened cinder of the forest. It looked like a MOAB strike. The twisted remains of his two hundred and thirty-three thousand-dollar Urus hunkered in the burn pit like the bones of some dinosaur. Gary dumped the pig guts at the far side of the pit. Let the gators and birds have 'em.

He looked wistfully at the empty pool. Fuckin' gator.

In the garage, Gary used a flensing knife to remove the pig's skin, wondered what he could do with it. Pigskin gloves? His own football? Like he had money for taxidermy.

"Don't be an ass!" he snapped at himself.

Gary methodically cut up the pig into ribs, hams, bacon, put the meat in big plastic zip-loc bags and stored them in the restaurant-style freezer he'd had installed in the garage. He gathered up the hard parts, bones and hooves, put them in a plastic bag and put that in his garbage can. He used a hose to wash the blood down the drain.

Holding his jeans at arm's length, he returned to the main house, entering through the kitchen. Krystal was at the counter brewing a Keurig. She looked at him, screamed, and dropped her mug.

"What happened? Are you all right?"

Gary looked down at his near naked blood-smeared body. "It's not my blood. I was just chopping up that pig. Chill. El Cheapo will be here shortly."

"Don't track blood in the living room!"

Gary used a dish towel to wipe himself off as best he could, then tossed it in the laundry room, beyond which lay another bathroom. He went upstairs and stood for long minutes under the multi-nozzled Kohler jet stream shower, the water lukewarm. Stepping out, he dried off with one of the massive luxurious Turkish bath linens Krystal had bought at finelinens.com, spritzed his underarms with deodorant, slapped on some Giorgio, put on a fresh set of Carhartt jeans, a Victory Motorcycle T-shirt, and slipped his sockless feet into gator-skin loafers.

Walking down the second-floor hall, he looked in at his exercise room and thought of pumping some iron, but he'd just taken a shower. He entered and admired himself in the full-length wall mirror, with barre. The room contained a weight bench, weights, a Pellotron, a treadmill, and a Bowflex Max Trainer on which you could pump weight, exercise your quads, your lats, and your nads, facing a fifty inch flat screen TV. One wall was all glass with a sliding patio door overlooking the backyard.

Gary went out and inhaled the humid air, redolent with the smell of burning weeds and animal flesh. Out front, a car honked. Gary skipped down the marble steps, crossed through the tiled foyer and out the front door. El Cheapo had pulled up in an anonymous panel van. El Cheapo and another man, who was built like an Abrams tank, got out.

They went around to the back, opened the van, and began hauling out equipment, including a steam cleaner and many plastic containers.

"This is my associate, Manny," El Cheapo said.

Manny stuck out a ham, completely enclosing Gary's fist.

"Come on in. Lemme show ya the damage."

Gary led them through the foyer into the living room where they stared in disbelief at the destruction. There was blood all over the place, a smashed glass table, and dirty dishes.

"What the fuck happened, essay?" El Cheapo said.

"Hey, some of this shit is left over from Sunday. The blood's new. Fuckin' feral pigs, man. Somebody left the patio door open."

"Whadja do, shoot 'em in the house?"

Manny examined the back of a Finish chair blasted with shotgun pellets.

"Yeah, I probably should have chased 'em all out first, and then shot 'em. But you never know. Some of those feral pigs are fuckin' ugly. They'll turn on ya. My old man had a coon hound and they ate it. I hear there's ferals back in the swamp that weigh over a thousand pounds."

"Yeah, well before me and Manny get to work, this is gonna cost you a thou."

"Fuck, man. I ain't got a thou."

"How you win the lottery and ain't got a thou?"

"Man, I spent it all. But shit. I got shit in this house that's worth way more than a thou. What do you need? A Pelloton? You want one of those flat screens?"

El Cheapo looked around. His gaze fell on the Steve Rude velvet Elvis.

Dressed in Kelly-green jumpsuits, El Cheapo and Manny went to work, hauling out the stained carpet, the ruined sectional, and loose pieces of furniture, returning with a twenty gallon Craftsman shop vac which they used to hoover up the shredded glass and copious hog hairs. They sprayed and scrubbed. Two hours later, the living room was down to its hardwood floor, half the furniture was gone, and it smelled of Pinesol.

Krystal appeared on the second-floor balcony, smoking a cigarette. "I'll order a new sofa from American TV."

"You ain't ordering shit. Didn't I just tell you we're in debt up to our eyeballs?"

Krystal spat smoke. "How is that even possible? We're millionaires!"

"I took a cash settlement. That came to five and a half million dollars. I put five down on the house."

"Five million dollars?" Krystal was bug-eyed.

"Yeah. My old man always told me to put down as much as you can for a low mortgage. That brought our mortgage to a little over three thou a month which normally wouldn't have been a problem except we got a little carried away with the partying and the catered dinners and all that shit you buy."

"I buy? What about those two jet skis out in the yard? And that fucking Mustang you never drive?"

"They repossessed the Mustang!"

It had disappeared in the middle of the night.

The front door opened and closed. Jen and Barb entered in bikinis with huge straw purses looped over their shoulders, wide-brimmed straw hats on their heads and wrap-around sunglasses.

"Hi! Do you mind if we use the pool?"

"Pool's empty. Ain't got around to filling it again."

Jen and Barb advanced into the living room. Barb whistled.

"What happened?"

"Fuckin' feral hogs. Somebody left the patio door open."

"What're those funny pale stains?" Barb said.

"I shot 'em."

"Why didn't you chase them out of the house before you shot them?"

Gary threw his hands in the air. "You had to be here."

"The hot tub's still full," Krystal said.

Jen fanned herself with her hat. "It's too hot for a hot tub! Can't you fill it up now?"

"No. It's a twenty-five thousand-gallon pool. It takes twenty-four hours to fill, and I still gotta clean out all the gator parts and shit."

Jen went into the kitchen and pulled a bottle of Chardonnay from her purse, which she put in the freezer. Barb sat on the remaining sofa in the living room, pulled out a baggie and papers and rolled a joint on a copy of Hunting & Fishing.

Putting her hat back on, Jen went out the sliding kitchen door onto the back patio, put her hands on her hips and gazed at the ecological disaster across the rutted lawn. "You should have this place declared an environmental disaster and apply for federal funds."

Gary followed her out, beer in hand. "Do you think I should? Do you know how to do that?"

Jen laughed. "Hell no."

Gary eyed her butt. "Omma have to sell this place."

Jen turned on him. "What? You've only been in here six months!"

"I know, I know, but I'm broke. I don't know where the fuck it went. I never had much money, so I was never any good in spending it. Maybe I should have bought something more modest and invested in gold or something."

"Well if you're serious about selling, I know a realtor. She's a good friend of mine."

"Why don'tcha write that down for me."

"I will, but I'll tell you right now, the first thing she's gonna do is have you take down those chains."

"My house suspenders? Why should I take them down? That's like an added attraction. That should add like twenty thousand dollars to the price!"

"Oh Gary, grow up. They're hideous. No one wants those draped over their house."

"You don't know shit, Jen."

Up went the hands. "What evs! I'm just trying to help."

"So was Missus O'Leary's cow."

Jen stared at him. "What are you talking about?"

"Never mind."

They went back inside where Krystal and Barb were bent over the surviving coffee table. Krystal inhaled, spread her arms and leaned back in ecstasy of chemical acceleration. She got up. "I'm gettin' a drink. What do you want, hon?"

"Is that Chardonnay chilled yet?"

Krystal strode toward the bar. "Fuck Chardonnay. Vodka and tonic."

"Yeah," Barb said.

"Me too," Gary said.

Krystal grabbed a bottle of Grey Goose. Soon they'd be back to Popov. She made four drinks and handed them out. Gary sat on the sofa and did a line, snorting and running a finger beneath his nose.

"Got any more valium?" he asked Krystal.

"I think so."

"Good. I really need a good night's sleep."

Jen's phone sang "Kiss Him Goodbye" by the Supremes. She got up and walked toward the patio.

"Say hello to Yodel for me!" Barb called out with gusto.

Gary looked up. "Who's Yodel?"

"Her latest boyfriend. A Cuban rapper."

"You're kidding?"

Barb effected a Cuban accent and used jazz hands. "'Hey mamacitasan, meet me with your red dress on...meet me in your rayon thong, hey mamacitasan'."

"You're kidding?"

"You wish. He wants me to sing back-up, but he really just wants to fuck me."

"Who wouldn't?"

Barb ran her hand down Gary's thigh. "Would you like to fuck me, big boy?"

Krystal reached over, grabbed Barb by her long blonde hair, and yanked her sideways.

"I was just kidding!" Barb protested, pulling her hair free."

Krystal stood. "Move your ass out of there. Sit over there."

Barb stood, started. "Someone's here."

Gary looked up. "Ain't nobody at the end of this road but us."

"I heard tires."

Door pounding commenced. Gary felt his testicles shrivel and his heart race. He knew that knock. He got up, went to the front door and looked out through a glass side panel to observe two county cars parked in the driveway, two county mounties standing by the rear car, two more on his doorstep.

Gary opened the door.

Sheriff Ralph Hunnicutt looked like George Washington, Rushmore version, save for the amber aviator's glasses.

"Gary, I'm real sorry to have to do this, but we got a court order to evict you. The First National Bank of Okeechobee has seized the property. Normally, I'd give you twenty-four hours, but somebody at the bank has a real hard-on for you, so me and the boys will observe while you and Missus Duba pack, then we will escort you off the property."

Gary gaped. "Are you shitting me?"

Sheriff Hunnicutt spread his hands. "I'm sorry."

Krystal came out clutching her vodka and tonic. "You can't just throw us out!"

"I'm sorry, Missus Duba, but we can."

Krystal threw her drink in Sheriff Hunnicutt's face. Sheriff Hunnicutt slugged Krystal on the jaw. Gary charged, bowling the Sheriff over backward and taking him down to the ground.

Two deputies landed on Gary, peeled him off the sheriff, threw him face first to the ground, and cuffed him painfully behind his back, a knee pinning him between his shoulders. Gary twisted his head around to see if Krystal was okay, but he couldn't spot her.

The Sheriff got up. "Gary, that was a real dumb ass move. Now I gotta charge you with assault, and the judge, she don't cotton to people who assault the law."

"How do you know what the judge is gonna do?"

"Experience, dumb ass. Get him up. Where'd the woman go?"

A young deputy and potential linebacker stepped up. "She went in the house, Sheriff."

The sheriff spread his hands and bulged his eyes. "Well?"

"Sir, don't we need a warrant to go inside?"

"She threw a drink in your face, dumb ass! Go get her. Try not to hurt her."

The young deputy squared up. "Yes, sir."

"Buva, you go with him."

A squat uniformed Mexican followed the deputy inside. The Sheriff and the remaining deputy, a tall Latina, pulled Gary to his feet.

Krystal exploded from the open door holding the two-foot dildo overhead, samurai style.

"YAHHH!" she bellowed, leaping at the Sheriff and WHAP right across the side of the head and then WHAP back again.

The female deputy uncorked a can of Mace and let Krystal have it right between the eyes. She immediately dropped the dildo and fell to her knees, rubbing her face.

"Don't rub it," Gary said. "It will only make it worse."

The sheriff and one deputy shoved Gary into the back of one cruiser. The other two deputies cuffed Krystal and shoved her in the other. They got in their cars and drove away.

No one noticed Jen filming the whole thing on her camera on the second-floor balcony. She wore a black bathing suit and hid behind potted palms. She kept filming until the cruisers disappeared around a bend. Barb stood next to her the whole time.

"Ho Lee shit," Barb said.

Jen laughed. "I need a drink."

"No fucking kidding."

They went inside, down to the rec room with the wet bar as Barb mixed more vodka tonics.

Barb handed Jen a drink. "Whaddaya gonna do with that video?"

"What do you think I'm gonna do with it?"

"Do you really want to piss off the police?"

Jen sank her drink and smiled lasciviously. "Fuck that shit! I don't live in this county! Of course, first, I gotta do a little editing. I don't just slap whatever footage up on Youtube, you know? I studied film in college, and I've acted in feature films."

"You mean Splay Misty For Me? Or Thighscraper?"

"Laugh all you like, but I got paid for both those jobs and I didn't fuck the leading man, if that's what you're insinuating."

"Who did you fuck?"

"The director. Do I look stupid?"

The girls squealed.

Jen sent the video to her laptop, on which she edited it down to a hard-hitting sixty seconds. She uploaded it to her Youtube channel, Just Jen, on which she talked cosmetics and thrifting.

30 | WHOMP THAT SUCKER

Gary spent the night in the Glades County Jail and was taken to the magistrate, along with a dozen other hapless shmucks, at nine in the morning, where they were left cooling their heels until the judge was good and ready to hear them at eleven.

Judge Ellen Haversham was a tiny ginseng woman who looked like she belonged on the Supreme Court. Gary offered silent thanks it was not Judge Murphy. He stood before Judge Haversham with Habib Rodriguez in his court clothes, a sober three-piece navy blue suit from Men's Wearhouse. The judge was looking at Gary's record. She looked up.

"Mister Duba, you've been in trouble with the law since you were a teenager. Up until now, most of your offenses have been petty, but assaulting a police officer is not petty. Bail is one hundred and fifty thousand dollars."

"Your honor!" said Habib. "Mister Duba has strong ties to this community! He is newly married and just moved into a new house. The only reason he struck the officer was because the officer struck his wife! He acted in the heat of passion."

"Mister Rodgriquez, many criminals do. That does not excuse their behavior. One hundred and fifty thousand dollars."

BAM.

"Next."

The bailiffs hustled Gary out of the courtroom into the crowded hall, followed by Habib.

"May I have a word with my client?"

The bailiffs knew every lawyer in town. "Go ahead," one of them said.

Gary was incensed. "One hundred and fifty thousand dollars?!"

"Relax. You only have to come up with ten per cent."

"How'm I gonna do that? I'm broke!"

Habib sighed. "I ain't even gonna ask."

"Can you bail me out?"

"Sorry. I don't have two dimes to rub together. I had to hire a lawyer to fight these ridiculous charges."

"Can you get Krystal out?"

"Sorry. She struck a police officer. Pretty sure her bail will be less than yours, though."

"Well I guess I'm screwed."

"That video of her braining the cop with the dildo is everywhere."

Gary was silent for a minute. "What?"

"Oh yeah! Didn't you know? Somebody posted a video

of Krystal swinging that thing. It's all over the internet! Do you own that footage? You could monetize that. I'll bet it's got over a million views by now."

"Holy fuck!" Gary said, mind racing. Had to be Jen. She was always filming. "Since that's video of us, don't we own it? Can they do that without our permission?"

"Well you can always sue, but you'd have to prove damages."

The bailiffs reclaimed Gary. "How goes the cockfighting?" one of them asked Habib.

"It's bullshit, Bob. I was only there to meet a client."

"You don't raise cockfighting roosters?"

"No. And I wouldn't spread that around, if I were you."

When Gary returned to the holding tank, the prisoners were whooping and hollering. He heard them before he even turned the corner.

"WHOMP THAT SUCKER!

"YEEEEEE-HAH!"

"DO IT AGAIN!"

As the guard unlocked the door to the tank, every prisoner in the room stood facing him and applauded. Gary put his hands up.

"Thank you, thank you."

A series of benches faced the flat screen TV bolted high up on the wall. There was Krystal braining the cop. She was replaced by a serious-looking woman with dark hair and glasses.

"This video, of Missus Duba attacking Deputy Ross

Evans with an adult toy, has been viewed over ten million times."

The prisoners parted, indicating Gary should sit in the front row. A big black man wearing a blue work shirt sat next to him.

"Hey Duba. How do you blow seven million dollars?"

"I don't know, but I had a good time."

"Whooooo-EE!" The man enthused, holding up his hand for a high five. Every prisoner lined up to slap skin with Gary.

"Man, you have one righteous old lady!"

"They oughtta make that into a stamp!"

"Man, if you put that on a shirt, you'll make a million dollars!"

"Dude, you're a fuckin' inspiration!"

Gary blushed. "I'm still the same redneck who likes to get shit-faced, shoot at cans, and watch the Dolphins."

Hoots and hollers. A squat Mexican with a Zapata mustache sat on Gary's other side.

"How's your lawyer, meng?"

"Habib Rodriguez."

The Mexican grinned hugely, showing off a gold tooth. "Joo know, my sister-in-law got rear-ended last year in Tampa and the focking insurance company wouldn't do shit, so she went to Habib, and he got her five hundred thousand dollars!"

"Did she do an ad for him?"

"No. Does he pay?"

"I think they do them for free, after he gets them a big settlement."

"I will ask her. So, I guess you didn't make bail then."

"I ain't got fifteen thousand dollars."

"Well joo know, meng, you could sell those shirts with your old lady whackin' that cop with a two-foot dildo!"

Those within earshot cheered.

The Mexican extended his hand. "I'm Manny Huerta."

They shook. The Mexican slapped Gary hard on the back and pointed at the TV. "Look! Look! Is your meng!"

Habib Rodriguez appeared resplendent in a gray shark-skin three-piece and mauve tie, standing in front of a street fresco of Justice as a blind, break-dancing black woman with a 'fro out to here.

Manny stood and faced the noisy room, waving his hands. "Shut up shut up! That's Gary's lawyer!"

"Have you been involved in an auto accident? Did the insurance company fail to live up to its promises? If you feel you've been short-changed, call the law offices of Habib Rodriguez. Justice is our only concern."

Hoots and hollers.

"Bottom feeder!"

"Fuckin' ambulance chaser."

"Shut the fuck up. He's my lawyer too."

The Habib detractor shoved the Habib protector and suddenly they were on the ground rolling.

A corrections officer ran his billy along the jailhouse xylophone.

"Knock it off or I turn the TV off."

Other prisoners pulled the two apart and calmed them down. Gary wondered where he was going to get the money. Maybe this was it. Maybe he wouldn't get out of this bind, and they'd find him guilty of assaulting a police officer and he'd have to do some serious time. Gary hadn't been in jail since he was eighteen and found guilty of being a public nuisance and exposing himself to a woman in Winn-Dixie. He couldn't even remember. He was doing a lot of meth back then.

If he ever got out, the first thing he'd do was to see about using Krystal on a T-shirt. But that would turn every cop in the country against him. They'd be on his ass. As leery of the law as he was, Gary didn't want that. He riffled through his mental rolodex of money-making schemes. House suspenders was his best idea. Maybe he could get on Shark Tank, using his own home as an example. He'd have to look into that.

The day passed with excruciating slowness. Inmates played scissors, paper, rock, talked about their big scores and the scores yet to come, the ideal floozies waiting for them upon their release, and Miami's chances in the play-offs.

At five p.m., the jail guard reappeared.

"Duba, let's go! You're bailed out."

Gary gaped in astonishment.

"Who paid my bail?"

"Fuck if I know. Let's go."

The same female desk sergeant who'd checked him in returned Gary's personal belongings and had him sign release papers. Gary heard laughter and excited voices from beyond the door separating him from the booking desk.

"What's going on?"

"Seems we have a celebrity," the woman said, sliding Gary's possessions across the counter in a plastic bin.

"Who is it?"

"Some football player. You're free to go, Mister Duba."

She buzzed him out.

Waiting on the other side of the metal detector was an elderly black man in an old black suit with an unbuttoned white shirt. It took Gary a minute.

"Quincy!" he said, stepping forward. "What are you doing here?"

"Bailing your white ass outta jail."

"What? How did you even know?"

"I musta watched that video of your old lady beaning the popo 'bout a dozen times. I guess by now everybody in the country knows. She's famous. And since you're her old man, you're famous."

"Quincy, I don't know how to thank you, or pay you back. I'm flat broke."

"I don't care 'bout dat. You don't have to pay me back. You stopped when I needed help and that's all I need to know."

"But where did you get fifteen thousand dollars? That's not chump-change."

Quincy gestured to a dozen people including five cops surrounding someone, laughing, clapping their hands. "Not to my boy. He spend that much at dinner for four."

Gary looked, but couldn't see who was in the middle of the scrum.

"Who's your boy?"

"Roebuck Simms, running back for the Dolphins."

The crowd parted and a buff young man in Armani slacks and jacket, short black hair and a Van Dyke approached smiling, arm outstretched.

"Mister Duba! Thanks for helping out my pops. Let's get out of here and go get something to eat."

The cops regarded Gary with respect. Roebuck addressed the room.

"Y'all don't know this, but my pops Quincy here, his car broke down on a dirt road, and this man Duba stopped, diagnosed his fuckin' carburetor, took it apart and put it back together again in the middle of the night, and that's how my pops got home!"

A smattering of applause grew into an intense chorus. A few cops opened a corridor as Gary, Quincy, and Roebuck left the building. Out front, a dozen people had gathered. Word spread fast in a small town. Roebuck paused to sign autographs and pose for a few selfies, then with a grin he waved them back.

"Folks, gotta run. But I appreciate your support!"

The crowd watched, perplexed as the trio walked down the street to a parking garage. Who was the white guy?

They went up the stairs to the second-floor where Roebuck beeped open a BMW X5M. Gary got in the back seat, ran his hand over the leather.

"Sweet! I had one of those Lambo Uruses."

"No shit! How'd you like it?"

"I liked it fine for the two months I had it. It accidentally caught fire."

Roebuck drove down and paid the ticket.

"Ain't familiar with this here burg. Where's a good place to eat?"

"Turpentine's ten miles down the road. You want Mel's Barbecue."

"I could use me some barbecue," Quincy said.

They reached Mel's at six. It was a hole in the wall in a crumbling mall, between a vacant storefront and a cigarette store, which also sold vapes.

Mel was a middle-aged black man with a bald head and

a white apron, and a good spokesman for his product. He smiled as Gary entered.

"Mister Duba! I seen the video! That's some wife you got."

"Mel, it's my own modest contribution to Turpentine."

Mel did a double-take. "You look an awful lot like, nah-hhh."

"Mel, that's Roebuck Simms and his old man Quincy."

Mel gaped like a grouper. He came out from behind the counter to shake their hands. He had his sous chef Lupe take pictures of the four of them. Roebuck ordered a plate of ribs, Quincy ordered the pulled pork sandwich, and Gary had the brisket sandwich. Roebuck insisted on paying. They took over a booth in the back.

"We're playing the Steelers Sunday night. Got box tickets if you want 'em."

"Thanks, Roebuck, but we don't hardly get down to Miami no more."

"They're yours if you want 'em."

People kept coming in. Mel kept them at bay until the boys were done, then Roebuck spent a half hour signing autographs and posing with people. When they were done, he said, "Where can we drop you?"

Gary still had to bail out Krystal. "They still got my wife."

Roebuck smacked his forehead. "Why didn't you say so? Let's go get her!"

Krystal's bail was five hundred dollars. Roebuck paid it

in cash and got a receipt. Krystal stank of cigarette smoke, body odor, and stale perfume. She threw herself into Gary's arms.

"Thank God! Thank God!"

Gary partly disentangled. "Thank Roebuck. He paid your bail."

She peered at him. "Well thanks a lot! Why did you do that?"

"Because your old man Gary here helped my old man Quincy here, when Quincy broke down on a country road."

"Remember?" Gary said. "That was the night I drove to WaWa for more cigs."

"Now can we drive you home?" Roebuck said.

It was dark by the time the Simms dropped Gary and Krystal off at the trailer. Gary's truck remained in the yard. It was the only vehicle they had left, since the police had impounded Krystal's Edge, the jet skis, and the Harley. Someone had dumped a load of trash in their front yard through which raccoons and gulls burrowed and pecked like housewives at a thrift store.

"Who the fuck?!" Krystal seethed.

"Yeah. I'll go through that trash tomorrow, find out who dumped it, and cart it back. They probably dumped some old bills or magazines with their address or something. I'll teach those motherfuckers to use my yard as a dump."

"I have to shower, lover, and then I'm going to devour you alive."

"You go first."

Krystal applied a wet, steaming kiss to Gary's lips while stroking his Johnson. They went up the steps, unlocked the door and went inside. Gary turned on the lights. Palmetto bugs scurried for cover. Krystal stripped off her clothes and went into the bathroom.

"SHIT!" she screamed.

Krystal exploded out of the bathroom into his arms.

"What?"

"There's a fucking snake in the toilet."

Gary put on a thick leather motorcycle jacket he'd bought for thirty bucks at an ARC Thrift Store and a pair of leather work gloves. He went into the bathroom, seized the snake by its neck, carried it out on the deck and hurled it toward the swamp.

"GET OUT AND STAY OUT!"

When he returned to the trailer, he heard the shower running.

32 | WHO COULD POSSIBLY HAVE FORESEEN THIS?

They boogied in the living room, they boogied in the kitchen.
They boogied in the bedroom 'til the sheets needed stitchin'.
Gary rode Krystal like a wheelbarrow. She threw him down
on his back and climbed on top, as seen in Game of Thrones.
They drank Canadian Club on the rocks, smoked ganja and
snorted a little oxy. They went down for the count.

The morning began, as so many others, with someone
banging loudly on the door. Pressing his thumbs to his temples, Gary sat upright in bed.

"Who the fuck!"

It was not an official bang, characterized by metronomic
pounding. This was an amateur bang marked by intervals,
odd rhythms, and shouted but muffled exhortations. Snarl-
ing, Gary pulled on his jeans, strode through the house, and
ripped open the door to reveal a morbidly obese man wearing an XXXL Deng Gak Hurricanes jersey, with a puffy,
florid face and mean little blue eyes sunk deep in the dough

like blueberries.

Gary balled his right fist, calculating trajectories, mass, and weight. "What the fuck do you want?"

The man seemed to calm a little. "Is Krystal here?"

"Who wants to know?"

The man re-inflated. "I'm Marvin Claggett, her husband."

What an astonishment! "How many fuckin' husbands does she have?"

"Is she here?"

"Marvin, you asshole," Krystal hissed from within, wearing elegantly shredded blue jeans and a floppy gray sweatshirt, her red hair gathered in a ponytail. "What are you doing here?"

"I heard you was in the money." He held out a large, soft hand. You owe me two thousand, nine-hundred and fifty-five dollars, bitch. Where is it?"

Gary turned. "How many husbands do you have?"

"Bullshit! The guy who married us wasn't even a real preacher. He got his diploma from the Universal Life Church!"

Gary could feel the trailer and deck subtly adjusting as Marvin shifted from foot to foot. "She worked on me for two weeks to go to an eBay convention in Vegas. When I got home, she'd cleaned me out! Appliances, archery supplies, everything I owned! She took my collection of Batman figurines, and they were worth a lot of money."

Gary got right up in his face. "How about you get the fuck

outta here before I kick your nuts up between your ears?"

Marvin took a step back. The deck shifted. "Oh, a tough guy, huh? Yeah, you're real tough. We'll just see how tough you are."

He lumbered down the steps and headed toward his crapped-out PT Cruiser, opened the rear gate and rummaged around.

"Shit!" Krystal said. "That motherfucker's always packing. Wait here."

Krystal dashed back to the bedroom and returned a minute later with Gary's Taurus, and shoved it in his hands. "Don't take any shit from him."

Gary leaped to the ground as Marvin came toward him clutching an automatic that looked like a licorice bar in both hands.

"What now, tough guy?" Marvin said.

"You tell me. You're on my property threatening me with a gun. Who you think they're gonna blame?"

"Won't matter to you."

"Why not?"

"'Cause you ain't gonna be alive to see it."

Gary began slowly circling clockwise, twenty feet from Marvin, who mirrored his march.

"Make your move, you fuckin' manatee."

Marvin spread his tree trunk legs, gripped the pistol and fired. Gary felt something whizz by his ear as he instinctively raised the Taurus and fired. A hole appeared in the middle of Marvin's chest. Smoke curled up through the hole.

Marvin looked down. Marvin went down.

"Ho shit," Gary said. "Now I've killed the stupid son of a bitch."

"Nice shot, honey," Krystal said from the deck.

Gary knew from experience he would not be able to bury Marvin.

"Just take him out in the swamp and dump him," Krystal said. "The gators'll take care of it."

Gary looked up, still gripping the gun. "Fucker's got to weigh over three hundred pounds! How'm I gonna move him?"

"You moved that gator, didn't you? Use the truck."

Gary stuck the pistol in his belt and pointed at her. "Bingo."

He got two hundred feet of stout Strand Manila rope, tied a tight noose around Marvin's ankles, and fastened the other end to the hitch on his F-150. He drove the truck in a wide loop, pulling Marvin's carcass through the grass and weeds, roughly parallel to the shore just off his dock. He then untied the rope from his truck, went to the end of the dock, looped it around a steel pole jutting up through the water, and re-fastened it to the truck. He wrestled the old sofa sideways to get it out of the way. As he drove slowly away from the dock, the rope tightened until it was taut. Very slowly, Gary engaged first gear until the corpse began to move reluctantly toward the end of the dock, where his flat-bottomed swamp boat was tethered.

Gary returned to the dock, working his way around

Marvin the way a cat passes a sleeping dog. There was a one-foot drop from the end of the deck onto the boat, which was powered by a Pratt & Whitney aircraft engine mounted on the rear, driving an airplane propeller.

It was loud.

Gary hoped the combined weight of the engine and Krystal would prevent Marvin from pulling the front end down. But how to get the three hundred-pound sack of shit into the boat? Gary could press three hundred pounds, but that was different from moving a blob of dead weight. If he and Krystal both and ten-foot levers, they could tilt Marvin up and slide him into the boat. It would require precision work.

Gary had three ten-foot poles for his tipi, but he hadn't put it up in several years. They lay under the house. He got the poles and Marvin's gun, which he threw into the boat. He explained the plan to Krystal, then snugged the prow tight up against the end of the dock.

"You go sit in the back of the boat. That engine's gotta weigh more'n three hundred. I think we got it sussed."

Krystal leaped into the boat and sat on the stool in the rear, just in front of the propeller, which resembled a giant house fan in its steel cage. "Now what?"

"I forgot. I need you to help push him into the boat. Come back here."

With grunts and twirls, they got the poles under Marvin until the tips peeked out from beneath his jersey, which hung down to his knees. They gripped the poles in both hands and faced each other.

"Ready? Heave!"

Straining and grunting, knees bent, Gary and Krystal raised the poles.

"Higher! We're almost there!"

Sweating and cursing, they brought the poles up to head height and Marvin slowly slid into the boat, landing with a thump and a splash that shook the dock. The boat quickly resettled. Gary turned toward Krystal with a grin and held up his hand. They high fived.

"All right, little lady, let's rip!"

33 | TREASURE IS WHERE YOU FIND IT

The boat had belonged to Gary's dad Ron, who died in a freak swordfish accident. The six-cylinder engine ripped the sky as they cruised away from the dock. Gary watched his trailer peeking above the saw grass, civilization dwindling until they were out of sight of any sign of modernity, save a tiny slice of highway briefly glimpsed twixt swaying palms. Perhaps with the engine off they would hear traffic from the nearby highway, but as far as they looked, there were no buildings, docks, or houses.

Fortier's Swamp extended deep into Hendry County, all the way to the Big Cypress Indian Reservation, encompassing hundreds of square miles. The shattering sound sent cranes flying. They watched alligators sunning on cypress hummocks, unfazed by the din. Forty-five minutes in, Gary came to a spot he frequently fished, a bewildering backwater of ponds and hummocks standing six inches out of the water. He cut the engine. The sudden silence was hallucinatory. Even with the earplugs, it would take a few minutes for their hearing to return.

The boat's momentum carried it beneath overhanging cypress dripping with Spanish moss until it bumped into a hummock, sending a gator scooting into the water. Gary used one of the poles to turn the boat around so that the prow faced outward, toward deeper water, then used the pole to back the boat up again until it bumped. Leaping off, Gary used the rope to tie the boat firmly to some cypress roots. Then he and Krystal used the poles to dump Marvin in the swamp. It was easier this time because the boat's construction allowed them to slide the poles beneath the body.

Marvin landed with a great splash, sinking quickly out of sight in the green water. They watched the expanding circle of ripples. They waited for gators. Krystal opened a quart bottle of Gatorade, slugged some and handed it to Gary.

"I know a place to dump his car," Gary said. "Is anyone gonna come looking for him?"

"Ha!" Krystal scoffed. "That loser? He's got two sisters who hate him. Probably not working. He got a bullshit disability claim done by some sleazebag lawyer because of his back. Well if he didn't weigh three hundred and fifty pounds, he wouldn't have that problem."

"How'd you hook up with him?"

Krystal eloquently molded a statue in the air. "I don't ask you about your exes, so don't ask me about mine. We shoulda gone through his wallet though. He may have had some cash."

Gary snapped his fingers. "Damn it!"

"Hey. What's that?"

Gary looked at Krystal, who was peering across the swamp at something. "Over there. In those rushes. It looks white. See it?"

Gary squinted. He could just make out something white poking among the weeds, something that didn't belong. "It's probably just trash."

"Let's take a look?"

"Why?"

Krystal put her hands on her hips. "What else have you got to do?"

Gary picked up the anchor, put it in the skiff, and shoved off, climbing aboard with his feet wet. The white thing was no more than fifty feet away so rather than start the engine and send twenty thousand birds screeching, he just poled over. As the skiff pushed in against the tall grass, Krystal went to the front of the boat and knelt.

She reached down and pulled what looked like a Styrofoam picnic cooler into the boat, two feet by two feet by eighteen inches, wrapped with duct tape and trailing green slime.

Gary came forward. "Fuck is it?"

Sitting on the floor, Krystal hefted it between her legs. "Feels heavy. Let's open it."

"Not here. Let's take it back to the house."

"Why not here? What if it's a human head or something?"

"Not likely. Just hold your horses. We'll know soon enough."

They screwed their earplugs back in and Gary let 'er rip. They could probably hear the boat from the highway, which flickered in and out of vision two miles to the east, a horizontal white strip on which zipped cars.

Out of the corner of is eye, Gary saw what looked like a fire hose drooping from a low hanging mangrove tree. He cut the engine and stared as the loop slowly uncoiled and drooped to the ground like a giant slinky.

"Would you look at that," Gary said, pointing.

Krystal followed his finger. "Holy shit. What is it?"

"One of them pythons they keep talkin' about. That thing could eat a goat."

The trailer poked up among the cypress, thatch and cabbage palms, not unlike a big silver picnic thermos. With Krystal crouching in the prow, Gary cut the engine and let the boat glide the final fifteen feet until it gently bumped the dock. Krystal climbed up with a rope and secured the boat. Gary hefted the thermos out of the boat onto the dock and got out.

A loud snort caught his attention. Three feral pigs were rooting among the trash in the driveway.

Gary ran down the dock.

"GET THE FUCK OUTTA HERE! GO ON! BEAT IT!"

The pigs placidly regarded him until he was ten feet away, then turned and moseyed off into the brush. No hurry. They had all day. Gary thought about getting his rifle, then remembered he'd left it at the new place. The only firepower he had left was the revolver stuck in his belt. He pulled it out and cocked it.

"FILL YOUR HAND!" he shouted, aiming for the nearest pig.

BOOM! The bullet clipped the pig's ear, sending a spray of blood into the air as the pigs scattered. He ran after them into the brush. A wounded pig could be dangerous. He heard them squealing as they fled. The fever of the chase was upon him!

Nah. He'd caused enough racket for the day, not that there were any neighbors to complain. That trailer park was his nearest neighbor and it was a mile down the road. He turned around and tramped back to the trailer, passing the garbage dump, which smelled like rancid meat.

On the deck, Krystal was wiping down the cooler with a damp cloth. When she finished, she used a dry towel. Gary pulled his knife from his pocket, flipped it open, and squatted, inserting the blade carefully along the seams. Whoever had taped it shut had done a bang-up job. He had to cut the tape all around the top. It came lose with a Styrofoam squeak, revealing an inner black plastic bag, also sealed with duct tape. He upended the case and a block slipped to the deck. Inserting his knife, he cut the tape and reached inside, pulling out a tightly wrapped brick of white powder.

He cut the plastic wrapping and withdrew the blade with a white mound on the tip, in which he dipped his wetted finger, bringing it to his mouth. He rubbed it on his gums, and they went numb.

He rubbed some in his nose. Within seconds, an electric

charge whipped through his veins galvanizing him to further action.

"Holy shit!"

"Is that what I think it is?"

Gary held the brick out to her. She borrowed his knife, brought a tiny pile to her nose and inhaled.

"Holy shit!"

There were eight kilos of coke in the cooler.

34 | ONCE AGAIN, EL CHEAPO

El Cheapo pulled into the yard shortly after eight p.m. in his Escalade. Gary and Krystal were on the deck, the cooler between them, gyrating to Jerry Reed's "Amos Moses".

El Cheapo climbed the steps. "What's that pile of garbage doing in your yard?"

"Some motherfucker dumped it when we weren't home. Makes me want to install a camera, track him down, and beat the sumbitch with a baseball bat."

"That happen often?"

"First time. Hey, thanks for coming. Got a proposition for ya. First, try a snort of this."

Gary proffered a chipped orange china plate with several lines neatly arranged like Brazilian riot troops. El Cheapo pulled up a plastic chair, set the plate on his knees and hoovered up a line, leaning back with eyes shut.

"Oh yeah, baby!"

He noticed the cooler filled with bricks. "Where the fuck

did you get that?"

"We found it in the swamp. Must have drifted in. Eight keys. What do you think that's worth?"

"A key of good blow goes for twenty in Miami. That's one hundred and sixty thou, retail."

"How'd you like to take care of this for us? We'll give you half."

"Yeah, yeah, I might be able to help you. That's El Nariz's territory, but I think I can get around that."

"Who's El Nariz?" Gary said.

"He's the main source of blow in Miami. He supplies the gangs in Coral Gables and West Miami. I think he's Nicaraguan."

Krystal went into the house and came back with a bottle of Canadian Club and three paper cups. Gary filled the cups and held his up. "Here's to luck! Just when you think you're down and out, fortune hands you a box full of blow!"

They drained their cups. Krystal lined up more blow. "Aren't you afraid of stepping on Nariz's toes?"

El Cheapo lifted his shirt to reveal a snub-nosed revolver tucked in his belt. "I'm not afraid of anyone. I spent four years in the military. I know what I'm doing."

"What military?" Gary said.

"The Presidential Guards. That's how I was able to save enough money to come to America!"

Gary rubbed thumb and forefinger together. "Baksheesh?"

"La Mordidaaaaaa," El Cheapo said with a grin and a

cheap Mexican accent, drawing out the last syllable like a cartoon villain. "We would also hire out as personal bodyguards because of the threat of kidnapping. I remember one time, a famous American actress came to Mexico City with her lover, a Latin Lothario in the Rob Lowe mode. He was twenty, I think. The actress, forty-seven, but she looked great. She had the trainer, the gym, the pilates. Which reminds me what do we pronounce pilate pill-lot-tee, when we pronounce Pontius Pilate, pilot? Are pilates not descended from Pilate's teachings?"

Gary bent to the plate. "Ya got me there, El. So, how'd that go? Anyone try to kidnap her?"

El Cheapo laughed uproariously. "We staged for her a fabulous drama! It was like a Mexican soap opera! I wrote it! We made up this whole mysterious background for Jaime. That was pretty boy's name. That he was descended from noble Spanish stock, his great great grandfather was a hero of the Civil War, that they owned thousands of acres and a bull breeding service in Seville, and they owned tens of thousands of acres in Mexico, where they grow Oaxacan gold, which goes for five hundred dollars an ounce in Brentwood and Beverly Hills, and that a rival syndicate planned to snatch Jaime and hold him for ransom. The actress perceived this as the greatest insult! What? They didn't want her? They wanted her boy toy?"

Gary and Krystal were laughing. El Cheapo got to his feet and put on a show.

"Madame! You must retreat to the inner courtyard! The

kidnappers are in the neighborhood!"

Changing posture and voice, El Cheapo minced and vogued. "Oh no! I had my heart set on visiting the Laredo Market today!"

He shoved his hands in his pockets and switched back to El Cheapo. "You can go to the market. It's Jaime I'm worried about."

El Cheapo drew himself up to his full height, five six. His face contorted in horror. "Denial!" He snarled and beetled his brow. "Anger!" El Cheapo on one knee, supplicating. "Bargaining!" El Cheapo slumped in a chair like Blanche DuBois. "Depression!" El Cheapo froze like a felon caught in a spotlight. "Acceptance?"

"There was no acceptance! She wasn't that good an actress!"

"Who was she?" Krystal begged. "I promise not to tell!"

"Who she is is not important. I signed a confidentiality agreement. Let us just say she has been nominated for four Oscars. Now she goes to rallies. She makes speeches. She gets arrested. Save the androgynous skink."

"Did you know the Jamaican iguana is an endangered species?" Gary said.

"I did not know that. You know, if I step on the blow a little, we could double our sales."

Gary's mouth dropped open. "You can't do that!"

"Why not? Is very simple. I cut it with baby laxative. It's going to make you shit anyway."

"What about my integrity?"

El Cheapo barked. "Have you ever dealt blow before?"

"A little, when I could afford to."

"And you have a name on the streets as a blow dealer of integrity? A standard to uphold?"

"Well no, but this shit fell into our laps just the way it is. It's a sign from God. We should pass it on the same way."

"When was the last time you sold blow?"

"I don't know, eight, nine years ago."

"So, you are known on the streets as a man of integrity who will not step on his blow?"

"Well no. But it was already cut when I got it."

El Cheapo pulled out a cheap cigar and lit it with a cheap lighter. "So, you're saying that although no one knows where the blow came from, you don't want it stepped on because you're concerned about your reputation?"

"I'd know. I don't want to have to live with myself knowing I came into possession of high-quality blow and cut it for the sake of profits! This cocaine is a gift from God! Not only would I know, God would know. I think eighty grand each is a decent payday. Then something else will come along. You know I'm going to set up my own company to manufacture my house suspenders. I just need some seed money to get started. I don't want to get greedy."

El Cheapo muttered in Spanish. "Hokay. I do as you say."

"What about El Nariz?"

El Cheapo waved his cigar. "Don't worry about El Nariz. He won't be a problem. I have put the velvet Elvis in a place of honor in my home. And now, my friends, I have to go."

"You sure you're okay to drive?"

El Cheapo stood and stretched, thrusting out his barrel chest. "The coke counterbalances the liquor."

35 | HOWARD

In the morning, Gary put on a pair of leather gloves and hip waders, backed his truck up to the garbage dump and shoveled. It did not take long to unearth the dumper's identity, as he had foolishly discarded unopened solicitations featuring his name and address. Citibank. Franklin Mint. Liberty Insurance. The Friendly Flyer. Guns & Ammo.

Howard Perkins lived in the Wokenoki Trailer Park, too stupid and feckless to go through his own garbage and pull his identity, not to mention the sheer laziness of driving two miles down the road to dump in his nearest neighbor's yard.

Why couldn't he have dumped his shit in the ditch? In front of the salvage yard? Did Howard Perkins think the property was abandoned? That no one would notice?

The load filled Gary's truck bed. As he closed the tailgate, Krystal came out on the deck in a white terrycloth robe, cigarette dangling, hair wrapped in a towel, drink in hand.

"Where ya goin'?"

"Omma drive up the road and return this asshole's garbage. Wanna come?"

"Aw I'd love to, hon, but I just tinted my hair."

Gary took off his gloves, tossed them in the truck and drove away. Four feral hogs crossed the road in front of him. Seemed like they were getting worse. What caused this recent explosion in the feral pig population? Could it be global warming? They were a good source of protein and if things got worse, Gary would do most of his shopping in the forest with a gun. He wished he still had that commercial freezer he'd left behind. A one hundred and twenty-pound pig yielded at least sixty pounds of meat. The bacon tasted a little gamey, but Gary liked gamey. One pig could feed them for two months. Some people claimed to have seen monster feral hogs back in the forests and swamps. Thousand pounders. You needed more than a twenty-two to stop those monsters.

Or they could just be legends, like Sasquatch, the hodag, and the Loch Ness Monster.

A stucco arch framed the entrance to Wokenoki Village. Some of the letters had fallen off and it now read Woke... illage. Dusty date palms stood sentinel on either side, more growing beside the road that wound through the village, which looked like it dated from the seventies, with about sixty trailers splayed out according to the serpentine streets. Most were of the three-bedroom, two bath design, with extended living rooms, broad awnings, raised above their concrete foundations, fading in the sun. Howard Perkins lived at 1229 Whaler's Way in a gray house that looked like

FLORIDA MAN   **203**

a shipping container, with an attached carport throwing
shade on a dull red Dodge Ram. Gary backed up so that
his tailgate was ten feet from the two wood steps leading to
Perkins' door, put on his gloves, stuck his pistol in the small
of his back, opened the tailgate and started shoveling.

Five minutes later Perkins' front door opened, and
Perkins appeared, shirtless, flabby chest covered in white
fur like an angora sweater, gut flopping over his brass belt
buckle, wearing floppies, a high red forehead surmounted
by a wisp of white hair.

"What the fuck do you think you're doing?" Perkins
croaked.

"Are you Howard Perkins?"

"Fuck you! Get the fuck out of here before I call the
cops."

"This is your shit, you dumb ass. You dumped it in my
yard last night, or don't you remember?

"How do you know that's my shit?"

Gary reached into his hip pocket and pulled out a solici-
tation. "Your subscription to Underage Pussy has elapsed."
He tossed it to the ground. "You might want to renew."

Perkins looked ready to explode. He shook in fury. He
went back into his house and came out a minute later holding
a samurai sword. "Now you get the fuck outta here before I
do some serious damage."

Gary reached behind him and held his pistol at his side.
"Look here, motherfucker. Where do you get off just dumping your shit in my yard? What kind of man are you?"

"I'm a veteran, you piece of shit! I was in the Army! I was in Iraq! You ever serve?"

"You think that gives you the right to just dump your shit on somebody else's property? Have you no shame, sir? At long last, have you no shame?"

Perkins stared hard. He deflated. He looked down. The samurai sword hung at a sad angle. "Awright. You got me. I was having a bad night." He doubled over and coughed into his fist. He coughed and coughed. The last cough trailed into a rattle of phlegm. Perkins regained his composure. "The trailer park threatened to evict me if I didn't get rid of my shit pile. I'll tell ya what. Let's you and me load it into the back of my Ram, and then I'll drive sixty miles to the nearest landfill. But I ain't got jack for the fee. They charge fifteen bucks."

"You want me to pay your dumping fee?"

"I'm just telling you the facts. That shit still here at sundown, I'll be homeless. You want a homeless veteran on your conscience?"

Gary admired Perkins' brass. He pulled out his wallet. "How do I know you're gonna do it? Maybe I better come with ya."

"Hey, if you ain't got nothin' better to do, we could use your truck."

Gary handed Perkins the shovel. They put all the garbage back into Gary's truck and headed out, turning right on Brody Street. Fifteen minutes later they headed east on Eighty toward Belle Glade. Perkins smelled like tobacco and booze. Even with the windows open at sixty miles per, it was hot in the truck. Perkins had a coughing fit. Gary reached into the door bin and handed Perkins a napkin from Burger King.

"Who the hell are ya, anyway?" Perkins said.

"Gary Duba. I live at the end of Brody on the swamp."

"Yeah, I'm real sorry about that, my eyesight ain't so good anymore. I don't even remember seeing a house. I just thought it was the end of the road. There was a lot of junk there already."

"That's my stuff, and I don't know how you could miss my trailer. It sits four feet off the ground."

"Yeah, well, like I said, I'm sorry. I appreciate your helping me."

"Ain't got nothin' else to do."

"What you do for a living, Duba?"

"I'm a roofer. Sometimes I help a friend who's in pest control."

Perkins hawked and spat out the window. "Florida ain't lackin' for any pests, that's for sure."

Twenty minutes later they pulled into the West County Transfer Station in Belle Glade, stopping at the gate to fill out forms and pay the fifteen-dollar fee. A man in a yellow hard hat directed Gary into a warehouse-like building, where he backed up to an iron rail above a steel container. Another worker opened the gate and motioned for them to transfer the load.

On the way back, Floyd called. "You up for a little pest control?"

36 | AN UNUSUAL PROPOSITION

The house was in an older subdivision in Pahokee, stucco with Spanish tiled roof, that peculiar lawn endemic to Florida that resembled astroturf, with old palm trees lining the street and shading the front yard. Floyd's truck was parked in the driveway when Gary arrived at eleven. The occupants had left for the day. Floyd greeted Gary in the driveway.

"Simple job, I just need an extra hand. I got three jobs today."

"What are we dealin' with? Palmetto bugs?"

"Termites. We're gonna have to fumigate. Full body armor and gas masks."

Gary suited up. "You want a little pick-me-up?"

"Did you bring coffee?"

"No, man. Blow."

Floyd pulled on his one-piece orange coverall. "You need money so bad, don't waste it on blow."

"No, man. I come into a supply. We was out scootin'

around in the swamp and we found a sealed picnic container filled with the stuff. I got El Cheapo selling it and we're gonna split the profits."

Floyd lit a cigarette. "You gotta be shittin' me. You ain't got enough problems you want to get busted for dealing?"

"No, man. El Cheapo assumes all the risk. What do I know about moving wholesale blow? I just need a little money to tide me over."

"Help me tent the house." Together, they manhandled the tightly folded house tent out of the rear of the van and began unfolding it in the front yard. The process took over an hour. Once unfolded, Floyd remained on the ground using a pole to hand the back end of the tent to Gary on the roof. They had the house fully tented by one-thirty.

They hooked the portable generator up to the blower and began to fill the tent with sulfural sulphide. Neighborhood kids skated by with flat-brimmed hats turned sideways. The chug of the generator vied with lawnmowers in a symphony of suburban clang.

"You need money so bad I know a guy who will pay you big bucks to smuggle tarantulas into the country. He's done it numerous times. He's got a system."

"You're shittin' me."

"His name is Rolf Panny. Lives in Kissimmee."

"What kind of name is that?"

"I think it's Rumanian or something."

"Well why not? Can you give me his phone number?"

"Let me call him first."

Panny and Gary agreed to meet in Yeehaw Junction at seven. Gary phoned Krystal. When they were done fumigating the house, Gary took a yard shower with a garden hose and changed into clean clothes he kept in his truck.

They met in the Cracker Barrel on Forreston Road. Panny was easy to spot, seated at a corner table wearing a striped red and black shirt, metal-framed rectangular glasses, with a greasy comb over that looked like music paper. Gary introduced himself and ordered a cup of coffee.

"How do you know Floyd?" Gary said.

"We belong to the same Civil War Reenactment club," Panny said with a thick Eastern European accent.

"But aren't you from Rumania?"

"I have always been fascinated with American history. I will pay you ten thousand dollars to bring in three hundred Mexican red kneed tarantulas. There is no risk to yourself. I have perfected a system. You will fly to Mexico City and return the same day. The tarantulas will be confined to a piece of checked-through luggage filled with plastic compartments. I have an arrangement with customs officials in Orlando."

"What do you do with them, if you don't mind my asking?"

"Some people prize them as pets. Others use them for environmental control. They are not ferocious; they do not creep upon you while you're sleeping and bite. They have an insatiable appetite for insects, beetles and crickets. They are shy, nocturnal creatures."

"Yeah, all right. When do you want me to go?"

"The tarantulas are ready for pick-up now. Can you leave tomorrow? I will give you the money to purchase a round-trip ticket in and out of Orlando. I will pay you half in advance, half on delivery. At the Mexico City Airport, you will meet a colleague of mine who will give you the suitcase. She will greet you upon your arrival. She will wear a green blouse. Her name is Maria. When you see her, say 'My uncle is sick, but the highway is green.'"

"My uncle is sick, but the highway is green."

"That is correct. I want you to take United Flight #234, which leaves Orlando at ten-fifteen tomorrow morning."

"That don't leave me any time to go home. Time I get home, I'll just have to get up and drive up to Orlando."

Panny passed Gary an envelope. "Here is five thousand four hundred and fifty dollars. The four hundred and fifty is for travel expenses. Take a room at the Orlando at the Day's Inn. You can leave your vehicle in their parking lot. I will greet you upon your return and drive you to your vehicle."

Gary tucked the envelope into a pocket of his cargo pants and extended his hand. "Mister Panny, we got ourselves a deal."

He sat in his truck with the windows down and phoned Krystal. "Babe, I got a gig, and I won't be home until tomorrow evening."

Krystal sounded hyped-up. "Okay. Jen and Barb are over, we're having a little wine party."

"Wine? You sound like Mickey Mouse on helium."

"Don't be a spoil sport! What's the gig?"

"Well it's kinda hard to explain. I'm a courier, sorta."

"You ain't trying to courier no drugs, are you?"

"Fuck no. You think I'm stupid?"

Gary checked into the hotel at ten-thirty. The clerk didn't bat an eye as Gary handed him two hundred-dollar bills. The clerk made change and handed Gary his key card.

"There is a complimentary breakfast every morning between six am and ten-thirty."

"Do they serve meat?"

"Alas, no. It is mostly cereals, juices, fruits, muffins and doughnuts."

Gary thanked him and rode the elevator to the sixth floor. It was a standard hotel room with a king-sized bed facing the flat screen TV, a bland landscape hanging above the bed. Gary cranked up the AC, took a shower, lay on the bed in his skivvies and turned on the television. Non music accompanied scrolling pictures of hit movies, resorts, and other Day's Inn delights. When the Sandals ad came on, Gary switched off the television and the lights.

37 | WHOLE FOODS IS BROKEN

Krystal woke at ten Friday morning and realized they were out of toilet paper. Head pounding from last night's soiree, she threw back a couple ounces of Canadian Club, smoked some killer ganja, and did a couple lines. She dressed in pedal pushers and a long-sleeved white men's shirt with the sleeves rolled up and the tails tied across her taut belly with the FiFi tat, got in her old blue Pontiac G6, unlocked the glove compartment and raided her secret stash for her food stamps. Gary would shit if he knew. He was a proud man.

Krystal flitted from job to job like a butterfly. Dollar Store cashier, Chili's waitress, Merry Maid cleaning service. The only reason she worked was to fulfill her twenty-hour per week requirement for the food stamps. She made a little money playing poker with the girls. She hoped to test her mettle at the Seminole Hard Rock in Tampa. Krystal had upped her poker game to the point where none of her friends would play with her.

Was she ready for the big time? There was only one way to find out. Last year she'd won twenty-seven thousand dollars playing video poker at Seminole Brighton Casino on the other side of Okeechobee. It had been her main source of income. She dreamed of playing in high-stakes poker games like her hero, Annie Duke.

She drove to the Whole Foods in Belle Glade. The lot was almost full. She parked in the row farthest from the restaurant, easing her Pontiac in between a BMW SUV and a Tesla. She did a line. The parking lot was filled with Lexuses, Infinitis, Mercedes, Leafs, Priuses, and trail-rated Jeeps. The broad entrance was festooned with hanging flowers exuding a pleasant aroma. She caught a glimpse of herself in the store's gleaming facade, her hair now copper. She liked the new tint.

Inside she grabbed a cart and deliriously cruised the halls of plenty. She plucked a Cabernet and a Merlot in the wine aisle, asparagus and broccoli in the RESPONSIBLY GROWN aisle, fair trade coffee, two packages of Moon Cheese, cruelty-free boneless chicken breasts, and two frozen lobsters.

Three of six check-out lanes were open, all with long lines. Most shoppers brought square-bottomed grocery bags emblazoned with Whole Foods, or Gold's Gym, or Hialeah Chamber of Commerce. Krystal was dying to light up. She'd been standing in the same place for five minutes staring at a magazine rack displaying Sustainable Living and Living the Keto Way. What was the hold up? She stepped out of line to see a stout woman in black hip huggers and a super baggy shirt that said, "HOP! HUMANS OFF PLANET!" The woman had brought six of her own bags and staked her territory from the end of the conveyor belt to where it disappeared beneath the cash register, the space filled with bags of nuts, organic kale, organic beets, ancient grains and quinoa breads. As the cashier waited patiently, the woman was going through her feedbag purse looking for just the right amount of change.

A Problem Shopper.

Why did they always get in front of Krystal? At the post office, there was always some skinny Asian guy trying to ship a machine gun to North Korea and pay for it with a bank draft or a personal check.

Krystal wanted to grab the Problem Shopper by the back of her neck and throw her to the ground. God, she needed another line and some bourbon. Hang in there, baby! The end was in sight.

She wondered about Gary's new gig. What if he were lying when he said it didn't involve drugs? But why would he lie? Gary wasn't a liar, and they were already sitting on top of eight keys. Well, one key, since they gave the rest to El Cheapo. Krystal wondered if it had been wise to keep so much around the house. There was always potential for abuse.

Someone tapped her and she jumped.

"Eep!"

She turned to see a gaunt old man with white hair grinning. "Sorry! The line is moving. You better close up before somebody sneaks in there."

"Oh. Oh! Thank you."

Finally, it was Krystal's turn. She placed her items on the conveyor belt. The pierced and inked woman cashier said, "Plastic or paper?"

"Paper, please. We use them over and over."

As the cashier rang up each item, Krystal bagged them herself in two large paper bags, placing the frozen lobsters in last.

"One hundred and eight dollars and seventy-nine cents."

Krystal smiled and handed over a hundred dollars in food stamps. "I'll pay the rest in cash."

The cashier stared at the food stamps. "I'm sorry, ma'am. You can't use food stamps to purchase alcoholic beverages."

"What do you mean?" Krystal sputtered. "I've used food stamps here before."

"Yes, but you can't purchase alcohol with them. That's the law."

"ARE YOU SHITTING ME?"

The clerk looked around anxiously for back-up. Shoppers paid attention. "Ma'am, I'm going to have to ask you to step aside while I call the manager."

"WHAT? AFTER ALL THE MONEY I'VE SPENT IN THIS SHIT HOLE?"

The manager, identifiable by his shirt, tie, and determined expression, steamed her way. He stopped in front of her.

"Ma'am, you'll have to leave."

Krystal grabbed the frozen lobster out of the bag, ripped it free, and hurled it end over end like a shuriken across the breadth of check-out lanes. Shoppers marveled at its rotation and speed until it struck a potted ficus tree in the plants department and fell to the ground.

"That's it," the manager declared. "I'm calling the police."

Seizing the other frozen lobster, Krystal fled. As she approached her car she wondered if she had time to do another line before she skedaddled. Better not. No doubt Whole Foods had the cops in their pockets.

As Krystal headed out of town on Marigold Boulevard ten miles over the limit, two cop cars passed her, lights blazing, sirens whooping, going the other way. In her rear view, she watched them both stand on the brakes and pull a U-turn in the middle of traffic. Damn. Someone must have followed her out to her car.

Krystal hit eighty on Eighty, took the Fanouk exit, which ran along the Fanouk Canal. She thought she'd given them the slip when the flashing red and blue appeared in her rear view. She didn't have a plan. She'd always had trouble with authority figures, which was one reason she and Gary got along so well. They saw eye to eye on so many things.

Abruptly, the crumbling gray blacktop, the consistency of goat cheese, dissolved into pure dirt which wouldn't have been a problem except that a turtle appeared abruptly right in Krystal's path and she swerved instinctively to avoid it.

The car hit a hummock, was momentarily airborne, and belly-flopped into the canal.

Krystal sat there a minute breathless. The airbag didn't deploy. What a rook! What if she'd been in an accident? She should sue the manufacturer.

The whoop of sirens drew her attention. Water was up to her knees as the vehicle settled to the bottom of the canal. Krystal extricated herself through the driver's side window and climbed on top of the vehicle. She waved the frozen lobster.

"COME AND GET ME, COPPERS!"

38 | EL NARIZ

Eleven p.m. Thursday night found El Cheapo parked at the curb across the street from Tango's Night Club in South Beach. He'd put the word out and received word back. An old clubbing friend, Tomas Villaneuve, would meet him in five minutes. A transplanted Columbian, Villaneuve ostensibly worked as a booking agent and talent scout for the many South Beach and Miami night clubs.

El Cheapo waited with the windows down, listening to the Afro/Cuban All Stars playing softly on his CD player, smoking a Cohiba, wearing Emporio Armani men's jeans, Skecher loafers, and a silk shirt in a purple and yellow pattern. He spotted Villaneuve in his rear view, sauntering up the sidewalk wearing a narrow-brimmed fedora, carrying a man purse, a tall man with a Frank Zappa nose and mustache. El Cheapo waved through the open window. Villaneuve came up on the passenger side and slid inside bringing with him the scent of Versace Dylan Blue. Villaneuve had never really recovered from Versace's death.

They slipped skin.

"Hombre!" Villaneuve said.

"Tomas. How are you doing?"

Villaneuve shot his cuffs revealing a Tag Heuer on his left wrist. As a young man, Villaneuve had raced Formula One for Honda. Two races. He failed to place, yet he was an expert on all things automotive.

"I am doing great, my friend. I have bookings from one end of Miami Beach to the other. I have sexy babes from one end of the beach to the other. And if you are looking to install a sound system in your car, I am your man."

He looked around. "A vehicle such as this deserves a superior sound system. What are you running?"

El Cheapo used the steering wheel control to crank the volume until the vehicle, the boulevard, and the very waters themselves were doing the Latin boogaloo. Giggling young women, boys on boards, spandex-clad cyclists all looked his way. Laughing, Villaneuve put his hands to his ears.

"All right! All right!"

El Cheapo turned the volume down and started the engine. "Let's take a drive." They took Venusian Way to Miami where El Cheapo pulled into Duarte Park, stopping the vehicle beneath a spreading acacia tree. A handful of other vehicles were scattered around the parking lot, some glowing softly, others burbling with bass. El Cheapo opened the center console, removed the brick of blow and set it in Villaneuve's lap. He handed Villeaneuve an amber bottle and a tiny silver coke spoon.

Villaneuve did a one and one. His head snapped back. "Whoa, Mama!" He reached into the front pocket of his pants and pulled out an envelope. Turning on the cab light, El Cheapo quickly counted the cash. He started the engine and headed back for Miami. His next appointment was at midnight.

El Cheapo waited for a Panamera to pull out of a space on the boulevard, then expertly parallel parked his massive Cadillac. Villaneuve slipped the brick in his man purse, got out, saluted, and dashed across the boulevard toward the Cameo Lounge. Elbow in the breeze, El Cheapo smiled at the pretty young things walking his way, listening to the surf and the faint bass boom of a nightclub across the street. Traffic was busy but slow, with jaywalkers dashing across the four-lane highway. A thick Samoan dashed right up to El Cheapo's car, slid in, and stuck the muzzle of an automatic beneath his chin.

"Hey," El Cheapo protested. "Hey! You got the wrong guy!"

"No, I don't, motherfucker," the Samoan said in a soft voice. "Drive or I'll splatter your brains all over the ceiling."

Tossing his cigar out the window, El Cheapo pulled out into traffic, following the Samoan's directions as they once more headed across the causeway to Miami.

"Listen," El Cheapo said. "Do you know who I am?"

"Yes, motherfucker, I know who you are. Do you know who El Nariz is?"

A cold metal settled in El Cheapo's gut. He knew what was coming. The Samoan directed El Cheapo to a warehouse west of the Orange Bowl, the retractable door sliding up into the roof. They drove into a vast, dimly lit space with hundreds of cardboard cartons stacked against the walls. The door closed with a flesh-shredding shriek. There were three other men at the far end of the warehouse, one seated behind a gunmetal desk on which sat an old fashioned banker's lamp with a green shade, the other two standing behind him, looking at El Cheapo as the Samoan marched him up to the table and shoved him down onto an old wooden chair with arms. Goons two and three swarmed out from behind the desk and fastened El Cheapo's wrists and ankles to the chair with plastic wire harnesses.

El Nariz was a huge man with a conning tower nose and a receding chin which he tried to hide behind a black brillo beard, his eyes gleaming raisins beneath a beetling brow.

"Do you know who I am?" he growled in a South American accent.

"El Nariz. We both worked for El Mordito back in the day."

"I don't remember you."

"I was just a lowly lieutenant. You were a colonel."

"Ha!" El Nariz barked. "So, we are brothers in arms!"

"We both came here for the same thing, my colonel. A new life, a new opportunity. I am in no way threatening your operation. I have my own list of clients. I did not mean to poach on your territory."

"And yet here you are." El Nariz reached into his desk and pulled out the brick El Cheapo had just sold to Villaneuve. Villaneuve must have handed it off as soon as he got out of the car.

"I did not know you and Villaneuve were doing business! I never would have sold to him."

"I own two nightclubs in Miami. I know Villaneuve well."

"He sold me out. How do you know he won't sell you out?"

El Nariz held up a finger. "Excellent point. I know because there is no one higher up the ladder, and because he knows what will happen to him if he does. Search him."

The Samoan expertly went through El Cheapo's pockets removing his wallet, his gold-engraved pocket-knife, his phone, and several packages of gold Trojans, which he placed on the desk.

El Nariz calmly went through the wallet, removing and lining up the cards, counting the money. Setting the phone aside he picked up a package of Trojans between index and middle finger.

"Safe sex."

"My colonel, if you're willing to overlook this indiscretion, I can tell you where I got the blow. I swear, I'll never set foot in Miami Beach again!"

El Nariz reached down and set a machete on his desk. "I have no doubt that you will tell me everything."

39 | THE BLACK DILDO

They booked Krystal into the Glades County Jail Friday afternoon. The bored woman cop who fingerprinted her said without looking up, "Look who's back."

"Nice to see you too, Edna."

A matron wearing blue latex gloves walked her back to the big holding cell, steel benches bolted to the floor, holding a dozen women. Two huddled in a corner. Six sat rapt in front of the flat screen TV behind the chain mesh grill tuned to The Shopping Channel. The other four sat by themselves. As the door slammed shut behind Krystal, a big, wiry black woman who looked like she played pro basketball stared at her in amazement. For an instant, Krystal thought she was going to get in a fight, but the woman's expression morphed into delight.

She came right up. "Ain'tchoo the Black Dildo?"

Krystal put a hand to her face. "I am so embarrassed."

"What for, girl! You should hold your head up! I watched

that video myself about a dozen times, and everybody I know loves it! They should give you some kind of medal!"

The woman turned to the room. "Hey! Y'all know who this is? This is the Black Dildo!"

She grabbed Krystal's hand and held it up like the winner of a fight.

Every woman except one sad soul in the corner stood and applauded.

"ALL RIGHT!"

"YOU GO, GIRL!"

They crowded around, reaching out to touch her as if she had healing properties.

"How you like that big black cock?" asked a wan white woman with a blue neck tat.

"It was a wedding gift. I got me a real man. I don't need no lady's aid."

"I hear that!" whooped one.

A statuesque black woman with short blonde hair closed in. "You swing my way?"

Krystal smiled. "Nope. Sorry!"

"Well lookee here. With your moves, you ought to wrestle. You ask for Downtown Brown at the Roxy. You tell him Cleo the Magnificent sent you."

"Are you serious?"

Cleo the Magnificent's chin hung low. "Duh! I'm tellin' you, you already got the name recognition. First time you appear, I betcha you'll get a full house, and if you're lucky, they'll televise it. My real name's Latisha Forbes."

The basketball player stuck out her mitt. "Airwrecka Jones."

"Krystal Duba." They shook. Then everybody else wanted to shake, high-five and fist bump.

Airwrecka pushed people back. "All right, all right, give her room. Whatchoo in for?"

"I tried to buy wine with my food stamps. So they called the manager and I threw a frozen lobster at him. Then the cops chased me, and I went into a canal."

Airwrecka nodded sagely. "Been there myself. Now look here. You got name recognition, girl. I don't know who put up that video, but you a private person. You got the right to your own video. People will pay big bucks to advertise. You got a Youtube channel?"

"No."

"Who put up that video?"

Suddenly, Krystal saw things clearly. "Jen. Jen put up the video."

"Who Jen?"

"My best friend."

"She ax your permission?"

Now Krystal was getting mad. "You're right! That's me on the video. I didn't give her no permission!"

"You should sue her."

"No, she ain't got shit. What I should do is take over ownership of that video and start selling ads, like you said."

"Now you're talkin'. Now omma do your hair."

A female guard came up to the gate. "Duba, it's your

call."

Krystal perked right up. "Who? What?"

"It's your turn. You get one phone call."

The guard accompanied Krystal to a wall phone where she phoned her mother.

"Trixie, it's Krystal. I'm in jail again."

"Whazzat you on the news?"

"What for?"

"Crazy lady waving a lobster."

"Yeah. Can you bail me out?"

"How much?"

"Won't know 'til morning. Probably a thou."

"Jesus, Krystal honey, I ain't got that kind of money and neither does Stanton. Did you call Gary?"

"Gary's out of the country right now. You call him. He should be back this evening."

"What do you mean out of the country?"

"He took a job to fly down to Mexico City and bring something back."

"What do you mean, bring something back? He ain't involved in drugs now, is he?"

"Of course not! It's just a favor for a friend."

"Well I'll try him right away, but he ain't got any money neither."

When Krystal got back to the holding cell, Airwrecka went to work braiding her hair into corn rows, using a comb. First, she washed Krystal's hair in the stainless-steel sink, using liquid soap from a dispenser in the wall.

"Then I part the hair in rows from front to back," she explained as she went to work. "Then I divide the first row into three small sections, and make the first braid stitch…"

"How do you know this?"

"I got a degree from the Fuhrman School of Cosmetology in Miami. I'm licensed to braid, dye, cut, and curl. I been workin' at Miss Thing's Hair Salon down in South Miami."

"How'd you end up here?"

"Girl, that's a long story."

"We ain't goin' anywhere."

"That's true. Well my man Graham come up with a plan to sell pedigreed papillons."

"Oh, I love papillons!"

"Me too. They are so sweet. Anyhow, what I din' know, Graham was making up those pedigrees himself. He's a printer, see, so he knows how to make up all sorts of things. Fake certificates and documents, things like that. He just did it as a goof for his friends all these years, you know, when someone retirin', they ax Graham to make up a certificate World's Biggest Crybaby, or World Fart Champion. He make up all these impressive seals and things, you look at 'em you swear they're real. There's elected officials who have Graham's certificates on their walls and they don't even know they're fake."

"Where'd he get the pups?"

"Well Graham knew a lady breeds 'em from painting her house. These was unplanned pregnancies. Her Papillon and a schnauzer. That's what tipped 'em off I think. Those Papillons, they didn't look quite right. They call 'em 'Butterfly Dogs' on accounta the ears, but these here, they was more like moth dogs or somethin'. Anyway, they had moth ears."

"I told him, Graham. You may as well make up new certificates that say these here are Moth Dogs, and you tell 'em it's a new breed, and you're waiting to hear from the American Kennel Club 'bout recognition. But he says to me, don't you worry about it, sweet thing. These people don't know a Chiuahaha from a pitbull. 'Cept he was wrong about that, and when this lady tried to verify her pup's pedigree, the AKC set her straight.

"Graham was ready to give her her money back, but no. She wants to go on Judge Judy. So, we got tickets for the show. You can bring one guest. So, we fly out there, they put us up in a nice hotel, and then we do the show. She was a nasty bitch, that woman who sued Graham. Her name was Nancy Something, from Palm Beach. Just nasty. She makin' all sortsa racist comments and shit. She brings the dog. Judge Judy looks at that dog and says, 'I know dogs. And that's no Papillon. Judgment for the plaintiff for five thousand dollars. Step out, please'."

"But that was in Los Angeles," Krystal said, trying to keep up.

"I know it was, but then I saw that bitch down at the Quik-Mart last night and I put her on her ass. And that's why I'm here."

40 | IN OLD MEXICO

Benito Juarez International Airport smelled like ozone and diesel until Gary reached the main concourse, when it acquired a subtle fish aroma, with overtures and undertures of human sweat. It was eleven in the morning. Gary was to meet Maria in the Caramba Lounge, a tropical-themed bar at the head of the main concourse. Gary wore a pale-yellow Banlon golf shirt with the tails out as he paused by the green rail and gazed into the interior, dimly lit with bamboo blinds covering the windows, fake macaws, a bamboo bar, and plastic palm trees. It took a minute for his eyes to adjust to the gloom, but once they did, Maria was easy to spot, sitting in a corner banquette with one shapely leg draped over the other, wearing a pleated skirt and iridescent green blouse, nursing a drink with a tiny parasol, smoking a cigarette.

Gary walked over. "Maria?"

She regarded him from beneath palm frond lashes, glancing at the bench.

"Sit."

Gary slid in. "I'm Gary from Florida."

"I know who you are."

Gary wondered what to do.

"Do you have something to say to me?" she said with a soft Mexican accent.

"Oh. Oh! My uncle is sick, but the highway is green!"

"Yes. Would you like something to drink?"

"I wouldn't mind."

Maria raised her hand and immediately a young man in black slacks and white shirt appeared. Gary ordered a Bohemia. Maria raised her almost empty glass indicating a refill.

"My flight ain't for an hour. Where the spiders?"

Maria blew smoke at him. "Don't say spiders. They are here, in this suitcase." She toed a large black suitcase with concealed wheels. "You will have to check it through at the boarding gate. There are no worries. Everything is prepared."

The waiter appeared with their drinks. Maria insisted on paying.

"Thanks for the drink!" Gary said, holding up his bottle. They clinked. "So, what do you do, Maria?"

She looked at him for a minute. "I sell luggage."

"Ahuh. Well I'm a roofer."

"You are not roofing now."

"No, I'm between jobs. Waitin' for the next big blow. That happens, I'll be busier than a tick on a dog. I hate good weather. It's bad for business. But I got a plan. I ain't gonna roof forever. I have invented something to keep your house tethered during a big blow. Here, lemme show ya."

He brought up a picture of his house and showed it to Maria. She stared at it for a second, then her eyes slid off. "You had better get going. You have a ways to go."

"Ahuh, sure. You're right." He slugged the rest of his beer and took the big black suitcase by the handle. Twenty minutes later, he stood outside the gate waiting for his group to be called. He noticed a skinhead in an oversized gray hoodie several people in front of him, the hood back to display his pale orb with blue frogs inked behind the ears. The skinhead checked a small suitcase.

At last they called Gary's group, condemned to find the odd middle seats toward the back of the plane. The skinhead found a middle in row twenty-two. Gary's only choice was a middle seat in the second to last row between an old woman with a parrot perched on her shoulder, wearing a tiny pájaro de terapia vest, and an austere businessman in cheap gray suit in the aisle seat. Smiling, Gary edged past the businessman and took his seat. The parrot was on the woman's left shoulder. It turned toward Gary.

"CHINGA TU MADRE!"

The woman colored and turned. "Cantinflas! Be nice. I am sorry, senor. My parrot has very bad manners. He was this way when I got him several years ago. His previous owner ran a bar."

"No problem. Gary Duba, outta Turpentine. Where you headed?"

"I am Lupe. I'm going to Orlando to visit my daughter. I suffer from post-traumatic stress syndrome, so I must have Cantinflas with me to keep me calm."

"I'm sorry to hear that, Lupe. Were you in the army?"

"No. You cannot tell it, but I had very bad plastic surgery done on my breasts. I was once a beautiful woman."

"Lupe, you're still a good-lookin' woman. Anybody tells you different, they're fulla shit."

"Thank you, Gary. I have never been to the United States. This is my first trip. I am very nervous. I am praying to the Virgin that they will not quarantine Cantinflas when we arrive. I don't know what I'll do if they take him away."

"Is your daughter meeting you at the airport?"

"Yes."

"You ask her to take you to Universal Studios. It'll blow your mind!"

"Oh, I have heard of it. And Disney too!"

"Either one's a good time."

They could see the flight attendant working his way toward them in steerage. Eventually he arrived, a middle-aged man with a hairline mustache, handing out cold soft drinks and tiny packets of albino peanuts. Lupe fed a peanut to Cantinflas. The skinhead two rows up fussed his way into the aisle, entered one of the rear water closets and stayed there for fifteen minutes while other passengers worked around him. He bothered Gary. Gary didn't know why. Something about his demeanor.

Lupe pulled out her camera and showed Gary pictures

of Esmerelda and her two-year-old son Joaquin, photos of Cantinflas dressed as a gaucho with a little sombrero and kerchief around his neck, pictures of her cactus garden on the porch of her Mexico City high rise.

After twenty minutes, a flight attendant knocked on the water closet door and the skinhead skulked back to his seat.

Gary nudged Lupe. "You see that dude?"

"What dude?"

"The skinhead?"

"Yes, I thought he looked odd when he got on."

"He makes me nervous."

"Oh, do not even joke about such things! I prayed to the Blessed Virgin for a safe flight."

"Can't hurt."

She took his hand in hers. "Let us pray to the Blessed Virgin together."

"Can't hurt."

Lupe mumbled softly in Spanish.

A woman screamed.

A man leaped to his feet from his aisle seat, swatting frantically at his pants.

More screams. People popping out of their seats like prairie dogs. Confusion! Hysteria! Lupe gripped Gary's hand with white knuckles. Something tickled the back of Gary's hand. It was a tarantula. Cantinflas hopped from shoulder to arm and snapped it up. Its hairy legs protruded from the parrot's beak.

The seat belt sign came on. Moments later, the captain

spoke.

"Ladies and gentlemen, please remain in your seats with your seat belts fastened. We are aware of the situation. Please remain calm. Tarantulas are not aggressive by nature and if you don't attack them, they will not bite. Their bites are not usually fatal. We have contacted Miami International and will make an emergency landing in forty-five minutes. In the meantime, flight attendants will go through the cabin and try to collect the tarantulas in plastic garbage bags. We apologize for the inconvenience.

"Chinga tu madre!" Cantinflas squawked.

41 | BOOM!

The remainder of the flight was like a horror movie with people moaning and scrambling despite the captain's warning. Attendants tried to assure passengers that the tarantulas were not life-threatening, to little avail. A few brave souls used their vomit bags to trap the bugs and hand them to the attendants, who walked up and down the aisle clenching black garbage bags.

When a tarantula crawled up Lupe's leg, she flicked it into the corridor with her finger. "These are very common where I live. If you don't bother them, they won't bother you."

The only person who did not look alarmed was the skinhead two rows up, who remained absorbed in his personal device.

People moaned in terror, shrieked, prayed out loud in English, Spanish, and Farsi. Babies screamed.

A man raised his hand in triumph. "GOT ONE!"

"DIE YOU BASTARD DIE!" cried a woman with her shoe in her hand.

The plane gully whumped.

"CAN I GET A DRINK BACK IN HERE?" yelled a man several rows in front of Gary and Lupe.

The pilot came on. "This is your pilot. This is a difficult situation. Please don't make it worse by acting out or leaving your seat. There are two flight marshals on board, and I won't hesitate to ask them to restrain and charge any passengers who are disruptive."

"DISRUPTIVE?" a woman cried in disbelief.

"CHINGA TU MADRE!" a young man bellowed.

"CHINGA TU MADRE!" Cantinflas seconded.

The flight attendants worked their way up and down the aisle, hanging on to the seat backs for support, making eye contact with every passenger. Some were bent over with their head on their arms.

"I'm sorry, ma'am, you have to put the tray up."

And so it went, destined to be a Tom Hanks movie. Gradually the shrieks and exhortations tapered off as the flight attendants collected every loose tarantula in giant plastic bags. Several bumptious boys chased them down on hands and knees, using napkins and vomit bags.

"This is your captain speaking. We are landing in ten minutes at Miami International Airport. Folks, I want to get off this plane just as badly as you, but please. Keep your seat belts on until the plane has stopped taxiing. We will be landing at an unused runway and we will facilitate your deplaning as expeditiously as possible."

Ten minutes later they were on the ground. Ten minutes after that, the plane lurched to a halt, the passengers threw off their seat belts and as many as possible crowded into the narrow aisle. Through the window, Gary watched several vehicles approach including Airport Security, Transportation Security Administration, a Miami PD cruiser, a fire truck, and a panel van.

Stair vehicles drove to the front and rear exits. The doors opened. The people surged. Flight attendants called for calm and an orderly departure. People sucked it up. Parents held crying infants. Some passengers clutched their emotional support animals including a peacock, an aardvark, and a pig. Cantinflas perched steadfast to Lupe's shoulder.

People hastened down the steps as fast as they could as first responders rushed, eager to help. An ambulance pulled up. Airport Security, TSA, and the Miami PD held an ad hoc confab. More police arrived, directing the deplaned toward a ten-foot concrete abutment that served as the side of the runway.

"Over here, folks!" declaimed a police veteran wearing a ball cap, aviator shades, and a Stalinesque mustache. "We'll have water for you shortly, and nurses for anyone with medical conditions. If any of you have suffered spider bites, please go see that man in the white coat."

As Gary reached the bottom of the steps, he heard a scuffle behind him, turned around, and saw an angry woman facing the skinhead behind her. "Stop pushing! You're not helping!"

The police waved them on. It was at least a thousand feet to the concrete abutment where several emergency vehicles had stopped. It looked like the Children of Israel crossing the Red Sea. The column moved fitfully, with the young singles leading the way, some helping the elderly. Gary and Lupe were in the middle. The panel van pulled up, the rear doors opened, and two nurses, one man, one woman, got out with kits. The man cupped his hands.

"Is anyone experiencing a medical emergency?"

Gary's pulse red lined. Sooner or later they'd search the cargo bay and discover the source of the infestation. He looked around for a back door. No way was he going to leap to the top of that ten-foot barrier, and there was no concealment. The moment he broke from the pack the cops would be on him like Cantinflas on a spider.

Fuck. Fuckity fuck fuck fuck. They were gonna bag him for smuggling wildlife and there was no one left to bail him out. Not at those prices. The judge would take one look at his record and throw the file at him. With his luck, it would probably be Judge Murphy. He would never see the light of day again. They'd call it an act of terrorism. He would spend the next twelve years in Raiford clearing brush or breaking up rocks.

He still had his phone. He dialed Habib, but the noise from jets passing overhead made conversation impossible. All he could do was yell into the phone, "Habib! It's Gary! I'm stranded at Miami International! They may arrest me for smuggling! Please come and find me!"

Lupe smiled at him uncomprehending.

The skinhead lurked at the edge of their group bobbing up and down, looking nervous. A woman fainted, drawing law enforcement attention. As soon as the mustache cop turned his back, the skinhead bolted, running along the edge of the wall which stretched to infinity, like a Kafkaesque video game.

"Hey!" the cop yelled. "Stop!" He took off running.

Someone from the TSA took note, got in a plain sedan and gave chase. Everyone watched the wiry skinhead bound along with the cops at his heels. He had run perhaps an eighth of a mile when the TSA pulled in front of him and got out with their guns. The skinhead put his hands in the air as they forced him to his knees, and then on his belly, where they handcuffed him, raised him up, and put him in the back of the sedan.

The captain and crew were the last to deplane. As they walked by themselves across the blistering tarmac toward the wall, the passengers broke into applause. Even Gary found himself clapping and cheering. Emergency responders had not yet entered the plane, as there was some discussion of fumigation. Gary wondered if he should give them Floyd's card.

The plane bulged comically like a silver party balloon before it leaped in the air and split in the middle like an overcooked bratwurst. Seconds later, the shock wave hit them, and then the boom.

42 | THE PEANUT MANIFESTO

Runway Fourteen D looked like a war zone, with emergency vehicles surrounding the smoldering wreckage of the airplane pumping water. The airport set up a triage unit in a United hangar where doctors and nurses treated the injured, deciding who should be sent via ambulance to three area hospitals. Not only was the airport closed-down stranding thousands of travelers, airports up and down the East Coast closed-down.

Gary, Lupe, and Cantinflas were not even knocked down. Lupe's daughter was on the way from Orlando. Krsytal didn't answer her phone, but Trixie had called.

"Gary, Krystal's in jail again in Glade County. Causing a public disturbance and resisting arrest. Gary, I'm afraid she's on drugs again. Oh honey, I don't know what to do! Call me."

Gary called her back and left a message. "Don't worry, Trix. I'll get her out."

After calling Trixie, Gary called the jail and learned that Krystal was being held on a thousand dollars bail. He asked Lupe if her daughter would give him a ride to Turpentine. By the time they passed through customs and stepped outside onto Northwest Twenty-First Street, it was nine p.m. A smiling tourist in a Tyrolean hat and patched elbows approached them at the curb.

"Nice parrot!" he said in a German accent.

"CHINGA TU MADRE!" Cantinflas replied.

The man tipped his hat and moved on. Lupe raised her arm and waved as Esmerelda pulled up in a Nissan Rogue, hopped out, and embraced her mother. Cantinflas danced onto the daughter's shoulder.

"Thank God you're all right! What a terrible thing to happen! It's a miracle no one was killed!"

"Yes, it was just terrible. I wasn't worried. I have dealt with these spiders before."

A police officer pointed at them and waved for them to move on.

"This is my friend Gary. Would you mind giving him a ride?"

"Of course! You have no luggage?"

Gary spread his hands. "It was destroyed in the explosion. I left my truck in Orlando."

Gary got in back. Cantinflas perched on Lupe's seat back and gave him the hairy eyeball.

"Don't start with me," Gary warned.

Esmerelda negotiated the tricky exchange onto Nine Fifty-Three heading north, expertly inserting herself between a semi and a Mercedes, working her way over to the second of four lanes. Miami gleamed like a jeweled crown to their right.

"Joaquin is dying to see you!" Esmerelda said.

"I can't wait to squeeze him! And how is Faustino?"

"He's fine but he works too hard."

Esmerelda's husband was an optometrist in Winter Park. Mother and daughter talked family.

"And you, Gary. What do you do?"

"I'm a roofer."

"What were you doing in Mexico?"

"I was, uh, just visiting a friend for a few days."

"It is a miracle that we survived! Can you imagine! How did those spiders get on the plane? Not just one spider, but hundreds! Do you think they had anything to do with the explosion?"

"I doubt it," Gary said. "Spiders don't know much about bombs."

"And they have no idea who set the bomb off?"

"Yeah, I got an idea, but I don't know nothin' about him."

Esmerelda turned on the radio and switched around until she found WIOD.

"Police have arrested Ronald Baitch, a twenty-five-year old Uber driver from South Miami. Last night, Baitch posted a bizarre manifesto from a Mexico City cyber-cafe. It reads in part:

*I have warned the airlines repeatedly, and United in par-
ticular, that their peanuts are deadly to people of allergy. I
have tried to raise awareness about this situation for years.
I have spoken. I have posted. I have tried to contact them
over and over. But they will not listen. I have also warned
them about the pretzels. They will not listen until it's too
late. Well now it's too late. I have also warned them about
the Funko Pops...*

"Ronald Baitch is in police custody," the news reader said,
"and while he doesn't deny setting the bomb, he claims he
knows nothing about the tarantula infestation which caused
the plane to make an emergency landing one hour short of
its scheduled landing in Orlando. Baitch has a long history
of threatening establishments that sell peanuts. He was arrested last November for creating a disturbance at a Safeway
in Coral Gables..."

"Wow," Esmerelda said. "That guy really doesn't like
peanuts."

"You have to admire him. He was willing to give his life
for his cause. I'm not crazy about airline peanuts myself."

"No one likes them," Lupe said.

"PEANUTS!" Cantinflas erupted. "RAWWK! PEA-
NUTS!"

"Almost nobody."

Traffic was heavy until the Five Ninety-Five, which was
a straight shot to Twenty-Seven, where traffic was light.
Esmerelda dropped Gary at the hotel at two in the morning.

It was five a.m. when Gary finally pulled into his yard. The predawn light showed two feral pigs rooting around beneath the trailer. Gary was too tired to even shout at them. He pissed in the yard, went inside, and collapsed, falling asleep almost immediately.

He dreamed he was being chased by feral hogs through the swamp, but his path was blocked by a massive alligator. Suddenly a green parrot landed on the gator's head.

"CHINGA TU MADRE!" it shrieked.

Gary woke up. It was two in the afternoon. Krystal was still in jail. He used the broom handle to check the toilet. No snake. Even so, he was nervous as he perched on the throne. There was no telling when some water moccasin would swim up through the depths and bite him in the ass. Although the bites were seldom fatal, no one wanted them. Gary showered, put on his last pair of clean pants and a T-shirt printed with a tux and tie so as to appear respectable, and headed out to the Glade County Jail.

It was three when he pulled into the visitor's lot and walked around to the front door. LIZARD ON A STICK was parked across the street. Gary did a double-take and crossed the street where four people stood in line. When it was his turn, he stepped up. The fresh-faced Dominican gave him a cheery smile.

"What can I make for you?"

"You don't remember me?"

The kid squinted. "You look familiar."

"I owe you from last week." Gary slid a twenty across

the counter.

"Oh yes, now I remember. Thank you very much. You want anything?"

"No, I'm here to get my baby out of jail."

"Well hokay then. Good luck."

Gary crossed the street, entered and went to the booking desk. Bail was one thousand dollars. The bored clerk took his identification and ten hundred-dollar bills.

"Wait here."

Ten minutes later Krystal collected her things and exited, looking like a Barbie doll that had been chewed up and left in the rain, her hair in corn rows. She threw herself into Gary's arms. They left for home.

"What was that all about?" Gary said.

"I tried to use food stamps to buy some wine. You'd think I shot up a church!"

"Who did your hair?"

"Airwrecka. She says I should check out pro wrestling. Also, we got to get a hold of Jen. She put up that video and it's getting millions of hits. We could be making money."

"I'm all for that."

43 | SNAKE FREE ZONE

Gary owed the IRS four hundred and twenty-three thousand dollars. They sent him a threatening letter. He laughed. He sat at the folding Formica topped table that was their breakfast nook reading portions of the letter to Krystal, who, in a rare moment of uxorial energy, was frying eggs on the little electric stove.

"How you want these eggs?"

"Over well. Jesus. How long we been together? You know how I like my eggs!"

"Down, Fang! What crawled up your butt and died?"

"All I ever think about is money. This trailer's all we got. What happens if the IRS comes and takes it away?"

"Nobody wants this trailer. This trailer is a piece of shit. It doesn't even have wheels. If it's a mobile home, why doesn't it move? Now Panny's gonna be pissed I didn't deliver his spiders."

Wearing an old terry cloth robe, her feet in fuzzy bunny

slippers, Krystal put her hands on her hips, spatula jutting at a forty-five-degree angle. "If you're so worried about money, I talked to this gal in the joint who used to wrestle professionally. She says with my reputation I would have no problem finding a manager and getting on the pro wrestling circuit."

"Huh?"

"That's right."

"What reputation?"

"Helloooo! I'm the Black Dildo!" she used a double-handed grip on the spatula to reenact her moment of triumph.

"Seriously?"

"If I'm lyin', I'm fryin'."

"You are fryin'."

"I meant if I'm lyin', I'm flyin."

"Who's this pro wrestler?"

"Cleo the Magnificent, but her real name is Latisha Forbes. You can look her up. She was never in the top tier, but there's a lot of women wrestling out there. Events all over the country, at state fairs, Masonic Temples, local arenas. She was with the Pro Wrestling Alliance. They got a lot of leagues. Chick Fight, Gorgeous Ladies of Wrestling, Naked Women's Wrestling League, Women Superstars Uncensored, Shimmer..."

"Uncensored, what does that mean?"

"Use your imagination."

Gary used his phone to look up Cleo the Magnificent. He marveled at his ability to operate this futuristic device, straight out of a comic book, and yet his seeming inability to make a living. Maybe if he got one of those talking helpers like Siri or Alexa.

Alexa, how do I make money?

Cleo the Magnificent was a statuesque black woman, six two, one hundred and seventy-five pounds, not an ounce of fat on her. She looked like she could suplex a mule.

"But you can't wrestle!"

"The fuck I can't! You wanna try me, tough guy?" She struck a McGregoresque pose. "Come on. Let's go. If yer yella, we can just arm wrestle on the table!"

Gary laughed. "Have you ever wrestled?"

"I told you I wrestled in high school."

"Your high school had girls' wrestling?"

"No! I trained with the boys. It was fun! I did it when the coach wasn't around. Those boys were all eager to grapple with Krystal, 'til I got 'em on the mat. My brother Lester wrestled, and he taught me all the moves."

"Did she tell ya who to call?"

"Yeah, she did. Let me think...Brown! Downtown Brown!"

"Who the fuck is Downtown Brown?"

"He's a fight promoter down in Miami. Runs events every Friday night in Little Havana. Place called the Roxy."

"You gotta be shittin' me?"

"I got Seminole blood."

Downtown Brown had his own website dedicated to Moxie at the Roxy. The next event featured Miranda Rights versus Junkyard Mama in the heavyweight division followed by a long list of colorfully named contenders.

Brown himself struck a Duke Ellington-like pose in tails and top hat, a light-skinned black man with a pencil mustache.

"But he's a promoter. How's he gonna rep you and host these contests?"

Krystal slapped two hardened discs down on Gary's chipped china plate. "We won't know unless we ask. Don't worry your pretty, little head about it. I got his number."

"Well what the fuck. Ain't like I got something else goin' on."

After breakfast, Krystal took a shower while Gary patrolled the property with his handgun looking for feral hogs and rabid raccoons.

"I'm livin' on the fuckin' frontier out here," he muttered. "Critter paradise. Well, you lunkhead, you chose to live on a swamp."

Gary bought the property nine years ago using money he got in a settlement resulting from a traffic accident. That's how he'd met Habib.

Gary picked up trash that had floated or blown in and stuffed it in a plastic garbage bag. By the time he got back to the house, it was half full. He'd spotted a couple gators out in the swamp, but they were too far away to plug.

Florida's alligator population was out of control. If one attacked your dog, it was against the law to shoot it. What kind of sense did that make? Didn't these fucking morons who passed law own any pets? Last year, gators killed twenty-five dogs. They found a woman's arm in one gator's belly. Out in the swamp among the loners and indigenous, no one kept track of death by gator. Official figures put last year's tally at two, but that was almost certainly low.

If a gator was willing to throw itself into a rich man's pool, they would stop at nothing. They were all over the golf courses. The National Golf Association was convening on whether to pass a gator "by" to the rule book.

When he got back to the house, Krystal was sprawled on the deck in an Adirondack, wearing capri pants, a halter top, and cat's eye sunglasses, talking on the phone. She held up a finger as Gary came up the steps. He went inside, cranked the roof-mounted AC to the max and took a shower. He checked the toilet. It was a snake free zone.

He got all his laundry stuffed into two bulging duffel bags and put them in the back of the truck. Krystal came dancing down the steps.

"I just got off the phone with Downtown Brown! He wants to meet with us this afternoon!"

"Aw, I ain't drivin' into Miami today. Be like a zoo."

"He says he's willing to meet us at Weston."

"Fuck what else I got to do?"

44 | DOWNTOWN BROWN

The Cracker Barrel lay in the lee of a mall that also housed an empty Sears, a defunct Waldenbooks, an empty Montgomery Ward, a thriving vape shop, a liquor store, an American Black Belt Academy, and a tropical fish store. It was four-thirty when they entered the restaurant, doing brisk business that Sunday afternoon. Downtown sat at a table by the window wearing a chocolate au lait three-piece suit and gleaming ruby tie, hair slicked back in the manner of Cab Calloway. He looked up as Gary and Krystal entered, an enormous grin appearing on his face.

He stood, extending both hands to clasp first Krystal's and then Gary's.

"Love your hair!"

"This is my husband Gary."

They sat. Gary ordered a coffee. Krystal ordered a vanilla milk shake.

"Here's the deal," Downtown said in a rich baritone. "I'm

a fight promoter. I can't take a proprietary interest in the fighters or no one will trust my fights. But I know a headline marquee when I see one! Krystal, I don't have to tell you that you are now a household word."

"I'm so excited!"

"What I aim to do is to hook you up with a manager friend of mine who'll put you on the roster, put you through a little training, and land you a gig."

"Ain't that a conflict of interest?" Gary said.

"No sir. I'm a promoter. How'm I gonna make a living unless I know the managers and trainers? Ain't no thang. We all know each other. That's how it is in the fight game. I useta box. I was four and six in light heavyweight with the Global Boxing Federation in 1999. But I weren't no champ. I could see that. Decided to get out before I lost my mental faculties. I'd wrestled in high school, and I always loved pro wrestling. It's a way for me to make a living and stay in the fight game."

He turned his brown eyes on Krystal. "Whatchoo weigh?"

"'Bout one hundred and thirty, I reckon."

"You don't look like you need to lose much weight. You can wrestle at one twenty-five."

"When do I start?"

"Not so fast, honeychile. I wouldn't throw you to the wolves. You got to do a little boot camp first. Ludlow will see to that. Ludlow Kudlow. He manages Charmaine Pain, Ella the Propella and Queen Kong."

Krystal stared blank-eyed.

"Ahmina have to bring you up to speed." Downtown reached into the Gladstone sitting on the chair next to him and handed Krystal a pair of DVDs. Best of Ladies Wrestling, volumes one and two.

"This'll help familiarize you with the game. Also, you're gonna have to change your name."

"What's wrong with Krystal?"

"Not that name. You can't call yourself the Black Dildo for obvious reasons. Now I've been thinkin'. How does Steely Danielle sound to you?"

Wrinkled foreheads. "It's okay, I guess."

"You're not familiar with the provenance of Steely Dan?"

"Well I've heard of them, sure."

"Hey, that's just my two cents, as a seasoned promoter. I already spoke to Lud, and he's very excited about you joining his roster. He asked you to call him."

Downtown slid a card across the table.

"What does Ludlow want me to do?" Krystal said.

"Believe it or not, pro wrestling is a serious business. Wrestlers are real athletes, even if the outcome is predetermined. He will put you through a training regime and teach you the basic moves. He's got a gym in Lauderdale, has a few rooms for athletes to stay over so you don't have to drive back and forth."

Gary took Krystal's hand. "You up for this?"

She shrugged. "What else I got to do?"

"You gotta have a look," Downtown said.

"I already got a look."

"I guess you do."

"I got a hairdresser. Airwrecka. She'll help me out. She's a big fan."

"By the way. The league tests for drugs. Is that going to be a problem?"

Gary looked up. Krystal looked away.

"What makes you think we're drug addicts?" Gary said.

Downtown put both hands up. "Hey, I'm just sayin'. I have no interest in your personal lives, but they are gonna test you. But that's a while off."

"Are we talking about marijuana, or what?" Gary said.

"Yes. I know it's ridiculous, but if you have traces of THC in your blood you can't wrestle."

"How'd you come to be a promoter?"

Downtown grinned. "Graduated Martin Luther King High School and thought I was hot shit. Played football, wrestled. Tried my hand at boxing. I got ranked in Golden Gloves, but my pro record was four and six. Play a little guitar, so I started playin' the blues down around here. That don't pan out, so I worked construction 'til I fell off a scaffolding and says to myself, fuck me, there's got to be an easier way to make a living.

"One night I was down on Bustillo Boulevard in Little Havana and I see they're having a ladies' wrestling match at the Roxy. So, I go in there. And fuck me, if that didn't turn my life around! 'Cause some of these women I got to know playin' the blues, they wanted to rassel. They practically begged me to represent them. So, I went to being a trainer. Hoosier Mama was my first star. Second she starts winnin', along comes Broderick Burke, big fish in these waters, steals her away from me. I could see any time I come up with a winner, Burke, or Fazula or one of those fuckers would steal 'em away from me. Now I always had a knack for gab. And I got the voice. So, when I heard they was lookin' for an announcer, I jumped. Guess it was meant to be."

"You make a living?"

"I got me a couple hustles. I still play blues, Sunday's, at Macy's Bar in Coral Springs. Y'all come down. There's no cover charge. I only get tips, but we get a lot of pale white northern customers who think they're listenin' to Robert Johnson, so I do all right. I also buy cars at auction, fix 'em up, and sell 'em. Whatchoo do?"

"I'm a roofer."

"Well I don't mean to pry, but I heard you won seven mil in the lottery. How come you're out here hustlin' your old lady?"

Gary sighed. "It's a long story."

"I love long stories."

"So, the first thing I do is I buy this house."

"Don't forget the Lambo," Krystal said.

45 | ASSORTED PESTS

The truck was their only vehicle now that the popo had impounded Krystal's G6. They stopped at the laundromat in Turpentine and stuffed their laundry into two machines. While the machines whirled, they walked down Main Street window shopping. Krystal stopped outside the Turpentine Bakery and gazed longingly at the cakes and cookies in the window.

"Don't let me go in there."

"No way."

"I'd eat everything in that window if I could."

"You got to think about your training."

"I been thinking. I have an idea for an invention. It's like a cookie dispenser that delivers one cookie per hour, only it's like a safe. It would weigh about a hundred pounds, be made of steel, and you couldn't tamper with it. Maximum rate, one cookie per hour."

"That's a good idea," Gary said. "We should start a think

tank. You ever eat iguana?"

"Just that once. Why?"

"It's not bad. Tastes like chicken. I'm thinkin' a chain of iguana restaurants would do well down here. They eat 'em all the time all over the Caribbean. Lots of people from all over Latin America would flock to a good iguana restaurant."

"Yeah? Who's gonna run this operation?"

Memorial Park featured a plaque commemorating Civil War volunteers who made up the XIV Turpentine Regiment, which served under Stonewall Jackson. Gary and Krystal took a bench beneath a banyan tree and watched board punks do stunts. "Maybe I can show you some of my old wrestling moves."

Krystal put her hand on Gary's thigh. "Maybe you can show me that when we get home."

They returned to the laundromat, transferred their clothes to the drier, and walked hand in hand the other way on Main Street, past the Cinemax which was showing Fast and Furious 19, Star Wars Episode XXXIV, and a new animated Pet Sematary.

"When's the last time you took me to a movie?" Krystal said.

"That was about three Fasts and Furious ago. Why? You wanna go?"

"No. There's nothing I want to see. Last time I was in a theater was with Jen last year when we saw I, Tonya."

When they returned to the laundromat their laundry was

dry. Holding a freshly laundered shirt to her face, Krystal declared, "This makes me want you inside me really bad."

Gary felt himself quicken. "Fresh laundry makes you horny?"

"I can't explain it. Let's go."

They piled the laundry into their plastic bins, but them in the truck bed and raced home. When they were almost to the trailer, two feral pigs cross the road in front of them. Gary laid on the horn and shook his fist.

"GET OUT OF HERE! GO ON!"

"Why don't you run them over," Krystal said.

"I don't want their blood on my truck! If we're gonna eat 'em, I'll kill 'em fair and square."

Each grabbing a laundry bin, they went in the house, tossed the bins on the floor and turned toward each other like two lampreys mating. Krystal drew her finger up Gary's crotch. He gripped her left boob like a necker knob.

"Why don't you go put on your Burger King crown?" she whispered.

"I'll do that, little lady. Why don't you put on something filmy?"

"Do you want me to dress up as a squirrel?"

"No, those animal outfits don't turn me on. You know there's people who dress up as all sorts of animals and they have orgies and you can't tell who's screwin' who. It's just a bunch of fuzzy shapes grindin' and gruntin'. I don't get it."

"You don't have to get it, big guy. Want to do a line?"

"No, that shit makes me limp. And I'm tossin' it all out in

the morning. We got to get serious about this wrestling biz, which means no more blow for you."

"Awww, you're no fun!"

Gary went into the bedroom, stripped, and found the cardboard Burger King crown in the closet. Krystal went into the bathroom. Gary heard the water run, guessed there weren't no snake, and wondered what she was doing in there.

She came out wearing crotchless silk panties, a domino mask, and fake vampire teeth. Gary threw her on the bed, and they wrestled, her on top then him on top. Up close, he could see the white rim around her nostrils. She was a machine. Gary was going to come but then he thought about all the money he owed and throttled back. They screwed like animals. Their brain patterns were the same. They weren't thinking about dinner or advanced trigonometry. Sure, people thought about those things, but not during sex. Gary had never heard of Sigmund Freud, but he knew how important sex was, and how often it figured into decisions which, on the surface, had nothing to do with sex.

They screwed in the bedroom, then they screwed in the living room. Finally, he lined her up on the kitchen counter. Gary yipped like a coyote. Krystal tossed back her head and swooned, "Oh, oh, oh!"

Gary fell to the floor, exhausted. Krystal jumped down. "Are you all right?"

"I'm more than all right, little lady! I am energized!"

"Seriously?"

Gary held up his hand. "Well I need help getting up."

They put on shirts and curled up on the sofa to watch Swamp People. Two swamp people wrangled with a six-foot gator. One pulled on the line while the other awkwardly aimed a rifle. The gator kept spinning and spinning. "Shoot it!" the line wrangler exhorted.

"Y'know, if she'd use a pistol, they wouldn't have this problem," Gary said. "The gator's right there, for fuck's sake! Just use a pistol!"

"All these gators look alike to me," Krystal said.

"You call that a gator! Wished I hadn't burnt that gator back at the old place. Now that was a gator."

"What would you do with it?" Krystal said, laying out a line on a smeared hand mirror.

"I'da stuffed that sucker and put it on the wall."

Krystal leaned over and snorked. "Ain't room on the wall."

"Was at the old place. You better enjoy that blow while you can, 'cause come morning, I'm flushin' it down the toilet. Maybe the snake'll want it."

"What if it's different snakes? What if they're comin' up for a look-see? Then they go down and tell their pals."

"What's to tell? Ain't nothin' but a bare-bones trailer bathroom. Not exactly the Breakers. These snakes ain't readin' Town & Country. Fuck if I know how they get in there. Must come through the septic tank or somethin'."

Tires crunched on gravel and light swept the room.

Krystal leaped up and grabbed the mirror. "Shit! We got company! Who's gonna come out here this time of night?"

Gary went into the bedroom and pulled on a pair of jeans as heavy steps came up the wooden stair. Gary turned on the porch light and opened the door. Rolf Panny stood there in a baggy gray suit and a face like a bulldog. Gary opened the door.

"Rolf! Come on in. How the hell are ya?"

Panny entered, looked around with a hint of disapproval. "I've come for my money."

"What money?"

"I advanced you five grand to deliver those spiders. This you failed to do."

Gary's Adam's apple oscillated. "What the fuck! I was nearly killed! You know we had to make an emergency landing in Miami! And why do you suppose those spiders got out? I never messed with the luggage! That's on you!"

Rolf reached into his baggy trousers and pulled out a small automatic pistol. "Nevertheless, the fact remains that you failed to deliver and now I need my money back."

Krystal entered wearing blue jeans and a Shazam! T shirt. "Who the fuck are you?"

"Rolf, Krystal. Rolf hired me to bring in those tarantulas and now he wants his money back."

"Are you shitting me? It's a miracle he wasn't blown to bits! The only reason anybody on that plane is still alive is because of those tarantulas!"

"Yes," Panny said, "well you see, that's to my credit, isn't it? Do you think it would occur to Mister Duba to fly down to Mexico City and bring back those tarantulas? Of course not. He hired on to do a job. He failed to deliver. I'm only asking for what's mine."

"What are ya gonna do? Shoot me?"

"Don't test me, Mister Duba. I served in the Rumanian Army. You may keep two hundred dollars for your trouble."

"Well, see, there's a problem. I had to pay some bills and I had to bail Krystal out of jail. Lemme see what I got."

Gary turned to go into his bedroom.

"Not you," Panny said. "Sit your ass down on that sofa." He pointed the gun at Krystal. "You. Go get his wallet."

Gary sat. "Do as he says." His gun was in the truck. He only had thirty-five-hundred of the original five thou due to expenses and bail. He hoped Panny wouldn't shoot him over that.

"Y'know, Rolf, I kept my end of the bargain. Ain't my fault if some nut decided to blow up the plane. Weren't for those spiders, we'd all be dead. Don't that count for nothin'?"

"I congratulate you on cheating death. I'm happy for the passengers that survived. But this is business. You acquitted yourself well. Perhaps I will consider you for future jobs."

"Don't suppose you'd consider that five an advance?"

Panny grinned like Mr. Sardonicus. "It's just business, Mister Duba. I'm sure you understand. Another time, I might let you hang on to it. But I've encountered a run of bad luck."

Krystal stomped back in and forked over Gary's wallet. Panny took out the cash, tossed the wallet on the sofa, and counted it.

"You're fifteen hundred dollars short."

"I had expenses."

Panny stuffed the money in his pocket and looked like he was about to go when a shape loomed behind him in the open door. A machete snaked around his neck, and with a brutal swipe, cut Panny's neck. Blood spewed on the gnarly throw rug as Panny fell on his face from a shove in the back. The man with the machete completely filled the doorway. He had a nose like a conning tower, a GI Joe beard that failed to disguise his receding chin and wore a serge blue suit with a white dress shirt, open at the collar. Ruby cufflinks gleamed on his wrists.

Stepping on Panny's back, El Nariz entered. Panny gurgled and blood spewed. Krystal emitted a bird-like chirp.

El Nariz pointed the blade at Gary.

"Do you know who I am?"

"I honestly have no idea."

"They call me El Nariz."

It took a minute for the dime to drop.

"Oh! You're the coke guy from South Miami!"

"Do you know why I'm here?"

"You're pissed about something."

"You are not what I imagined. Who's your supplier?"

"Well you may not believe this, but we found that coke all sealed up in a picnic cooler in the swamp."

El Nariz regarded Gary with tiny eyes beneath a beetle brow. "Even if that were true, what made you think you could sell in my territory?"

Gary put up his hands in supplication. "Hey. I don't know nothin' about nothin'. My friend El Cheapo said he could move it, so I gave it to him. I didn't know he was gonna step on your turf."

"I killed El Cheapo with this machete."

Gary's Adam's apple bobbed. "Did you have to do that?"

El Nariz pulled a small automatic from his pocket with his left hand and pointed it at Krystal.

"Bring me all the coke you have."

Krystal went back to the bedroom and returned with a quart plastic container filled with blow.

"Lay out a line," El Nariz commanded.

Krystal knelt before the smeared mirror on the coffee table, used a plastic restaurant spoon to scoop up the gleaming crystal, shook it on the mirror, and used a Harley Davidson playing card to lay out a line.

"Hand me that straw."

She handed the gangster a plastic straw cut to two inches. Without taking his eyes off Gary and Krystal, he placed the pistol in his pocket, picked up the mirror, placed it on the kitchen counter and hoovered up. He blinked.

"Isn't it lucky that you just happened to find all that yayo floating in a picnic cooler. Wow o wow. This is the real deal. Feels good to me. CARAMBA!"

"Why don't you just take it and go?" Gary said. "We don't have any money. You see how we live."

"Lay on the ground and put your hands behind your back. Don't even think about making a move. I will stomp your ass to jelly."

Gary did as he was told. El Nariz knelt with his knee in the small of Gary's back, set down the machete, pulled a plastic wire harness from his pocket and fastened his hands tightly behind him.

"Roll over."

Gary rolled over. El Nariz used another wire harness to lock his ankles together so that Gary lay on his back, unable to move except like a shrimp. His eyes fell on the discolored yellow headliner. Once it had been white. He really did live close to the bottom.

El Nariz stood and motioned at Krystal with the machete. "Now I'm going to take a shit. You're going to stand right outside the bathroom door so I can keep an eye on you, and when I'm finished, we will decide what is appropriate for your transgression."

He leered at Krystal. "I like redheads."

Prodding Krystal before him, El Nariz pushed her back against a cabinet and went into the bathroom. He set down the machete and took out the automatic.

"Don't make a move."

"Oh God, this is gross," Krystal said.

"What's the matter? Haven't you ever seen a man take a shit before?"

Krystal looked away. In the living room, Gary had wormed his way to the sofa and was trying to leverage himself back onto the seat. He kept a Buck folding knife between the cushions. He got to his knees and pushing against the floor succeeded in regaining his perch.

"What are you looking at?" El Nariz snapped.

Krystal turned away. "Nothing."

El Nariz grunted. There was a splash. A fetid odor drifted out. Krystal stared at him in disgust. El Nariz' eyes bulged. His mouth opened. He stood and with his pants around his legs, shuffled as fast as he could out of the bathroom and toward the front door, bellowing like an ox, a black tendril attached to his buttocks.

47 | ONCE MORE INTO THE SWAMP

Krystal ran out on the deck and watched as El Nariz made fifty stumbling paces toward his black Escalade and collapsed face down in the dirt. The snake attached to his butt let go and slithered toward the swamp.

"Ho. Lee. Fuck," she said.

"What happened?" Gary asked from the sofa.

"Snake got 'em."

"The snake?"

"That's right."

"Come in here and cut me loose."

Krystal used a pair of shears from the kitchen to cut through the plastic. Gary sat on the sofa rubbing his wrists.

"Fuck an A," he said.

Krystal giggled. Krystal barked like a dog. She and Gary laughed like hyenas as they shoved each other back and forth on the sofa.

Gary stood up. "Fun's fun, but now we have to get rid of

these bodies."

"What's the plan?"

"Same as Marvin."

Gary knelt and searched Panny's pockets, keeping his cell phone and a gold money clip containing two thousand eight hundred and fifty-nine dollars. He picked Panny up by the arms. Krystal took the legs and they carried him carefully down the steps, out on the dock, and tossed him into the boat where he landed with a thunk. The boat dipped minutely.

El Nariz was another story.

Gary got his pistol from the truck and approached the inert thug. A cottonmouth bite wasn't necessarily fatal, but Gary wasn't certain it had been a cottonmouth. Gary used his right foot to stomp El Nariz' outstretched hand. No response. The man was dead. Maybe he was allergic to snakes. Maybe he had a heart condition. Coke'll do that to ya.

"Search his pockets," Gary said, holding the pistol on the drug kingpin's head just in case. Gary had seen too many movies where the villain roars to life after being presumed dead.

Krystal reluctantly hunkered down and probed the big man's pockets, pulling out a snakeskin wallet. Irony! She pulled out the .32 Beretta and car keys and set them aside. She peeled a gold Riesling watch off his left wrist, and the ruby cufflinks.

She went through the wallet. "Holy shit," she said. "Holy

shit."

Gary gestured impatiently. "Gimme!"

Peeling off several hundreds and sticking them into the tight front pockets of her jeans, Krystal handed Gary the wallet. He stuck the pistol in his belt. The wallet contained over eight thousand dollars in cash, and four credit cards, two in the name of Emmanuel Ortiz, one with Eduardo Sariba, and one with Emilio Farrengetti.

"Finally," Gary said. "A little cash-flow. Awright. Ahmina drag this piece of shit down to the end of the pier like I did Marvin. He ain't no lightweight, but he ain't no Marvin either."

It was one in the morning by the time they loaded El Nariz into the pond skiff, the moon hanging low in the southern horizon. A light mist lay over the swamp as they roared away from the dock. Theirs was the last house on the road. There were no neighbors to upset, and sound from the highway a half mile away would drown them out.

Gary turned on the big spotlights mounted to the frame arching over the wheel. The skiff lay low in the water due to the weight up front. Slowly, Gary navigated the swamp, keeping his eye out for gators. He used a hand flash to look at surrounding hummocks. The hand flash picked up two sets of glowing red eyes close to the ground. Gators.

"Din din, boys!' Gary sang. "Din din!"

As they headed toward the hummock, the gators glided into the water. Gary cut the engine. Eerie silence followed for a few seconds. Then the frogs, loons, crickets and mosquitos got back to work. The night chirped and hooted. Working together, Gary and Krystal strained to tip El Nariz's two hundred and eighty pounds into the water. It hit with a splash and the front end bobbed up.

Panny was easier. They just picked him up like a sack of garbage and heaved him over the side.

Glowing eyes slithered from their perches on the surrounding islands and converged at the body dump, which churned frothy white, tails whipping, as the gators went to work.

"Hellfire!" Gary hooted. "Look at them gators eat!"

Krystal pulled a doobie from her tight pants pocket and lit it with a Bic, inhaling deeply and blowing a plume of smoke into the swamp. She passed the joint to Gary, who inhaled, exhaled slowly and inhaled again via his nostrils, like water flowing uphill.

The boat rocked gently in the ripples created by the gators. It was like a hot dog eating contest. Gradually, the thrashing subsided with each gator heading off in a different direction clutching its prize.

Gary looked at Krystal. "What a night."

"Let's head back."

Gary was about to start the engine when he noticed something pale floating in the water just off the stern. He used a boat hook to draw it in. It was a picnic cooler sealed in duct tape. He hauled it into the boat, took out his pocket-knife and slit the tape. They opened it up. It contained eight keys of blow, presumably of the same quality.

"Aw hell no," Gary said, tossing the open carton back in the water where it slowly filled and sank.

"Coked-up gators would make a good SyFy movie," Krystal said.

"Yeah. Giant coked-up mutant gators."

Gary started the engine and let 'er rip. They cruised toward home leaving a rippling wake in the glassy waters, the only sign of civilization the headlights of cars on the nearby freeway. When they got back to the dock, Gary put on a pair of blue latex gloves and searched the Escalade, finding a diamond tennis bracelet on the floor, a loaded .357 magnum in the glove compartment, and the complete works of Herb Alpert and the Tijuana Brass in the center console.

Gary handed the gloves to Krystal. "We'll leave it at the Palm Beach Airport."

Dawn was creeping up in the east by the time they left the Escalade in long-term parking. They stopped at an IHOP on the way back for breakfast, arriving home at nine-thirty in the morning.

Gary flushed the bin of coke down the toilet. The night's proceeds came to just over ten thousand dollars. After meeting current expenses including interest on their credit cards, they had a six thousand-dollar surplus, not counting what they owed the IRS, Visa, Mastercard, and AmEx.

Tuesday, they drove to Fort Lauderdale to meet Ludlow Kudlow, a dead ringer for Disney's Gipetto the Dollmaker in Pinocchio, with brushy gray hair and mustache. Ludlow wore Banlon pants, a pale-yellow knit golf shirt, penny loafers, horn-rimmed glasses and a yellow fedora. They met at Mitch's Crab Shack in West Laurel, a nautical-themed restaurant with thick hawsers separating the outdoor eating area from the street, mounted marlin over the bar, and fishnets festooned with colored glass floats.

Ludlow was there when they arrived, seated outdoors beneath a Cinzano umbrella. He stood and smiled, showing yellow teeth and a hint of yellow in the 'stache, shook hands, and felt Krystal's biceps.

"Very excited to work with you," Ludlow said in an Australian accent "Even with no wrestling experience whatsoever, I believe that we can make a nice profit."

"Not if she gets her teeth knocked out," Gary said.

Ludlow laid both elbows on the table and grinned. "No worries. Every move is choreographed. The point of training is to teach you to perform the stunts without injury to yourself or your opponent. I have a gym here in town and some dorm rooms. I would like to start as soon as possible. I believe you will be ready for your first bout in a month."

The waiter, a slim young Haitian in white shirt and black pants, took their orders: mimosas, crab, swordfish, and chicken.

"I'd like to start as soon as possible," Ludlow said.

Gary looked at Krystal. She shrugged.

"Ain't like I got anything else to do."

"Can you start today?"

"What?" Gary squawked.

Krystal put her hand on his. "Gimme some of that cash, big daddy. I'll buy what I need."

"It's unfortunate that you will be deprived of the delightful Krystal's company, but it's only until the weekend. I'm not a slave driver."

Krystal held out her hand. Gary peeled off a thou and passed it over.

"I need a car," she said.

"Hell, I got enough money to get your Pontiac outta hock."

"It's ruined. It was door deep in the canal. Let 'em have it."

"Well honeychile, we don't got a lot of spare cash at the moment. I know you think we do, but we still owe hundreds of thousands of dollars."

Their food came. While Gary and Krystal chowed down, Ludlow held up a finger. "This is not a get rich quick scheme. But it could be. First, you've got to win a few matches. Then we start crawling up the rankings. You've already got name recognition so that should guarantee good box office, but the real money comes when you join World Wide Women Wrestling. That's the premier promoter. Fortunately, they are headquartered in Atlanta and they come down here all the time to see what's goin' on. I'm also working on a deal to televise the bouts on Telemundo."

While Ludlow paid the bill, Krystal leaned in close and whispered in Gary's ear. "I'll call you tonight, big daddy, and tease you until you burst."

"It's a date."

Gary kissed his wife goodbye and headed toward Turpentine. He stopped at the post office for his mail. The post office didn't deliver out where he lived. The box was fat with bills, solicitations, coupons, and real estate fliers. Someone had tracked down his old address and assuming he was flush, was trying to interest him in another multimillion-dollar home.

The trailer felt empty with Krystal gone. Gary didn't mind. His life had been crowded since that rabid raccoon appeared. He welcomed a little peace and quiet. He turned on the television. If he didn't pay his Direct TV bill soon, he would lose all four hundred and twenty-seven channels. Swamp People was his favorite show. He loved to see them gators roll. Fetching a Dixie from the kitchen, he settled down in front of the television and rolled a doobie.

Every week the same thing. Gators. Got to get that gator population down before it threatened the kids. Two good ol' boys were trollin' for gators in a Caymas with a ninety horse Johnson. They were about to plug a six-footer when it broke for a commercial.

Habib Rodriguez stared stolidly at the viewer in a charcoal three- piece suit with gold tie, his hair slicked back.

"Have you been in an auto accident and your insurance company has failed to give you what you deserve? Call me, Habib Rodriguez, the Long Arm. I'll get you what you deserve."

A young woman with an aw shucks expression said, "I was stopped at a red light when I was rear ended. The insurance company wouldn't give me what I deserved so I contacted Habib Rodriguez, and he got me ninety thousand dollars!"

Back to Habib. "I can't guarantee that your injury is worth ninety thousand dollars, but we won't know until we look. Call me. The consultation is free, and you don't pay a cent unless we get a settlement."

Back to the gators. Two women in a swamp boat, Lucille and Esther, with a stout pole reeling in an eight-footer. Thick as a linebacker, Esther wrestled with the line, wearing leather gloves while Lucille hunkered at the gunwale holding a big automatic in both hands.

The gator surfaced.

"Shoot it, girl! Shoot it!" Esther exhorted.

Coolly, Lucille double tapped the gator in the head.

"WhooooooEEE!" Esther crowed. "That's shootin'!"

As they hauled the gator into the boat, Esther addressed the camera.

"We make the finest quality gator leather wallets, belts with Grade I and Grade II belly and back skins!"

Lucille held up a gator leather purse. "Y'all come see us at Lucille and Esther's in Pahokee! If we ain't got it, you don't need it!"

Car tires crunched and light flickered across the room. Gary pulled his pistol from between the sofa cushions and went out on the deck. A beige Toyota Corolla had pulled up near the base of the steps and a spindle-shaped man in baggy trousers, a soiled white shirt and a beaten tie got out.

"Are you Gary Duba?"

Gary hid the pistol in the small of his back. "Who wants to know?"

"I'm Andy Wurster. I'm manager of the Wokenoki Trailer Park. You know a Howard Perkins?"

"I just met him. Why?"

"Howard died last night, and he left a letter that says he wants you to have everything in his trailer. We gotta get that place sorted out 'cuz I got renters waiting to move in. How soon can you come over?"

Gary came down the steps. "How did he die?"

"He blew his brains out in his truck."

49 | PERKINS' TRAILER

Perkins' trailer smelled of dust, cigarette smoke, and desperation. The living room was so crowded with paper boxes Gary had to turn sideways to make his way through to the kitchen. The kitchen counters were heaped with dirty dishes and the detritus of dishes past, including pizza cartons, empty Cheeto bags, empty beer cans, empty bottles of Peppermint Schnapps and Popov, and ashtrays heaped with used butts.

The letter said, "Dear Duba: On acount you had the balls to round up my shit and help me get rid of it without going to jail or some such shit, I'm leaving you all my stuff. Some of it's good. That's all. I'm checking out."

Gary called the nearest chapter of the VFW, which was in Belle Glade and left a message.

"This is Gary Duba of Turpentine. Just want you to know that Howard Perkins killed himself last night. Howard said he was a veteran so y'all need to look that up."

Gary tracked down Wurster, who was having coffee on his west-facing deck at nine in the morning. "What about Perkins' body?"

"Coroner took it away afore you got here. You don't want 'em sitting around in this heat."

"Did he have any family?"

"Not that I know of. Maybe you can find something."

Gary cleared a space on the threadbare cloth sofa, moved when he sat on a broken spring, and began going through the boxes. One box held nothing but men's adventure paperbacks from the sixties including The Avenger, The Executioner, The Destroyer, Matt Helm, Sherlock Holmes and the War of the Worlds, Matlock, McCloud, Combat, Garrison's Gorillas, Go Down Fighting, Dan Marlowe, and Jim Thompson. Gary knew from thrift stores that some of those books were valuable, but now it became a question of logistics and time. Did he have the logistics to move this shit to a warehouse location, and then did he have the logistics to post it up on eBay and ship it out?

Hell to the no.

There was Billy Bob and there was Alex Chow. There were two thousand other pawn shops up and down the coast. Gary envisioned himself driving from pawn shop to pawn shop looking for the best deal. He needed an expert. Somebody who knew collectibles, like those guys from Pawn Stars. Having watched a lot of Pawn Stars, Gary had a few ideas of his own, but the proliferation of cheap-jack reality shows like Pawn Stars and American Pickers had led to a generation of Americans looking to strike it rich with no effort. Gary knew from experience that making a profit from trash was hard business.

Nevertheless, he heaved the big cardboard box of old paperbacks off the crowded table, out the door, and into the bed of his F-150. Next was a box containing Franklin Mint models in their original boxes. This was more like it. Some of those old Franklin Mint cars were worth hundreds of dollars. Gary did a quick search on his phone. A used 1948 Tucker brought four hundred and fifty dollars on eBay. Likewise, the 1956 Nash Metropolitan, a 1953 Cadillac Eldo, and a '63 Studebaker Avanti. That was eighteen hundred bucks right there, minus his time and trouble. They went in the truck.

Next was a box of VHS tapes, mostly porn. Perkins had been fascinated by certain body parts. Gary set those aside. Nobody wanted VHS. A heavy box yielded a complete run of National Geographic from July 1969 through January 1984. Nothing there.

There were unopened cases of Junket pudding, Tab Diet Soda, Cott's Diet Soda, Moxie orange soda, Mr. Pibb, Vault, Tab, and Jolt. A case of Weasel Peters. Two hours later, he made it to the bedroom which barely had room for the queen-sized bed. It still bore Perkins' indentation. Perkins' closet contained a green cowboy suit with white piping, a yellowed ten-gallon hat, a dozen belts in cow, gator, and snake leather with some unique buckles, and the samurai sword.

Gary picked up the sword and eased it out of its enamel

scabbard. The handle was wrapped in gold thread, with a faux gold pommel and hilt. It had been made in Spain. But it was not a cheap sword. It was made from high-grade steel and had been sharpened to a razor edge. Gary drew it all the way out, took it in both hands and made a few slicing moves, cutting the dusty window blinds.

There was a pair of boots from Lucille and Esther's. Perkins wore a size twelve. Someone would want them. Perkins kept his jewelry in a faux leather box on his dusty dresser. Several bolo ties in silver and turquoise, some cheap Mexican silver rings, and a golden wedding ring engraved on the inside with "forever—Joan". Only by clearing the massed boxes of wallets and pen knives was Gary able to reveal the mirror behind, in whose frame rested several yellowed photographs including one of a very young Perkins with a full head of brown hair and an aw shucks grin, holding a smiling, pretty brunette in a knee-length dress.

Gary took the photo and went in search of Wurster, whom he found in the trailer park offices talking to a young couple with a coon hound on a leash. Gary helped himself to the cardboard-tasting coffee and coffee mate and sat in a molded plastic chair flipping through the latest issue of Trailer Life until the couple left.

Wurster raised an eyebrow.

Gary showed him the photo. "Did you know Perkins was married?"

"No. Hardly knew the man. Been here fourteen years. Perkins been here nine. Trailer park's a small place. You usually get to know your neighbors pretty good. Someone's brewin' meth or turning tricks, that's hard to hide in a trailer park. But Perkins? Didn't know nothin' about him. Paid his dues on time, kept to himself, but he was always putting out trash. Way too much trash. I talked to him about it on numerous occasions. He had a junk pile goin' just beyond the property back there near the swamp and I give him twenty-four hours to get rid of it or I was gonna ask the health department to condemn his property. That was last week."

"He dumped it in my yard."

"What?"

"Yeah. That's how I got to know him," Gary explained. "All I did was bring his trash back here, and then help him take it to the dump. And he leaves me all his stuff? That's just sad, man."

Wurster shrugged. "He may have had kids, all I know."

"Well fuck. Now I gotta go through all his shit and find out. Christ. Somebody should know. It ain't right that he leaves all his shit to someone he just met."

"Yeah. How soon can you clear out that trailer?"

Gary put up his hands. "Hold on there, podnuh. Ain't my job to clear out his trailer. You just said he left me his shit. That's it. I'm takin' what I can use and leaving the rest."

Wurster put his chin in his hands. "What if I was to pay you?"

Gary thought about the six thou in his pocket. It wouldn't go far, and he wasn't above getting his hands dirty. "How much?"

"Two hundred and fifty."

Gary did a quick calculation. Loading and making the round trip to the "recycling center" would take at least three hours each time. That was at least fifteen hours. That was only sixteen bucks an hour.

"Can't do it. Ain't there any kids around here? They'll do it."

"I wouldn't trust these kids to carry a bucket of water."

"Why don'tcha call them American Pickers?"

"I got to have that plot cleared out by the weekend. That trailer's just junk now. Gonna cost me a thou just to have it hauled away. Well it ain't your problem. How soon before you're done?"

"Gimme another hour. Ahmina see if I can find any clue to his family."

50 | A VISIT FROM BURT

The old vinyl three-ring binder lay in the press-board dresser's bottom drawer, beneath a collection of balled up socks. Someone had painstakingly snipped articles from the local papers, glued them to construction paper and saved them in the binder. The first notice was from the Port Charlotte Herald, announcing the Harriet Tubman High School's valedictorian for 2003, Haley Beth Perkins. The old black and white photo could have been any seventeen-year-old girl.

Six months later, also from the Herald, young Haley had won a free trip to Washington to participate in Student Government Day, as a senator. It was four years until the next clipping, this one from the Tallahassee State Journal announcing that Haley Beth Van Droot had graduated cum laude with a degree in sociology at Florida State University, and planned to pursue her Masters in Law.

An ancient colored photograph showing the young Perkins, Joan and baby Haley at an outdoor picnic somewhere with palm trees in the background. Scrawled handwriting on the back said, "Swayne Family Picnic, 1987. Me, Joan, Haley."

Somewhere between 2003 and 2020, Perkins and Beth had divorced.

When Gary came out with his last load, Wurster was waiting with two kids, a stout Mexican and a wiry white boy, both wearing leather gloves.

"You done?" Wurster said. "Can we get in there?"

"Go crazy. What you gonna haul it in?"

Wurster pointed to Perkins' Dodge Ram underneath the desiccated fiberglass roof. "I got the keys."

It was none of Gary's business whether Wurster intended to appropriate Perkins' truck. Gary wondered why Perkins hadn't left him the truck. He'd let Haley know, if he found her. Gary drove to Belle Glade Pawn. Alex Chow offered him five hundred dollars for the ten Franklin Mint models. Chow wasn't interested in the paperbacks.

He went into Center State Bank in Turpentine and deposited eight thousand dollars in his checking account, which would disappear as soon as he caught up on bills, leaving him with net debt in six figures. Next stop was the Turpentine Library to research some of the items. His phone just didn't cut it. Staring at his phone, Gary always felt as if he were looking through a keyhole. He toyed with the idea of buying a regular computer with a flat screen monitor, but there really was no place to put it except the kitchen table, and he was afraid he'd spill beer on it. He'd barely gotten started when the librarian announced that the library was closing.

He pulled into his yard a little after seven, took the box of paperbacks and samurai sword into the house, returned to the yard and covered the truck bed with a tarp, tying it down with bungees. Heavy clouds scudded in from the west and there was a flash of lightning. He checked the swamp boat to make sure the rear drains were open and scampered up the steps just as the first heavy drops began to hit.

The aluminum trailer amplified the rain so that it sounded like a military barrage. Gary rolled a doobie, got a can of beer and turned on the television. No dice. The storm had knocked out service. He called Krystal.

"I'm wiped," she said. "I've been doing calisthenics and shit all day. Ludlow's a slave driver."

"He feed ya?"

"He bought me dinner at Chick-Fil-A. How's it with you?"

"You promised to talk me through my orgasm."

"Gary, can I get a rain check? I'm just bushed. All I want to do is hit the hay."

"Are you refusing me phone sex?"

"I'll make it up to you. Promise."

"I've half a mind to call a professional."

"You do and I'll cut off your nuts off with a rusty can."

There was nothing left to do but take a shower. When Gary got out, he edged up the toilet seat with his foot. A snake curled comfortably in the bowl. It may have been the same snake it may have been another. Gary didn't know if snakes were like bees, who died once they sank their barbs. He'd have to look it up.

"That's all right, li'l buddy. In light of your service, ah-mina just go outside and pee off the deck."

The moment he stepped outside he was drenched to the skin. It didn't matter because he wore no clothes. He went back inside, toweled himself off again, put on a pair of skiv-vies. He flopped on the sofa and picked up a Destroyer novel from the Perkins Collection. There was nothing else to do.

While he was asleep the rain stopped and he was visited by the ghost of Burt Reynolds, who wore an Elvis-like white and gold jumpsuit and held a golden harp.

"How could you lose seven million dollars like that?" Burt asked.

"It was easy! First we bought this house."

Burt held up his hand. "That's enough. I don't want to hear it. I talked to you about financial planning. Didn't you visit that adviser?"

"Burt, all I think about is money! I got plans! My house suspenders will revolutionize the building industry."

"Okay I might be able to help you on that. You're gonna need a video set-up to catch the next hurricane, to prove that it works. Once we get that video, we put it up, it goes viral, you're in business. The money will come rolling in."

"Burt, I got another idea! A cookie dispenser that only dispenses one cookie per hour. Tamper proof! It would weigh a hundred pounds and made of case-hardened steel."

"Why don'tcha just not buy cookies? Don't have 'em in the house."

"It's for rich people with poor impulse control."

Burt covered his face, turned away, and made a gagging noise. "Son, rich people can afford to hire others to eat their cookies for them. And if this thing's hooked up to the internet? Forget it. Fifteen minutes after you turn it on it's gonna be spewing cookies all over the house like a machine gun."

"I can make good money smuggling spiders."

"No, you can't."

Gary was exasperated. "Well what do you suggest?" he said a little too stridently, considering it was Burt Reynolds.

"Grilled iguana. Up 'til now, it's just been treated as a novelty meat, but I'm telling you, millions of people throughout Latin America consider it a primary source of protein. You can't call it Lizard On A Stick, 'cause that's already taken. You start with one anchor location, a fancy, but not too expensive place called The Lizard Lounge. You can serve some fish and chicken if you want, but lizard's the main attraction."

"Are you serious?"

But Burt was gone.

It was morning and something was scratching at the front door. Gary opened the door to see a raccoon standing on its hind legs trying to get in.

"What?" Gary demanded.

"My name is Inigo Montoya. You killed my father. Prepare to die!"

Having competed in gymnastics in high school, Krystal was better prepared than most for Ludlow's syllabus: the power-slam, the powerbomb, the brainbuster, the backbreaker, the paddling blow fish, the foaming pipe snake, the piledriver, the Boston crab, the doomsday device, the suplex, the sharp-shooter, the figure four, and the camel clutch. Despite their gruesome names, the moves were designed to be performed without injury. That was the whole point. Of course, you could also use the moves to inflict injury on the unprepared.

Krystal had never paid much attention to pro wrestling. It always struck her as fake, and it was, in a sense. Pro wrestling was a morality play with heroes and villains, a serial soap opera in which a hero could prolong his or her career by becoming a villain, and vice versa. The Mexicans had it down to a science, called Lucha Libre.

Lucha Libre meant "freestyle wrestling", characterized by bizarre masks, elaborate scrambles, and aerial displays as wrestlers launched, leaped, and somersaulted off the ring posts in death-defying maneuvers designed to elicit oohs of awe. A luchadore's mask is highly symbolic, and a symbol of pride. The most extreme form of lucha libre involved matches in which the loser agreed to forfeit his mask, a defeat so humiliating it often caused permanent withdrawal from the sport.

Ludlow's gym was a converted warehouse with a ring, a trampoline, a padded floor, and three monastic dorm rooms upstairs. Krystal's window overlooked an alley. There was a communal bathroom down the hall with two shower stalls. After a week of training she could feel the changes. Her muscles had become hard. The tiny bit of fat around her belly had disappeared.

Following Friday's intense workout with Ella the Propella, Ludlow took both wrestlers to a nearby Qdoba. After they got their food and settled at an outside table beneath dusty palms, Ludlow said, "I know we're moving fast, but if you feel you're ready, I can get you a bout with Honey Badger in two weeks at the Roxy."

"Who's Honey Badger?" Krystal said.

Ella the Propella looked up from her taco. She was a stout Mexican with square shoulders who'd come off the Lucha Libre circuit. "She's bad news. She gave Wampus Cat a torn Achilles tendon."

"Listen," Ludlow said. "I had a sit-down with her manager, and she promised me no shenanigans. You two will meet several days before the match and finalize your routine. You don't get to come into the league and start winning, so it will go to a decision which Honey Badger will win. But it pays five thousand dollars. That's four to you once I take my cut."

"I'll do it!"

"Good. I was hoping you'd say that. When we get back to the gym, we'll watch some videos, so you know what to expect."

Honey Badger, whose real name was Ruth Katchatorian, was a mesomorph from South Africa with a butch haircut, the top dyed white. She weighed one hundred and seventy pounds, and whenever she face-planted or suplexed an opponent, would hunch over, arms clenched, and snarl to the four corners of the ring.

"Be careful of her initial rush. She'll try to bowl you over."

"I thought this was all choreographed."

"It is, and that's her signature move. You have to be ready. You have to jam to the side, go low, and leave a leg out to trip her."

Krystal and Ella got in the ring and worked until they both needed showers. Later, Krystal phoned Gary.

"Does this mean you're coming home soon?" Gary said.

"I can have Sunday off. Did you get me a car?"

"I got three thou. You want a three thousand-dollar car?"

"Let's hold off. I'm getting four thou for my first fight."

"Fat City! I'll pick you up."

They had breakfast at an IHOP in Belle Glade. Two tables away sat a husband and wife who collectively weighed six hundred pounds and their four kids, aged two to six. The eldest child, wearing an appropriate striped top like a prisoner, sailed pancakes across the dining room like Frisbees while shouting, "UFO! UFO!"

Management huddled to deal with the problem. A pancake landed in front of Krystal, who forked it onto her plate, added butter and syrup, and chowed down. The little boy came over and stared petulantly.

"That's my pancake."

"It's my pancake now."

The little boy's face twisted in rage and confusion. "MOMMEEEE!"

The manager spoke to his parents.

"EUSTACE, YOU GET YOUR ASS BACK HERE RIGHT NOW!"

Eustace glumly returned to his table.

"That kid's got a hard row to hoe," Gary said.

"Do you think we should have a baby?" Krystal said.

Gary's heart seized a piston. "Jeez! Kinda early to think of that, don'tcha think?"

"You're thirty-six. I'm thirty. If we lived a hundred years ago, we'd be grandparents by now."

"Well you're about to embark on a career as a wrestler. Can we wait and see how that goes?"

"Of course. I just think about it every time we go to an IHOP."

"Is this about your sister?" Eve lived in Tallahassee with her husband Marc, an IT guy, and had two children whom

Gary had never met. Krystal had planned to invite them down to the new house, but now it was too late.

"Of course not. I just look around at all these happy families..."

Gary nodded toward Eustace.

The dad grimly shoveled food into his mouth. The mom poked and prodded at her phone. The children kicked one another beneath the table and fussed. It was warm in the IHOP despite the air conditioning and smelled of bacon and coffee.

The waitress dropped off their check. Gary stuck his credit card in the vinyl folder and set it upright. The waitress took the card and returned a minute later.

"I'm sorry, sir. The credit card company is denying your card. Do you have another card you'd like to use?"

Gary blinked. "What? Run it through again."

"Sir, I tried that. Not only do they deny the card, they asked that we take the card from you and destroy it. I'm not comfortable doing that. Do you have another method of paying?"

Gary reached for his wallet, paid in cash, leaving a five-dollar tip.

52 | MOXIE AT THE ROXY

The combatants met at the Roxy Friday afternoon to meet review their routine. Honey Badger was fifteen minutes late and walked with the exaggerated swagger of a bronc buster, accompanied by her manager, a cadaverous ectomorph named Eli, and her trainer, a dynamic, thick-set woman named Martha Grieves. They shook hands with Krystal, Ludlow, and Gary.

Katchatorian shook hands with a dead fish, didn't look Krystal in the eye. They went into the ring where Ludlow and Grieves walked the wrestlers through their moves.

"Now we all understand that this is Krystal's first professional fight, and she doesn't win, but she can't look like a newbie either. We're all trying to make a living here."

"I'm just thrilled to be here," Krystal said. "And I want to thank Ruth for the opportunity."

Honey Badger did a half wave. With her black sides and white top, she reminded Krystal of a Starbucks' pastry.

Clutching lists, Ludlow and Grieves acted out the bout, beginning with Honey Badger's charge which would spring Steely Danielle into the ropes, from which she would rebound, performing a handstand reversal, her legs swinging around Honey Badger's neck and taking her down. The bout proceeded through the powerbomb, brainbuster, and paddling blow fish, ending with Honey Badger pinning Steely Danielle with a face down leg lock. Krystal got to perform an aerial wurlitzer, a pro-bionic, and a fluffex. She would fight brilliantly, but inevitably succumb to a bigger, stronger opponent, thus setting her up for her next bout.

After the walk-through, Krystal and Gary went to a Cuban restaurant. They both ordered Cubanos, roasted pork loin, sliced ham, swiss cheese, mayo, and dijon on home-made bread. When they returned to the theater at five, Airwrecka was standing out front. Krystal rushed to her and they embraced.

"Girl! Thank God you're here! You need to do my hair!"

"Well get me in there, girl! I invited a friend. I hope that's all right?"

"You bet. I'll leave the name with the box office."

Krystal's backstage dressing room contained a sink, a mirror surrounded by lights, and a mini-fridge stocked with mineral water and two suspicious Styrofoam boxes. Gary pulled one out and opened it, releasing an earth stench.

Holding the box at arm's length, he went out into the hall and dumped it in a thirty-gallon plastic tub. The old theater smelled of sawdust, sweat, and makeup. He heard hubbub

emanating from other dressing rooms in English and Spanish.

Downtown Brown appeared in a cafe au lait three-piece
with flared trousers, a black shirt, ruby tie, and a matching
Fedora with a pheasant feather thrusting gaily from the gray
silk band.

"Mister Gary Duba!" Downtown sang coming forward
with open arms. "How's our girl?"

"She's getting her hair done. We feel pretty-confident
after the walk-through. Everyone is very professional."

"Ain't they? Well excuse me, I got to make the circuit. I'll
be dropping in on Krystal shortly."

"Wait a minute, Downtown. When do we get paid?"

"Well you know first we have to add up the house receipts."

"Oh horseshit! You don't run a show like this pocket to
pocket! How 'bout half up front or my girl walks."

Downtown did a double take, assuming a wounded expression. "You don't trust me? After bringing you into the
game?"

"All we've seen is a lot of hard work and sweat. Come on,
Downtown. Cough up."

Downtown grinned like a Steinway Grand, pulled a roll
from his pocket and peeled off twenty-five hundred in hundred-dollar bills."

"Only because I like you!"

"We like you too, Downtown!"

Back in the dressing room, Krystal sat in front of the

mirror while Airwrecka braided her hair into cornrows. Airwrecka wore a tie-dyed shirt, red hot pants, and three-inch stilettos, her hair topping out at seven feet.

Even without makeup Krystal was beautiful, with the upturned nose of a country girl. Gary opened three mineral waters, set two on the makeup counter, glugged the third. He heard the faint susurrus of the faithful arriving through the walls. The Roxy was built in 1925 and was on the Register of Historic Buildings. It had housed vaudeville, the silents, the talkies, rock and roll, rap, boxing, and now pro women's wrestling.

There was a knock and Ludlow entered, wearing wide pleated pants and suspenders. He hip-checked Airwrecka, stood behind Krystal, kneading her shoulders. "How's my sheila? You ready?"

Krystal held her thumb up. "I'm ready!"

"That's my girl. Remember. This is just your first show. Let 'em see your personality. Play to the audience. Have fun out there."

The thumb. "I'm down, Ludlow!"

"You go through the moves? Everything copacetic with Honey Badger?"

"We're all pros here," Krystal said.

"Excellent."

There was a knock and Downtown entered.

"How y'all doin'? Krystal, you're third on the ticket. The bouts start at seven and each one runs for about ten minutes, so I'll be callin' you at around eight-fifteen. Make sure you're at Door C and ready to go a few minutes before that. You need anything? Water?"

"We're good," Gary said.

Downtown moved on. Airwrecka finished Krystal's hair. Krystal had chosen a red one-piece leotard, nixing Gary's suggestion of a black dildo silhouette.

"I want to be classy."

At seven, Gary, Krystal, Airwrecka and Ludlow heard the PA system emit a preparatory squawk, and, like flies to sugar, were drawn to the arena where they took seats just off the main floor in shadow. The ring, four-feet off the floor, was surrounded by folding chairs laid out in rows. The theater, which could hold twelve hundred, held about one quarter that with boisterous families commandeering whole rows down front, two ringside long tables for sleazy announcers already slouched in their chairs drinking rum and tequila from paper bags, a couple of photographers roaming, and a sky cam attached to guy wires moving around over the stage.

Downtown held a cordless microphone.

"LADEEEEEEZ AND GENTLEMEN! WELCOME TO THE ROXY THEATER'S WEEKLY SERIES FEATURING THE GORGEOUS LADIES OF WRESTLING!"

Pause.

"¡DAMAS Y CABALLEROS! BIENVENIDOS A LA SERIE SEMANAL DEL TEATRO ROXY QUE OFRECE A LAS MARAVILLOSAS SEÑORAS DE LA LUCHA !"

"We have an exciting and dynamic card for you tonight,

climaxing with the rematch for which you've waited four-teen months, SWEET MOTHER OF MERCY VERSUS MANDY MANGLEBAUM!"

Again, in Spanish.

Screaming, clapping, stomping, vuvuzelas. People kept streaming in. It was a surprisingly diverse crowd with many Latinos, blacks, frat boys, whole families including infants. The concession in the lobby was mobbed.

Downtown gestured like a matador. "And now, our first bout of the evening in the women's one hundred and sixty-five-pound class,ZORRA versus TAWDRY AUDREY!"

The fighters entered from opposite corners. Zorra was a box-like Mexican with a fade leaving a thatch of red hair on top of her skull like a strip of Velcro. Tawdry Audrey was a rawboned hillbilly with freckles, her red hair incongruously done in corn rows like Krystal's. Zora's trainer and cut man were men, while Audrey's were women.

Krystal nudged Gary and pointed toward Audrey's trainer. "That's Pitbull Pauline. She used to be a Chick Fight champ."

Downtown gestured toward the stars. "OUR REFEREE TONIGHT..."

He looked around, feigning surprise.

"OUR REFEREE TONIGHT!"

A wide body in an XXXL striped sport shirt with the tails out bounded down the corridor and rolled into the ring.

"OUR REFEREE TONIGHT IS LEVON LEVIN!"

Levon Levin gestured the wrestlers to the center of the

ring where they flipped each other the bird. Levon stood between them, his hand in the air.

"And…"

Chop.

"Fight!"

Downtown got out of the ring faster than Bruce Lee.

53 | UNRETURNED BOOMERANG

As Downtown announced the winner, Ludlow took Krystal's hands in his and looked her in the eye. "Let's go backstage. You have to get your mind right before you enter the ring. I want to go over the fundamentals."

Gary, Krystal, and Ludlow went back down the corridor to an outside hall filled with fighters going through their routines. Some stretched. Some walked around muttering to themselves and throwing punches. Ludlow led them to an alcove with some institutional chairs.

"The first thing she's gonna do, she's gonna bull rush you. You let her hit you about four feet from the ropes and hurl yourself backwards as hard as you can, up off your feet, and use the ropes to spring you back toward her. Then you go down on your hands..."

"I go down on my hands, do a backwards spring, and seize her head between my legs. I rotate like a spinning alligator and bring her down."

"That's it! You got it?"

"I've practiced it with Ella, and Honey Badger's about the same size. I'm ready."

"Okay. Remember, she's gonna try to sharpen her bad girl credentials with a lot of huffin' and puffin' and maybe calling you names under her breath. Don't let her get under your skin."

"I can run the dozens same as her."

People streamed out of the arena during the break to purchase popcorn, hot dogs, soda and booze, from the full bar in the lobby. Money changed hands.

From inside, Downtown announced the next bout in a stentorian voice.

"Next on our ticket, two outstanding contenders in the one hundred and twenty-five-pound category! Hailing from Havana Cuba, a bronze winner in Women's Wrestling in the last Olympics in Fuji, Japan, fourteen and three since joining the Gorgeous Ladies of Wrestling...standing five four and weighing in at one hundred and twenty-five pounds, Los Glorious de los Los Arroyos, YANNICO THE PLANNICO ALDEMA!"

Chanting, screaming, cheering, vuvuzelas.

"And her opponent, hailing all the way from Minsk, Belarus, a former Girls' Night Out flyweight champion, two-time Olympian, standing five six and weighing one hundred twenty-four and a half pounds, THE MINX FROM MINSK, NOVA STEPOVA!"

Cheers, screams, flying shoes, applause, vuvuzelas.

Ludlow bade Krystal sit. "Five minutes of meditation."

Krystal sat in a folding chair while Gary stood behind her massaging her shoulders and arms. She felt like an athlete. Gary was stoked. Finally. After years of struggle, they would triumph, not through chicanery or luck, but through Krystal's honest and heartfelt skill as a wrestler!

She was an entertainer, like Stevie Ray Vaughan or Larry the Cable Guy! With her buzz, there was no telling how far they could go. Someday they'd look back at this and realize that his luck in winning the lottery had been a mere blip, a hiccup in life no more notable than a free haircut. Someday they would live in a magnificent new home and laugh! Maybe they'd even buy back the old place!

It was still on the market. People said it had bad juju.

Airwrecka whipped around the corner and zeroed in.

"Y'all better get your ass out there. The Minx just pile drove the Planet."

Wearing a towel with a hole cut in it, Gary behind her, hands on shoulders, Krystal waited at the entrance while patrons skittered hither and yon. Downtown stood on the ground talking to one of the reporters. Levon blew a whistle and pointed at his wrist.

Holding the wireless mic, Downtown stepped up and climbed into the ring, straightening his hat. He stood in the spotlight in the center of the ring for a minute, hands on hips, watching people flow back into their seats. Now the theater was half-full and there was an electricity in the air, a sense of anticipation.

Gary heard people whispering, "Black Dildo." He hoped the name change wouldn't hurt them.

"AND NOW! EL MOMENTO DEL DESTINO! THE MOMENT YOU'VE BEEN WAITING FOR! THE TOP SPOT IN OUR PRELIMINARIES! PRESENTING HER GORGEOUS LADIES OF WRESTLING DEBUT, FIGHT-ING AT THE CATCH WEIGHT OF ONE HUNDRED AND THIRTY-TWO POUNDS, AN OVERNIGHT SEN-SATION. HAILING FROM NEARBY TURPENTINE, THE ONE, THE ONLY STEELY DANIELLE!"

"BLACK DILDO! BLACK DILDO! BLACK DILDO!"

Gary craned his neck to see who was doing all the chanting and was surprised to see it was a mostly black section with Airwrecka on her feet leading them. They were joined by some leather-lunged rednecks and a contingent of goombahs in knit cotton shirts who looked like they'd been transplanted from Brooklyn.

Led by Ludlow, Krystal marched toward the ring, eyes straight ahead, Gary's hands on her shoulders. Halfway to the ring, Patrice and Floyd lunged to the corridor and threw out their hands for slaps. Eyes straight ahead, Krystal slapped dozens of palms. All three climbed into the ring where Krystal bounced around burning off nervous energy and acknowledging the crowd with upraised hands.

"AND HER OPPONENT, HAILING FROM JOHAN-NESBURG SOUTH AFRICA, FIGHTING AT THE CATCHWEIGHT OF ONE HUNDRED AND SEVEN-TY-TWO POUNDS, WITH A RECORD OF FOURTEEN

AND THREE, HONEY BADGER!"

Vuvuzelas sounded. Honey Badger trotted toward the ring accompanied by Eli and Martha Grieves. She climbed through the ropes and ran around the ring, stopped in front of Krystal, shook her finger in Krystal's face, and did two back over flips returning to her corner.

Levon called the combatants to the center to touch hands. They glared at one another and returned to their sides. Levon pointed to each in turn.

"ARE YOU READY? ARE YOU READY?"

The hand dropped! Honey Badger put her head down and launched herself like a howitzer so fast, Krystal didn't have time to get ready. Honey Badger bulled Krystal into the ropes, keeping her scalp in Krystal's gut, reached up, grabbed Krystal by the neck and threw her to the ground. Honey Badger stooped, picked Krystal up by the crotch and neck, held her overhead and did the propeller. Honey Badger rushed to the edge of the ring and threw Krystal to the crowd.

Krystal flew six feet through the air landing in the first row of spectators who caught her, going over backwards into the second row.

Downtown Brown leaped into the ring signaling the match was over with crossed hands. Gary and Ludlow rushed to where Krystal was struggling to get to her feet.

"WINNER BY UNRETURNED BOOMERANG, HONEY BADGER!" Downtown bellowed.

The crowd screamed, cheered, jeered, stomped its feet,

blew vuvuzelas. Several fights started. Gary and Ludlow each grabbed Krystal by an arm and whisked her out of the arena, down the hall into her dressing room, where they sat her in a chair and handed her a glass of water.

She took a sip. "What the fuck was that?"

"I think we got screwed," Ludlow said.

54 | THAT WENT WELL

During the intermission between the under card and the main event, Downtown appeared in the doorway to the dressing room with an expression of contrition.

"Are you okay?"

Krystal looked up angrily. "What the fuck was that?"

"I know, I know, that wasn't part of the agreement. Profoundest apologies. I really have no control over what the individual wrestlers do once they get in the ring. Are you okay?"

She clutched herself. "I'm fine."

Ludlow rounded on the promoter. "We took this bout in good faith. What are you going to do about it?"

Downtown spread his hands. "There's not much I can do. She was supposed to win anyway, and none of those moves are illegal. If I sanction her, she'll just go over to Girl Fight."

Gary held out his hand. "Pony up."

Downtown waved his hands. "Oh no. You got to wait 'til

we add up the receipts, just like everybody else. And don't go tellin' anybody I gave you half up front. Look. You want some advice?"

Gary crossed his arms.

Downtown pointed at Krystal. "You either learn how to wrassle or find another gig."

Krystal's jaw hit her knees. "You told me I was ready!"

"Yes, and you still have marquee value. In fact, you can use this to build up anticipation for your next bout."

"How about no more catch weights?" Ludlow said. "That girl had forty pounds on our girl."

"I didn't mean to cast aspersions on your training."

Ludlow got in his face. Ludlow only came up to Downtown's collarbone. "Well that's what you're doing. I've had three world champions!"

"Yeah, but not in a long time."

Gary got between them. "Where do we learn how to wrassle?"

"There's an old witchee woman lives back in the swamp, used to be quite the scrapper back in the day. Name's Madame Delilah. Tell her I sent you. I'll text you how to find her when I got a minute."

"Well how long is that gonna take?" Gary said. "We need money."

"It takes as long as it takes. You go see Madame Delilah. When she says you're ready, you're ready."

Gary and Ludlow waited out front while Krystal showered. They smoked cigs and watched life skate, ride, roll, hop, skip, jump and amble by. It was nine-thirty by the time Krystal came out and night had fallen, the street lit with flashing neon and cruising cars.

Gary put his arm around Krystal's shoulders. "How you feelin', baby?"

"Like I got rode hard and put away wet."

"Let's go home. We'll look into this Delilah thing tomorrow."

They cruised north on Twenty-Seven, Gary scrupulously obeying the speed limit. He was in enough trouble. A vehicle roared up on their ass, unable to pass due to southbound traffic. After a few minutes of tailgating, the vehicle turned on its brights. Gary stuck his arm out the window and gave them the finger.

The vehicle gyrated, hoking and faking dashes into the oncoming lane until at last the left lane opened-up and the vehicle busted loose, like a junkyard dog, roaring alongside. Gary was reaching for his pistol between the seats when the girl in the passenger seat hurled something, the car hunkered down, laid rubber, and shot ahead, pulling in front of the truck and slowing down so that Gary had to stand on the brakes.

The fish sailed past him and landed in Krystal's lap.

"EEEEYUUUUU!" she exclaimed, picking it up by the tail and hurling it out the window. It appeared to be a perch.

Gary laid on the gas. "All right, motherfucker."

Krystal grabbed a pen and wrote on an empty Burger King bag. "I got the license! Let it go! We ain't got no more bail money!"

Gary put the pedal to the metal. The F-150's V8 surged. The rear end skipped on a wet patch. But the vehicle in front had a bigger engine and roared off into the night with fingers flying from both windows.

"Asshole!" Gary snarled.

"Pricks!" Krystal snapped. She turned on the radio, roamed around, found a country station out of Fort Myers playing Patsy Cline's "Walkin' After Midnight". A sense of calm permeated the cab as Gary returned both hands to the wheel and hummed along.

Far ahead, red and blue lights lit up the corridor, strobing off the trees on either side. Gary slowed to a sensible fifty-five as they passed a FSHP car pulled up behind the fish flipper, a tall trooper in a Smokey hat at the driver's window.

"Yes!" Gary fist pumped. "There is a God!"

"Fishing without a license!" Krystal crowed. They slowed as they passed and smiled at the fuming driver.

They were driving south on Weldon Way between the trailer park and home when the headlights picked up two feral hogs tearing at something in the middle of the road. Gary blinked the high beams, honked the horn and shook his fist.

"GET THE FUCK OUT AND STAY THE FUCK OUT!"

The pigs glared back, sullen and defiant. Gary drove straight at them. At the last second, they split, one right, one left, and the truck rolled over something. Gary pulled off a few feet ahead, took the flash out of the console and walked back.

A dead goose lay in the dirt, torn in two by the hogs. Gary spotted buckshot holes in its breast. He got back in the car.

"Someone shot a goose."

"Those fuckin' geese are everywhere," Krystal said. "Stoppin' traffic, shittin' all over everything."

"No shit. If they tasted good, it wouldn't be a problem. But they taste like shit. You can shoot 'em, but you can't eat 'em."

As they pulled into the yard the clouds parted and a bright moon emerged, shimmering over the swamp. An alligator mooned itself on the dock.

"How the fuck did it get up there?"

Krystal swung down using the hand grip on the A pillar. "It hadda come up on the beach and get on the dock. Leave it be. It ain't botherin' anyone."

Gary thrust his hands in his pockets. "Fuckin' Wild Kingdom. This is why we have to make some money, so we can move outta this garbage pit."

"We made some money, and we still got a gator in the pool, remember?"

"Oh yeah."

Wearily, they made their way up the steps and into the trailer. Gary switched on the lights. Krystal headed for the bathroom, did a U-turn in the hall.

"It's back."

"Leave it be. It's the only critter around here workin' with us."

55 | MADAME DELILAH

Madame Delilah lived deep in the Big Cyprus Seminole Indian Reservation, at the end of a twelve-mile dirt road that wound among hummocks, cypress elbows, mangrove, and the odd oak. They passed gators sunning, ducks and geese gliding gracefully onto mirror surfaces, white cranes perched on one leg, and what may have been a monitor lizard.

They passed a bottle tree.

Thicker forest signaled denser, drier ground. They passed a tree holding a dozen hex signs made from colored Popsicle sticks. Through the mangrove they saw an odd, brown building and when they pulled around the last curve, they saw that it was a geodesic dome finished in brown shingles, twenty feet tall with a low conning tower jutting up and triangular windows and a satellite dish. A hand-painted sign nailed to a tree said WARNING—PRIVATE PROPERTY. Another said BEWARE OF DOG.

A pit bull appeared before them, bandy legged and barking. A wiry woman with a brown scarf wrapped around her head wearing a full-length brown, black, and turquoise African print came out the front door, hands on hips.

"Belial," she said in a whiskey-soaked contralto. "Hesh up now."

The dog immediately stopped barking, turned around and sat at its master's feet.

"Y'all come out. He won't bite."

Gary picked up the bottle of Buffalo Trace he'd brought, and he and Krystal got out of the truck. Delilah held open her front door.

"Come on in."

The big main room was dark and rich in texture, from Navajo throw rugs, wicker furniture, African masks carved from black wood, and a raven on a perch. A round table with a wood inlay of a pentagram sat in the center surrounded by four mismatched wooden chairs. Framed posters of Judas Priest and Edgar Winter, candles everywhere, and what looked like a shrunken head. The kitchenette included an oven, a sink, a refrigerator, and a rack full of clean dishes. A door led to a bathroom. An iron spiral staircase went up to a loft, from which a ladder led to the crow's nest. A ceiling fan hung from the loft. The room smelled of incense and patchouli.

Delilah motioned them to a brocade love seat while she sat in a Barcalounger facing them. Belial sat at her side, grinning with his tongue out.

"How did you know we were coming?" Gary said.

"Brown called. I like to bust a gut when you whacked that cop with that dildo."

Gary handed her the bourbon. "This is for you."

Delilah set it on a low table. "Thank you kindly. Got any money?"

"Fuck no. I had some, but I blew it."

"I get twenty-five per cent of your next five wins."

Gary looked at Krystal. Krystal nodded.

Delilah sat forward, bony elbows on her knees. "How'd you run through five mil so fast?"

Gary shrugged.

"Okay, here's the deal. You leave girl here with me. She can have Sundays off. We start training tomorrow. But I gotta warn you, there's a lot more unscripted shit goes on in Gorgeous Ladies of Wrestling than some other sanctioning bodies."

"Like what?" Gary said.

"Dirty fighting. Low blows. I will teach you about those."

"Tell me about your qualifications," Gary said.

Delilah leaned back and looked down her nose. "You're here, aren'tcha?"

"Yes, we are. Downtown Brown recommended you, but he didn't say why."

"I'm the seventh daughter of a seventh daughter. My grandfather, Nathan Knute Krabong, wrestled on the Sepia Circuit back in the fifties. He started teachin' me when I was knee-high to a grasshopper. I used to wrestle with the boys, and let me tell you, those boys could wrestle. By the time

I was fifteen, wasn't a boy in the tribe would take me on. Too humiliatin'. I'm familiar with all the wrestling moves. I focus on conditioning, acrobatics, and sparring. I throw in a little Southern Spider Style."

"What's that?" Krystal asked.

"Type of kung fu from Mississippi. Also gonna teach you how to catch and prepare game."

"I gave her an iguana and she didn't know what to do with it," Gary said.

"Don't you worry none about that. I know how to skin an iguana, and any other critter you care to name. Don't eat gator. Don't like it. Sometimes I gotta put a couple down they get too aggressive." She put a hand on Belial's head.

"This here dog, he brings home enough game for both of us. He's pure hell on waterfowl and nutria. Once he brought me a python, but I threw it back."

"Where'm I gonna sleep?" Krystal said.

Delilah pointed to a fold out futon sofa. "Don't worry none about Belial. He sleeps with me."

"How does he get up in the loft?"

Delilah pointed at Belial. "Where's your squeaky toy? Get your squeaky toy!"

Belial loped up the spiraling staircase and ducked out of sight, returning an instant later to stand triumphantly with some kind of furry toy in his mouth.

"SQUEAK! SQUEAK!"

"Good boy! Come on down."

Belial came down slower than he'd gone up, holding a toy

beaver in his jaws.

"Well do we need a contract or somethin'?" Gary said.

Delilah pointed two fingers at him. "You play straight with me I'll play straight with you. You don't, you'll wish you had."

"You ever put a hex on someone?" Krystal said.

"Oh honey, don't let me commence!"

"Can people, like, pay you to put a hex on someone?"

"It's been known to happen. Ain't got no complaints, neither."

"Who you wanna hex?" Gary said.

"Honey Badger."

"That was a fucking mismatch. We never should have agreed to that. She had forty pounds on you!"

Delilah shook her head. "That's on Downtown's head. He sent me the video."

Gary stood. "Well I'll get your overnighter."

Belial followed him as Gary walked to the truck, grabbed Krystal's bag from behind the front seat and went back in.

Krystal got up. "I'll walk you out."

They stood by the truck hugging.

"Don't you worry about me. I'm up for this!"

"I don't worry about you, baby doll. I worry how ahmina get through these next couple of weeks without you."

"You'll manage."

They kissed. Gary got in the truck, did a Y turn and headed back up the long dirt road which wound serpentine around sinkholes and hummocks. As he rounded a corner, he paused for a line of Canadian geese, like elderly tourists crossing the road. The weeds erupted and a gator scrambled out of the muck, snapping its jaws on the lead goose, sending the rest honking and running down the road, taking flight.

Gary stepped out of the truck and shook his fist. "THAT'S RIGHT! RUN! FLY BACK TO CANADA, YOU HOSERS!"

56 | SAMSON

Wearing a one-piece yellow and black jumpsuit from Game of Death, Delilah hung upside down from her knees ten feet above the marshy ground while Krystal, wearing gray sweats and over the ankle sneakers watched from below. Delilah swung her torso up, gripped the branch between her legs and pulled herself up to a sitting position.

"Been climbin' trees all my life. Feel real comfortable up here. Now watch." With surprising ease, Delilah stood, hanging on to an overhead branch for support. "You start that spin the instant you launch. Don't hesitate."

She leaped into the air, tucking her head, drawing in her knees and putting her arms around them, unwinding just in time to land on her feet.

"Holy shit," Krystal said. "I hope you don't expect me to do that?"

Delilah picked up her backpack, slipped it on, and gestured at the tree. "Get on up there."

"That's ten feet off the ground! The ring posts are only five feet!"

Delilah pointed. Krystal leaped to grab a handful of oak six feet off the ground and pulled herself up until she clung to the tree on the branch vacated by Delilah. She looked down.

"You expect me to somersault off this tree? Are you nuts?"

"It's not as difficult as it looks, and the ground is very marshy. Didn't you say you were a gymnast?"

"Yeah, but that was on a mat!"

"Did you do aerial somersaults from a running start?"

"Yeah. Maybe I should try doing that again before I try it from here."

"That tree provides motivation! You crouch and leap up, spinning as you go, tuck your knees, put your hands around them. When it's time to unfurl you'll know. It all happens very fast." She clapped her hands twice. "BAM BAM!"

Krystal crouched on the branch, one hand on the trunk, heart in mouth.

"Leap, tuck and roll!" Delilah commanded. "Now!"

Krystal jumped forward off the branch, tucked her head, throwing her whole body into the turn, and immediately extended her legs. To her surprise, she landed on her feet. She didn't even stagger.

"Wow!" she said.

Delilah applauded. "Now that you know you can do it you can do it off a ring post and plant your feet on your opponent's chest. Come on let's run."

Krystal followed Delilah down the rolling game trail, occasionally stepping in water that splashed up over her ankles. The weather was hot and humid, but their motion kept the mosquitos at bay. Delilah led them in a mile loop that ended up back at the house.

Delilah pointed at her outdoor shower fed by a fifty-gallon drum strapped to a tree.

"Shower. Then we'll eat. Then you'll meet Schneider."

"Who's Schneider?"

"Schneider is your Kung Fu instructor."

When Krystal came out wearing blue jeans and an Explorers Club T-shirt, Delilah was frying bacon in a cast iron skillet. They sat at the pentagram table, eating bacon, cornbread, oranges and peanuts. Krystal did the dishes, stacking them neatly in the wood rack.

"Okay," Delilah said. "Let's go meet your Kung Fu instructor."

Krystal followed Delilah out the front door. Delilah crouched at the base of her home, held her hand out palm up next to a tiny hole and whistled.

Nothing happened. Delilah whistled again. Two minute black prongs appeared, followed by a two-inch wolf spider.

"Good morning Schneider! How are you today?"

Schneider dutifully crawled onto Delilah's hand, standing on its back four legs and stretching the front four like a cheerleader. Delilah deposited Schneider on a chainsawed mangrove stump.

"Watch."

At first the spider was still, but then it began to move in what looked like an elaborate dance, turning to face the four corners of the earth, its forelegs describing arabesques. Delilah straightened and keeping her eyes on the spider, followed along, turning with a dancer's grace, her arms emulating Schneider's. She looked at Krystal.

Krystal took her place opposite Delilah and they flowed around the stump performing an intricate spider kata.

"Hang on," Delilah said and veered off, returning a minute later holding a cricket between thumb and forefinger. She knelt, held the squirming cricket where Schneider could see it, then tossed it to him. Schneider seized and pounced, holding it down with while its mandibles attacked the cricket's eyes.

"You see how it gets on top and immobilizes its prey?"

"I only got four limbs."

"Doesn't matter. That's how you do it."

"When do I get to practice this shit with a sparring partner?"

Delilah rocked back on her heels with a shit-eating grin.

"Uh oh," Krystal said.

"It's time for you to meet Samson."

"Who's Samson?"

"He's your sparring partner."

Krystal had not seen or heard from another human being since Gary left yesterday, and there were no dwellings anywhere near the dome.

"Is Samson coming over?"

"No, we'll go to Samson. Let's get some water. It's a

hike."

Fifteen minutes later they were tramping through the everglades, Delilah pointing out psilocybin, used in native rituals, and boletes, puffballs, chanterelles, indigo milk-caps and ganodermas, sandhill cranes, nutria, dragonflies, and gators.

She paused by a swampy inlet, pointing to what looked like an army helmet poking up out of some weeds. "Here's one of them nasty snapping turtles, got a neck like a snake. Don't go near 'em."

Onward, until Krystal stopped to drain her bottle of water, her clothes already soaked through. "Where does Samson live? On a boat?"

"We're almost there. Please don't make any comments about his appearance. He's very sensitive."

"Too sensitive to live among people."

"A lot of people that way. I count myself among them."

"Well I reckon you're right. Me and Gary are perfectly happy living off by ourselves in a trailer without no noisy neighbors."

Delilah stopped in a natural clearing surrounded by mangrove, like a crown. "This is where Samson lives. Don't make any sudden moves. Don't worry about Samson. Samson will not hurt you."

"What kind of person lives out here without a house?"

"Oh, Samson's not a person."

Delilah wolf whistled. Krystal heard some snorting and shuffling, and a brown bear shuffled into the clearing.

"You have got to be shitting me?" Krystal said, trying to remain calm.

"Samson won't hurt you. Samson is a gentle bear."

"It's a fucking wild animal, Delilah!"

"Please keep your voice down. Samson and I have rolled many times. Samson taught Ella the Propella how to roll. Now Samson will teach you."

"What about its claws?"

"I will give you ten dollars for every cut Samson inflicts. And please don't refer to him as an it."

Krystal laughed. "All right. Tell me what to do."

"Bend over in a wrestler's crouch, smile, and motion for Samson to come to you."

Krystal did as she was told. Snorting, Samson shuffled sideways causing Krystal to do the same. They circled each other until Delilah sharply clapped her hands.

Samson lunged forward, butted Krystal in the gut knocking her down, and sat on her, forepaws extended in triumph. The bear weighed over two hundred pounds. Krystal lay on her back, chuffing for air, trying to boost him off.

"Now what?" she said.

Delilah clapped her hands on whistled, motioning for Samson to come toward her. The bear rose and lumbered forward. Delilah handed it something out of her pocket.

"He likes Cheetos."

Krystal picked herself up. "And what am I supposed to learn from that?"

Delilah laughed. "Next time he comes at you, you grab the fur on both shoulders and rotate clockwise, pivoting on your left foot and moving your right foot to nine o'clock."

"He weighs two hundred pounds."

"Get low. The lower your center of gravity, the more force you generate."

Krystal put her hands on her hips. "I've watched pro wrestling. It's all so patently fake. Why don't we just choreograph the fights ahead of time like everybody else?"

"How'd that work with Honey Badger? She used you to score easy points. That bout was supposed to go at least five minutes.

"The Gorgeous Ladies of Wrestling is not well refereed. There's a reason it hangs on to the lower rungs. Now I got nothin' against Downtown. He done alright by me. And bringing you to my door shows me he wants you to win. So, from now on, you got to stipulate you ain't fightin' above your weight. I'd like to put a clause in the contract that says if one of the fighters refuses to abide by the agreed-upon choreography, she'll forfeit the match. But I can't do that. Until you showed up, I had no dog in this fight."

"So, what's next? Anacondas? Gators? An Everglades puma?"

"No. But let's you and me practice that move you're gonna use against Samson."

"If I throw him to the ground, won't he get angry?"

"Laws, no. Samson's just a good ol' bear! Ain't that right, Samson, sweety?"

She dug in her pocket and pulled out a handful of Cheetos. Samson happily munched.

"Now let's you and me try it. What do you weigh, one-thirty? I go about one forty-five, and I ain't carrying any fat. You remember what I told you?"

"I remember."

They faced off in the clearing. Samson sat and watched, munching Cheetos. Delilah rushed arms forward to grab Krystal, who ducked, grabbing Delilah on both shoulders, pivoted clockwise and sweeping Delilah to the spongy ground where she executed a nifty somersault and came up on her feet.

"You got it. Ready to try Samson?"

Krystal made the gimme sign. "Bring it on!"

Delilah motioned Samson to his feet. Krystal wondered if they had some kind of telepathic or magical connection. The woman was a witch, after all. Nobody called her a witch, but what else do you call a woman who communes with spiders and bears? Krystal had often played the witch as a child with her sisters and cousins.

Samson walked on his hind legs to the center of the clearing and faced Krystal, who motioned him forward. Samson sat down.

Delilah stood in front of him. "Come on, big guy. On your feet." She made rising gestures. Finally, she held a Cheeto over Samson's head and he rose. Delilah walked behind Krystal and held the Cheetos bag overhead.

"COME ON SAMSON LET'S GO!" she shouted, startling Krystal, who almost lost her concentration. Samson lumbered forward. Krystal went low, gripped the bear by the fur on both shoulders, and swung him in a clockwise direction. Samson swatted her away with the back of his left forepaw like she was a fly, seized the Cheetos bag from Delilah, sat down and tore it apart.

Krystal landed on her ass.

"You okay?" Delilah said.

"What else you got?"

Delilah helped her up. "Maybe you should just train with me instead of Samson."

"That would be good. Not that I don't like Samson. He's a hell of a bear. He's the greatest bear I've ever met, and he's got pretty good manners, for a bear."

Samson belched loudly.

"You're not supposed to eat the bag!" Delilah said. "All right. Let's head back to the house. That's enough for the day."

Delilah tossed Krystal a bottled water from her back-pack. They headed back down the trail with Delilah in the lead. Paths led through the swamp like a bowl of spaghetti dumped on the floor. Without Delilah, Krystal would have been lost.

After about an hour, Krystal caught a glimpse of the odd dome through the trees.

"Almost there," Delilah said.

As they entered a dense patch of overhanging mangrove and cypress, two feral pigs emerged from the forest on op-posite sides of the trail and turned to face them, malice in their mean little eyes.

Krystal put her hands on her hips. "Huh! Don't they just look like two fuckin' muggers waiting for some marks?"

"Yeah. The way they both stepped out from opposite sides. That's very unusual."

The hogs pawed and snorted, sporting two-inch tusks.

"What are we gonna do? You got a gun?"

Delilah swung off her backpack and reached inside. "Of course, I've got a gun."

Krystal stared in surprise at a black Colt .45 1911. "What the fuck is that?"

Delilah lifted her hand just enough to reveal the Duke's profile inlaid in gold on the barrel. "This here's my John Wayne commemorative pistol. Look out. Here they come."

The hogs rushed.

"Cover your ears."

Krystal barely had time to slap her palms to her head

before John Wayne roared. The first hog stumbled and went down in a heap. The second veered off into the undergrowth and vamoosed. Krystal cautiously approached the dead hog.

"Ho shit! You got it right between the eyes!"

"I been practicin'," Delilah said. "Let's grab that sumbitch and see what it tastes like."

58 | AN EXCITING CONTEST

Belmont Pest Control was parked in the driveway of a stucco ranch-style house in Belle Glade. The house was completely enclosed in a giant translucent plastic bag patched with duct tape, a five-inch pleated tube running from a nozzle at its base by the front door to the back of Floyd's truck, which faced the street.

It was two o'clock on a sunny afternoon. The boys had been wrapping the house in plastic since eight in the morning and they were soaked with sweat. They had stripped off their hazmat suits and were down to ragged jeans and tank tops, both wearing sunglasses, an old blue bandanna wrapped around Gary's head.

"All I think about is money," he said.

"You should get on one of those game shows, like Jeopardy or something."

"Yeah, right. First, you gotta be in California. Then, you gotta know the producer or something. Then they get a kickback."

"Fuck they do."

"Fuck they don't. Plus which, I'm supposed to know who played third base for the nineteen forty-nine Pittsburgh Pirates or something. I might as well play the slots at Hallandale. I got to be my own boss. There's got to be some way I can get some savvy dude to fork over a few mil for me to start my house suspenders program."

Floyd lit a heater, inhaled and exhaled through his nose. "There ya go. Shark Tank."

"Fuck izzat?"

"It's a show where entrepreneurs go on and try to pitch their companies to these millionaires. 'Course they don't come in empty handed. Whatever it is they're selling, some gizmo or a new style shoe, they got that with 0'em. They got finished product."

"I got finished product! Just look at my house."

"Yeah, look at it."

Gary leaned against the van and lit a cigarette. His house wasn't exactly House Beautiful. Esthetically, it had its draw backs. But any house would look a little odd the first time you fixed the suspenders. What he needed was graphic evidence that it worked. What he needed was a hurricane. Set up a video cam and hope for the best. But where could he set a video cam where it wouldn't be destroyed? He imagined a concrete bunker, a pillbox with a mailbox, and in the mailbox, the video cam aimed at the house.

Gary had no intention of testing his invention with him

and Krystal in the house. Hell no. They'd bug out and hope for the best.

"I need video," he said, tossing his cig to the drive and stepping on it.

"You need a lot more than that. Alright, ahmina start the blower. Open the valves."

Gary climbed into the truck and opened the valves on four fat greet cylinders filled with formaldehyde and dazomet, each marked with a yellow bio-hazard symbol.

Floyd gripped the pull cord on a lawnmower engine that had been converted into a blower. The blower roared to life contributing its cloud to ozone depletion, and the insect hungry gas flowed through the tube into the tented house. As the gas reached the house, the giant tent puffed out. Floyd kept a close eye on the tank gauges and the tent, and when the tent looked like it was about to take to the air, he cut the blower.

"Now we wait," he said.

They leaned against the side of the truck watching the house. An alligator launched itself through the living room picture window, shattering glass and bouncing off the interior of the tent. The alligator leaped up, seized the plastic in its jaws, and ripped it asunder. The alligator flopped out of the jagged hole and high-tailed it for the canal in back.

Floyd looked at Gary. "Don't that beat all?"

"Well are we gonna have to patch that shit? I mean, is it gonna take?"

"Yeah. Shut off the valves. Grab that roll of plastic and

the duct tape. Better suit up, too. There'll be gas slipping out."

Gary put on leather gloves and the gas mask. To hell with the hazmat suit. It was too hot. The rip was about a yard long. Floyd used shears to cut a big plastic oval and held it in place while Gary secured it at twelve, three, six, and nine. Once it was firmly in place, they worked their way around the perimeter sealing it all up. The tent had deflated so that they had to hold the thick plastic from beneath to provide a firm backdrop on which to press the tape.

They retreated to the truck, started the blower, and watched the tent billow. A tiny black bat escaped from the top like a cinder. More bats followed until a dozen had taken flight. Four escaped behind them but were overcome with fumes, fell to the tent and slid off into the front yard.

"Izzat gonna put a cramp in it?" Gary said.

"Naw. Hole's too small. We just keep pumpin' the gas until it runs out, should kill every termite, palmetto bug and rat in the house."

"They got rats?"

"They had a fuckin' alligator. Why not rats?"

"Did you know that gator was in there?"

"Surprised me, hoss. Shouldn't. Shit I seen. One place had a fucking Burmese python in the bathroom."

"I know the feeling."

"Which reminds me. You want some fast cash, some billionaire's offering a lot of money to whoever catches the biggest python in this year's python hunt."

"For reals?"

"For sure. But what the fuck do you know about catching pythons?"

"I'm a hunter. You think I can't bag a python? I seen 'em out in the swamp behind the trailer."

"Yeah, but this bird wants the biggest python."

Gary pulled out his phone, which he could barely operate. "Okay, okay. Lemme look this up."

He searched for python hunt and billionaire offers reward for biggest python. First up was an item from the Miami Herald: THE HUNT IS ON! Fonebone CEO Orin Houtkooper of Palm Beach is offering $100,000 to whoever brings in the biggest snake in this year's annual Python Elimination Program. "Invasive species are killing the Glades," Houtkooper said. "STAYBAK is committed to preserving the environment. Besides. I want to hang it on my wall."

Next was a public service announcement:

The South Florida Water Management District Governing Board is taking aggressive action to protect the Everglades and eliminate invasive pythons from its public lands. Starting in March 2017, the Python Elimination Program incentivizes a limited number of public-spirited individuals to humanely euthanize these destructive snakes, which have become an apex predator in the Everglades. The program provides access to python removal agents on designated SFWMD lands in Miami-Dade, Broward, Collier and Palm Beach counties.

"I sent this shit to Krystal. She'll get it printed out at the FedEx."

"Where she at?"

"Off training the swamp with some witchee woman."

Floyd waggled his eyebrows. "How's that?"

"Oh yeah. She got bum rushed in her first bout so Downtown Brown hooked us up with this old witchee woman in the swamp, trains wrestlers."

"You got to be shittin' me."

"I don't make this shit up, hoss. It just finds me. You wanna help me catch this python? I'll split the reward money."

"What python?"

"The world's biggest python. I seen it out in the swamp behind my place. Motherfucker's the size of a storm drain."

"Yeah, all right."

59 | LO, THE MIGHTY HUNTER

Gary purchased thirty pounds of chum from Alfred's Bait in Turpentine and hauled it out to the end of his pier in two five-gallon plastic buckets. He loaded his pistol with dum-dums he'd made himself with a buck knife and sat on the spongy old sofa smoking a cig, waiting for Floyd to arrive. He wasn't about to tackle that python by himself. No sir.

The sofa was damp from rain and smelled like a dead rat, and in fact, Gary figured it had some dead rats in it, but he wasn't ready to dump it. Not yet. Usually he covered it with a tarp during rain, but he'd forgot the last couple of times, so he just laid the folded tarp on the seat so the moisture wouldn't seep up into his pants. One hundred thou would go a long way toward alleviating his problems. He'd still be in debt, but he wouldn't have creditors breathing down his neck like he did now.

He wished he'd paid cash for a new truck when he had the money, but no. He had to buy that Lambo, and the insurance wouldn't pay off because they said he caused the fire.

Well maybe.

Nothin' against hard work. Gary worked like a dog. Always had. But with his mind, he should be far ahead in the game at this point. Never mind the lottery. That was a fluke, unlikely to be repeated. If only he'd earmarked money for House Suspenders!

Gary slapped himself hard. He slapped himself again.

"Boy, you a fuckin' idiot! When you going to get your hands on that kind of cash again?"

Reduced to hunting pythons for a lousy six-figure pay off. Well it was a start. A year ago, he couldn't wrap his mind around a hundred thousand dollars. He made so little he didn't even bother to file for taxes, another reason the IRS was on his ass.

Floyd's van crunched into the yard and Floyd got out wearing fisherman's shorts, flip-flops, a Dolphins jersey and a fisherman's vest. An ugly purple scar covered the inside of his left calf. He pulled a backpack and a shotgun case out of the truck and walked to the end of the pier, creaking with every step.

Floyd set down the shotgun, put his hands on his hips and surveyed the grassy swamp, a series of green pools interspersed with reeds, mangrove, cattails, and kudzu, the Creeping Charlie From Hell, that covered the state like a furze of green fungus.

"So what, we're just gonna toss chum in the water and that'll make this snake appear?"

"It's a fucking science, Floyd! I've seen that snake. It hangs out rightchere, in this backwater. Snakes smell with their tongues. I looked it up! One whiff of this shit and that big boy'll come runnin'. Then we just drill it through the head and collect our money."

"Boy, you got it all figured out."

"I'm just gettin' started."

Floyd pulled a fat doobie out of his vest and lit up, exhaling mightily and passing the joint to Gary. Floyd sat, took his Remington Twelve Gauge out of the leather case and reached for a box of shells. One by one, he inserted the shells in the magazine. Gary took out his magnum, opened the cylinder to make sure it was fully loaded, and flipped it shut. Standing, he jammed the gun in the back of his belt, picked up a metal soup tureen, scooped chum and cast it into the water in a wide arc, like a painting chimpanzee.

Floyd headed back to the truck and returned with a boom box and a six pack of Funky Buddha, wrestled two out of the plastic yoke, popped one and passed it to Gary.

"Threw about three gallons out. Now we wait."

They sat back on the reeking, squeaking sofa and quaffed beer. Mosquitos attacked. Deep in the swamp, loons howled. The sun beat hard on the backs of their necks. Floyd popped open the cassette hatch on the boom box and slipped in a cassette.

Hank Williams sang "Your Cheatin' Heart."

"That's the real deal, right there," Gary said.

"Hank Fuckin' Williams. Accept no substitutes."

"This shit they call country today, how does rap make it country?"

"Don't get me started."

"Taylor Swift..."

"She's not country."

"Dierks Bentley..."

"Not country."

"The Dixie Chicks..."

"Fuck 'em."

A delta of ripples headed their way in the glassy water.

Gary hefted his pistol. "Oh oh. Here it comes."

Floyd pulled down on the bill of his cap. "Where?"

Gary pointed. They watched the ripples intently until fifty feet from the pier it stopped.

"You sure that's a snake?" Floyd said. "Could be a gator."

"Could be."

The boys waited in breathless anticipation. A big bird glided in and cruised gracefully on its belly for several feet.

"Fuck izzat?" Gary said.

"That's a big bird. A big fucking bird."

"Looks like some kind of crane."

The gator rose up chomped the big bird at the neck, dragging it under.

Floyd brought the Remington to his shoulder. "Kill! Kill the sumbitch!'

The boys unloaded a mighty fusillade. The gator rolled and writhed, the bird in its jaws. After what seemed like an eternity but had only been nine seconds, gator and bird lay locked in death's embrace in a spreading circle of blood. Soon, other deltas appeared heading their way.

"Great," Gary groused. "A fucking gator con."

Floyd grabbed a boat pole off the swamp boat, snugged tight to one side against old tires. "I'll go drag it in. Like to see what the fuck it was."

"Shit, Floyd, you'll get your ass chomped in two! Look at them sumbitches! Hold on. We'll take the boat."

Untying the swamp boat, they poled out fifty feet where Floyd roped in the bodies. Wearing heavy leather gloves, they rolled the dead gator and its giant prey into the boat.

"Some kind of crane. Big fucker."

As they were tying up, red and blue lights flickered off the underside of the old oak and mangrove lining Gary's property.

Gary tied up and got on the pier. Hands on hips, he looked skyward.

"What?" he demanded of the gods.

Sheriff Ralph Hunnicutt approached in Smokey hat and amber aviators, followed by a gangly deputy.

Sheriff Hunnicutt walked up to Gary on the pier. "Gary, what the fuck you doin'? I got people calling me from the trailer park talking about gang warfare."

"I'm real sorry about that, Sheriff. We was just pluggin' a gator."

"Gary, you know you need a license to hunt gators. Do you have a license?"

"Well I do somewhere. Can I get back to you on that?"

"Did you plug a gator?"

"Yeah."

"Where is it?"

Gary led the way back to the boat where Floyd was tying up the other end. Sheriff Hunnicutt stared at the mess of scales and feathers swimming in blood shaking his head and grunting, "Mm, mm, mm."

"What?" Gary said. "I suppose I need a permit for that bird too."

"Gary, do you know what that is?"

"Hell, no."

"That's a whooping crane. There are less than a thousand left. That there's a federal crime."

"Fuck!" Gary howled to a heedless god.

"Boy howdy," Gary said gazing into the sunset. "I got the Duba Curse."

"What's killin' that bird gonna cost?" Floyd said.

"Don't know. Sheriff says he'll contact the Department of Fish and Wildlife. I didn't even kill that bird. Fuckin' gator killed it."

"Least he didn't take our guns."

"How'm I gonna get seed money for House Suspenders when all I do is fuck up?"

"Don't let it get you down. We all have our bad days. Other day I was out ridin' my Fat Bob, pulled into an S&S to get some duct tape and beef jerky, I set the side stand and get off. Only it's so fuckin' hot, the tarmac's like taffy and the kickstand just sinks and the Fat Bob goes over. So, I get around, stoop down with my ass to the bike, and hoist it back up, only I hoist too far, and it goes down on the other side. So, I go around to that side and I hoist it up and I'm wearing shorts, and the straight pipes burn the fuck out of my calf! If a car fulla nuns hadn't pulled in, I'd probably still be there flippin' it from one side to the other."

"What about the nuns?"

"They pull in, three nuns in a run-down Dodge, see me gruntin', and hung on to the bike until I could push it over onto hard concrete. They was on an ice tea run. So, I get my duct tape and jerky and go to the ER. They tell me there ain't much they can do."

"How's the Fat Bob?"

"Got a few scratches, nothin' I can't handle."

"You ever eat iguana?"

"Nope. Why?"

"I'm thinkin' the first person opens a grilled iguana franchise is gonna clean up."

"Why?"

"Well I had some and it was good, and this kid with the cart says it's a main food of people in the Caribbean. Eat it all the time. There's hundreds of thousands of people here from the Dominican Republic and I don't know what all, love iguana and would snap it right up."

"I'll tell ya what might be better."

Gary gazed at the setting sun through mosquitos. He wore a yellow repellant bracelet which made no difference. "What could possibly be better than iguana?"

"Nutria."

"Huh?"

"Nutria. They're big fat water rats and there's already a

shitload of restaurants in Louisiana got 'em on the menu."

"You're shittin' me?"

"Nope. Russia? They can't get enough nutria. People are gettin' rich shipping nutria to Russia."

"Are those those fat fuckin' rodents that look like were-hamsters?"

"Yeah."

Gary pulled out his phone and searched for nutria. They looked like beaver with curved orange teeth that grossed him out. "Don't look too bad 'cept for the teeth."

"Yeah, you don't serve 'em with the head. You hide that meat 'neath a sauce."

Gary set his phone on the seat. "Shit. They're all over the place. But they're like rats. Who wants to eat rat?"

Floyd pulled out a fat doobie. "They're rodents, they're not rats. Rabbits are rodents. Ever eat rabbit?"

"Shit, yeah."

"Well there ya go. They call it hassenpfeffer so it don't sound like rabbit. And they remove the ears. Somebody didn't tell you it was rabbit you'd think it was some respectable game like raccoon or possum."

"You ever eat nutria?"

"No, but I've thought about it."

Floyd lit the joint, inhaled, exhaled into a mosquito battalion. They fell in droves. Others flew around erratically smashing into each other. He passed the joint to Gary.

"A marijuana-based insect repellant," Gary said.

"Ya think?"

"Watch."

Gary cruelly targeted a dense cloud of bloodsuckers, dispersing them like a cucumber tossed into a box of cats.

"Yeah, but then you're wasting good smoke on bugs."

"Not if you just inhale, and then exhale. It serves two purposes."

Gary stoked that joint and let fly.

"They're too dumb to know this ain't good for 'em."

Gary handed the joint back to Floyd. "You got a point. We just keep gettin' higher and the mosquitos just keep comin' back. There's more of them than there are of us. We could smoke dope all day and not make a dent in the mosquito population."

Floyd reached down into his pants and scratched his balls. "Neither one of us is gonna get rich gassin' palmetto bugs, that's for sure."

"Seems like wildlife got it in for me, startin' with that raccoon you shot."

"What you mean?"

"Think about it. I get the new place and that fuckin' 'gator lands in my pool. Next thing I know, the swamp's on fire and they're finin' me for shooting a gator and setting fire to the swamp. Next morning, feral hogs invade my house. Now I got this whooping crane hangin' around my neck like an albatross."

"They're fuckin' endangered, too."

"Hell. I wouldn't be surprised if an albatross shit on my head right now."

They gazed westward into the fading light, two old friends, each lost in their own thoughts. Six Canadian geese glided in and coasted on the mirror-smooth water. Gators plunked into the water heading their way, but the geese were wise and took off in a flapping, honking dance.

A tendril of smoke rose from a corner of the old sofa.

Gary held out his hand. "Where's the doobie?"

Floyd snapped out of his reverie and looked around. "Do you smell something burning?"

The sofa erupted in flame, sending its occupants flapping and honking to the end of the pier.

"You moron!" Gary said. "You dropped the fuckin' joint in the sofa!"

"I guess it ain't too wet to burn."

"Come on. We gotta boost it into the water before it sets the dock on fire."

They went to the side that wasn't engulfed in flames, got down, and shoved the burning sofa over the edge. The burning side hit the water with a hiss, leaving the other side on the pier. The water was only two feet deep.

"For fuck's sake," Gary said, stooping and picking up the end. He cake-walked to the edge of the pier and threw it in.

Floyd pointed. "Dude. Is that your phone?"

"Fuck!" Gary jumped into the water, reached for his phone, and went down. Floyd watched in fascination as Gary thrashed about and rose, triumphantly raising his right fist, clutching a fat nutria.

"Got one!"

61 | CASSOWARY

Friday night and crowds thronged Bustillo Boulevard in Little Havana, lined up outside the Comedy Club and the Roxy Theater. The Roxy's line was four times the size of the Comedy Club's because the Roxy was a much larger venue and tonight was an eagerly anticipated bout, pitting the much-hyped Steely Danielle versus the twelve and four former Chick Fight champion Cassowary.

After Danielle's ignominious defeat at the hands of the Honey Badger, many pundits observed that it had been a travesty throwing a novice in against a seasoned competitor who outweighed her by forty pounds. This time the opponents were more evenly matched. They weren't even the headliners.

The old-fashioned marquee jutting out over the sidewalk said

GORGEOUS LADIES OF WRESTLING PRESENTS
ALICE "OCELOT" CELINE VS. LA CHUPACABRA
HEDDA HEADFAKE VS. THE GIANT RAT OF SUMATRA
CASSOWARY VS. STEELY DANIELLE

Low riders, Ubers, choppers and beaters cruised the four-lane boulevard, elbows and arms hanging out. Papi chulos wolf-whistled women and deployed pick-up lines.

"Hey, little mama! Lookin' for a good time?"

"Hey, girl! You must be a brick 'cuz you hit my heart hard!"

"Hey, girl! Your name must be Coca Cola, because you're soda-licious!"

"Somebody call the cops. It's got to be illegal to look that good."

A lowered '79 Chevy slowed to the curb outside the Roxy. A chulo leaned outside the shotgun seat and called to a tall woman in a towering platinum beehive and three-inch heels, "Girl, you are a skyscraper and I want to climb you!"

Patrice, wearing Ralph Lauren jeans and a sleeveless sequined silver top, stepped out of line, wig bobbling as she leaned over the car.

"I'd crush you like an insect," she said in a throaty contralto.

The chulo slapped the side of the car. "Drive! Drive!"

Patrice and Alfredo, his companion for the evening, a proper Mexican gentleman in a rust-colored suit and string tie, had barely settled into their seats in the fourth row when

Downtown Brown climbed into the ring, holding a wireless mic.

"LADEEEZ AND GENTLEMEN! SENORS Y SENO-RITAS! WELCOME TO FRIDAY NIGHT WRESTLING AT THE ROXY! TONIGHT'S OUTSTANDING CARD CULMINATES IN A RUBBER MATCH BETWEEN THE OCELOT AND CHUPACABRA!"

The crowd of four hundred, with more streaming in, erupted and shouts, whoops, vuvuzelas, and whistles.

Gary, Krystal, Kudlow, Delilah and Airwrecka could hear Downtown through the walls. Two hours earlier, Krystal and Cassowary had worked out their routine in slo mo, and medium mo. Krystal would still lose, but this time she would look much better doing it, would demand a rematch which Cassowary would instantly grant. Cassowary, whose real name was Meg Wakia, was a dark-skinned Australian, her brown black hair sculpted into a cassowary cap making her resemble an Indian cabinet minister. Cassowary stood five feet six inches tall and weighed one hundred and thirty pounds.

Gary had brought a black nylon backpack which he treated with reverence.

"TONIGHT, WE HAVE A TRULY INTERNATIONAL CARD! HOOCHIE MAMA VERSUS COOTCHIE CUTIE! HEDDA HEADFAKE VERSUS THE GIANT RAT OF SUMATRA! AND NOW, TO START THE FESTIVITIES, MOSCOW MULE VERSUS KENYA DIGGIT!"

Delilah patted Krystal on the shoulder. "You're next."

Krystal rose, her hair in tight cornrows, and stretched, wearing a one-piece black leotard with the Belmont Pest Control symbol, a dead cockroach in a green oval, on her chest and back. Krystal pulled on a brightly colored Mexican blanket with a hole cut in the middle and with Delilah leading and Gary's hands on Krystal's shoulders, the retinue headed for the ring. They paused at the end of the corridor looking down the aisle as the Moscow Mule, a towering big-boned woman with a Slavic jaw, contended with Kenya Diggit, a lanky Kenyan with hair like a black tennis ball, while Levon Levin danced around.

The Mule got Kenya down in an arm lock, but in a seemingly impossible move, Kenya pivoted like a break dancer, freeing her arm and wrapping her legs around the Mule's neck. Down went the Mule. Kenya straddled her from behind and went for the can opener. But in a seemingly impossible move, the Mule bucked her off and hopped on her back. Leap frog!

Kenya won the match with a tap-out at three minutes and fourteen seconds. Downtown held her hand up high. Krystal and Cassowary quick-stepped to the ring from opposite sides. As agreed, they entered simultaneously, dancing around the ring with their arms up. Gary and Delilah got in with Krystal. A huge Aussie with a shaved skull and a handlebar mustache and an Abo shaman got in with Cassowary.

"OUR NEXT MATCH PITS THE INTERNET'S FAVORITE COP BOPPER, STEELY DANIELLE..."

He paused.

"BLACK DILDO!" the audience screamed.

Patrice stood and pumped his fist. "BLACK DILDO!"

"BLACK DILDO, BLACK DILDO, BLACK DILDO!" chanted the crowd.

Downtown nodded knowingly. "Yes, I know...BUT WE CALL HER STEELY DANIELLE! HER OPPONENT, A PREDATORY BIRD NOTORIOUS FOR ITS FEROCITY, ALL THE WAY FROM DOWN UNDER, CASSOWARY!"

They met in the middle of the ring.

"No eye gouging, groin shots, or fish hooking," Levin recited by rote, ordered the fighters back. He dropped his hand and danced back as the wrestlers circled. Krystal felt an almost preternatural calm as she closed with Cassowary, each putting their hands on the others' arms like collegiate wrestling. They circled. The juked and jugged. Cassowary went down on one knee and attempted a hula hoop, but Krystal did an aerial somersault coming up behind Cassowary, who shoved her greasy pompadour in Krystal's face.

Krystal's eyes burned. The bitch put something in her hair! All bets were off!

"Whadja put in your hair, bitch?" Krystal hissed.

"Fuck you, you racist fuck!" Cassowary hissed back. "How are you the Black Dildo? No white girl can be Black Dildo!"

They closed again. "You want to be Black Dildo, then you have to beat Black Dildo!"

Cassowary turned abruptly and threw Krystal over her hip to the mat, coming down with all her weight on Krystal's gut, knocking the wind out of her. Cassowary got on top and rained down blows.

"Buck!" Delilah urged. "She ain't no Samson!"

Krystal bucked Cassowary free and got to her feet. Cassowary charged.

"Spider dance!" Delilah said.

Krystal leaped up and spun around with a reverse crescent kick, striking Cassowary in the chops. The action ebbed and flowed, the crowd on its foot whoopin' and hollerin'.

"Aerial pomegranate!" Delilah urged.

With perfect timing, Krystal ran at the charging Cassowary, leaped in the air and as she was overhead upside down, sunk her fingers deep into Cassowary's greasy black helmet, dragging the Aussie to the mat on her back. Krystal quickly moved to an arm bar, planting her knee in Cassowary's back and forcing her to tap.

Cassowary's handlers were outraged but knew better than complain lest their ploy be exposed.

The opponents gathered in the ring with Downtown in the middle. As he took Krystal's hands, an expression of horror rippled across his smooth facade.

"Tell ya later," Krystal said out of the side of her mouth.

"AND THE WINNER, BY TAPOUT, IS FLORIDA'S OWN STEELY DANIELLE!"

"BLACK DILDO, BLACK DILDO, BLACK DILDO!"

62 | NUTRITION

When it came time to collect, Downtown was nowhere to be found. An angry mob of wrestlers and their handlers gathered outside Downtown's office on the third floor overlooking the avenue. Chupacabra vowed to suck his blood. The Ocelot swore she would tear his face off. Camel Bat called the cops. The cops came.

A flustered black cop with a brush mustache took their report. "Look, I'm a wrestling fan too. We don't know what happened to Mister Brown. All I can do is take down your report, and if he doesn't show up in forty-eight hours, we'll put out a missing person."

"This is bullshit!" Chupacabra snarled.

The cop shrugged. "Sorry. That's all I can do. He turned to his partner, a diminutive Dominican woman in a peaked cap with a glossy black bill. "Let's go."

The wrestlers stomped, swore, issued exhortations. Several of them decamped to the Comedy Club bar next door.

Gary grabbed his backpack. "So, what if Downtown ran off with the money? We won! We did it! You did it!" He picked Krystal up and swung her around while she squealed.

"What we do now?" Delilah said.

"I ain't letting nothin' ruining this night! We're going to the Capital Grill to celebrate!"

"I can't afford the Capital!" Ludlow croaked.

Gary waved dismissively. "I got it!"

Krystal took his arm. "Where you got it?"

He hoisted his backpack. "I got it in my man bag."

"What? What money? How much?"

"Relax! I just opened a new credit card with Wells Fargo. I'm a preferred customer."

"What the fuck!"

"I know, right? It surprised me too."

While Gary and Krystal drove in the trunk, Delilah, Airwrecka and Ludlow Ubered to the Capital Grille on Brickell Avenue. The inked, pierced, and enhanced driver said, "Be sure to give me a good review!"

Gary flashed him the thumbs up.

"I thought the horns were a little much, didn't you?" Airwrecka said.

At ten-thirty, they did not have to wait long for a round table in the corner. Rum flowed as freely as tequila. Cuba was liberated. Even at this hour, the popular eatery was mostly full. Tourists, South American businessmen, rich kids.

Their waiter was an elegant young matador, whisking

dishes up and down with masterful grace. They passed around appetizers. Airwrecka and Delilah ordered the sushi-grade sesame seared tuna with gingered rice. Krystal and Ludlow ordered slice filet mignon with cipollini onions, wild mushrooms, and essence of fig. Gary ordered a steak.

"What are we gonna do about the money?" he asked Ludlow.

"We're gonna have to wait a few days and see if Downtown surfaces. We can probably get the cops to search his office, dude hasn't paid his taxes in years. I'm baffled. Downtown's got roots. He's been here twelve years. I can't believe he'd throw everything away for the sake of one lousy payday. I mean, how much can he pull in? The house was about six hundred, ten bucks a pop, that's only sixty gees. The building's worth more."

Ludlow shook his head and looked down. He smiled and looked up. "Unless he's on the run. Unless Downtown owes money to one of the cartels or something and had to vamoose. No time to tell anybody. He sees them coming down the aisle. He knows he's fucked. It's like that scene in The Godfather when Sonny goes after what's his name, the worthless brother in law."

Delilah sipped gin. "Do you have any reason to believe this?"

"I'm just speculating. But with Downtown, anything is possible. Did you know he played football for Clemson? And that plays blues on weekends? He may have been abducted by aliens. Anything is possible."

Gary thought about Downtown in space.

"What about Krystal? Where do you think we should go from here?"

"Well first off, there won't be any more deals with the Gorgeous Ladies of Wrestling."

Delilah pounded the table. "Hear, hear."

"Minx Tussel has made us an offer. They will pay you ten thousand dollars to fight Ann Thrax."

Even in that rarefied atmosphere, people kept glancing at them, wondering who they were. Maybe it was the swagger that came with the win. Maybe it was their mixed bag of nuts. A white redneck, a white redneck woman in a blinding sleeveless white T-shirt, hair done in cornrows, a Yosemite Sam manager type, a six-foot seven-inch black woman in a Grace Jones jacket, and an older cafe au lait woman in brown blouse, brown jodhpurs and alligator boots.

A little girl approached Krystal, her doting parents looking on.

"Are you the Black Dildo?" the child asked.

Krystal bent forward. "Yup! What's your name?"

"Georgia."

"Oh, that's such a sweet name!"

The grinning father walked up. "I'm sorry, I hope we're not intruding. We saw you online, I mean...you know."

Krystal dimpled. "It's okay. I thought maybe you knew me by my wrestling career. I've only had two fights."

"We just came from the Roxy," Gary said. "She tapped out Cassowary!"

"That's great!" the man enthused. "Can I get a picture?"

Krystal rose and came around the table to pose with the man while Gary took the picture.

"Honey," his wife called.

"Gotta go. Have a nice evening!"

They watched him go.

"You are a hit with normal people," Delilah drily said.

The matador whisked away their dishes. A waitress brought them a celebratory cake. They ordered coffee. After much laughing and sloshing, came the bill.

Eight hundred and ninety-five dollars. Gary took out his wallet and proffered a brand spanking new credit card. The matador bowed and vanished.

"Anybody need a ride?" Gary said.

Ludlow pulled out his Blackberry. "I'll just Uber."

Airwrecka pulled out her Galaxy. "I'll Lyft."

"I could use a ride," Delilah said.

The matador returned with a frown. "Sir, I'm very sorry, but your card would not go through?"

Gary looked at him in consternation. "It's a brand-new card. I'm pre-approved."

"Yes sir. Sir, not only did the system reject your card, we received a call almost immediately asking us to impound and cut up your card."

"Those bastards!" Gary said.

"Sir, do you have another means of paying."

Gary looked around the table, then reached for the back-pack at his feet. "Yes, I do. I was hoping to hang on to this, it's worth a lot more than this dinner, but now it seems I have no choice. Will you give me a moment?"

The waiter backed off. Gary looked around.

"Will everybody please stand?"

Everybody stood. Gary opened the backpack dumping the nutria on the table.

63 | JUSTICE IS SERVED

Everybody ran like hell. Delilah was first out the door. Could that woman run! Gary and Krystal were right behind her, veering down the street to where they'd parked the truck. It was every man jack for himself and devil take the hindmost.

They piled into Gary's truck, Krystal in the middle, Delilah at shotgun, and rolled! They rolled north like Bonnie and Clyde with federales on their trail. They joined the river of steel and chrome flowing north.

Delilah pulled a pipe from her backpack. "Ha!" she barked, slapping her knee. "I like to bust a gut when you dumped that rat on the table!"

"It's not a rat," Gary said. "It's a nutria, and some people consider them a delicacy."

"Oh, I know all about the nutria. Cooked a few myself. They ain't half bad if you know how to prepare them."

At one-thirty in the morning, traffic was thick on the Interstate, FHP lurking in the weeds in the median. Gary flowed in the middle of the pack, just another old truck among thousands. No one at the restaurant knew what he drove. Aside from his guests, no one saw him dump the nutria. They owed that nutria dinner!

"You got any good recipes? I'm thinkin' of cooking some up myself."

"Sure, I got lots of recipes. Been thinking of doing a book."

Krystal twisted around, snagged her backpack, and dug around for a cig. Gary held out his hand. All three smoked contentedly, contrails flowing out the open windows.

"Actually," Gary said, "I've been thinking of opening my own restaurant. We'd serve nutria and iguana."

Delilah spoke with clenched pipe. "Everybody knows nutria's just a water rat. Iguana's got a lot more cachet, you ask me."

"That's what I'm thinkin'. A chain of iguana restaurants could go big. Bigger 'n Chick-Fil-A."

"Now you're talking chain," Krystal said. "A minute ago, it was one restaurant. And what happened to your house suspenders?"

"I'm just brain storming. We got to find some cash flow, know what I'm sayin'? You trained six weeks for that bout, and what have we got to show for it?"

Delilah looked out the window at a big couple on a Gold Wing with a teddy bear bungeed to the sissy bar, towing a little trailer flying an American flag. "Krystal's got talent. She can make it as a wrestler. We just have to be more careful. I never thought Downtown would take a powder like that. I can't help but get the feeling he's on the run. Maybe have nothing to do with the show."

Krystal exhaled through her nostrils. "Like maybe he had an affair with some top gangster's girlfriend? And the gangster found out and sent some torpedoes to kill him?"

"More like he got an acute case of gonorrhea and had to get to the ER," Delilah said.

Krystal wrinkled her nose. "Eeeeyuh!"

"Yes, Downtown cuts quite a swath with the ladies. Used to be married. Four times. More likely, he owes big money to some shylocks and absconded with the proceeds to prevent injury or possible death. If that's the case, you ain't gonna see him again."

"He a gambler?" Gary said.

"'Fraid so. I would not put it past him to take an interest in his own bouts."

Gary pounded the wheel. "Son of a bitch!"

Krystal turned on the radio. A man with a wheezy voice said, "They're watching us right now. And not just one or two, but literally dozens of UFOs from six or seven advanced civilizations. And the reason they're monitoring us, they're trying to decide whether to exterminate the planet. Just blow it up. 'Cause they don't like what they see. I see Marion from Huron, South Dakota is on the line. Welcome, Marion."

"Thanks for having me on, Ferd," Marion said in a deep drawl. "I been seein' 'em all my life. My cousin Delbert was abducted by the aliens and kept for over a week."

"Did they sexually abuse him?"

"You bet."

"I gotta take a short break, right now, but we'll be right back with Marion from South Dakota."

"Men," a sultry voice said. "Do you show up too soon at the party? Do your fireworks go off before the Fourth? Do you leave your partner gasping and fuming? This is Billie Jo McGonnigill for Saturn Booster, the new wonder drug for erectile dysfunction. Why pay forty or fifty dollars or more for Viagra, which only contains one tenth the boosting power for Saturn Booster? Call in the next ten minutes and I will send you a free sample. Don't be a loser! Use Saturn Booster!"

"My man don't need no Saturn Booster," Krystal said, twisting the dial to WBCW, Florida Country Radio. Merle Haggard singing "Momma Tried".

Gary picked it up on the chorus. "I turned twenty-one in prison doing life without parole. No one could steer me right, but Mama tried, Mama tried..."

Krystal and Delilah joined in, Delilah taking bottom. They were in key and harmonized sweetly. The song ended and Toby Keith sang "Down in Mexico."

"I think you passed my turn-off," Delilah said.

"Oh hell, I'm sorry. Why don'tcha just come with us. You can spend the night on the sofa. I'll take you back tomorrow."

It was three o'clock when they finally reached the end of the road, the swamp glittering silver by the light of the lowering moon. Two feral pigs snorting around beneath the trailer ignored them as they tromped up the steps.

Gary turned on the light. Palmetto bugs headed for the exits.

"You need to take a shower?" Gary said.

"I wouldn't mind. Got my toothbrush."

"Check the toilet. Might be a snake."

While Delilah showered, Krystal got a couple mismatched sheets and a wool surplus Army blanket and put them on the sofa. Delilah emerged wearing sweats from her backpack.

"Thanks so much," she said. "It certainly has been a memorable evening."

Gary turned off the light in the main room and took a shower. Krystal was waiting for him in the bedroom, wearing a black peignoir.

"Stick it in me, Big Daddy," she cooed.

They rocked and rolled. There was a pounding at the door, flashing red and blue lights on the drapes.

"Open up!" cried a cop.

"What the fuck?!" Gary groused, hurriedly pulling on his jeans. He went through the darkened living room where Delilah was sitting up on the sofa.

Gary opened the door to a tall sheriff's deputy in a Smoky hat.

"What can I do for you, officer?"

A nutria wearing a tracking collar scratched his ankle.

Gary looked down. The nutria looked up.

"Are you gonna take that rat's word for it?"

The deputy leaned on the rail. "Gonna have to take you in, Gary. We got witnesses, and we got your credit card."

64 | A SERIOUS OFFER

Gary was chagrined to once again find himself in the Glades County Courthouse with only one phone call. He left Habib a message on his machine. It was Sunday morning, and he was unlikely to get bailed out before Monday. He sat on a bench engraved with gang signs, tags, genitalia, big-titted gals, indecipherable scrawls done with felt markers, some kind of gouging device, or by tooth.

An enormous man who looked like Li'l Abner sat next to him wearing a yellowed wife beater exposing his blue and green tribal sleeve. He had a chin like a bulldozer and a glistening black pomp for which Elvis would have killed. The cracked, flat-screen TV mounted on the wall opposite the cells showed a silent game show.

Habib appeared twice before the big man said out of the side of his mouth, "You won the lottery?"

"Yup," Gary said, eyes on the television.

"You married to the Black Dildo?"

"Yup."

They sat in companionable silence.

"My name's Earle." He stuck out a shovel.

There were a dozen people in the cell, a wonderfully diverse group, some of whom poked each other and pointed at Gary. They smiled approvingly and gave him the thumbs up.

"Warn't she gonna rassle?"

"She did. First time she lost. Second time she won but the promoter took off with the money. Nobody got paid."

"So, how'd you get in here?"

Gary sighed. "I dumped a nutria on the table to avoid paying the bill."

Earle nodded sagely. "That's a good idea. But choo din't get away."

"Got all the way home but they tracked me with that nutria. They put a tracker on it, and it led them right to me. I had that nutria at home for several days and I guess it got attached to the place."

They watched a half-hour infomercial about an all-pur-pose exercise device.

"How'd you run through ten mil so fast?"

"It wasn't ten mil, it was seven, and it wasn't so fast. We was in that house a good six months before they kicked us out."

Gary tried to sleep on the floor against the wall, Earle sitting next to him, when the deputies brought in some hepped up board punks who'd been caught spraying swastikas on the local synagogue.

Gary slept fitfully, wakened numerous times by beefs, splats, squeals, raps and smacks.

He woke at one am to the riddum of an aspiring rapper.

"My dong is long. My shlong is strong. Let it feed like an eagle eating eagle in the weed."

Groaning, Gary saw the hip-hop artist, a gawky black kid in chinos and an artfully ripped Tupac muscle shirt.

"That don't even make sense!" a man bellowed from a bench.

"You want to test me, broheem?" the rapper said. "Step right up. I ain't what I seem."

To these soothing tones and others, Gray drifted off to sleep.

Someone shook him by the shoulder. He woke with a start to find a young man wearing a blue cotton Armani suit, a blazing white shirt with the collar outside the suit jacket, and black Brunos, reeking of Paco Rabanne. He had a fashionable three-day stubble on his handsome chin, and rich black hair.

"Mister Duba?" he said. "Mister Duba?"

Gary sat up and looked around. Where was Earle?

The man seemed comfortable on his haunches. "I'm Sid Saidso. I'm a programming executive with Netflix. I've been following your exploits and I'd like to talk to you about possibly doing your own reality show."

Gary sat up, rubbing his eyes. "My exploits?"

Sid Saidso's smile was a thousand-watt bulb. "Since the

lottery! I'm executive producer on What's Your Snoblem, which is in its second season, and Barfalo, which debuts in November and stars Bruce Willis and Brie Larson."

"Barfalo?"

"A bulimic buffalo terrorizes settlers in eighteen-eight-ies Nebraska. But never mind about that. I believe in deep preparation. I'm not a drive-by guy. I know how you won the lottery. I know about the alligator in the pool. You were on that plane that exploded. They said it was filled with scorpions."

"Tarantulas," Gary said.

"Exactly. You're a fascinating dude. Your wife is even more famous. Sponsors would pay plenty to feature your exploits. It won't be cheap. It won't be exploitative. I respect what you do."

Gary scratched his head. "What do I do?"

"That's what we'll find out."

Sid Saidso dipped in his jacket and extended a white linen card between his exquisitely manicured first and second fingers. It showed the black silhouette of Charlie Chaplin dancing with his umbrella, and said,

SID SAIDSO

SAIDSO PRODUCTIONS

LOS ANGELES AND ROME

There was a website, an email address and two international phone numbers. Gary tucked it in his front pocket.

"What are you doing in here?"

"I heard you were in here and slugged the first cop I could find."

Gary regarded Sid Saidso. "No shit."

"Kidding! They said I was veering all over the street. Now I ask you. Do I seem the slightest bit impaired to you?"

Saidso held his right hand out like the head of a snake, steady and level to the ground.

"Did you see a big guy? Looks like Li'l Abner?"

"No, I just got here. Here's what I'm thinking. My team will follow you around. They're very unobtrusive. You won't even notice them. We use drones. We'll wire your house to the extent that you'll allow. I'm looking at either forty-four of fifty-six minutes to be aired weekly. I believe I can get you a seven-figure deal."

Gary counted on his fingers.

"I know Roebuck Simms bailed you out of jail, but I don't know why. I think I can get him on the show."

"You know about Steely Danielle?"

"I was there! I tried to talk to you then, but some thug kept getting in my way."

"What thug?"

"A six-foot seven Jamaican transsexual. Not that there's anything wrong with that."

"So why ain'tchoo bail us out?"

"Believe me, my lawyer is on the way. As soon as I'm out, you're out. By the way. The nutria." Saidso made the 'OK' figure with thumb and forefinger. "Brilliant. I even have a nutria wrangler."

A guard named O'Malley who looked like El Capitan in Yosemite came back. "Duba, let's go. You're bailed out."

Saidso followed Gary to the gate. "How do I get in touch with you?"

"I'll call you."

Habib waited in the reception area. Gary collected his things and signed the forms.

"Thanks for bailing me out."

"What can I say, I'm sentimental. Also, I have three properties need new roofs."

65 | MAN VS. NATURE

Gary phoned Krystal.

"Where were you?"

"I'm sorry, hon, I had to drive Delilah back to her place. Then my mother called and now we're having lunch. Did you get out?"

"Yeah. Habib bailed me out. I'm with him now."

"I hope it wasn't too horrible for you?"

"No, in fact I met a guy wants me to do a TV show. Says he'll give us a million dollars."

Krystal barked like a seal. "Okay, hon. You tell me about it when I get home. You all right?"

"I'm fine."

Habib led the way into a nearby parking garage and went up two flights. He opened the back hatch of his Mercedes SUV and pulled a manila envelope from his bursting barrister's case.

"This is a list of my properties. They all need new roofs.

You take care of this in a timely manner and I'll consider us even."

Gary got in the shotgun seat and looked at the properties. There was a sheet for each including a color photograph, assessed value, and features.

Habib started the vehicle and wound downward via ramp. "They all got hit by heavy hail last week."

Habib paid the parking lot attendant. The gate lifted and they pulled out onto Magnolia Avenue. "I'll drop you off at your place."

"This is gonna take me at least three weeks, boss," Gary said. "If I do it alone."

"That's your problem. What else you got to do?"

"Dude says he wants to put me on my own show."

They drove past Arby's, KFC, Taco John, Taco Bell, Les Schwab Tires and Farmer's Insurance.

"What dude?"

Gary pulled the card from his pocket. "Sid Saidso."

"Who said so?"

"Sid. Produces a show called What's Your Snoblem?"

"I've heard of that," Habib said. "Neighbors get together and bitch. What's your show?"

"Says I should have my own reality show. You know. They follow me around and film me doing things. I could shoot alligators."

"They already got a show for that."

"I could shoot pigs."

"They already got a show for that."

"I could show off my house suspenders."

"There ya go. Maybe you'll find some backers."

Habib dropped Gary at the end of the road at ten-thirty. Gary went inside and took a shower. No snake. He found a personal deep-dish pizza in the freezer and nuked it. It tasted like dough. He grabbed a Mason jar of shine, grabbed Henry Perkins' samurai sword, and went out on the end of his pier to drink, think, and spear catfish. He'd thrown the sofa away, replaced it with two springy metal kitchen chairs he'd found at an ARC thrift center.

He swigged acidic shine, gazing out over placid waters above which moved clouds of mosquitos and flies. Blue-winged dragonflies swooped from cattail to cattail. Ducks coasted near shore.

Gary hiccupped. Gary belched. Gary hiccupped and belched simultaneously. He wondered if that was some kind of achievement. Would people like to see that on his show? He felt very sorry for himself. Here he was, thirty-six years old, stalled like an abandoned locomotive. He'd had it all and he'd spent it all. He lived in a trailer and owed money all over the state. Why hadn't he invested his lottery winnings in the house suspenders?

"Gary," he snarled, "you are one stupid motherfucker! How many chances do you think the good Lord's going to give you? You just about used up all your luck. It's a miracle you haven't been run over by a truck. You got a good woman in Krystal. You should give this wrestling thing another chance."

After all. Gary had been generous. Gary had paid for everything. Now it was Krystal's turn to pull the cart. Downtown Brown invaded his brain like a cloud of mustard gas. That motherfucker. Not that the measly five they'd been promised would have ended their problems, but it would at least have kept the creditors at bay for a few days.

But supposed Downtown had been abducted?

What if he'd bugged out one step ahead of a hitman?

What if he'd gone to Brazil?

How much were the receipts?

He almost wished they'd get a hurricane so he could film it not blowing his house away. With his luck, it would blow him away and leave the house intact. If it happened right now, he could film it on his smart phone. It would look like crap. He needed a professional. Maybe Sid Saidso could help him. He pulled out the card and called Sid. Went straight to voice mail.

"Sid, it's Gary Duba. Give me a call when you're able."

Sighing, he jammed his phone in his pocket and took another slug of shine. It was almost as if nature itself had declared him the enemy. The snake. The raccoon. The alligator. Sliding the sword in and out of its scabbard, he looked around for nutria. What did they taste like? Maybe he should find out. The public might find a nutria-tasting event fascinating. Same for iguana. Inspired by Robert Kiyosaki, Gary vowed to produce new streams of revenue.

The Lizard Lounge!

Nutritious Nutria!

Perhaps Sid Saidso would be interested in financing these as part of the show. It wouldn't take a lot. Gary knew of several restaurant locations in Turpentine, right on the main drag. He could hire Floyd part time.

A pelican cruised in, plopped down, and glided toward the mangrove which dominated the shore. The pelican dipped its beak and stuck its ass in the air as it went down for a morsel. An obscene cable, like Brock Lesnar's bicep, dipped from the mangrove and wrapped itself around the startled pelican. The pelican thrashed and the cable looped and looped until it fell from the tree with a splash.

It was the mother of all pythons.

Gary leaped off the deck, his sandal-clad feet sinking an inch into the muddy bottom as he set off for the trees, clutching his sword in both hands. He pounded through the water twenty yards to where the python—the biggest fucking python he'd ever seen—was trying to jam the pelican down its gullet, its jaws at seventy-five degrees.

Holding the sword in both hands, Gary whacked off its head. The massive body continued to writhe.

Birds took flight. The snake's head still did not let go of the bird, which hung limply in its coils. The python's body roiled like the devil's lariat and fell down over Gary's head and shoulders. Gary elbowed and fought as the coils began to contract, and then stopped. The thing went limp and slipped off him like a loose robe. Gary looked down. Holy fuck.

It was the biggest python ever. Grabbing the spade-shaped head, he ran for his truck before the gators got it.

66 | FONEBONE

Gary pulled his old truck into the gated entry to Orin Houtkooper's Palm Beach estate at ten o'clock Tuesday morning,
truck bed covered with a tarp. Krystal was with him. He
leaned out and pressed the buzzer, eyeing a camera mounted
on the brick wall.

"Yes?" said a voice.

Gary got out, facing the camera.

"I'm going to uncover the bed of my truck. Can you see
what's in it?"

The camera swiveled. "Yes, I think so. What's this
about?"

Gary untied the tarp. "I understand Mister Houtkooper
is offering a reward for the biggest python. Take a look at
this baby."

He whipped the tarp back uncovering loop after loop.
"This baby's eighteen feet long and weighs one hundred and
eighty pounds. Sorry about the head, but I figure a good

taxidermist can fix that."

The camera focused on the head, which was attached to the body with several rolls of duct tape.

"Please wait one minute."

Gary squeezed a pimple. Krystal picked at her nails.

The speaker squawked. "This is Orin Houtkooper. Whom am I addressing?"

"Gary Duba. I bagged this bad boy near my place up by Turpentine last night."

"Mister Duba, I'm opening the gate. Please drive into the courtyard and pull up in front of the main door."

The steel gate silently split to either side. Gary drove in and parked in a brick turnaround surrounding a fountain featuring an aquamarine dolphin. Gold koi swam in the fountain, along with lily pads. The two-story house was Italian villa style, with a red tile roof, Florentine arches, and statues of nymphs. A burley man in tan coveralls and a newsboy cap came toward them from the four-vehicle garage.

"Hello," he said. "I'm Ames Butler, Mister Houtkooper's chauffeur and mechanic. I'm going to help him measure the python."

A second later, Houtkooper emerged wearing torn jeans, Versace Medusa pool sandals, and a Beach Boy-themed Hawaiian shirt. He was hale, buff, and bald in designer sunglasses. He shook Gary's hand with a strong grip and calloused palm.

"Hello. Thank you for coming. I'm Orrin Houtkooper.

And you are?"

"Krystal."

"Well let's take a look at this bad boy. How long ago did you kill him?"

"Less than twelve hours. He don't stink too bad yet. Whatcha plan to do with him?"

"I'm going to have him stuffed, but really, I'm just trying to do my part to protect Florida from invasive species. I plan to do this every year."

Butler was already wrestling the snake out of the bed, using rubber gloves. They got it on the ground stretched out and measured it from tip to tail.

"Eighteen feet," Butler said. "Just like he said."

Houtkooper rubbed his hands together in glee. "What's the story on the neck?"

"It's all neck."

"I mean the duct tape."

"Killed it with a samurai sword. One swipe. Swoosh!" Gary reenacted his triumph.

"Wow oh wow! I'm so excited. Would you like to come inside?"

The foyer contained another fountain with a nymph, Italian tile floor and a soaring atrium with a stained glass dome depicting Eden, or the San Diego Zoo. Marble stairs swept up on both sides to a second floor. Houtkooper led them through the house with a lush living room on one side and a dining room on the other, out onto a marble deck overlooking the canal. They sat on the deck looking over the marble balustrade at luxury boats moving slowly up and down, leaving churning white wakes in the green water.

Minutes later, a Dominican maid in a white smock wheeled out a cart with coffee, cream, sugar, mangoes, orange juice, bananas and doughnuts.

"Mister Duba, I will write you a check before you leave. Tell me how you came to kill this python."

"It started with a snake in my toilet. And now I'm gonna be the star of my own TV show. Let me tell you how it happened."

An hour later, Gary sat back.

Houtkooper stared at him in wonder. "You're either insane or the greatest liar I've ever encountered."

Krystal leaned forward. "Google black dildo Florida."

They sipped coffee while Houtkooper consulted his state-of-the-art notepad, the shape and consistency of a sheet of paper. He watched Krystal's moment of fame, then watched it again.

"Were you arrested?"

"I sure was! That's where I met my hairdresser."

"You can Google me too," Gary said. "Lottery winner shoots gator in swimming pool."

Houtkooper Googled.

"What's a Fonebone?" Gary said.

Houtkooper held up his gossamer notepad. "This is a Fonebone." He reached into his pocket and withdrew a sleek device. "And this. Its built-in software prevents anyone from tracking or recording you. I built the prototype in my parents' basement. I never went to college. I started fooling around with computers when I was seven. Built my first computer when I was ten.

"I hope you can stick around for the photographer and the taxidermist. They're on their way."

Gary put a hand to his head. "Oh mannnnnnnn...I didn't get a license for that python."

Houtkooper poked, searched, and read. "Pythons can be killed on private lands at any time with landowner permission - no permit required - and the FWC encourages people to kill pythons on private lands whenever possible. Pythons must be humanely killed at the time and site of capture and may not be transported alive off of the private property without a permit from FWC."

"The python didn't suffer!" Gary said. "Now I got this whooping crane hanging around my neck."

"Tell me about that."

Gary explained. "I never shot that whooping crane! I shot the alligator. The whooping crane just got in the way."

"I might be able to help you with that," Houtkooper said.

Butler came out to the patio and whispered in Houtkooper's ear.

"The photographer is here. I think we'll take this in the front courtyard. There's no point in dragging that snake all over the house."

They went out front and held the snake. Gary, Houtkooper, Butler and the taxidermist, a small man with a mustache and a bad comb over. The snake was eighteen-feet long. The photographer was a bald ex-biker named Bill who moved around the courtyard snapping with abandon.

Afterward, they loaded the snake into the taxidermist's van, went back out to the courtyard, and Houtkooper wrote Gary a check for one hundred thousand dollars.

That hundred thou was gone. Gary took a job at Vootie Burger, from four to midnight. Gary stood at the second window handing out the food. He saw all sorts of things. He saw a man in a pick-up truck with a badger riding shotgun. He saw a twenty-foot limo with smoked windows. After he forked over the burgers and the limo started to move, he saw a Hollywood star in coitus with two willowy women, one wearing a Carmen Miranda banana hat, the other a beret.

Gary had given up trying to collect. Downtown Brown was in the wind. The Miami Herald ran an article. PRO-MOTER ABSCONDS WITH PROCEEDS. Krystal went to work keeping the books for Ludlow and some other promoters. She still trained and visited Delilah when she could.

It was eleven Friday night. The drive-through had been non-stop. Except when it stopped, and meth heads would lean on their horns and get out of their cars to fight. Gangsta rap, The Eagles, The Berlin Philharmonic poured from myriad sound systems. Some made the ground thump. Gary would look into creating some kind of jammer that could knock out trunk-mounted bass.

A gang banger with two inked teardrops leaking from his left eye and a red bandanna on his head held out his hand.

"Ayyyyyyy. Bout the fuck time."

Gary filled it with Vootie Burger.

An older woman with a copper wig and a schnauzer pulled up. Gary forked over two burgers.

"Thank you so much," the woman said, unwrapping a burger on her lap and handing it to her companion.

A disgruntled black man with a bullet head and brush mustache pulled up. Gary waited for the order. He kept glancing at his phone.

"Where's that order?" Gary said.

The burger landed in front of him. He placed it in the bag with the napkins and handed it to the man. "Thank you."

The man removed the burger, unwrapped it, lifted the bun and stared. He hurled the hamburger through the window and hit Gary in the face.

"I SAID NO PICKLES!"

Gary launched himself out the window like a top fuel dragster, trying to remove Bullethead's head with his knee. The man was immensely powerful, and they tussled, feet jamming the car into gear. They crept forward at an angle, thumped over the curb, over the median into oncoming traffic. Screech, squeal, KABLOOEY.

The impact stunned both combatants as the car careened

out of control and was struck once more. The window was shattered. No crash bag.

"No crash bag!" he said, bleeding from his scalp.

"Motherfuckers!" said the driver, who looked like the actor Charles S. Dutton.

"You should sue their ass!"

"Motherfucker!"

A Latina with a yellow hat approached. "Are you all right?"

People stood on the curb, filming. Sirens.

Gary lay there until the police arrived, wrenched open the door with a crowbar, and handcuffed him. He sat at the curb next to the driver.

Next stop: Glades County Jail. The jailer greeted him by name. Bullethead's name was Major Sutton. A couple inmates called out when Gary entered holding. He looked around for Sid Saidso, Earle or Patrice. He was on his own. He sat on the oak bench, intricately inlaid with genitalia and gang symbols. Major Sutton sat next to him. He wore gray slacks and a white dress shirt that had seen better days.

"You know I didn't make your burger?"

"I'm having a bad day."

"I know how that goes."

Several seconds passed. Gary stuck out his hand. "Gary Duba."

"Major Sutton."

"What do you do?"

"I do stand up. I host a game show."

"You mean like you're a comedian?"

"Yes. I have a game show too. What's Your Snoblem?"

"I've heard about that. What's that about?"

"People bitch about things."

"Do you know Sid Saidso?"

Sutton's mouth went oval and he pointed at himself. "Do I know Sid Saidso? He's my producer."

Gary guffawed. "This is where I met Saidso! He wants to do a reality show with me."

Sutton went pop-eyed. "You're that guy?"

"I just caught the biggest python in Florida history!"

"I saw that! Congratulations!"

"What do contestants win?"

"Boob jobs, penis enhancements. My sponsor was Doctor Vanderlay Mukerjee. The winner would receive free plastic surgery."

"Didn't he go to prison for murder?"

"Manslaughter and malpractice. And now we need a new sponsor."

"So, What's Your Snoblem is not on the air?"

"Not currently, but Sid has Noxitril lined up."

Gary had called Krystal, but it was too late. There was nothing she could do until morning. Jerry Springer was on the tube, sound turned off. Subtitles ran in a strip. "You XXXXX XXXXXX!" "XXXX you, you XXXX!"

Habib appeared in white Stetson, turquoise and silver bolo, and a yoked jacket. Gary silently recited, "Have you been in an accident? Do you think you have not been fairly compensated? Contact the Long Arm at Rodriguez Law Offices to find out how much your injuries are really worth. You don't pay us unless they pay you."

Sutton and Gary found a corner and flaked out. The lights never dimmed. Gary slept fitfully, dreaming of giant nutria, half hearing men puke, curse, or piss into the stainless-steel pisser. Someone took a shit crouching and grunting like a hellish toad, releasing stench throughout the wing.

"For the love of Christ!" a prisoner cried. "Give us some matches!"

In the morning, a jailer handed out boxed breakfast consisting of cold egg and potato burritos with flecks of unknown meat, a banana, and orange juice in plastic bottles. One inmate traded his for a fix. Another reached over, snagged his neighbor's and added it to his. A third turned the cardboard and plastic container into an ocarina and played "St. James Infirmary".

Dutton was sitting up clutching his knees when Gary woke.

"Did I miss breakfast?"

Dutton handed him a sealed box. "I got your back. You come see me at the Comedy Club. It's next to the Roxy."

Gary sat up, unwrapped the unsavory burrito and bit in, chewing mechanically, swallowing with a dunking sound. "I know where it is. Krystal fights at the Roxy. We just fought there."

Gary told him about the bout.

"I was working that night! I remember the marquee! So,

Krystal's Steely Danielle? How'd you get that name?"

"Cuz we can't call her the Black Dildo."

Sutton's mouth morphed complexly. He leveled a cigar-like finger. "Krystal's the Black Dildo?"

Gary nodded.

"I musta watched that a half dozen times. Man, she let that cop have it!"

"She's got a temper, that's for sure."

The bailiff banged on the bars. "Duba, let's go. You're bailed."

68 | FREEBIRD

Krystal was waiting for him in front. He signed for his things and stepped out into a sunny parking lot.

"Who bailed me out?"

"I did. I saved some of that money you gave me."

"How much is left?"

"Fourteen thousand and eighty-five dollars."

Gary did a slow whiplash. "How is that possible?"

"Income tax took most of it. I had to give Habib some. He wants you to get started on those houses right away. The rest went to Visa, MasterCard, and American Express."

"How'd you get here?"

"Floyd let me borrow his old van. It's a rolling bomb. We could use it to clear out half the mosquitos in Glade County. I'm fighting tomorrow night. They're paying me ten thousand dollars."

She pointed to Floyd's old gray van. The dead cockroach in the piss-yellow oval symbolized Gary's career prospects.

His myriad failures loomed before him like the Pittsburgh Steelers' defensive line. He hoped he could find Sid Saidso's card. A reality show didn't sound too bad right then. The only shows Gary ever watched was Judge Judy and Jerry Springer, which he pulled in out of thin air with an old rabbit ear antenna and aluminum foil halo. Floyd had cable. Gary saw Swamp People and Deadliest Catch at Floyd's place and realized what he was missing.

Gary had spent thousands on state-of-the-art audio and video for the new place, but the creditors had hauled it away.

"Who's paying you?"

"Webster Mantooth. He's the new manager of the Roxy. I told him half up front."

"Any word on Downtown?"

Krystal put her fingers to her lips and made a kissing sound.

"Who you fighting?"

"Chupacabra."

Floyd's listing van smelled of formaldehyde and bug killer. The seats creaked. A diagonal crack ran from the upper left to the lower right of the windshield. Krystal fired it up releasing a dense cloud of dark gray smoke from the rusted muffler. They drove down the highway leaving thousands of dead mosquitos in their wake.

"I thought you were fighting the Yellow Rose of Texas."

"She had to pull out. Chupa was the best they could do. She outweighs me by forty pounds but I'm not worried." She clenched her fist. "I have the powa. I have the knowledge.

I know the paddling blowfish. I know the foaming pipe snake."

"Ten thou, huh?"

"You bet. When they told me I was fighting Chupa, I threatened to pull out. I just deposited the check."

"That's what I'm talkin' about!" Gary said, high-fiving Krystal.

They drove with the windows open because the AC didn't work. Buckets and canisters rattled around in back. They passed a Ford 350 pulling a motor home towing a Jeep, with a motorcycle bungeed to the rear bumper and an aluminum skiff upside down on the roof. They were passed by twelve members of the Tasmanian Devils MC. They passed a flashing FHP cruiser that had pulled over two bicyclists, each bike laden like an Indian train, the bicyclists wearing multi-colored spandex and backpacks the size of refrigerator units. They were passed by a flotilla of U-Haul rentals with New York plates heading south. They passed four discarded tire carcasses. They were passed by a Ferrari with the Beast with Two Backs in the driver's seat. They were passed by a screaming FHP cruiser. They passed the cruiser with the Ferrari pulled over, the passengers by the side of the road, the woman pulling on her panties.

When they pulled into their yard, two feral hogs were rutting by the steps. Krystal put her hand on Gary's thigh. "Let's go, you old weasel."

They went inside. Krystal lifted her T-shirt and flashed her tits. Fifi LePew batted her eyelashes. "Take a shower!

I'll be waiting."

Gary took a shower. No snake. He was beginning to like the snake and wondered how he could get it to return. When he came out, Krystal lay on the rumpled bed sheets, wearing a nothing but a Harley T-shirt pulled up. "Stairway to Heaven" played on the boom box. Gary gave a rebel yell and pounced, sliding right in. They rutted like a paint mixer and fell off the bed with Krystal on top. She leaped up, stuck out her ass and ran into the living room. Gary caught up with her and pulled her down with him on the sofa. She sat on his lap and they did the wild thing.

A raccoon entered through the screen door. It stuck its little paw in the crack and swung it open like a teenager returning home and skittered behind the couch. Gary froze. Krystal said, "What?"

Gary pointed. "It's Inigo Montoya!"

Krystal squeaked, leaped up and ran for the broom. Inigo Montoya slithered behind the sofa.

"It was Floyd!" Gary pleaded voice tremulous. "I didn't pull the trigger!"

Krystal rushed back brandishing the broom.

"Get rid of it! Get it out of here!"

"My gun's in the truck."

"Fuck the gun! That gun is bad luck! Here." She thrust the broom at Gary, who yanked the cheap-jack Big Lots sofa away from the wall with a jerk exposing the trash panda who lurked like Fu Manchu, rubbing his paws. Gary herded the critter toward the door where it showed itself out.

Gary stood with broom at port arms, panting.

"Why did you talk to it?" Krystal demanded.

"Months ago...before our luck changed, and changed again, and then changed back, when you were in jail for licking that manager. There was a rabid raccoon in the yard. Floyd shot it with my magnum. We buried it in the yard. It was a rabid raccoon! What choice did we have? And then several months later, that other raccoon showed up at my door and accused me of murdering its father!"

"Gary, that don't make a lick of sense."

Gary threw the broom over his shoulder. "Nevertheless."

It was only then that he noticed that his flag was at half-mast. Krystal advanced like a storm front.

"Don't worry, big boy. I can fix that."

Soon they were back at it, rocking the kitchen table until it collapsed. They retreated to the bedroom while "Freebird" soared on the radio. Their sex was brobdignagian! Their sex lasted for hours! In centuries to come, bards would sing of their sex! They could have filmed their sex and paid off their credit cards. Who wouldn't want to see the Black Dildo in action? But Black Dildo was now Steely Danielle and she had a match tomorrow.

They collapsed in a heap, covered with sweat.

"Now what?" Krystal said.

"Try to get some sleep."

69 | BLACK DILDO VERSUS CHUPACABRA

Under the watchful eye of Webster Mantooth and referee Levon Levin, Krystal and Chupacabra went over the fight three hours ahead of time in the empty arena. They shook hands in the middle of the ring. Chupa was a stocky woman in a leotard that said Taco Power, Wonder Woman boots, hair cropped short and dyed platinum blonde. She was four and oh, but Krystal's last victory had been unexpected amid bizarre circumstances, increasing her marketability exponentially. A freckle archipelago traversed Chupa's pug nose. Her manager, Vassily Shuvelov, looked like a buzzard with a pronounced larynx and climbed in the ring alongside her trainer, Sylvia Wrath, a pink-haired fury.

They agreed that Danielle would come out swinging, Chupa would duck under, grab her and do a wurlitzer and throw her to the ground. Danielle would roll onto the small of her back and do a break dance sweep, bringing Chupa to the canvas. Danielle would go for the arm lock, but Chupa would bounce off the ropes with altitude and kick Danielle in the chops. They agreed on a sequence of thirteen maneuvers at the end of which, Danielle would perform a flying scissors take down and a leg lock whereupon Chupa would tap out. It was all settled. They all shook hands.

"Have you heard from Downtown?" Gary asked Mantooth, a mild-mannered middle-aged Methodist with a pronounced under bite.

"No one's heard from Downtown since he vanished. I pray they don't find his body in the belly of an alligator on the twelfth green at Lakewood."

Levon wore gray sweatpants and a long-sleeved Waldo shirt. "I have a feeling we'll never hear from him again. Just one of those unexplained disappearances."

The show was sold out. Univision was there. Gary had to reserve tickets for Airwrecka and Patrice, who was bringing his boyfriend Manfred. Two hours prior, Krystal sat in her dressing room while Airwrecka braided her hair and Delilah whispered in her ear.

"Remember what we practice. The spider dance. The paddling blowfish. The foaming pipe snake. Remember your koan."

"Euripides, you menda dese. You bend a blended bar with ease."

"And when they circle back to sneeze," Delilah prompted.

"THAT'S WHEN THE WEASELS SEIZE THE CHEESE!" they shouted in unison.

Airwrecka dropped her scissors which fell point first

and stood upright quivering. Ludlow Kudlow started and clapped his hands "Is it time?"

Gary was nonplussed. "Not yet, Lud."

Lud reached inside his jacket, removed a silver flask, unscrewed and imbibed. He offered it to Gary, who passed. Delilah took the bottle and chugged until it was empty. She handed it back. Ludlow shook it.

"I'll catch you on the flipside, baby," Delilah said.

A boy in a hoodie stuck his head in the door. "Five minutes."

They formed up, Gary leading, Krystal's hands on his shoulders framed by Delilah and Ludlow, with Airwrecka bringing up the rear. From twenty feet away, they felt the crowd's sound and heat. It was a hot August night and the joint was packed. Various factions sported banners like states at a national convention. Chupa's fans commandeered a solid block waving Chupa banners.

"CHUPA! CHUPA! CHUPA!" they chanted.

Krystal's fans unfurled their Black Dildo banner, despite the promoter's pleas to call her by her real fake name.

"BLACK DILDO! BLACK DILDO! BLACK DILDO!" they chanted, waving black dildos. Univision was taping, as well as Shoddy Productions which marketed off brand wrestling DVDs. Many individuals held their smart phones aloft taping Krystal's advance to the ring.

Wearing a black tux, blue shirt, and white tie, Webster Mantooth appeared in the center of the ring.

"DAMAS Y CABALLEROS! WE COME NOW TO ONE OF OUR FEATURED FIGHTS OF THE NIGHT!

FIGHTING OUT OF PECADILLO MEXICO WITH A RECORD OF FOUR AND OH! THALIA 'CHUPACA-BRA' ESTEFAN!"

The Chupa peopled clapped, cheered, shook their banners and blew their vuvuzelas as Chupa climbed into the ring followed by Vassily and Sylvia Wrath. Chupa danced around the perimeter with her hands in the air.

"HER OPPONENT, WHO CAME OUT OF NOWHERE WITH HER STUNNING DEFEAT OF CASSOWARY, HAILING FROM TURPENTINE, FLORIDA, STEELY DANIELLE!"

Patrice leaped to his feet waving a hard rubber schlong. "BLACK DILDO!"

"BLACK DILDO, BLACK DILDO, BLACK DILDO!" her people chanted waving their rubber shlongs.

Levon met them in the middle of the ring. "Obey my commands at all times. Shake hands."

They slapped five and retreated to their corners. Levon chopped down.

"Fight!"

Krystal came out swinging. Chup ducked under, grabbed her and held her aloft for the wurlitzer. Her hand slipped and Danielle fell to the canvas, automatically going into her break dance sweep, right leg catching Chupa behind the knee, sending her down on her ass.

"Puta!" Chupa hissed.

They bounced to their feet and circled, careful rehearsals forgotten. Chupa shot for a take down as Delilah shouted ringside, "Spider dance!"

Krystal leaped up into a reverse spinning crescent kick which sent Chupa sprawling into the ropes. Krystal stalked her along the ropes. Vassily stuck his cane through the ropes, hooked Krystal by the ankle, and pulled her flat on her face. Paper cups, pieces of clothing, and vuvuzelas rained down. Chupa's followers got up and surged around the ring toward Krystal's followers. Patrice rose to his feet, gripping his three-foot dildo like a baseball bat. Chupa's fans unveiled chains, brass knuckles, and nunchucks made from two plastic water bottles filled with plaster of Paris, connected by a short rope.

The camera crews were torn.

Gary rolled through the ropes and ran across the ring to get at Vassily, while Levon blew his whistle. Gary rolled out the opposite side and faced off with Vassily who hunkered in a fighter's stance, his cane forgotten. Sylvia Wrath jumped on Gary's back for the rear naked choke, but Delilah appeared out of nowhere and applied Dim Mak, the death touch, to Shirley's neck and she fell unconscious to the floor. Vassily picked up his cane and advanced like a fencer. Gary picked up a folding chair and held it in front of him like a lion tamer. As the Russian thrust, Gary whirled around backwards and whacked him on the elbow. Vassily dropped the cane. Gary picked it up and hurled it into the crowd. Vassily went after it. It was a very valuable cane.

Krystal climbed the ropes and brought Chupa down with a flying scissors kick, landing on Chupa's back and pulling her leg back into a painful lock.

Chupa tapped out.

Flush with spending cash, Krystal, Gary, Delilah, and Ludlow floated down the sidewalk past the Comedy Club. A familiar voice intruded on the warm night air.

"White boys love Hornitos. They think it's Mexican Viagra."

Gary gripped Krystal's arm. They looked at the peg board next to the door.

STAND-UP TONIGHT: Major SUTTON

"Come on! I know that guy."

"Not me, hons," Delilah begged off. "I got to get back to the bayou."

"I'm going home, kids," Ludlow said.

Gary and Krystal found a table in the back. Three dozen people crowded the small round tables or the bar, watching Sutton wearing a Navy blue suit and white shirt open at the collar, the spotlight gleaming off his polished brown head. Several college boys were clustered front and center. The tables were so tightly packed, the waitresses had to move sideways. They ordered tequila and water except for Ludlow, who had an iced tea.

"I had to fly to Cleveland. I'm in line for security," Major said. "I keep seeing the same people over and over. Young woman with baby. Rapper in a hoodie. Lumber jack with skateboard. Along comes a TSA agent with a dog on a leash, sniffing for drugs. Dog stops at this businessman pulling a suitcase on wheels. You can just tell this guy's flying business class on his way to an interstate manager's meeting. Dog starts barking. Agent says, 'Sir, would you open your suitcase?'

"'What, here?'"

"'Yes, right here, sir.'"

"Guy opens his suitcase. The dog snags a summer sausage and wolfs it down. 'Thank you, sir. You may proceed.'"

Gary and Krystal laughed and applauded. Major shielded his eyes.

"Ho shit! It's my man Gary Duba, soon to be a major motion picture!"

Gary waved.

"I get to the gate. The gate is full but there are no agents. There's nothing happening. Sign says on time, but there's no plane at the gate. Back in the day, you brought a gun to the airport to make sure the plane left on time."

A young man with a beard and a manbun said, "Wow, man. Just wow."

"Did you assume my gender?" Major said.

The young man and his two companions crossed their

arms. One hissed.

One said, "Lame."

Major pointed at himself. "Am I bombing up here?"

"You suck!" said one.

"That's sick, man," said another.

"Lame," said the third.

"What time does a Chinaman go to the dentist?" Major said.

The three stood. "That's it," said the manbun. They trooped out. A young couple raced to take their seats. Major bowed at the waist.

"Welcome. You can have those drinks."

The couple giggled. She looked like Cleopatra Jones. He looked like Napoleon Dynamite.

"Finally, we're on the plane. I'm flying Cattlecar Airlines. I'm sitting next to a woman with a support ocelot. Behind me there's a guy with capybara wearing a vest. Across the aisle's a young woman with a garter snake wrapped around her neck. I told her it was in the wrong place. I'm the only guy there without a therapy animal. I'm feeling antsy. But get this—I can rent one for one hundred and sixty dollars. I call the attendant.

"What can I rent?"

"'Sir, all we have left are coon cats.' I look him in the eye. Is that what you think of me? That because I'm a person of color, I should rent a coon cat?"

"'That's all we have left. We had a very limited selection.'"

Major took a sip of water. "I threaten to sue. Five minutes

later, the attendant brings me a check for fifty thousand dollars and a complimentary coon cat.

"He hands out dwarf peanuts. The ocelot is gulping them down. I order the mozzarella and roasted red pepper agnolotti in vodka sauce, served with kale, fire-roasted peppers, a petite soft baguette and apple wheat berry grain salad for eleven ninety-nine. I've had MREs that taste better. Each MRE comes with a pouch of water, a heating sleeve, an entree that may contain beef stew, chicken, muskrat or possum, crackers, raisins, and Skittles."

The audience tittered. The audience drank. Major peered around.

"Folks, Omma hand the mic over to the somber and funereal Alice Prosciutto. Alice!"

A skinny, pale woman with an amazing poof of red dandelion hair took the stage, wearing a dress she'd rescued from Goodwill where it had been serving a forty-year sentence.

"In the meantime," Major said, "Try the mozzarella and roasted red pepper agnolotti in vodka sauce, served with kale, fire-roasted peppers, a petite soft baguette and apple wheat berry grain salad."

Warm applause followed Major as he walked to the rear of the club, following a serpentine pattern. Gary rose to greet him. They hugged. Gary introduced Krystal. Major went down on one knee and took her hand.

"I am in awe. I am in your thrall."

"Get up, Maj. You'll tear your knees."

"I talked to Sid. Wants to know when you're going to get

back to him?"

"Hell, let's go," Gary said. "Let's do it. His lawyer and my lawyer. Hell yeah."

Krystal slammed her fist to the table. "Fuck an 'A' Bob."

Major ordered a vodka gimlet, "and whatever they're having."

"My friends," Alice Prosciutto said, "did you ever accidentally shoot your neighbor six times?"

Major pulled out a card and wrote something on the back. "That's my address. I'm having a barbecue Monday. Why don't y'all come 'round bout three?"

Gary tucked it in his pocket. He needed a card.

Major pulled out his phone. "Let me give Sid a call. He's usually around."

The call went through. Major cupped his mouth. He put it away.

"Sid will be down in fifteen minutes."

"Seriously?" Gary said.

"He's right up the street at the Drunken Monkey."

Fifteen minutes later, Sid swooshed in, resplendent in Gene Kelly khakis, a flowing yellow and blue Hawaiian shirt, and a yellow porkpie hat. He too embraced Gary as a long lost brother and gushed over Krystal.

"The marketing possibilities are infinite," he said, taking a seat and ordering absinthe. "Anybody need anything? You hungry? Anybody need a bump?"

Krystal raised her hand, but Gary grabbed it by the wrist and forced it down, like a parking brake. "We're good."

Sid framed a scene with his hands. "Here's how I see it. Florida Man. Gary Duba's having a bad day. There's a snake in his toilet, a rabid raccoon in the yard, and his girl Krystal's in jail for getting naked at a Waffle Hut and licking the manager. With his best friend Floyd, Gary sets out to sell his prized Barry Bonds rookie card to raise the five hundred for bail. But things get out of hand."

Sid sat back, smug, hands open to accept bouquets.

"Then what?" Krystal said.

"Then what? Everything! All of it! The lottery! The alligator! The python! You're a legend! This show is pre-sold. Huge overseas market! And you!" He pointed at Krystal.

"The Black Dildo! 'Nuff said!"

Gary couldn't keep himself from beaming. Maybe this was it. The pot of gold at the end of the rainbow. It wasn't often a man got a lucky break. Gary felt he must be some kind of freak, but this was his fourth or fifth major break. It was like God was testing him to see if he was worthy. He knew he wasn't worthy.

"What happens next?"

"I'll put together a proposal and an offer. We'll shoot eight initial episodes. I already have a crew lined up, and a writer structuring your story. You'll walk us through it and of course participate in meaningful reenactments."

"We have all of Krystal's fights."

"She only just whupped Chupacabra's ass three hours ago."

Sid beamed. "That was my team down there."

71 | THE LIZARD LOUNGE

They parted outside. As Gary and Krystal walked to his truck in a garage, they passed Lizard on A Stick. Gary went to the window. It was the same Latino kid with the shock of black hair. He smiled when Gary came up.

"Ola! You want lizard? It's on the house."

"Naw, I'm flush. What's your name? I'm Gary."

"Julio."

The boy expertly skewered grilled lizard, added green peppers and mushrooms, wrapped in wax paper. He handed them out. Gary gave him a twenty.

"Where do you get the lizards?"

"I catch them."

"What are they?"

"Iguana."

"How do they taste?"

Julio just smiled and pointed. Gary bit into the charcoal grilled meat. It tasted just like chicken, with just the right blend of peppers and sauces.

"Julio, how'd you like to come work for me?"

Julio rapidly nodded his head. "Doing what?"

"Cooking iguanas. You know all the recipes, right?"

The next day, putting on a roof on one of Habib's properties, Gary spotted the perfect location, a former Friday's in a corner location in a trendy new strip mall near Turpentine. Using python money, Gary leased the property and with him and Floyd doing most of the work, renovated it. Gary took the Florida Man offer to Habib who promised to get back to him but didn't get around to it for two weeks. By the time everyone had agreed, and Gary signed, it had been a month since the meeting at the Comedy Club and the Lizard Lounge was set to open.

It was a hot November day and Christmas was on full display. Poinsettia festooned the light poles. Red and green was everywhere. The Lizard Lounge had been finished with a South Pacific Tiki theme, despite the prevalence of iguana throughout the Caribbean. Bamboo strips lined the walls. The bar lurked under thatched straw. Tiki gods looked down from the walls and up from the mugs. Sid's film crew was there. Krystal, who waited tables, wore a hidden body cam.

The first patrons arrived at eleven fifteen, shortly after opening. Gary greeted them at the door, wearing cargo pants, a Hawaiian shirt and a pith helmet. The man, of medium height and appearance, wore a gray seersucker jacket over a Jimmy Buffet shirt and Jeans. The woman, slim and prim with her brown hair cut short.

"Welcome folks! You're our first customers."

"Is that right?" said the man.

"How'd you find us?"

"We were just walking down the street, looking for a place to eat and decided to give it a try," the woman said. "We're from Minnesota."

The man grinned. "Fresh off the farm!"

Gary led them to a table looking out on the patio and handed them Tiki themed menus.

> *Lizard cacciatore with kale guacamole*
> *Barbecued Lizard*
> *Lizard brochettes*
> *Lizard chili*
> *Pan-broiled lizard*
> *Lizard casserole*

Back in the kitchen, Julio dervished from salads to tapioca to the fresh iguana he'd prepared.

"What can I do?"

"Grill arugala, mix with ancient grains and coconut oil."

As Gary mixed, he noticed a ferocious lizard in a cage by the back door.

"Fuck is it?"

"Is monitor lizard, Mister Gary. Is no good for eating. Stupid cousin bring it in this morning. I tell him to go climb a tack."

"What are you doing with it?"

"I will get rid of it when I get a chance."

"Well ahmina put it in the truck. I don't want it hanging round in here."

Wearing a grass skirt and a black wig, Krystal sashayed up to the Minnesotans. "Welcome to the Lizard Lounge folks! You're our first customers."

"We're very excited," the woman said.

"We're from Minnesota.

"Can I get you something to drink?" Krystal said. "We carry fourteen rums and twelve tequilas."

"Bit too early for me," said the man. "I'll have an iced tea."

"Just water," said the woman.

When Krystal returned with their drinks, they ordered. Four more customers arrived. Perched in the middle of his culinary powerhouse, Julio was an octopus of activity, flipping, mixing, baking and cutting with masterful flair. Watching him, Gary thought about moving the kitchen to the center of the dining room a la Ginza of Tokyo.

Now the place was humming. Now the place was happening. People slowed as they passed to look at the window graphic, a sunglass-wearing iguana lounging poolside with a pina colada. Sid's soldiers surreptitiously slithered and stalked. Directional mics picked up every word.

In short order the Minnesotans' entrees arrived at their table on a black lacquered tray, covered with clay lids. Krystal brought them in for three-point landings and whisked the lid off madame's entree, roast lizard. There lay the succulent lightly browned protein, a broad-leaf of kale over the neck. Madame used her fork to dislodge the leaf exposing the head, its staring eye, its rictus grin.

Once again, Gary returned to the Glades County Jail. There were no familiar faces. All the talk was about alleged serial killer Vanderlay Mukerjee who was being held overnight until he could be transferred to a more secure facility. Scuttlebutt had the fiendish doctor performing hideous experiments on his already dead subjects, molding their flesh into grotesque parodies.

Monday morning, Gary found himself hauled before the magistrate. He stood in the docket wearing a cheap blue suit off the rack at Men's Wearhouse, next to Habib, who wore a bolo tie, a tan Western-style jacket with a yoke and elbow patches, a belt buckle the size of a dinner plate, and hand-tooled Western boots. Krystal stood with Sid Saidso at the back of the courtroom.

"Mister Duba, you have appeared before this bench six times in the past two years. While individually, your transgressions don't compare to those of, say, Vincent 'The Chin'

Gigante, you are shaping up to be something of a public nuisance.

"Do you have any compelling reason why I shouldn't sentence you to jail time?"

"Your honor," Habib said, "I have two witnesses who will speak to Mister Duba's character."

It was late on a Thursday afternoon, the day after the grand opening and the closing. Judge Walter Wilberforce was tired and cranky. Outside, the sky was overcast and the weather people were in a frenzy over Hurricane Gretchen, gathering force in the Gulf. The Judge had reservations that evening at Bistro Bastille, a new French restaurant that was getting rave reviews.

"Mister Rodriguez, I'm sure Mister Duba has many fine qualities, but I don't see how they alter the facts of the case. Operating a restaurant without a license. Employing undocumented workers. He still owes six figures in federal taxes. There are federal agents waiting outside this courtroom."

"Nevertheless, your honor, Mister Duba is a well-known and long-established member of this community. He represents zero flight risk and he is not the bloodthirsty fiend portrayed in the media."

"Very well, Mister Rodriguez. You may have five minutes for each witness."

Habib turned and motioned. Patrice, wearing a burgundy superfly suit with flared trou, lapels the size of bomber wings and a 'fro out to here, took the oath and the witness chair.

"Your honor, I am Miss Patrice Talley, formerly of Kingston, Jamaica. I had hardly known Mister Duba for a few hours when he offered to pay for my sex change operation. And he did. He is a very good man."

The assistant district attorney rose. "May I ask the circumstances of your meeting?"

"How is that relevant?" Habib said.

"It's very relevant, if they were engaged in an illegal activity. Your honor?"

Wilberforce nodded. "Answer the question."

"Mister Duba and I were fighting after I caught him trying to take pictures of myself and a good friend engaged in a private business."

Habib beamed. "Your honor, that only speaks to my client's generous nature. One minute they are at each other's throats. The next, he is paying for Mister Talley's sex change operation."

"Call your next witness."

Quincy Simms took the stand, wearing a sharp three-piece cotton suit with a pale blue shirt and a Dolphins tie. "Your honor, Mister Duba came across me in the dead of night when my car gave out, and spent an hour taking my carburetor apart and putting it back together. He literally sucked the palmetto bugs out with his mouth. I had never seen him before. He had no idea who I was."

"And who are you, Mister Simms?"

"I'm Roebuck Simms' father."

Like any red-blooded Floridian, Wilberforce was a die-hard Dolphins fan.

BANG!

"I'm dismissing Mister Duba on his own recognizance. Don't make a fool out of me, son."

As they danced down the courthouse steps, a mob of media surged up. Sid Saidso tracked them with his video cam, affixed to a sweatband around his head. Here came stacked and vivacious anchor babe Cloris Sanchez, formerly a Mexican weather girl.

She paused to say hello to Sid, whom she knew from her stint on the entertainment circuit.

"What's going on, Cloris?"

"Alleged mass murderer Vanderlay Mukerjee is about to be sentenced. I'll phone you later, Sid."

News vans double-parked in the street, disgorging gangs of smartly-dressed content providers.

Habib left them at the street. "I need you to jump on those roofs."

"I'll do it today. Sorry about the delay. I don't know why these things keep happening to me."

"Well I got a theory," Habib said.

"What?"

"You sure you want to hear it?"

"Come on, Habib. You ain't gonna shock this good ol' boy."

"You know how there are certain individuals who have been struck by lightning multiple times and survived?"

"No."

"Well there are. You can look it up. It's like they've got some weird kind of lightning magnet in their bodies. Well you've got a weird magnet."

"Oh, come on, Habib! What happened to me could happen to anybody!"

Sid turned to Habib. "Will you be representing the Dubas for the reality show?"

Habib shrugged. "Sure. Send me the contracts." He waved and walked on.

Sid Saidso beamed. "BAM! That little bit in the courtroom this morning, that's gonna make the show."

"When do we start?"

"I'll get you a proposal by the end of the week."

Gary's truck was waiting for them in the parking lot behind the restaurant. They got home at eleven. Keeping an eye out for Inigo Montoya, Gary and Krystal went up the steps. He unlocked the door. Krystal went around opening all the windows.

Gary slumped in the sofa and turned on the TV. There was Cloris Sanchez, high color in her cheeks.

"...has escaped. The person they brought before the judge was not Mukerjee, but another prisoner whom the infamous plastic surgeon had altered to look like him. Mukerjee, who has been accused of twelve murders, is currently at large. The Chief of Police will give a press conference in one hour."

73 | WHO MONITORS THE MONITOR LIZARDS?

Major lived in a sun-faded white and yellow ranch style on Bluebird Lane in an older subdivision outside Belle Glade. His nearest neighbor, hidden behind a massive oleander, was unoccupied with plywood filling the windows. Gary and Krystal arrived at four p.m., Julio's unloved monitor lizard in a cage in the back. Gary had taken pity on the creature, kept it fed and watered in the shade. He couldn't very well just turn it loose.

They got out of the truck.

"That lizard is creepin' me out," Krystal said.

"I'm dropping it off at Lizards! tomorrow." Lizards! Was a pet shop in Turpentine.

"Why don't you just turn it loose?"

"It's an invasive species!"

"Well why don't you just shoot it?"

"In a cage? I should at least give it a running start."

Krystal threw up her hands. "Fine!"

As Gary approached the house, Krystal ran back. "I forgot my eyeliner!"

They smelled the tantalizing aroma of barbecue. A fat-tired black and blue mountain bike with TPD painted on the rail in white letters leaned against the wall next to the front door. A sign on the door said, "Come around back."

As they circled the house clockwise past hibiscus beaches, they came to the concrete slab patio surrounded by crab and scrub grass, a drainage ditch in the backyard. Major sat on a plastic chair from Walmart, leaning forward, his arms on his thighs. A small, dapper, olive-skinned man in a wide lapel burgundy suit with pink pinstripes, with a bizarre paste faced them holding a small automatic pistol. He looked up at the newcomers and gestured with his pistol.

"Come here. Sit down."

Gary ran through his options. He could turn and run, but what about Krystal? The little man was too steady. Cautiously, he advanced and sat on the bench of a wooden picnic table. Krystal sat next to him.

"What's going on?"

"I am Doctor Vanderlay Mukerjee," the little man said with precise enunciation, "plastic surgeon to the stars. Unfortunately, through no fault of my own, I am forced to flee my adopted country. This requires a grubstake. Mister Sutton assured me on countless occasions that he would steer clients to me, several clients in particular. I only just recently learned that Mister Sutton not only reneged on our deal, he talked smack of me to these clients, who subsequently sought out other plastic surgeons."

"Muk!" Major said. "You killed seven people!"

"Every one of those unfortunate persons failed to disclose to me certain medical conditions that would have precluded me from practicing my art, had I known."

Krystal could not stop staring. Mukerjee's face looked like a Picasso painting, with a sideways nose, split-level eyes, and a mouth going the other way.

"What's wrong with your face?"

Mukerjee gazed with placid eyes. "There is nothing wrong with my face. Everything you see is by design. When I realized the full scope of Sutton's betrayal, I knew I had no choice but to become a fugitive in my adopted country. Never in my wildest dreams, as a child in the slums of Mumbai, did I imagine that this great land of ours, the land of opportunity and freedom, would turn on me in such a savage fashion.

"I graduated summa cum laude from the UF Health Plastic Surgery and Aesthetics Center in Gainesville. Within a year, I was doing over a million dollars business. I improved the esthetics of two Miss Universe runner-ups and four Miami Dolphinettes. I would tell you of the many stars who proudly display my craft, but I am sworn by oaths of confidentiality."

"Sarah Jessica Parker?" Krystal asked hopefully.

"I cannot comment. I only want what's mine. I must now ask you all to accompany me to wherever it is Mister Sutton stashes his goods while he makes me whole."

"Muk! I was the one told Madonna about you!"

Mukerjee pointed the pistol at the comic. "No names. Move."

Sutton led them single file through the kitchen, down to the hall, to his office with a bay window looking out on undeveloped scrub grass. An old wood desk sat in a corner at an angle. Framed movie posters hung on the wall: The King of Comedy, The Original Kings of Comedy, Stormy Weather. A solid cube jutted against the wall covered with a tablecloth holding Sutton's trophies: Best Nightclub Comic Miami, 1999, Performer of the Year—Bilks, Stratton Tools, Man of the Hour—Glenn Burke Productions. Sutton silently moved them to the desk, pulled off the tablecloth revealing a steel Protex floor safe with an electronic lock.

"I ain't got jack shit," Sutton said.

Standing in the office doorway so that he could cover them all, Mukerjee pointed at the safe. "Nevertheless."

Grumbling under his breath, Sutton got down on his haunches and entered the code. The safe clicked. He pulled it open and stepped aside, gesturing like a stage magician. "See?"

Inside lay featureless black videotapes, a couple vinyl bank bags, a fat packet of legal papers, and some photo albums.

"Open the green bags on top of the safe."

Three slim wads fell out of the upended bags. Sutton picked them up and forked them over. Mukerjee glanced at them.

"This is disappointing."

"Yeah, well next time stick up somebody who has money."

Mukerjee stuffed the wads into his jacket pocket. "I will need your transportation.'"

"HA!" Sutton popped. "I took an Uber home last night. My car's in the shop. Go. Go and check the garage if you don't believe me. How the hell you get here?"

"I was forced to improvise." He turned to Gary.

"I will need your transportation."

Gary handed over the keys. "It's an old truck out front."

"Give me your cell phones. I am leaving you in good faith, and do not wish to be reported. Mister Sutton, yank the power cord from your computer and hand it to me."

"Fuck! Ahmina lose all the jokes I wrote this past week! That's some good shit!"

"They will come back to you."

Gary couldn't take his eyes off the dude's face. One eye fixed on Sutton. The other stared off to the northwest searching for pterodactyls. The nose went one way, the mouth the other, like an Art Spiegelman drawing.

"Now all of you in the living room. I am backing out. I am not causing trouble. Do not attempt to obstruct me. I am an ace shot. I was in the Indian Army."

"You told me you emigrated when you were twelve!" Sutton said.

"The Indian Army has a Youth Brigade."

They entered the living room.

"Sit."

They sat. Mukerjee backed out of the room, holding the pistol.

The front door opened and closed. They watched through the picture window as Mukerjee got in the truck and started to back up. He had withdrawn ten feet when he cried out, jerked the wheel, and stepped on the gas causing the truck to swerve into the drainage ditch, listing like an abandoned ship.

Mukerjee exploded from the driver's door, ran twelve paces and fell on his face.

Gary looked at Krystal. "Did you let that monitor loose?"

74 | SHOUTS AND ARMS

At twelve noon on Friday, they gathered on the broad front porch of the Glades County Courthouse. Gary, Krystal, Major, the Mayor, the Chief of Police, and State Senator Cicely Steuben to present the three friends with the Key to the City and a reward of two hundred and fifty thousand dollars put up by the Plastic Surgeon Association of America.

Sid Saidso's crew was there. Patrice and his new friend Fritz were there. Quincy was there with a beautiful woman named Chantelle. Trixie and Stanton had driven down from Orlando.

Mayor Hector Scaramucci had a black Beatles cut and wore a navy-blue suit, white shirt, red tie, with an American flag pin in his lapel. WFTV and WKMG were set up at the curb. A thousand people gathered on the sidewalks and in the street, which had been cordoned off.

"Fellow Floridians!" the mayor boomed. "Turpentine has always been a friendly place and we pride ourselves on our small-town atmosphere and lack of drama. Other than me, you would be hard-pressed to name a famous Turpentinian! Yet, in the past year, we have become aware of a man, a giant, a legend who walks among us! It's true, Gary Duba has lived here for the past eleven years, and nothing in his history indicated the greatness that was to come.

"In the astonishing breadth of one year, Duba has gone from triumph to tragedy to triumph to tragedy to triumph to tragedy too many times to tell. He won the lottery! He set fire to the glades! His beautiful and talented wife Krystal was by his side every step of the way until she herself stepped up to grab a little of that glory for herself!"

"BLACK DILDO!" chanted the crowd. "BLACK DILDO, BLACK DILDO!"

With a good-natured expression, Scaramucci tamped down the crowd. "My friends, please remember that there are children and Baptists present and show a little respect for your neighbors. Turpentine is all about friendliness.

"Then, when it seemed they had nothing more to achieve, Krystal entered the world of professional wrestling as Steely Danielle! We are proud she represents Turpentine. And then, when you thought it couldn't possibly get any better, Gary bagged the biggest Burmese python in Florida history, earning the respect and a paycheck from Orin Houtkooper, founder and CEO of Fonebone!"

"FONEBONE!" changed the crowd. "FONEBONE, FONEBONE!"

"An ordinary man would be content with those achievements. An ordinary man would quietly retire to his trailer in the swamp. But Gary Duba is no ordinary man! Now he has presented his masterpiece! A masterpiece of public service! He, Krystal, and local comedian and all-around stand-up guy Major Sutton captured the infamous mass murderer Vanderlay Mukerjee!"

"They din't just catch him!" yelled a voice in the crowd. "They kilt him!"

"Technically," the mayor said, "he had a heart attack. In any case, the world now breathes a sign of relief. Gary, come on up here!"

Gary sidled over to the mayor who put an arm around his shoulders. "I'm proud to call Gary Duba, Turpentine's Man of the Decade, my friend!"

Gary smiled, although he hadn't met the mayor until that morning.

They went inside for the press conference, where Gary, Krystal, and Sutton sat at a raised table facing a room full of media. Cloris Sanchez was first out of the gate.

"Mister Duba, were you among the passengers of United #591, which was forced to make an emergency landing in Miami last month, and blew up on the runway?"

"I was there. Thank God no one was hurt."

"What were you doing on that flight?"

"Flying."

A man with an immaculately groomed beard leaped into the fray. "Mister Duba, is it true you killed that python by cutting off its head?"

"Yessir, I did. I had recently come into possession of a samurai sword and I was thinkin' about ritual seppuku when that mother-- excuse me, when that snake appeared. It was killing a pelican. I like pelicans more'n snakes anyway. Wasn't like I'd been training for that my whole life, but I have seen The Seven Samurai."

Shouts and arms.

Gary leaned into the mic. "I want to give a shout out to Haley Beth Van Droot. Haley Beth, if you're listenin', I knew your father Henry, and I have a few things of his he wanted to pass along to you. You can contact me through Sid Saidso Productions."

Krystal leaned into the mic. "We got a TV show now! Y'all be sure to watch. It's on Vidflix."

Pandemonium. Sid Saidso came to the podium.

"I'm Sid Saidso, producer of What's Your Snoblem, which has been renewed, by the way, and I can confirm that we've struck a deal with Gary Duba Productions to do a reality show based on his life."

"Who's it gonna star?" cried a voice from the back.

Sid turned to Gary. "Why don't you tell them a little about the show?"

"Well, they're gonna follow me around while I do stuff. We already got shows about hunting alligators, snakes, and feral hogs, but this is mostly gonna be about me and my ideas. I still think a restaurant that serves iguana is a good idea. There oughtta be a chain of 'em. Lizard on A Stick. I didn't come up with that name, my good friend Julio did.

We'll license it from him, if we can find him.

"And y'all know about my house suspenders, right?"

"No," Cloris Sanchez said. "Tell us about it?"

"Y'all see soon enough. It'll be on the opening segment. It's what I invented to keep houses from blowing away during hurricanes. You anchor that house in solid concrete pillars sunk into the ground."

Krystal leaned in. "Tell 'em about your holistic hearing aids."

"Oh yeah."

A deputy entered the conference room from the back, went up to the chief of police and whispered in his ear. The chief stood and commanded the center mic.

"Folks, we've just received word from the National Weather Center that tropical storm Hermione is blowing in from the west and they are expecting eighty mile-an-hour winds. It won't hit for a couple hours yet, but I just wanted you to know, especially those who have come from farther away, that you might want to make plans to head back early."

Gary smacked is palm on the table.

"Finally!"

A LOOK AT BIKER—BIKER 1 BY MIKE BARON

MASTER OF THE ACTION ADVENTURE GENRE, MIKE BARON DELIVERS THE FIRST BOOK IN THE INTOXICATING BIKER SERIES.

Josh Pratt is an ex-con turned private investigator. Ginger Munz, a woman dying of cancer hires him to find the son she lost as a baby. The child's father is a sadistic sociopath named Moon who has vowed to kill her and Josh's girlfriend Cass, for ratting him out. The trail leads to the Sturgis Motorcycle Rally and west into no-man's land where Josh learns the monstrous fate of the stolen child.

Josh is the BIKER, caught up in a race for survival against a human monster on the road between heaven and hell at the end of which lies either salvation or damnation.

Baron spins a tale of unrelenting suspense and horror that moves across his narrative landscape like the roar of a chopper's engine.

AVAILABLE NOW ON AMAZON

ABOUT THE AUTHOR

Mike Baron is the creator of Nexus (with artist Steve Rude) and Badger two of the longest lasting independent superhero comics. Nexus is about a cosmic avenger 500 years in the future. Badger, about a multiple personality one of whom is a costumed crime fighter. First/Devils Due is publishing all new Badger stories. Baron has won two Eisners and an Inkpot award and written The Punisher, Flash, Deadman and Star Wars among many other titles.

Baron has published ten novels that span a variety of topics. They have satanic rock bands, biker zombies, spontaneous human combustion, ghosts, and overall hard-boiled crimes.

Mike Baron has written for The Boston Phoenix, Boston Globe, Oui, Fusion, Creem, Isthmus, Front Page Mag, and Ellery Queen's Mystery Magazine.

Made in the USA
Monee, IL
10 December 2019